GROENLAND

60°

P9-CPV-202

...loping Is.

...tung

BAFFIN BAY

NORTH ATLANTIC OCEAN

.Resolution Island

Fort Chimo

LABRADOR

50°

Arctic Voyage
of the
Whaling Bark
Escoheag
out of New Bedford

The
White
Dawn

An

Eskimo

Saga

by

James Houston

Drawings by the author

The White Dawn

Harcourt Brace Jovanovich, Inc. HBJ New York

First edition

ISBN 0–15–196115–8

Library of Congress Catalog Card Number: 72–134575

Printed in the United States of America

A B C D E

To Alice

Author's Note

Here is the first written account of the fate that befell the crew of a small whaleboat whose harpooner struck a whale that towed them far beyond return to their mother ship and into freezing fog and moving ice north of Hudson Bay, the very heart of the Eskimo world.

This saga is based on true events, related to me during the twelve years I lived in the Canadian eastern Arctic, roaming free in search of Eskimo art, and later serving as the first civil administrator of West Baffin Island.

The small camps along the barren coasts of West Baffin Island are thought by many to be the Athens of the Eskimo world, for here live the proud *Sikusalingmiut*, whose name means the people of the sea ice. They are clever sea hunters, splendid carvers and snowhouse builders, masters of swift dog teams, dancers, singers, storytellers, warm family people who help each other and respect their neighbors. I have had the good fortune to live on their winter campgrounds and, year after year, journey by dog team with them to their summer fishing camp. There I found the curious path, said to have been constructed by the strangers so very long ago, which is a part of this tale. I have built snowhouses with them near the entrance to the red canyon, where, on a winter's night, even when the moon is full, some are still afraid to enter.

I have changed all names—those of the whaling ship, its crew and the Eskimos involved—for the behavior of all those people is thought by many to be disgraceful, defiling the way of peace-loving people. Today some men confide that the hatred following the loving was all the fault of the old man I have called Sarkak, who tried to hold his place above all others. Some say openly that the trouble was caused by hot-blooded young girls and cunning old women. But most here believe that it was the intrusion of wild new customs and foreign ways that started to change the Eskimo people.

The final judgment of who was right and who wrong, of what was found and what lost, I leave to the reader.

JAMES HOUSTON

West Baffin Island
N.W.T., Canada
April, 1970

The
White
Dawn

Abstract from the log of the sailing bark *Escoheag*, 390 days outbound from New Bedford, Massachusetts

---

Tuesday, May 12, 1896
Light wind blowing from the SE until noon on this day when we sighted four right whales near the edge of the ice and put out all boats. All of them whales went into heavy ice and was lost to us. So ends this day.

Thursday, May 14
Wind from SE again this morning. Very cold today, crew complaining, but we do see whales. Three of them. But too much scatter ice to work the boats. So ends this day.

Saturday, May 16
Wind still SE, fair sky. Heavy fog banks to the south. Saw six right whales moving along near the ice. Put out all crews. Mr. Jamison in the starbord boat struck and kilt his whale. Stavos struck his whale from the larbord boat but it drawed his iron. The Portugese struck his whale good—but I saw it tow Billy's boat way up a long lead in the ice. Late afternoon the fog came over us. We hallooed on the horn and set out boats, but that night we did not find them. So ends this day.

Sunday, May 17
The damned fog cleared off this morning. Set out all boats searching, fired the gun in hopes they would hear us. The ice has changed—pressed tight to the land with this SE wind. Beyond this ice we can see cold mountains white with snow. No sign of them. So ends this day.

Monday, May 18

Wind stronger from the SW. Heavy ice moving towards us. Set out boats but not much hope for the missing crew. Late afternoon the search boats returned, and we left while we still could before ice reached us. It is hard to think that these six men—my third mate, Billy, young Nathan, Daggett, the Portugese, the Indian, and Shanks—are all lost to us. God rest their souls in their cold graves. We have no oil for our troubles. We is heading out of this bad-luck place to go back east to Baffin Bay. So ends this day.

Right Whale

1

When I awoke, the first sound I heard was the south wind whispering and moaning, forcing its foul warmth against the front of the snowhouse.

My dreams had left me with an uneasy feeling, a certainty that something new and strange was about to happen. I rolled over on my back and drew the caribou-skin robe up over my naked shoulders. It was cold and damp in the big igloo. The seal-oil lamp was almost out, and a gray fog caused by our breathing hung near the ceiling. I watched as the cracks between the snow blocks turned softly white with the coming of dawn. On the east side of the igloo I could see the melted places in the curved walls where the spring sun had licked them thin. The roof of the snowhouse would soon collapse, perhaps before the moon was full again. Listening, I could hear the soft calling of snowbirds newly returned to the land.

Suddenly the big dog, Pasti, lunged out of his sleeping place in the entrance porch of our igloo. A low growl rumbled from his throat. I could hear the sound of a dozen village dogs scrambling desperately to get away from him, for he was a savage fighter. Lao, my little gray bitch, was just coming into heat, and Pasti was determined to keep her for himself.

Every sound told me that winter had softened into spring. I did not need to go outside to know the weather or the look of our land when the pale white dawn came creeping out of the east. In my mind's eye I could see the stone hills rising behind our igloos, jutting steeply out of the snow. Smooth and worn they were, like the backs of walrus. This cursed south wind and the glaring sun of spring had wiped them clear of snow and dried them a rich red-brown. All the entrances of the igloos faced the sea, like seven dark eyes searching for food. Beyond the high meat cache lay our sealskin kayaks and our women's boat, long and sleek, lashed upside down onto their stone racks. From there the snow swept smoothly down over the hidden beach until it reached the barrier ice that had been thrown up by the tremendous force of the tides. These shattered fragments of salt ice stood like jagged blue teeth between the land and an immense field of snow-covered sea ice. The vast whiteness stretched as far as the eye could see to the east and west and seaward. It ended beneath dark fog rising from the open water, where each piece of floating ice was too small and dangerous for a man to walk upon and yet too large to let him force a kayak through.

In the open sea beyond the ice swam seals and walrus, whales and sea birds, riches greater than our wildest dreams. Yet we could not have them. Just one day of strong north wind helped by an outgoing tide would carry the loose ice away, but all our singing and our magic charms would not make it come to us. This broken ice had pressed against our coast for one whole moon and half another. We spoke of our neighbors, poor people living two days' journey north and east of us. We knew they must be starving, and before their dogs died, they would be forced to come to us for meat.

We were proud of our camp. It was the biggest on the whole coast. We had seven snowhouses. Other families visiting from far camps gasped at the size of our igloos, with their long tunnels and big outer snow porches. They wondered at our rich abundance; so many children, meat caches, kayaks, sleds and dogs. There was nothing like our village anywhere. You would need to count all the fingers and toes of two men if you wished to number the hunters, their wives, the old people and the children who lived in our camp.

But still the weather was our master. It could help to feed us or starve us to death, as it had done to other sea hunters who had lived here before.

Sarkak was the only man who did not believe this. Sometimes he acted in a proud and boastful way, as though he thought himself stronger than the weather, as though he could control everything. He was old and rough and powerful. He still had two wives living with him, even though four of his earlier wives had died, along with countless of his children. Three grown sons remained to him, good hunters, strong and willing to do his bidding. He also had me, Avinga, a bastard, half son, half cripple, half slave to his household.

But I will speak of Sarkak later, of his greatness and of his fierce jealousy. Now I wish to tell you what happened on that spring day and of the joyful and yet sometimes frightful days that followed. Listen carefully, for I, Avinga, am the only one who can tell you of these things. Imagine, I who was always the weakest, the poorest, I am the only person left alive from that whole camp. Even the children have died or have gone away.

Always, in the second moon of spring, the old pains return to me, shooting up my arm from the very tips of the two middle fingers of my right hand. This is impossible, of course, for long ago both these fingers were ripped away by an assassin's arrow. On the outside of me there are only these two small scars, but deep inside myself lies a memory so vivid and terrible that when it returns to me I sweat in the freezing blizzard and shiver in the summer's sun. I have never dared to recount all this until now.

At the dawning of the day that changed our whole lives, I arose early, for I knew that the camp needed meat.

Sarkak went outside and carefully surveyed the weather, then directed two of his real sons—Tugak, the eldest, and

Yaw, the youngest—and myself to take both of his sleds, harnessing five dogs to each, and go to open the last stone cache of walrus meat near the entrance to the long fiord. It was Sarkak's custom to leave his meat cached far from our camp, so he would not, in some wild party mood, be tempted to give all of us too much to eat. Perhaps he also feared that in his generosity he might give our great wealth of food away to visiting hunters. Because my arms were strong, I was sent to help remove the heavy stones, for when kneeling I could lift as much as most men.

Knowing that this was a season of quick violent storms and killing winds, we wore our inner pants and parkas made of caribou-fawn skin, with the hair turned in against our naked bodies, and over these we wore our oldest sealskin pants and parkas, not caring if they became smeared with walrus grease. We wore these with the hair facing out, to protect us from the icy dampness that crept in from the sea.

On our journey to the cache we saw no living thing, no sign of life in the whole country, save one faint string of fox tracks that trailed across the snow-filled valley. We opened the stone cache and loaded all of the meat onto our two sleds and then decided to return to the camp by another route, which would lead us across high ground, allowing us a wide view of the broken sea ice. We hoped to see some sign of change, some opening or shore lead where the tide had forced the broken ice away from our icebound coast.

As the two teams moved slowly forward through the immense white silence, I watched the hazy sun sink low and turn red in the freezing cold of the late afternoon. Each wind-carved drift cast a long blue shadow across the snow. We had not gone far when I saw a quick nervousness among the dogs pulling the lead sled. They bunched together, lifting their heads, turning their muzzles, trying to catch some faint scent that came to them. Then I felt my team's pace quicken, too. The dogs' heads jerked upward, and smelling the air, they whined with excitement.

I could see my two brothers carefully scanning the snow-covered hills before them, hoping to see a white bear. Their eyes searched the dark rocks that bordered the valley. They looked back at me to see if I had seen anything. My team pulled the heavier load of meat, but the dogs ran fast, following my brothers' sled, wanting to see everything that would happen.

Then in the snow we saw tracks cutting diagonally across our path. When we reached these, the dogs scrambled into them, heads down, sniffing wildly at the strong new scent. My oldest half brother, Tugak, jumped off to halt his sled and ran forward, followed by our brother Yaw. Kicking the excited dogs aside, they looked down at the tracks and followed them for a few paces, silently examining every detail. They stopped and looked at each other, and motioned to me.

"*Kalunait*," said Tugak, using the seldom-spoken word that means the people with the heavy eyebrows, strangers from some distant place. None of us had ever seen a foreigner, and yet we knew instantly that we stood in the tracks of one, fresh tracks.

"Four of them," Yaw gasped, snatching off his mitt in excitement. He hid his thumb and spread the fingers of his right hand.

"Sharp heels," said Tugak.

"Feet like giants," said Yaw. "Look how their paths stagger across the valley. That one's trail loops out like someone sick or crazy. See there, he fell. See how he pressed the snow. Look how long he is."

Tugak stared at the tracks and blew out his breath in amazement, saying nothing.

Shouting at the dogs, we moved back and untangled their long skin lines. I knelt down and ordered my team forward. Heaving the heavy sled into the new direction, I rolled onto it in my special way, kicking my worse leg into position. We did not need to urge the dogs to follow the rich smell along the new trail.

7

As we reached the high pass between the hills, we could see below us cold gray fog rolling in from the sea. We tried to slow the dogs, but they raced down into the valley, and it was then that we saw a dark form lying halfway up the opposite slope. Our two teams raced together like wolves in a pack, silent and intent, as though they pulled no sleds at all. They rushed in on the man's form. He lay face down on the snow, with his elbows jutting out unnaturally. His hands covered his face. The dogs knew, as we did, without really looking, that there was no life in this body, that the spirit had flown out of it and was gone.

I held my team back and watched as my brothers' dogs crowded around the dead man. Tugak ran forward. A growl more fierce than any animal's rumbled from his throat, and he lashed out savagely with the heavy butt of the whip. The big dog, Pasti, howled with pain, and the rest cowered away in fear.

Together my brothers rolled the dead man over. He was immensely tall and thin, but we could tell at a glance that he was young. His face was tight and narrow, white as frost in death, his nose long and thin. His blue-green eyes were half closed. When they drew off his tight black hat, a great mop of red hair was revealed. We could scarcely believe what we saw. Imagine, red hair!

Tugak pulled off the mitts that covered the dead man's hands. They were not like ours, for they had five separate fingers and were made of trade cloth, women's cloth, not animal skins. Dropping his own mitts on the snow, Tugak put both of these strange gloves on his hands. With difficulty my brothers next hauled the coat off the frozen man, and Tugak put it on over his shoulders. He also wrapped the long black scarf around his neck. Then my brothers discovered the knife. Broad and sharp and shiny it was, with a broken point and its hilt bound with cord. Tugak grabbed it and pulled the sheath from the dead man's belt. It was the most precious thing he had ever touched.

8

Next my brothers pulled off the big hard boots and the pants, which were to be Yaw's share. Remembering me, they drew out of the pants a leather belt with a shining buckle and threw it onto my sled. That was to be my share. We looked this strange man over in every detail, but seeing that he was in no way different from ourselves, save in his great length and body hairiness, we turned his naked body face down again, back to the position we had found it in.

Then, as though he had seen a terrible vision, Tugak flung the clothing off himself, and I believe that he feared the spirit of the dead man. But we gathered it again cautiously and shoved it under the lashings of his sled.

Once more we shouted and thrashed the big dogs away from the body, and started back onto the trail. Again we hurried on up the valley. Now there were footprints of three men walking, and we could see where they had stopped twice to urinate and shuffle in their own tracks. Two walked well, with long even strides, but the third man had sat down twice. It was wrong to sit on the snow, for it would chill him, and if he did it often, it would kill him. We could see by the mark of his pants that he was wearing only thin women's cloth, and the strong impression left by his buttocks showed us that he had not much clothing under this. If he sat for a time without moving, his bowels would stiffen, his blood would grow thick and he would freeze to death.

In the faint blue haze of evening I could see their trail stretching before us. The tracks of the three men went to the top of a small hill overlooking the sea. There the foreigners had stood for some time stamping their feet. Then foolishly they had gone down again toward it. We knew that the frozen sea could never help them, jammed as it was with broken ice. They had been walking, not in single file as we would walk, but side by side, each one breaking his own new trail, each one using too much of the little strength he had left.

We urged the dogs down through the rough barrier ice and out onto the snow-covered sea ice. We did not have to watch our path. The dogs ran in the wide trail, heads down, sniffing the strange human smell. Like a dancer, Tugak stood up on the sled, balancing himself while it was still moving so that he could see a greater distance. Finding that the strangers' trail led to the west along the barrier of broken ice, he jumped off and ran forward, shouting at the dogs, urging them westward. But they disobeyed him and scrambled forward with wild determination. Lying just ahead was a stiff cloth bag with a wide shoulder strap. Around the bag were scattered many yellowish-brown squares and countless black specks.

There were marks upon the snow where a man scarcely taller or heavier than ourselves had stumbled and fallen. The bag he carried must have dropped off his shoulder, but he had not cared, leaving behind him this precious possession and a strong thin coil of strangely twisted rope. Seeing the bag made us believe that these three men were not walking together at this time, for if they had been, surely the two who walked with stronger steps would have picked up the bag and helped this dying man.

For a short distance we followed the trail of the three men, examining it carefully, trying to gauge their size, their weight, their strength and their condition. We could read much of this in their footprints.

A little farther along their trail we could see where this smaller man had lain down against a snow-covered ice hummock. He had remained sitting there for some time, for the heat of his body had glazed the snow. It was fortunate that he had gotten up as soon as he did, for if he had fallen asleep, he would never have awakened. We could plainly see the place where he had struggled onto his knees and scooped up handfuls of snow to quench his thirst. Then he had staggered on alone, trailing after the others.

It grew dark, and heavy fog came drifting in around us. Freezing dampness rose from the ice-clogged sea and turned the dogs' coats white. It left us shuddering with the cold, as though an icy hand had touched our spines. But still we tried to follow the strangers' trail, which led along the very edge of the sea ice. Tugak walked out in front of the dogs, feeling carefully before each step with the sharp chisel end of his harpoon. The ice there had been broken and had frozen again many times, and a light covering of new snow hid all the dangerous places from our eyes. Sometimes Tugak's chisel broke through the thin treacherous ice, and dark water spread at his feet. We would retreat then and try another path, but soon we could see that it would be foolish to go any farther.

We waited together, silently trying to decide what we should do. Then Tugak cupped his hands beside his mouth and shouted, "*Iyoo, iyoo*," but his voice seemed to bounce back at us off the thick wall of fog. We listened and called and listened, but there was no answer, only the dismal cracking and groaning of the rising ice as the huge night tide swelled beneath our feet. We decided to go back to camp.

After turning the dogs and the sleds, we headed back across the sea ice toward the land. We were eager to show our father, Sarkak, the new-found treasures and to ask him what we should do. The dogs discovered our trail and backtracked home without any help from us. I sat alone, leaning comfortably against the load of frozen walrus meat lashed on to the second sled, following my brothers. I wondered where these giants with the hard-heeled boots had come from, and how they could have traveled so far to reach our land.

When we turned into our bay, it was dark, for the fog was thick and had spread over the whole coast. On the hills we could only faintly see the two stone cairns that marked our camp. The dogs broke into a run when they caught the familiar smell of home, and as we drew near the camp at the head of the bay, we saw the faint glow of lamplight through the ice panes above the entrance to each igloo. They seemed to blink at us like pale stars guiding us home in the fog and darkness.

We did not stop the dogs until they reached the very center of the village. Tugak pulled the strange clothing from beneath the lashings of the sled and drew the sheathed knife

11

from the safety of his high boot top. I hobbled as fast as I could behind him as we hurried toward Sarkak's big igloo. Crowding together into the long entrance passage, we tried not to make any noise and kept ourselves hidden from view.

Then, trembling with delight at the shock we knew we would cause, we flung all the riches into the lighted room: hat, coat, pants, boots, knife, belt, shoulder bag and all it contained. For a brief moment there was silence, and then a great rough shout came from Sarkak.

"*Tikitut kalunait tikutuk*. They have arrived. The people with the heavy eyebrows, the foreigners, have suddenly arrived."

We heard him clapping his hands together and shouting the words again and again. Then Tugak hunched through the doorway and, smiling, stood up inside the round snowhouse. Yaw and I followed him.

"Some of them have come to us dead," said Tugak. "But still they brought their gifts with them. Look at this knife and inside this bag. What are these?"

"Food and drink," said Sarkak. "Put some of those black specks into the hot water over the lamp. They will make the water turn brown and taste delicious. They call it *teemik*.

"Give me that," he said, and he took a huge bite out of one of the hard yellowish-brown squares. He chewed it for a moment, then blew the dry crumbs out over the bed. "It tastes awful, but those people with the heavy eyebrows, they love this food. I think it is why they look so pale and sick. They prefer it to meat. That is no wonder, for when they have meat, they boil it in water or burn it over a fire until it is gray and tough as walrus hide."

By this time the hunters Sowniapik, Atkak, Poota, Tungilik, Nowya and Okalikjuak, and as many wives and children as could stand, had crowded into the big snowhouse to hear the unbelievable news of the strangers. Sarkak sat quietly, examining the knife and listening carefully. His eyes narrowed as he heard his eldest son awkwardly relate this tale that

12

would surely become a legend. On the bed beside him sat his second son, Kangiak, the one the old man said was most like himself, for Kangiak had authority as well as skill with weapons.

When Tugak began to describe the dead man in the snow, the people gasped with wonder at his finding such a treasure. Tugak watched their faces as he told them of the three trails returning to the sea, of the square yellowish-brown food and of the sick man who had sat sprawled against the ice hummock.

"The man who lay against the ice, is he walking again?" asked Sarkak.

"Yes. He is following the others. But they have no harpoon to feel the ice, and it is thin and broken in places, dangerous in the dark. He may be dead now."

Yaw and I widened our eyes in agreement.

"Then we will have his clothes," said Yaw.

"And the other two?" asked Kangiak, with only a sidelong glance at his father.

"I don't know. Perhaps they will be frozen in the morning or at least before night comes again," said Tugak. "Then we will have everything."

"Go and get them now," shouted Sarkak. "You, Kangiak, go with Avinga. And Yaw, you go with Tugak," he called quickly. "Bring the *kalunait* in here to me now. Now. Do you hear me? Now. Bring all of them to me now!"

Harpoon with Ice Chisel

2

In all our lives we had seldom heard Sarkak shout with anger, and it terrified us to hear him. The women and children ran out of the big snowhouse, pulling up their hoods and hiding their faces in fear. Kangiak jumped off the wide skin-covered bed, snatched his mitts from the drying rack over the lamp and hurried out of the igloo. The rest of us followed, eager to be away from Sarkak, fearing he might shout again.

Kangiak helped me unlash the load we had brought from the cache. He and I shoved the heavy slabs of frozen meat off the sled onto the snow. Other men drove the hungry dogs away from the meat and dragged it off, heaving it up onto the high snow-block cache in the center of the camp, where we all kept our meat supply. Before our people had finished their task, we were moving. Oh, how I hoped that the foreigners were still alive!

We recklessly ran the empty sleds out through the rough barrier ice and onto the flat snow-covered sea ice, urging the dogs forward, for we could feel Sarkak's eyes boring through us. We made a new trail since we now hoped to meet the walking men as they moved westward. We traveled throughout the dark night, and when we reached the edge of the floe ice, we waited in the freezing gloom, waited for the coming of dawn. When it came and turned the fog pale gray, we saw them for the first time.

Two men were walking together along the floe edge beside the long twisting crack in the solid sea ice that stretched both east and west beyond our sight. They seemed too wide, too tall, the way things sometimes do in morning fog, on the edge of the white ice. A man can look like a giant or a dwarf in the mist, because there is nothing there with which to compare his size, only blank distance. These men seemed to float in the air just above the snow, marching awkwardly, stumbling blindly, not thinking or caring, not seeing us.

They stopped walking the moment they heard the dogs. I shook with excitement as we started toward them. Kangiak sat up straight before me, and I could tell that he was nervous and unsure of how he should meet these unknown strangers.

The other sled halted behind us when my brothers jumped off and dug their heels into the snow. They did not wish to risk any more of Sarkak's anger, and they wisely left the first meeting to Kangiak. Our dogs rushed at the two men, who now stood still beside each other, facing us, their backs to the broken ice that floated on the black waters of the sea.

"Now," Kangiak whispered to me, and I rolled off the sled and dragged myself like an anchor to slow it. I roared at the dogs and drove them sideways, lashing out with the heavy whip. Only the big dog, Pasti, still tugged forward, trying to reach the strangers. On his soft skin boots Kangiak ran lightly toward him and kicked Pasti in the ribs over the heart. The blow was quick and sharp. The dog dropped in his tracks, unconscious, his yellow eyes still half open.

Kangiak pushed back his fur hood and walked slowly toward the strangers. The long black lash on the dog whip trailed after him, wriggling through the snow like a living thing. When he was still ten paces from them, he stopped. Immediately both the strange men came a few steps forward. Unsure of themselves on the snow-covered ice, they watched where they placed each foot. Then they waited, and Kangiak took three paces forward and stopped again.

He called loudly to them, "*Tikiposi*. You have arrived."

The tallest one answered something to Kangiak, but I did not understand what he said.

Then Kangiak called to them to come to him, but they did not move. Dressed in black, they stood silently like big awkward children who did not understand.

Kangiak again called to them. "Come on the sled. Come to

our igloos for food," and he waved his arm, pointing back along our trail.

I know now that they did not know the meaning of his words but understood his gesture toward the land. Immediately they both stumbled forward and followed Kangiak to our sled. He warned the dogs away from them.

When the two strangers reached me, I sat and stared at them, keeping my face stiff, hoping that they could not see how I trembled with excitement. I could tell that they could hardly walk, they were so tired. But the first one smiled at me. I was terrified at the sight of his wolflike blue eyes that were pale and unreal, as though they belonged to some spirit of the dead. His nose was long and peeling from the sun and cold; his cracked lips were blue. On the lower part of his thin face he had yellow hair clogged with ice from his breathing. His black hat was pulled down over his ears and forehead.

When I looked at the second man, I felt the hair rise on the back of my neck, for he was dark in the face, as though he had been burned in a fire. He, too, smiled at me, showing his big white teeth. His nose was wide, but his eyes were dark, the color of a real man's eyes, and pierced through his left ear he had a shining yellow ring. He carried a bag across his back.

So, I thought, these are the *kalunait* who live south beyond the Indian country, half cousins to us, half children of the dog. I had heard of them as I had heard of ghosts, as songs of ancient times. Now, in one breath, I had them sitting on the sled beside me, crowding hard against my side, saying things to each other in rasping voices, speaking so strangely that I could not understand. I watched our team, wondering if perhaps the dogs could understand their words.

Kangiak and I managed to turn the sled with difficulty, for the two heavy strangers sat in the wrong position, holding on awkwardly like old women instead of jumping off to help us, as any real men would do. Pasti was conscious again and, like the other dogs, ready to go.

We came to the other sled, stopped and waited for one of the two men to change over and ride with Tugak and Yaw, to make the sled loads even in weight for traveling. But they sat together, staring at us, whispering to each other. They would not move. Finally Kangiak got up and pointed, and Tugak made space for another person. Slowly the big dark-eyed man stood up and stumbled over to the other sled and sat down. Then Kangiak called to the dogs, and we started off along the trail, retracing the steps of the two men, looking for the third.

We came to a place where the snow was tramped down and urine-stained like the rutting place of caribou, with tracks upon tracks, and we could see that the third stranger had walked all night, stumbling back and forth to keep himself alive, to save himself from freezing. It was not long after that we found the lost man. He leaned against a piece of ice, half squatting, his face in his hands.

The dogs rushed up to him, and I thought he was dead, for he did not seem to hear or see them, and when Kangiak drove them off, he did not even move. The tall, pale-eyed *kaluna* on our sled stood up and made his way forward. He and Kangiak held the crouching man and shook him gently. He was still alive. Kangiak drew the mitts off the stranger's hands and looked at his fingers. He rubbed them gently and blew his breath on them, and raising his parka, held them tightly against his own warm naked belly.

Together Kangiak and the stranger held him under the arms and dragged him back to the sled. I pulled the caribou skin out from under the lashings, and we wrapped this around him. I heard Tugak blow out his breath with wonder when he saw the bright yellow buttons on the jacket of this man who was almost dead. Kangiak and the stranger placed him on the sled, holding his limp body upright, and I tied his legs down lightly to keep them from falling sideways and being broken against the rough ice. The sick man coughed, and we knew he was half awake. I looked at his feet clad in those hard cold boots and wondered if they had been frozen too long to bring back to life again. If so, the green poison would creep up his legs, and he would die.

When we returned to the village, it was after midday. The sky was heavy with snow clouds, and big wet flakes drifted down to hide our trail. As we crossed the frozen bay that stood before the camp, we could see every person in the village standing motionless watching us, straining their eyes to gauge the immense size of the strangers. Our dogs had not been fed for two days, and they plodded wearily back along our night trail, their heads down, their tails uncurled, and their tongues lolling. But the magical smell of the gray bitch and of the open meat cache came to them on the land breeze, and they picked up their pace and ran toward the camp, heads high, drawing new energy.

When we came to the crack where the rough ice separates the land from the frozen sea, two of us held the sick man, and as the dogs raced through the jagged barrier, we managed with difficulty to hold him on. The two other strangers were thrown from the sleds when we hit the rough ice, and Kangiak quickly leaped off after them to point out the dangerous hidden crack. A young boy had fallen down into this same crack during the caribou moon and we did not wish to lose these precious strangers in such a stupid way.

I watched our people's eyes when they first saw the strangers. They did not look at the sick man, who was on my sled, but stared in horror at the other two, one dark and one pale. It was as though some awful dream had come true before their eyes. They stood in our camp, one like a dark night spirit and the other pale as death. They were like visitors from the world beneath, two ghosts walking among us, bold as giants. Was this pale one the eyeless kayakman, the spirit moved by maggots, and was the other man the black robed giant so long entombed beneath the ice, both spirits we had heard of all our lives?

At first, when everyone looked at the *kalunait*, they were so

18

shocked that they did not move at all. Then some women quickly put their hands over their faces to hide their eyes. They drew their fur hoods forward to shield the small children they carried on their backs from the terrible sight, and young people ran or hid behind their parents, sensing the new danger that had come to all of us. The youngest children set up a wailing, and the dogs answered with a fearful howling, as though they, too, knew that a strange and powerful new force had come into our village. Our hunters stood still, not knowing what to do, their muscles tense, their faces like bone masks.

Tugak and I held the sick man upright, his head sagging back in a way that could make one think only of death. The other two strangers stood together, tall and nervous in their black clothing. They were like powerful ganders that should have been able to rise up and sail away into the safety of their own distant world, and yet they were held down, bound to us because they were cold and lost and could not fly.

Thinking about them, I had not noticed Sarkak. Now he revealed himself to us. He had been standing quietly among the people, his hood drawn forward, his hawklike eyes appraising the strangers, deciding how he should act toward them.

As he stepped forward and pushed back his fur-trimmed hood, I saw the two tall men look at him, and I believe that they instantly sensed the fact that he was the man who held their lives in his hands. Sarkak stared at them for a moment, his eyes narrow, his long hair shifting in the light breeze. Then he cast his mitts down onto the snow, and in our formal way of meeting with strangers, raised both his hands above his head, pulling the sleeves back to his elbows to show that he concealed no weapon. He called out greetings to them, and the pale-eyed man answered in a way we did not understand.

Sarkak walked up and stood before these strange dog children. I knew they were tall, but I was shocked to see that their heads and shoulders towered above him. This did not seem

19

possible, since Sarkak had always been to me a giant, bigger in every way than all other men.

The strangers looked down and smiled at Sarkak, and he looked up smiling, showing them the whiteness of his teeth.

Without turning, he called to his wives, saying, "These two will stay with us. Get them food now. That sick man, let him sleep somewhere else. Let him sleep in Sowniapik's igloo. They will care for him."

Sarkak's wives turned and darted into the entrance passage of the snowhouse, hurrying to be in their proper places before any others could enter the igloo. Sowniapik and Tungilik supported the sick man, half carrying him away to Sowniapik's snowhouse.

Sarkak took the dark-faced man by the sleeve and, still smiling, tugged it. When the tall man moved with this slight pressure, Sarkak turned and led the two strangers through the crowd of villagers, who drew back to give them room. Sarkak was small beside the *kalunait* and yet seemed supremely powerful. I knew he was to be their master.

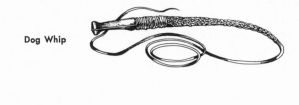

Dog Whip

3

Sarkak led them down into the winding passages of his big igloo. Crouching, we followed them, through the entrance passage and meat porch, past the side rooms, and finally into the big main room. Once inside, the two strangers hesitantly stood up straight again. The broad backs of their black jackets were white with snow where they had brushed against the tops of the low entrance. They stood blinking as their eyes became accustomed to the half darkness of the big dome-shaped room, whose smoke-stained ceiling kept out most of the light. I could see that the strangers were partly snow-blind, since they stood blinking at the bright square of lake ice we had set in for a window above the entrance. I knew that they must see everything through a bloodlike haze.

Sarkak's two wives sat in their places on the wide snow sleeping bench. It was high as a man's waist and took up more than half of the whole round room. They laughed nervously, calling out, "*Taktualuk, taktuvingaluk.* It's dark in here, very dark in here."

Their words, of course, were those they should say, insulting their own ability to maintain an even flame in the long stone seal-oil lamps. No one paid any attention to their politenesses, for we had all heard their words countless times before. We had new things to think about now.

Slowly I was beginning to realize that perhaps these strangers, these dog children, understood not one word that we spoke. I had sometimes heard it said that men from different lands speak with different tongues. It is also said that many Indian people cannot even speak like men, but only whine like dogs. But it is always hard to believe something until you actually see it, and before this time I had never seen anyone from far away.

I stood near the man with the shiny ring in his ear and said to him, "Who are you?"

He looked at me but did not answer.

Then, taking courage, I said quietly so others could not hear, "What is your name? *Keenowveet?*"

He only smiled at me. So then I knew certainly that he could not understand the words I said, or speak in our way.

He turned and started talking to his pale-eyed companion, and then I understood not one word. The whole rhythm of what they said was so fast that their words ran together, not at all smoothly. All I heard was "Cuck, cuck, cuck," spoken right from the front of their teeth. Their lips moved rapidly in a horrible way.

The two strangers were almost falling down with tiredness, and yet their eyes were bright with excitement. Both of them took off their tight black hats and caught them through their belts in some special way. At that moment, when we first saw the color of the pale man's hair, everyone gasped. It was long and white, yellow-white, like nothing we had ever seen before. The taller man had dark hair like our own, but his was tightly curled and bushy, springing up like tundra moss. They stood together like a giant black raven and a nervous white sea gull. I could not help but think of them as tall frightening birds.

I tried to go behind them to see the wonderful knives that they wore in their belts, but they turned so that no one could stand behind them. I noticed, though, that both knives had disappeared from their sheaths and must now be hidden some-where in their clothing. Perhaps they did not trust us.

In the center of our wide bed, in the softness of our deep-piled sleeping skins, Sarkak made room for the two strangers. Sarkak's older wife, Ikuma, and Nuna, his newer and younger wife, started carefully to draw off the two men's boots. These boots were high, almost like our own, but they were hard and heavy, stiff as stone, and smeared with an evil-smelling grease. Each boot bore a clumsy heel, thick as a man's hand and studded with frozen iron nails. Also from the *kalunait* the women took off two torn pairs of stockings, made of coarse, evil-smelling women's cloth, and these they handed to Nuna's mother, the old widow, to dry over her lamp at the far side of the igloo. Together we looked at the strangers' feet, and we were all pleased to see that they were blue-gray in color, not the deadly frozen white we had feared.

Nuna's lips curled with disdain at the nearness of the ghost-like yellow-haired man, but she pulled up the apron of her fur parka and held his stiff icy feet against her hot belly. Ikuma gently fed both strangers some warm blood soup, and as the warmth slowly seeped through their bodies, they eagerly drank quantities of the rich brown liquid. But they could eat only a little of the raw walrus meat that was offered to them.

We, who had driven the sleds, ate our fill of meat gladly, for it was our first unfrozen meal in two days.

After eating, when the strangers and Sarkak's family were seated in their places on the high sleeping platform, the villagers from the other snowhouses came in. Sowniapik and his brother, Tungilik, entered together, followed by their wives and children and Akigik, the midwife. Next came Okalikjuak, the good archer, with his wife and their daughter, Meetik. Poota and his daughter, Neevee, stood crowded beside the entrance passage.

Sarkak spoke to the two men in a loud clear voice, asking them where they had come from. But they rocked backward and forward, saying nothing. In the warmth of the igloo their faces burned like fire, and we could see they were falling asleep. Sarkak reached out his hand and poked them gently, then asked them again. This time they shook their heads, like wet dogs shaking off water, and made strange word sounds we could not understand.

Years before, Sarkak had seen many *kalunait*, we all knew, when he had visited Big Island, for they often came to that place to trade. It was far away from our camp, a whole summer's journey. Sarkak had tied his kayak to the side of their ship and had climbed aboard carrying the skin of a white bear and with his parka full of walrus tusks. These he had gladly traded for a few rusty iron nails and a small blue glass bottle that made the sun look like the moon when you held it to your eye. Sarkak often spoke to us about these sea travelers, and he had told how they would gladly give a single bright bead or a small iron nail just for the loan of a woman whom they always returned to you the next morning, unharmed. So eager were they for women that they stole nails from the ship's sides until there was danger that it might fall apart. These whale-hunting men had never come to our coast, because the tides were huge, the ice moved fast and the big whales did not come to feed here.

Because Sarkak had traded with them, we had always assumed that he could easily speak with them. Now finding that he could not make himself understood, his brow knit with anger and embarrassment. This was a bad sign. He fell silent and would not speak to us. Gradually the villagers turned and, one by one, left the snowhouse. Some perhaps thought less of Sarkak.

In Sarkak's igloo we were slowly becoming used to these two strangers and were not so frightened by their faces. Were they not sitting beside us helplessly like tired children unable to speak for themselves? And now they were being put to bed by all of us. I could see that already some of the women and girls felt pity and perhaps even kindliness toward them.

Sarkak motioned to me and said, "Go and sleep in the igloo of Sowniapik and help to care for the sick man. Watch everything. Remember that we found him and that he belongs to us. He belongs to this household. Tell me everything he does."

So for a time I went to live in the snowhouse of Sowniapik. That first night when I entered, I saw the third stranger lying in the middle of the bed. Dark patches of frostbite had spread over his cheeks, and sweat had gathered in beads across his forehead. His pale eyes, when they opened feebly, were red-rimmed and glazed with snow blindness and the coming of fever. The women had covered him with warm sleeping skins, and now Akigik, Sowniapik's widowed sister, laid a damp bird skin over his eyes to ease the pain. The fever caused him to shake and tremble, and the women covered him with more caribou skins and placed beneath him an amulet, a small ivory knife that would help to cut the fever.

Sowniapik's wife looked into his face and said to him with honesty, "You are dying. You will grow too hot, and you will die." But he did not understand the words she said, nor could he know how often she had seen death.

As I lay down near the stranger on Sowniapik's wide sleeping platform, I felt wildly excited. These foreigners had come from some far-off place. They had led different lives. Now we had them with us, and we could keep them and grow to understand them.

To impress this foreigner and to warm the house, Sowniapik's wife had made her lamp bright. A long streak of water had run down the inside of the dome and had freshly frozen, so that it reflected the lamplight. I fell asleep staring at it as it expanded slowly like the bright yellow edge of an owl's eye.

That night and the next day the stranger I had been sent to watch tossed restlessly in the bed. His head was hot to the touch, and he cried out many times, shouting harsh words we could not understand. I stayed with him, as Sarkak had ordered, but it was not necessary, for the women kept him covered, gave him water and cared for him like a sick child.

In the evenings I went to Sarkak's igloo for meat. There on his wide bed the other two men lay motionless, huddled under caribou skins. Sarkak's wives, Ikuma and Nuna, knelt on the right-hand end of the bed, sewing silently, and Nuna's mother, the old widow, sat quietly on the opposite side of the wide bed, tending a smaller lamp. Kangiak and Yaw spoke little.

On the fourth night I again lay down in Sowniapik's snowhouse, continuing to remind those in that igloo that Sarkak owned the brown-haired stranger. In the middle of the night, when everyone was sleeping, I was awakened by his calling. Probably he wanted water, but I could not understand his words. Softly he called at first, then louder, clacking his dry mouth with his tongue, and when he called once more, Sowniapik's daughter, Evaloo, sat up in the bed.

Evaloo leaned over toward the lamp and dipped a horn cup into the stone pot. She scooped the cup full of cold water, making the floating pieces of ice rattle, and drew back. In the faint light from the big lamp I could see the smooth curve of the girl's naked haunches as they flowed into her strong young back, now half hidden in a great cascade of loose black hair.

She leaned over her aunt, Akigik, who lay sleeping between us, and reached over me, her arm and whole body fully extended. Holding the cup in this way, she just managed to reach the stranger's lips, and he drank greedily. I felt the heat pouring down from her naked body as she shed her warmth over me. Then I saw her stiffen, and I could see that the stranger had grasped her by the wrist and would not let her go. I blew my hot breath upward between her breasts. It made her jump with surprise, and she jerked her arm away from his and recoiled back into her furry sleeping place.

She quickly drew the sleeping skins around her and whispered to both of us, "*Shogishiguluk*," calling us bad children.

But there was laughter hidden in her voice, for she knew at that moment, as did I, that this sick man must be getting well, for he was thinking of women, trying to draw one of them close to him. We were both glad. We could see now that he would live.

Horn Drinking Cup

4

Sowniapik's wife was the first to call the brown-haired stranger Billy. While we watched, he taught her his name by pointing at himself and saying it over and over again, as he lay with us on their wide bed. Soon we all spoke his name, the women saying it in a soft musical way that sounded like "Peelee." Sowniapik's wife liked the sound and often called to him, "Pilee, *aneiouveet?* Are you sick? Pilee, *kaktoteet?* Are you hungry?"

We could see that on the fifth day he was almost well again. His fever had gone, and he drank quantities of rich blood soup and water. When both of Sowniapik's daughters were in the snowhouse, I noticed that Pilee's eyes never left them for a moment. That day he first tried to talk to them. Sowniapik also tried to talk to Pilee, but nothing came of it. In the end we all laughed to hide our frustration.

Pilee showed us a wonderful tattoo that he had over the muscle of his right arm. Most of it was done with blue, almost the same color as our tattooing, but it also had another color: red. It was not at all like the straight soot-line tattoos that we have sewn under the skin of our wrists when we are young. Pilee's tattoo was an image of a large boat, with square wind sails of the kind these strangers use for travel. Around the boat were twisted lines and other strange marks. When it was known that Pilee had this different tattoo, and another one on his lower body, the news flew through the camp quickly. Every woman in the village came to see it, and even some of the men and children, too.

A swift storm came to us, and after it the sky was clear. A north wind blew over the land, and, helped by the tide, this wind that we had longed for forced away the great fields of broken ice. Beyond the smooth, heavy shore ice the open sea now spread before us. Seals appeared in great numbers, offering themselves once more to our hunters, who harpooned as many as we could eat. Our dogs grew fat again, and to hold the abundance of fresh-killed meat, the kayakmen built new stone caches along the coast. It was a time of plenty, a time of feasting. We had more seals than we could count.

I had slept in Sowniapik's igloo on each of the nights that Pilee remained there. Every day I told Sarkak about Pilee's condition, and one morning he judged the stranger to be well again. Sarkak told me to have a new snowhouse—wide enough for three persons to sleep—built against our family's igloo, with its only entrance leading into our passageway. Then, that evening, he sent his two strong sons, Tugak and

Yaw, to Sowniapik's igloo to bring Pilee carefully across the hard-packed snowdrifts.

Sarkak must have wanted the stranger a lot, for he should have spoken to Sowniapik, or sent word, before taking him. But he did not, and I believe that much of the trouble in our camp started at that moment. For, in taking Pilee without asking Sowniapik, Sarkak showed everyone that he considered these three strangers to be his personal property. He did not think of them as visitors, free men, who might choose their own home and friends.

With the coming of the strangers, our luck seemed to change. Sealskins with the thick yellow blankets of fat left on them now lay on the snow outside every igloo. The dogs that earlier would have killed each other for such a prize were now so full that they would not even look at the unguarded treasures. Our people stuffed themselves to bursting with the rich, red seal meat, slept long into the mornings, awoke, laughed with their neighbors and ate even more. Hunters, having little else to do, leisurely drew the naked infants from their wives' hoods, turned them upside down, and examined them, hugged them and bounced them on their knees.

Poota's wife, Mikigak, had been sick all winter and had been expected to die. We knew it could not be helped, but it was bad, for Mikigak was respected by everyone. She had always been a wise and kindly woman, who cared well for her three children and her mother, the oldest woman in our camp. It now seemed strange that Mikigak was so sick while her old mother, Ningiuk, who was as wrinkled and bent as a piece of driftwood, had the strength and step of a young woman and her youngest daughter of only fourteen winters to prove it.

After the strangers came, the sickness seemed to go out of Mikigak as if by magic. She left the bed and could be seen resting in front of the entrance passage of her family's snow-house, shading her eyes against the blinding brightness of the spring sun. Had the foreigners done this? We wondered. Had they some secret charm, some amulet, that had raised her from the bed?

Sometimes now we would also see the three strangers in front of Sarkak's big snowhouse, standing awkwardly, like black shadows in their foreign clothing. But for many days they scarcely moved or spoke to each other. They seemed afraid to venture far away, yet their eyes endlessly searched the open water beyond the frozen sea. To protect their eyes from the strong spring sun that glared off the snow in a blinding white light, Kangiak and I, from a scrap of driftwood, carved slitted goggles for each man.

But because the strangers were surrounded by such plenty and the safety of our igloo, they could not help but relax with us. I could see that they watched us closely, trying to understand our ways, as we did theirs. First they came to know Kangiak as their friend and then Sarkak and Yaw and me, and all the others in our family who slept in the big igloo. My brother Tugak, Sarkak's oldest son, was sleeping in Okalikjuak's snowhouse, for Tugak was in a trial marriage with Meetik, Okalikjuak's daughter. Kangiak was old enough to have a wife, but the girl who had been promised to him since her birth had died two winters before from eating poisoned whale meat. Sarkak had not yet chosen a girl to replace her.

Nuna's mother must have been the most difficult one in our igloo for the strangers to understand. The old widow always sat beside the lamp on her side of the igloo, leaving the house only after we lay down to sleep or at dawn before we woke. Often she only stared into space, while at other times she would sing to herself as she tried to sew with her gnarled fingers, her dim eyes scarcely able to see the sinew thread. I knew her well, since for some time I had been sleeping beside her in the wide bed. I knew the delicate blue tattoo lines in her face as well as I know the lines in my own hand. When she had first come to us and her mind was clear, she was always kind to me and often told me stories of the animals and about

29

ourselves and how this world was made. Now she had withdrawn from everyone into her own hidden world.

During the spring the strangers slowly came to know Sowniapik, because he had helped Pilee, and they easily recognized Atkak, because he was strong and fond of laughing. They also came to know Poota, Nowya, Tungilik and, last of all, Okalikjuak, because he was so shy. Gradually they came to understand who were these hunters' wives and who were their children. We had no language to explain ourselves to the strangers, and it is little wonder if they failed at first to understand our relationships. We were all related in our camp, being cousins, brothers, sisters, aunts, uncles, nephews, nieces, grandchildren, grandparents. There was also much adoption of children, and two husbands had wives who were younger than some of their children. Our young people acted like common property in times of plenty. They ran as free as foxes and ate and slept in any snowhouse they wished.

The women, following Sarkak's instructions, made each stranger long caribou fur stockings and a pair of knee-high sealskin boots. The *kalunait* seemed to like the soft, warm boots but found the smooth soles dangerously slippery on the hard snow. For them it must have been like learning to walk again.

The older children had been shy of the strangers at first. But once outside and away from their parents, they proudly showed the foreigners the snowbirds and lemmings they managed to catch, and they tried endlessly to teach the men words for many things in our language.

One day in late morning, when the mist on the mountains was fading and turning bright silver in the sun, the sky opened into large patches of blue. I saw the young people leading the three strangers up the hill behind the camp, showing them the best path. They were taking them up to the small wind-swept plateau in the hills, where they liked to play in the late spring and early summer when there was not much snow. They had hand-sized stones arranged there in the shapes of

30

igloos and kayaks and all manner of targets, set up for their throwing games.

Many of the dogs followed, howling as if they were trying to sing, so excited were they by the smell of these three new people. I was glad that the older children were with them, for I could see that the strangers knew nothing of the nature of our dogs and did not seem to fear them at all. We were always aware of dogs and would warn them off with stones if they were running in a pack and came too close. Well-fed dogs could often be the boldest. If a man fell down among our dogs, they would grab him, and in their savage excitement they would tear at him, injuring or even devouring him. This had happened to me.

Later, from the hills we heard the sound of shouting and girls screaming with delight in high-pitched voices. Kangiak and Yaw, who in the early morning had returned from seal hunting and had slept most of the day, awoke when they heard the noise. They got up and climbed over the hill to see what was causing so much excitement. Soon we heard them laughing, too, and shouting with the children and the strangers. None of them returned to the snowhouses until early evening, when the sky turned deep blue and the sun cast long shadows from the hills. Then they came back, walking in single file, still laughing and teasing each other.

"They have a new game, a new way of kicking a ball," said Kangiak as he passed me, following the three strangers into Sarkak's snowhouse. "When we fully understand it, we will show everyone how to play."

Eye Protectors

31

5

Inside the igloo I watched the tall foreigners bend down awkwardly to pick up seal ribs from the meat placed on the snow floor. They stood together eating. They did not seem to like the meat, and yet they were always hungry. The faces of the two pale men had turned red-brown from the sun, and they now looked more like real people, except that ugly hair covered their jaws and they had bushy eyebrows. How they must have envied the smooth beautiful faces and the short compact bodies of our people!

When we had finished eating, we all sat together on Sarkak's wide bed. Although the strangers had their own small igloo built off the side of our snowhouse, on most evenings they preferred to lounge on the bed with us. They listened carefully to every word we said, and I imagined that they were trying to learn our language.

On this evening the big brown man with the shining ring in his ear put his finger to his chest and said, "Portagee. Portagee. Me Portagee."

The other two strangers pointed at him and said, "Por-ta-gee. Por-ta-gee. He Por-ta-gee." That was how we learned that his name was Portagee. It was an easy foreign word to say, for it sounded to us like part of a song.

Now we had names for all three of the *kalunait*, for earlier it had been decided that we would call the other tall young man Kakuktak. We called him Kakuktak, meaning the white-haired one, because his yellow-white hair was so light.

That evening, when we were crowded onto the big bed in a way that makes it warm and companionable, I saw the tall man Kakuktak looking steadily at Sarkak, and I tried to guess what the stranger must be thinking of him.

Sarkak lay half naked on a thick pile of soft caribou skins spread over the wide bed. His long black hair had some strands of gray, and his face and hands were brown as old used leather, tanned from countless hunts out on the glaring sea ice. His nose was small, pinched and delicate, his cheekbones so wide that they drew his eyelids upward into narrow slits. Beneath the smooth hoods of flesh above his eyes, his merest glance was piercing, his pupils clear and black as stones that shine beneath the water. He was bent with age, but his chest was broad and smooth and hairless. His voice was rough as sharkskin. He wore new sealskin underpants, scraped free of hair and white as snow. These were cut wide at the knees for running, in memory of the days when he had been the fastest dog-team driver. His sealskin boots were black and beautiful in their fit, so finely sewn you could not see the sinew stitching. They had been chewed by his wives until they were soft as goose down.

Sarkak was born to lead men. Though the other six main hunters in our village were important persons, clever kayakmen, with growing sons and families, and strong and wise enough to have camps of their own with other men to help them, they had willingly come here. They stayed together under Sarkak, surrounded by more plenty than any other camp could hope to possess. There was almost always enough food and, with it, feasts and laughter and dancing, and many women and girls to choose from. Visitors came often and stood in awe of Sarkak's display of riches and power, such as they had never dreamed existed.

Sarkak's elder wife, Ikuma, was very wise. She sewed and cared for him and advised him quietly when no one else was listening. She was his original wife and had outlasted four others. She had cared for me as a boy. His newer wife, Nuna, was younger than I by two winters. She was smooth as a seal, red-cheeked and full of laughter. Sarkak had chosen her to play with, to joke with and to warm him in the bed at night.

Sarkak's three strong sons, who hunted for him, were his true riches. Kangiak, his favorite, was full of force like his father. The other two had brute strength and were willing to be led. Sarkak passed on to his sons his vast hunting knowledge of the land and sea beasts and the birds of the air. This was his only gift to his children, their only inheritance, and yet it was thought by all to be more than enough.

Sarkak was a sea hunter, a wanderer, with no permanent houses and no lands, for how can a man own the land or the air or the sea, things that are a part of him as he is a part of them? However, certain fiords and places on the frozen sea were recognized as Sarkak's hunting places, but even this slight sense of possession would end the day he died.

As Kakuktak watched Sarkak, I saw the old man close his eyes. Some said that when Sarkak did this, he could magically feel inside himself the changing migrations of the seals and walrus as they fed along the underwater reefs. Though Sarkak had now grown old and rarely hunted, he still remembered all the small signs of morning that could foretell the weather for a whole day. His knowledge allowed him to direct the hunters wisely. He understood the complex patterns of floe ice driven by the wind and the big tides, the rhythmic movements of the ice that could help a man to bring home heavy loads of meat or just as easily sweep him away to his death.

Though Sarkak had no possessions, he needed to hold power over this huge camp of men and women and children and dogs. I knew that some hidden longing forced him to try to dominate everything that lived. Indeed, to Sarkak, these three tall strangers, with their big bodies and sharp sea knives, were now personally his. They gave him power of a strange new kind. For who would not stand in wonder before a man who could organize and feed this camp, and command these three black-clad giants, these dog children, from another world?

My mother was the second wife that Sarkak had possessed. She had died when I was still young, but I often tried to remember her. Sometimes just at dawn, I felt that her spirit came near me, but before I saw it clearly, it would drift away into the other world. Her face and voice were gone from me,

34

but I will never forget the warm feeling of riding naked on her smooth back, within the dark protection of her hood.

In the year of my birth there had been a great killing of walrus, and during the midwinter Sarkak invited many hunters on their way inland to join him in a great feast. Out of snow blocks our people built a huge dance house. For five days and five nights they danced and ate and sang. The young people were wild with excitement, and many girls and women allowed themselves to be hauled into the smaller snowhouses to lie with the men, not once but many times.

I was born during the first storm of autumn and was carefully kept, for it was thought that I must be Sarkak's child. For the first two winters I was treated like a son. When I was still in my mother's hood, just entering the second winter of my life, Sarkak formally arranged my marriage to the first daughter of Tunu, who had not as yet been born. This would have been a splendid arrangement, for Tunu was a good hunter, with a heavy, clever wife. Unfortunately for me, Tunu and his wife produced only male children, and the one girl they did adopt, just to be my wife, was rolled upon and smothered in the bed before she ever saw a summer.

Sometimes at night I think of both those girls, one born and one unborn, as secret wives of mine. Beautiful pale-faced souls they are, with long hair and softly curving eyes. One comes to me in dreams and lies with me, slowly moving her hot buttocks against me. Sometimes I think the other one hides inside the gray bitch, Lao, peering out at me with all-too-human eyes.

But, as I grew older, it was seen that I looked in no way like Sarkak. When other hunters who had been to that famous feast came into our camp, Sarkak would draw back my mother's hood, point to me and say, "This one looks like you. He is surely your son." Then he would laugh, and the others would laugh, for by that time no one really cared whose son I was.

In the next two winters my mother grew thin and lost favor

with Sarkak. He took a red-cheeked girl of only thirteen winters to sleep with him. She was more like a child than a wife. Ikuma didn't seem to mind, for she was wise and durable and always kind to Sarkak. She made the young girl an elaborately designed parka and pants of caribou-fawn skins, and she treated the girl like a favorite daughter. Ikuma always held the important first-wife's place against the right-hand wall of the tent or snowhouse, and no young beauty could ever remove her. In front of her she kept the big stone lamp into which she fed chunks of seal fat. She rarely moved away from the lamp, yet she knew better than anyone else all the things that went on in the camp and out on the sealing grounds as well.

When I left the hood and could first walk, my mother was coughing and dying. By this time she and I had the poorest places on the far edge of the wide bed that stretched across Sarkak's tent.

Early one morning, while everyone slept, I left the big bed and ran outside. When people heard the dogs snarling and fighting, they rushed out of their tents, just in time to kick the dogs away from me and save my life. I had been bitten many times. My lower leg muscles were torn away from the bone. Sarkak, in his rage, slaughtered half of the dogs in his big team, for he believed that any dog that had bitten a human must be destroyed. People said I would surely die, but my mother kept me in her hood and nursed me. At last my legs healed, but they were not straight, and I was forced to limp forever.

Just when I could crawl again, my mother died. Sarkak, perhaps feeling sorrow for her and for me, allowed Ikuma to care for me, and she is the woman whom I remember best. Sarkak was kind to me when I was young and taught me to walk again on my crippled legs, and to refuse to be weak. I worked hard with my hands, stripping lines and scraping skin. When I learned to paddle a kayak, I strengthened my arms and the muscles of my back. Being crippled in both legs kept me from doing many things, but I sometimes went hunting if it was to be in kayaks or entirely by dog team. In certain ways I became stronger than other young men. My legs forced me to spend much time with the women, and I believe that I knew them better than any true hunter could ever know them. I learned secret things about the women of the camp, wild games they have among themselves, that men would find almost beyond their power to believe.

By the time the strangers came to us, I was treated more like a slave than a son, used by Sarkak for piling heavy stones, emptying urine pots, scraping skins and doing worse than women's work, to earn my food, the meat that others gained in the hunt.

When the two strangers, Kakuktak and Portagee, first crowded into our igloo and I was sent to watch over Pilee in Sowniapik's house, I felt certain that my own place on the wide family bed would be taken from me forever. I thought I would have to find a place to lie on the snow floor like a dog, but this great fear of mine did not occur. Instead, when Sarkak had a side igloo built for the *kalunait*, he gave them a position that was lower than my own.

Stone Seal-Oil Lamp

6

The *kalunait* had been with us for less than one whole moon when the domes of all our snowhouses collapsed. It happened late one morning after the men of our camp had been out hunting most of the night and were all asleep. The wind was still, and the heat of the spring sun was strong. Suddenly the snowhouses were filled with blinding light. I could hear people laughing at themselves, shouting to their neighbors, babies crying and dogs howling. It was always like this with us. When the roofs crumbled, we laughed at ourselves for our laziness in not cutting the domes off the igloos when we knew they would fall. We also laughed with joy at the thought of a new season coming to us and did not mind the piles of snow scattered over our beds. The three strangers must have thought, at first, that we had gone crazy, but soon they, themselves, were laughing as they, too, shook the fallen snow roof off their sleeping skins.

For a little while we lived within the crumbling walls of the snowhouses, and the women stretched makeshift roofs of sewn sealskins over them. The sun grew hot, and the melting snow revealed the vast gravel bank on the high ground behind the igloos. When the third moon of spring grew old, the big tides rose with mighty strength and carried away most of the heavy floes of winter ice that had clung outside our bay. The sea stretched endlessly beyond our land, sparkling deep blue in the sunlight

It was almost time to move into tents, and everyone grew excited at the thought of the change. It did not grow dark at all now, and at midnight the sun only hid behind the edges of the hills, then rose again and followed its ancient course through the sky. We tried but found we had no way to tell the three strangers what was about to happen.

Sarkak stood outside one evening, looking at the sky and at the snow turning icy hard in the coldness of the bright night air. He shaded his eyes and stared at the blue fresh-water pools that had formed over the remaining strip of sea ice that clung to the west side of the bay.

"The new boots, are they finished?" he called to the women. "Bring me the new boots."

The children, who had been playing near him when he called, ran to their families and whispered, "We're going.

Sarkak and the foreigners are putting on their new boots. They are getting ready to travel. We're going now. Sarkak will break this camp tonight."

The women looked through their peek holes in the broken snow walls and saw Sarkak's sons Kangiak and Yaw turning over their two heavy sleds and hauling the sealskin dog lines and harnesses down from the high poles where they were kept, away from the sharp teeth of the dogs. The children were right. The winter camp was ended. The women coughed until their husbands awoke and excitedly told them that it was time to move to the Big River, to move to the summer camp.

Everyone hurried in and out of the ruined passageways, their arms loaded with caribou skins, sleeping robes and bags stuffed with spare clothing. The children trailed after their mothers, carrying out stone pots, drying racks, scraping boards, snow beaters and loon-skin sewing bags. Ikuma wrapped her big stone lamp in an old yellowish bearskin and, with the help of Nuna, carried it out of the igloo and watched while it was safely lashed onto the back of the sled. The *kalunait* tried to help, but those poor creatures had no possessions to load on the sleds and did not know what we were planning to do or where we intended to go.

Now Sarkak's two sleds were ready to move. Each load was longer than a grown man and piled higher than his waist. The people from every other household quickly lashed their possessions onto their sleds, caught their dogs and harnessed each of them, with a long single line to the sled. Dogs too young to pull ran free around each team, and bags full of squirming young pups were tied on top of some sleds. Children too old to travel on their mothers' backs were also perched on top of the loads. For them it must have been the most exciting moment of the whole year.

We were ready to go, but still Sarkak leaned against the lead sled and waited.

"The houses," he said, and Kangiak went with Sowniapik,

Poota and Okalikjuak to destroy the front passages of the igloos. They kicked away the snow, to form new false entrances in the side of each crumbling snow wall.

We always practiced this custom carefully when we left a snowhouse, to confuse any evil spirits that might be lurking there and that might wish to follow us. Our people are plagued by many evil beings: dwarfs and giants, strange birds and weird two-headed animals of frightening proportions. In autumn Telulijuk, the woman who lives in the sea, is often heard sighing and screaming beneath the new-formed ice. To make the hunting go well with us, and to avoid sickness and disasters, we try to be careful to do the things that our shaman tells us to do.

I watched Portagee staring at the breaking of the entrance passages and then saw him talk rapidly with the other two strangers. I wondered if they, too, had broken their house entrances to ward off spirits when they had left the south, for something had protected these *kalunait*, something had kept them alive.

When all the real entrance passages had been filled in with snow to deceive the ghosts and spirits, we departed. Kangiak drove the first sled, breaking the trail that all the others would follow. He walked or trotted near the front of the sled, calling out directions to the lead bitch. To trim the course of the sled, he pulled hard on the crossbar lashed near the front or bumped the load with his hip. Sarkak rode grandly behind Kangiak, perched high on a white bearskin covering the load. He watched Kangiak, proud of his son's growing ability to command both dogs and men. Near Sarkak walked his two wives, one on either side of the sled. They were glad to be moving again and ran easily when the pace quickened. Their huge fur hoods were elegantly puffed with wind, and their long-tailed women's parkas, *amoutik*, floated out gracefully behind them. The garments were cut high on the sides, almost to their waistlines, to free their legs for running. Behind the women the three strangers walked together, foolishly fearless

40

of hidden holes in the ice, talking among themselves in loud voices.

Yaw drove the sled that followed Sarkak. It was heavily loaded, for Nuna's mother and I always rode on it. She, like myself, could not run, and when Kakuktak, Pilee and Portagee grew tired, they also rode with us.

After our sled came the other six teams in a long curving line, each following in the others' trail, until we were strung out—dogs, sleds and people—for almost the whole length of our small bay. Down the whole trail you could hear the crack of the long whips and the drivers calling. "Haar, haar, haar!" to their teams. All that remained of our village, as a sign that we had once lived there, was the big whale-shaped women's boat and the kayaks lashed upside down onto their high stone racks.

When Sarkak's sled thundered over the hard glare ice or swished, boatlike, through the shallow blue pools of water that had formed on top of the ice, Nuna and Ikuma jumped nimbly onto the loaded sled. There they sat whispering to each other, for they saw we were entering new country, and they knew human voices will sometimes frighten the sea beasts that have the power to understand the words humans speak.

The three strangers still did not know what we were doing or where we were going or how far we would travel. At first they were nervous about walking into the melted snow water that spread over much of the solid ice, and they carefully walked around the edges of these pools. The big brown man had the sure-footed gait of a bear, and yet he, most of all, feared the slippery blue ice. It must have been his great weight and height that caused him to hold back. I could see that he feared the spongy ice, thinking that it would open up, and that he would plunge downward into the freezing sea, leaving us smaller people around the hole.

Finally Kangiak and Tugak had to take the strangers by the hand and lead them through the big shallow blue pools to show them that the ice beneath would hold their weight. Then, when they found that their new sealskin boots kept out the water and that the sea ice beneath the pools was strong enough to support them, the three strangers skipped with delight like children.

After leaving our winter bay, we traveled east and then turned the sleds northward into the long frozen arm of the summer fiord. Often dozing on the slowly moving sleds, we rode through the long half-light of the spring night and into the soft brightness of early morning. But as the sun grew warm, we hurried on, for we knew that the trail would soon grow soft. We moved close to the land, trying to travel in the shadows beneath towering red granite cliffs laced with delicate tracings of snow. On the dark side of the fiord the stone hills lay wrapped in haze, waiting for the morning sun to turn them red and silver like leaping salmon. All those hills leaned in one direction, and it was said that some giant bird had drawn its terrible claw through them, but that was long ago, in ancient times, before our people came to this land.

Beyond us, as the haze lifted, we could see many seals lying on the ice. They were always wary, sleeping only in short naps, and as the dogs approached, the seals disappeared swiftly down their holes in the ice. We could have stopped to hunt them, but we had brought enough meat with us, and we were anxious to complete our journey.

Finally we could see the end of the fiord, the very place where we would make our summer camp. The drivers jumped off the heavily loaded sleds, urging the dogs forward, and after some time we could hear the surest sound of spring: the wild roaring of the river. It was still completely hidden by the snow, but we could hear it gnawing blindly at the winter ice, clearing its ancient summer pathway down from the inland lake toward the sea. So excited were the young people and stray pups that they ran out ahead of the dogs and sleds. They were eager to begin our summer life.

Our tiredness left us as we forced the dogs up over the big

gravel bank onto the land where we would make our summer camp. The rains and winds and snow had washed the ground clean again. The three strangers must have known that this was the place we sought, for all our things lay scattered on the ground, just as we had left them the year before. There were fish spears, tent poles, old stone lamps and blubber pots, for, of course, no human had been to this place since our leaving. The dogs were quickly unharnessed, and men, women and children hurriedly dragged their driftwood tent poles into position. Everyone helped to cover the poles with old sealskins sewn together into tenting, and then heavy rocks were placed around the edges of the skins to hold them down against the winds that often grow violent at the end of summer. We put up eight tents in all, with entrances opening south toward the end of the fiord or slightly west, in the direction of the river. Everyone flung their bedding and clothing and household things inside.

There had never been any pattern for the position of our new homes. Each family simply chose some high, dry place where they could easily gather stones to hold down the tents. But for the first time in my life, I noticed a curious separation in our camp. Sarkak's big tent and the smaller tent of the three strangers rose on one end of the high gravel bank. But I saw Sowniapik, Tungilik and the other hunters take their tents and move farther along the bank, toward the river, where the fish should soon run in countless numbers. A child could throw a stone the length of this split within the camp, and yet it was there.

The old woman, Ningiuk, and her shy young daughter went into the small tent belonging to the three strangers and fixed a new bed for them. Ningiuk, laughing and joking about geese and girls and men, made a bed using Sarkak's old sealskins over which she spread one of his thick white bearskins and some warm caribou sleeping skins. Portagee and Pilee pulled off their boots and pants and sang a wild, quick song to the two women. They tried to grab the girl, but Ningiuk

43

pushed her out of the tent and laughed at the boldness of the strangers.

We all ate quantities of seal meat, and almost before finishing we fell asleep, never thinking of feeding the dogs, for they could hunt lemmings for themselves and would not be worked again until the snow came in the early winter. I gave Lao, the gray bitch, some scraps of seal meat when no one saw me, for I hated to see her so lean from hunger. She looked bad enough as it was, with her winter coat of hair falling out in patches.

After our day-long sleep, we arose that evening and heard the first calling of the geese as they winged high above the tents, returning to their summer nesting grounds after their long winter in the south. Everyone started calling, "Kungo, kungo, kungo," imitating the sound of the snow geese. And when the big birds, pure white or sometimes slate-blue against the evening sky, answered down to us like old friends, "Kung-o, kung-o, kung-o," we held up our arms to them in greeting.

The three strangers called to the geese in their sharp voices, so delighted were they to see a familiar sight from their own land, and everyone laughed to hear them.

Some said to others, "See, they are really men like ourselves. They, too, can speak like geese when they wish to do so. We will show these dog children our ways. We will teach them to hunt like men."

From the coming of the geese until the darkness returned in autumn, people lost all track of time. The strangers, at first, tried to keep the order of days and nights, but soon it was lost to them, and they did not care, and we did not care. The sun wheeled endlessly above our heads, and we hunted and ate and laughed and lay with our women. Only the rise and fall of the tide had any meaning for us during the short softness of summer.

Dog Sled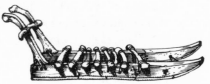

7

Late the following afternoon I heard Sarkak call to me, and I hurried out of the big tent. He was lying comfortably on the dry gravel bank beside the strangers' tent. The three of them sat near him, and he was gesturing and talking to them, as though they could understand his words.

"Bring one of the fish to me," he called.

Nowya's wife had walked up to the still-frozen lake, and finding a hole in the rotting ice, had jigged patiently for char, big sea trout, the best fish we have in our land. When we awoke, two huge char lay in Sarkak's tent as a gift for him. They were as long as my arm, with bright silver sides and deep red on the belly. We knew the sun would scarcely rise again before all the fish would slip beneath the ice of the river and rush into the safety of the sea, where they would remain until the fish goddess drew them back to us on the big tides near the end of summer.

Hooking my fingers through the gills of the biggest sea trout, I hobbled over to Sarkak and laid the fish on the clean white gravel beside him.

"*Shavik*," Sarkak said, as he drew out the dead stranger's knife that was concealed in the top of his long boot. Looking at the three foreigners, he again said, "*Shavik*," while gesturing with a cutting motion toward the fish.

All three men quickly nodded their heads up and down in their strange way and reached for their knives, for they had understood that he wished them to use their knives to cut the fish.

Kakuktak reached into the pocket of his short black coat, took out a flat, brown-covered thing and removed a long thin stick from a sheath in its side. When he opened the thing, I could see that it was white and smooth inside, with marks scribbled on it. Kakuktak looked at Sarkak and said, "*Shavik?*" while pointing at his knife.

Sarkak held it up and said, "*Shavik.*"

With the stick Kakuktak made some dark marks on one of the thin white skins attached between the brown covers. Our people often cut marks like these on bone and ivory and make the deep lines dark by rubbing them with black soot from the stone lamp, but it was the first time that I had ever seen anyone marking on something other than bone or ivory.

Sarkak pointed at the big fish and said, "*Ikhaluk.*"

Kakuktak nodded and scribbled again, slowly and carefully. Then he pointed to the tent and said, "*Tupek?*"

Sarkak also pointed and said, "*Tupek.*" Kakuktak marked once more on the white skin.

Sarkak quietly said to me, "These *kalunait* do some stupid things, like making their little marks. But, oh, I know they are wise in other ways. You should see the huge boats they have and the guns that belch smoke and fire and kill bears at great distances."

Bending forward, Sarkak slit open the belly of the huge sea trout and reached inside. He pulled out two long clusters of pink fish eggs. These he divided into four pieces, and holding back his head, slipped his portion of the delicate roe down his throat.

Kakuktak closed his eyes and did the same thing. Portagee ate his portion, but I saw Pilee slyly hide his in the gravel.

Then, with a quick movement of the knife, Sarkak slit the big fish lengthwise, from tail to head, cut the two pieces in half and cleverly stripped the meat away from the bones. Taking one quarter share for himself, he grasped the pink slab of meat firmly between his teeth, and with a great reckless slash of the deadly-sharp knife he cut off a slice just below his nose.

I had often watched him do this while eating in the company of visiting hunters, and it had always amazed them, for it was a wild unruly movement performed by one who either was an expert or scorned danger.

46

The strangers stared at Sarkak in disbelief as he wolfed down the portion of raw fish. They watched him as he sliced again and again with the same breath-taking accuracy.

Portagee tried gnawing the fish with his teeth, but the tough silver skin held the red flesh together, and he got almost nothing. Pilee looked away and would not eat the fresh raw fish. Kakuktak grasped a slab between his teeth, took his knife and hacked away beneath his nose until he sliced a mouthful free. He chewed it, swallowed it and bit into another piece, cutting it quickly, with the knife close to his nose, in imitation of Sarkak.

I saw Sarkak pop out the two fish eyes and slyly place them in his mouth, for he could not bring himself to share this special delicacy with the strangers.

"*Mumuktopaluk,*" said Sarkak, patting his big belly, meaning that it tasted good.

Kakuktak answered, "*Mumuktopaluk,*" in the true fashion of a hunting man.

Sarkak was pleased, and he looked straight at Kakuktak for a long time. I could see that he believed Kakuktak might become one of us, for this yellow-haired stranger was very quick and willing to learn.

I looked at Kakuktak, too, as if I were seeing him for the first time. He finished the fish and lay back on the gravel, resting his weight on one arm. He was long and lithe and graceful in his movements, like a young male caribou before the rut. His body was thin, and yet you could see that he was strong. His wrists were thick and square, but his hands somehow seemed too big for them. His neck was wide and curved gracefully upward, smoothly attaching itself to his well-shaped head. His whitish-yellow hair had grown longer since he had come to us and now caught the sunlight as it shifted in the faint breeze drifting from the sea. His nose was strong and bony and sharply separated his round deep-set eyes, which still troubled me, because they were not at all like the beautiful dark eyes of our people. But Kakuktak was no longer ugly

47

and frightening to me. When he smiled and his white teeth flashed, we all smiled back with pleasure. For now, although we could not speak together, we felt like brothers in a family. After all, this should be so, for the earliest story I remember is about a young woman of our people and a dog who slept together. Her father was ashamed of her and sent her to live on a remote island. There she had a litter of half dogs, half humans. She kept the best ones, but for those that were most doglike she fashioned and sewed a large leather slipper and sent the ugly children adrift to the south. When she tried to return to our people, her father killed her, and she fell into the sea and became a goddess. Now here were three of the great-grandchildren of that litter, relatives returned to us. In my mind at the time it was just as simple as that. These strangers having nothing and knowing nothing seemed very inferior to us, like overgrown children whom one must care for and protect against harm.

After they had eaten the fish, we lay together on the dry bank, watching the white clouds shift their dark-blue shadows across the green sea, for there were almost no words we could say to each other. The three strangers silently and thoughtfully looked around at our camp, watching the people and dogs moving between the tents. Their eyes also searched the waters of the fiord leading to the distant sea.

A little later Pilee jumped up and pointed, shouting, "Dag-it! Dag-it!" for that was the name the strangers called Kakuktak. The other two strangers leaped up and stared out to sea.

Sarkak said to me, "They think it is the white sails of one of their ships, but it is only a high drifting piece of ice."

Portagee, Pilee and Kakuktak sat down slowly, and again we all silently looked at each other and at the camp.

Our camp was on the east side of the riverbank, on the high ground above the place where the river, now breaking free, spewed chunks of ice out over the deep waters of the fiord. So well did the soft lines of our sealskin tents blend into the many russet-colored patches of the tundra that at first the camp was difficult to see. Between the tents there was a scattering of dark rocks and old tent rings and faint traces of the high gravel beaches where the sea had washed in ancient times.

Just above the camp a narrow stream ran down from the hills into the big river, and once a day you could see a young girl from each tent go to the stream, carrying a sealskin bucket. The girls would take their time filling the buckets and then would hurry back to the tents, imitating their older sisters' smooth stylish way of walking. It was the custom of our young women to walk quickly and gracefully over rough ground, even if they carried a load, so that they would look busy and alert and be seen by everyone to be good material for wives.

Almost all of the ice in the fiord had gone, and as often happens in summer, the water down its whole length lay dead still, reflecting the sky. Here and there a seal raised its black head to breathe above the water and then disappeared, leaving ring after ring, widening and shining in an outward course, increasing in size until the rings weakened and disappeared into the flatness of the sea. Long skeins of brown female eider ducks winged low across the horizon, where the broken drift ice stretched into high mirages that tapered, bent and shifted skyward in the waning light of early evening. High above us the snow geese drifted in from the south, flock after flock, calling, calling, searching for a place to land, for they had flown great distances. The high currents of wind that carried the sound of the geese back to us struck the black hills and swept down on our camp. A big cloud drifted across the sinking sun, and the gravel bank lost its heat and turned cold beneath our bodies.

Sarkak was the first to rise, stiffly, like an old man. He smiled at the three strangers and at me. Then he turned in silence and made his way slowly back to the big tent. Although it was still light, we could see the faint glow of the seal-oil lamp through the thin front wall of the entrance passage. We could hear Nuna humming to herself as she waited for him. She sang that tender wordless song women sing when they shrug their shoulders to comfort a baby in the hood. She had no child, but I knew she wanted one.

Portagee and Pilee stood up and rubbed their arms against the sudden cold, exchanged a few words and hurried inside their own tent. Then Kakuktak rose and walked down slowly to the water's edge. I saw him staring at his reflection, his other self, and I imagined that he was thinking of that far-off place that had been his home.

Sea Knife

8

Sarkak's summer tent, with its long entrance passage, seemed huge. It was much larger than any other I had ever seen, and of an ancient style that has now almost disappeared. Hair had been left on the sealskins that formed the rear half of the tent so that it would be dark inside, a good place to sleep during the bright nights of summer. For some magical reason the seal claws had been left on all the skins. The whole floor of the tent had been leveled with clean white gravel, more than a hand's depth of it above the half-frozen ground. The summer rains would run beneath this gravel and leave the floor dry. If anything was spilled on the floor, it would quickly run through the small stones and disappear. Sarkak had one vast bed that filled the entire back half of his tent, wide enough to sleep a dozen people, and made of deep layers of dry sweet-smelling heather covered with soft caribou skins. The long, high inverted-V-shaped entrance passage attached to the front of the tent served as another room. Its walls were made of *mumik*, the thin membrane stripped from the inside of the skin of the bearded seal that allowed a yellow-brown light to filter through. Here the women had a bright place to sew and gossip, and the children had a safe place to play, away from the dogs. The strangers often visited this bright porch, for they liked to be with people.

In our tent that night I heard Sarkak laughing and whispering in the bed with Nuna. They spoke together of the big brown man and the great physical differences that the women ascribed to him. Nuna said that she could not believe them to be true.

"You shall know," said Sarkak. "Tomorrow night I shall give him to you as a present. Later you can tell me what is true and what is not true."

"I would be too afraid," she said. But by the excited way she laughed, I could tell she would not be too afraid.

On the following evening Portagee found two children sleeping in his place in the bed. When he went to Sarkak's tent to speak of this, he found everyone lined up comfortably in the bed, waiting for him. There was one snug place left for him, right beside Nuna. Sarkak smiled at Portagee and waved to him, gesturing, insisting, that the brown man occupy the warm fur hollow beside his beautiful young wife.

Since Sarkak was the master of the house, everyone knew that he had carefully arranged all of this. Sarkak sighed with pleasure when he saw Portagee crawl, fully clothed, into the bed. Sarkak rolled over, confident that his wife would have the exciting truth for him in the morning.

I saw Nuna smile at Portagee, her loose hair spread around her as she lay naked beside him. Portagee raised his head twice to stare across Nuna at the broad snoring figure of Sarkak. He lay down again stiffly, perhaps with fear, for while I stayed awake he did not move or sleep. At dawn he hastily left the bed, still fully dressed.

"I think he was afraid," I heard Nuna say to Sarkak in the

morning. "I think you frighten him, even when you sleep. He smiled at me once in the night and even touched me once, but drew his hand away, as though my thighs were made of fire."

"Even so, I still believe all the wild things I have heard about him. He must be afraid of you," Sarkak replied.

She laughed. "I do not think he is afraid of me."

Early the following morning I hobbled outside. At the same time the stranger we called Kakuktak left his small tent and walked some distance away to urinate between two big stones. He turned his back in a shy way, hunching over secretly, as though he were ashamed of what he did and wished to hide his yellow urine from the sky. Returning to the tent, still buttoning his strange pants, he stopped and looked out across the fiord, watching as a big flock of snow geese set their wings and drifted low over our heads. I could tell by the way they gabbled softly to each other that they had not seen us and were about to land.

Just at that instant Kangiak, having heard them, slipped out of our tent, moving cautiously so that he would not disturb the geese overhead. He crouched and waited, motionless, until they were beyond his sight, and then he quickly gathered a slim three-pronged bird spear, a throwing board and six newly strung throwing bolas made by the women. He turned to me and moved his head in the direction of the geese, showing me that he was going after them. Carrying the spear and bolas, he started inland toward the place where he knew the geese would be landing.

Looking around, he saw Kakuktak and waved for him to follow. Kakuktak joined Kangiak quickly, and with a feeling of envy I watched the two of them make their way cautiously up the river valley. I saw them crouch as they hurried over the hill that led toward the great tundra beyond the half-frozen lake.

I returned to the tent and slept badly through the morning, for I was excited by the calling of countless geese flocking in from the south. I knew that every hunter must be out after the birds, and my mind walked with them where my legs could not carry me. I lay in the tent and tried to put the crazy chattering of Nuna's mother out of my mind.

I awoke to the sound of laughing and shouting, and when I limped outside, I saw Kangiak and Kakuktak standing like two fat snowmen that children make. Strung around their necks and across their shoulders they each had more snow geese than I could count on my fingers and toes. The great white birds hung down heavily, wings loose, dark feet dangling. The two hunters laughed and joked with Nuna and Yaw, and many women and children hurried out of their tents to see the catch.

Portagee and Pilee came out, too, when they heard Kakuktak's voice.

"Oooh-ho!" cried Portagee as he lifted the big clumps of birds from Kakuktak's shoulders. Holding them at arm's length, he rolled his eyes, laughed and shouted, "Heavy, heavy, heavy!" He pretended to stagger under the great weight of the geese.

We all laughed together and imitated his shouting. "Ooohoh! Hay-vee, hay-vee, hay-vee!"

Pilee looked at the two hunters, but his face showed nothing. He stood with his hands thrust deep into the sleeves of his jacket. That was often his way.

Kangiak said to me, "Kakuktak knows how to throw a bird spear, although I do not believe that he has ever thrown one before. He must live life well, for the geese crowd in on him from the sky. They land on the snow near him and seem to want to give themselves to him."

Sarkak stood nearby, listening to the words of his son, appraising the tall yellow-headed stranger. Perhaps he thought it was true that this man had good fortune, and perhaps he would bring meat in plenty to the camp.

Everyone standing there looked at Kakuktak in a new way. We thought there might be some kind of magic in him, for when he and the other two strangers had come to us in spring, the ice had left us, and more seals than we could eat had come to us. Now the hills around echoed with the calling of countless geese.

Some of the older women, laughing and smiling, took the welcome burdens of warm white birds from Kakuktak and Kangiak and walked across the stone beach to the water's edge. There they sat together and plucked them. To the spirits of the geese they hummed songs that caused the faint breeze to shift and blow northward, helping to carry the soft white down across the tundra. We believe that on this wind the spirits of the birds drift back to their nesting places.

It is the custom to give all birds to the women of one's household. The women may keep or distribute the birds as they wish. In this way the wife of a good hunter holds an advantage over other women. She has the great power of giving, of obligating others to her.

That evening Ikuma cut the first goose that Kakuktak had killed into many pieces, for she was acting as his mother. She flung them up into the air, and everyone in the camp, including the children and even the dogs, scrambled to have a piece of this sacred meat. It was Kakuktak's first kill among us, and it meant that he would always share with us as we would share with him.

Crowding around Sarkak's tent, everyone in the camp sat facing the sea that had sent us such riches, and together we ate our fill of geese. We ate the soft meat and sweet yellow fat until we were bursting and flung the guts and feathered skins and bones to the dogs that sat ringed around our feasting. We whispered among ourselves and laughed softly, for we knew that it was rather dangerous to eat or dance or sing under the open sky, where the spirits could see us.

Sarkak sat on a thick piece of winter caribou skin that his wives had spread on the gravel. In his left hand he held a whole goose carcass and cleverly stripped the meat from it, eating hungrily, without pausing to wipe the grease from his face. His eyes never stopped searching the faces of the three foreigners, and I knew that he was trying to decide how he would fit them into the life of the camp to suit himself.

I saw Sowniapik and Poota also looking at the *kalunait*. They told me later that they did not know whether to like or to fear these men, since they seemed so closely allied to Sarkak. They thought that gave him too much power. We were all trying to learn about these dog children, and as we squatted together and slowly ate our gifts of geese, I, too, looked at Kakuktak, Portagee and Pilee and wondered what they thought of my people, the real people.

Finally, when all of us had finished, an old man, the father of Atkak, rose and ran stiffly around us, shaking his bag of amulets at the spirits who lurk in the four corners of the world. Then entering the circle we made for him, he sang a song, imitating the soaring flight of the great white birds. He often turned directly to Kakuktak. He sang slowly, stamping his feet to set the rhythm:

> "*Ayii, ayii, ayii,*
> *My arms, they wave high in the air,*
> *My hands, they flutter behind my back,*
> *They wave above my head*
> *Like the wings of a bird.*
> *Let me move my feet.*
> *Let me dance.*
> *Let me shrug my shoulders.*
> *Let me shake my body.*
> *Let me crouch down.*
> *My arms, let me fold them.*
> *Let me hold my hands under my chin.*"

Atkak's father ended his powerful song with his vision of geese folding their wings and landing. Everyone exclaimed in wonder at the gracefulness of the old man's motions that seemed to burst from his wrinkled parka, as though some great bird spirit had possessed him.

During those days of early summer, whenever the three men sat in front of their tent, some of our people usually came and sat with them. Mostly it was the younger ones who went to visit, for many of the older ones were too shy and found it difficult because they could not speak together. Some in the camp stayed away from the strangers because they were angry with Sarkak and frightened by the new power that these huge foreigners had brought him. When geese and fish and seals were caught, Kakuktak, Portagee and Pilee were given a full share, just as though they were important hunters in our village, and some people were resentful because they thought them lazy and saw that only Kakuktak might learn from us to hunt for himself.

I could feel the camp breaking into two halves. There was a separation growing like a thickening wall of ice between our family and the strangers and the other hunters and their wives. It was strange to watch this separation, for the oldest people whispered that they had never known such a thing to happen. If a person or a family became angry with other people in a camp, it was the custom to move away quickly rather than risk quarreling or violence. But after the strangers' arrival, in spite of all the misunderstandings, everyone stayed together. I think it was curiosity about the *kalunait* that held the camp together, but I wondered if any good could come of this growing distrust.

Most of the young people did not seem to notice this feeling. They laughed with the strangers and tried endlessly to teach them to speak in our way. Kakuktak would make markings on his thin white bundle of skins, and we later knew that he needed only to look at these markings and he would remember many of our words. He also made delicate images of things with his thin sharp stick. He drew tall ships with wind sails, strange houses with high doors and too many windows, big-breasted women with thin waists and fat buttocks, wearing strange hats and ridiculous parkas that hung to their feet, and birds and whales and huge dogs that hauled rolling boxes with men in them.

Always, when Kakuktak began to draw pictures, many people crowded around him to watch. At first it was these pictures more than words that helped us to understand each other. By placing a harpoon in the backs of whales he drew, we knew that he was trying to kill them magically. These strangers were hunters, all right, but they did not know how to hunt in our way.

One day Kakuktak loaned Shartok, Tungilik's son, his little bundle of skins and the marking stick. Kakuktak and Pilee and Portagee seemed amazed at the quick, clever drawings Shartok made of the camp. His images showed the position of each tent, with our people and dogs, as well as some spirits that are usually unseen floating around the tents. He also drew the three strangers so cleverly that they could easily recognize themselves. I was not surprised, for I knew that Shartok was a poor hunter, good with his hands. Shartok was a skillful mimic, often full of jokes.

On this day he also made a drawing of Neevee, because he always wanted to lie with her. While she and many others watched, he drew her naked, carefully showing the details of how her legs fitted into her body. He outlined her breasts and copied her hair style and even the soft blue patterns tattooed above her wrists. When he was finished, Shartok held up the drawing so that Kakuktak and the two other strangers could see it. He pointed at Neevee, which caused her to laugh softly. She turned red with pleasure but ran away to her family's tent, because she was so shy.

The three strangers reached out for the bundle of skins and carefully examined Shartok's drawing of Neevee. In low mumbling voices they talked fast together and laughed among themselves. Portagee stood up quickly and watched to see into which tent she ran and where she slept. Outlined against the evening sky, Portagee looked immense, his one bright earring glistening, his nostrils blown wide. He kicked the gravel like a musk ox at mating, his legs stiff with yearning.

Skin Tent

9

It was during the fullness of the egg-gathering moon that the young women of the camp first started to work their wiles on the strangers. One clear white night I awoke and through my peek hole in the tent saw a pair of girls come nervously from the other side of the camp. They walked hurriedly, arms around each other's waists, whispering, leaning so close together that they looked like one person. To avoid the noise of gravel beneath their feet, they chose a soft path on the tundra behind the camp. I could tell that they were nervous. When they reached the strangers' tent, they scratched gently on the sealskin flap. The girls waited, scratched once more, and when the *kalunait* still did not wake, they hurried back to the tents of their families. It all happened in that quiet time before dawn, but in our camp I am sure that more than one pair of curious eyes followed the girls on this first night visit.

The strangers soon found that, like ourselves, they could not always sleep during the long white nights of summer, for the land was full of light and sound. Sometimes, hearing the endless calling of the geese, the howling of the dogs and the laughter of our young people, they got up and went walking. At that time I, too, was bothered by those long summer twilights and was often wakeful. Some nights I lay and thought of girls. I also dreamed about bears, which means that a man should try to lie with a woman as soon as the dream is ended. But this could not be for me. Sarkak would never ask any hunter to give his daughter to me, and I knew that if he did not speak for me, I would never have a wife.

One night I went out and, helped by the gray bitch, made my way up to the top of the hill behind the camp. I stopped to rest, with my back against a rock, breathing in the rich damp smell of the tundra. The sky curved down to touch the plain as it stretched endlessly away, rising slowly to meet the distant snow-peaked mountains, whose high white valleys lay almost hidden under long blue shadows. On the land itself only a few patches of old snow remained. The caribou moss had changed color, slowly spreading its soft gray-green magic across the tundra. The black rocks had reappeared, displaying their bright splashes of red and yellow lichen.

Out on the plain below the hill I saw Yaw and Shartok walking with Kakuktak and Portagee. They were spread out, moving slowly, searching for eggs. This was not hunting; this was women's work. But men also enjoyed the pleasure of discovering the hidden nests of warm green eggs.

With the first coming of true morning the sun's heat warmed the land, and everywhere white mists rose like steam. I saw Yaw pointing to a swan's nest, with the great white bird perched on top, its delicate neck a curved streak against the land. Swans are fearless fighters that can easily drive off owls and foxes, but this swan wisely flew away as it saw the four men approaching. Yaw and Shartok squatted by the nest and showed Portagee and Kakuktak how to crack open the big eggs and suck out the contents. When they were finished eating, I saw all four of them lie down on the high dry ground that the swan had chosen, and for a while I think they slept.

From beyond the fish lake I saw two girls come slowly through the mist, searching the ground for goose eggs, making their way back toward the camp. I could tell by their careful way of walking that they carried many eggs in their hoods and in the front aprons of their parkas. I looked toward the swan's nest and saw that the four men were awake, but they remained motionless as they slyly watched the girls approach.

Suddenly Shartok and Yaw jumped up like a pair of wolves hunting caribou and raced across the flat plain toward the girls. When Neevee saw them, she quickly knelt on the ground, carefully emptied her apron of eggs and desperately pulled them, one by one, from her hood. She could see that it was Shartok, and I knew that she didn't like him. He was almost on top of her when she leaped up and with deadly accuracy threw two goose eggs at him. He dodged sideways, too late, as one burst against his chest and the second splattered yellow on the side of his head. Laughing, Neevee whirled around and ran smoothly over the rough ground toward the camp. Shartok must have been embarrassed by having egg yolk on his face and parka, but he raced on after her through the mist. Somehow I knew he would never catch her.

Shartok's sister had short legs and did not even try to run from my brother Yaw. She carefully placed on the ground the eggs she carried in the apronlike skirt of her parka, just before he caught her by the wrists. Portagee and Kakuktak stood up with excitement as they saw the two wrestle gently, careful not to break the eggs in her hood, while he forced her slowly to her knees. It was like watching a game. She did not make a sound as he bent over, lifted the long back tail of her parka and possessed her, driving hard at her, quick and passionate as an animal. When it was over, he stood up, and the girl, too, rose cautiously. I saw them standing together, both feeling carefully inside her hood to see if he had broken any of the precious eggs. I guessed that he had not, for she calmly gathered up Neevee's eggs, as well as her own, and wandered away from Yaw. I heard her calling out to Neevee through the mist. As for Yaw, he hiked up his parka and carefully retied the drawstring of his pants. I could tell by the way he walked back toward the two strangers that he was somewhat pleased with himself.

The gray bitch whined softly at my feet. She watched my face with her pale eyes, as though she understood all my feelings of loneliness. I remember even now how my soul cried out for strong legs that could run a girl to ground.

On the following night, when the pale stars could scarcely make themselves seen in the east, I sat on the rocks behind our tent, scraping the handle of an old fish spear, binding new springing prongs of caribou shinbone onto the slim shaft. All the young people went up to the high plain behind the camp, and from their shouting and laughter I could tell that they were playing the kicking game. A little later I saw Pilee, Kakuktak and Portagee also walking up, and I could not make myself stay behind. I called the gray bitch, and holding tight to her neck ruff, I forced my way slowly up the steep path.

Once over the hill I sat on a dry patch of tundra where I had a good view of the game. Some of the young people called to me in a friendly way, but I do not believe that Portagee or Pilee or Kakuktak saw me, so absorbed had they become in the playing. All the clouds had melted together, turning the whole sky into a smooth gray skin that stretched evenly over our camp between the hills and the far horizon of the sea. It made the tundra glow in a strange way, like the silver guard hairs on a wolf.

Some woman had sewn up a sealskin ball that she had stuffed full of caribou hair. It was bigger than a man's head in size, stiff and hard, and would roll a long way when anyone kicked it. I watched with pleasure as everyone laughed and pushed and rushed back and forth, wildly kicking at this ball, and I imagined myself running and laughing and kicking with the rest of them.

Soon others came up from below. The old woman, Ningiuk, and her shy young daughter passed by the place where I sat. Ningiuk was puffing and blowing after the long climb and rested at the edge of the plain. Then she joined in the kicking game, and I was surprised that she could still run so fast. Young mothers carrying small children on their backs soon found them too heavy for running, and they let out of their hoods those old enough to walk. In no time these young chil-

dren were running, half naked, among the players, squealing
in delight, and everyone laughed, for the tops of their heads
scarcely reached the knee bones of Kakuktak and the gigantic
Portagee.

In a little while Pilee and Portagee set up two stones, side
by side, at each end of the plain and divided the people into
two groups. Then they showed each group how to go against
the other. They showed the players how to kick the ball violently and fight their way through their neighbors to reach
their goal. It was rough and unpleasant, puzzling to watch,
and when my people understood this new game, they were
shocked, for it was not a game of pleasure. It was more like
men fighting against each other in anger. But still they continued, for everyone wished to be polite to the strangers. In
our minds it would have been rude of us to offend them.

Slowly the young people changed the game so that it would
not be like fighting. They laughed and did not really try to
force their way to the other goal. Only the three strangers
rushed wildly after the ball, smashing into each other, kicking
and snorting like animals. It was terrifying to watch them.
Kakuktak's nose ran with blood, but he did not seem to care. I
turned my eyes away and stared out at the blankness of the
sea, for I did not want to watch their madness. I wanted to like
these *kalunait* and have them for friends. Later, when I looked
back, the three foreigners were lying down, exhausted, on the
tundra. The young people went on kicking the ball, some of
the older ones rudely joking and pretending to be violent.

After a while the strangers entered the game again, but
they were tired and played more gently this time. It was as if
they had run off some of their wild fighting energies and were
beginning to understand our joyful way of playing.

Panee, Atkak's daughter, stood at the edge of the plain,
whispering with her friends Mia and Evaloo. Panee was tall
and quick, with narrow hips and full breasts that swayed
wildly when she ran. As I watched her, she darted out at Portagee and tripped him. He fell and rolled over and stared up

into her laughing face. Then he jumped up as if it had not happened and ran after the ball again. It passed near me, and I tried to kick it while everyone was running and shouting around me, and for a second time I saw Panee slip her foot cleverly between the big man's legs and send him sprawling on the ground. He leaped up, looked surprised and pointed his finger at her, but she laughed again and made no attempt to hide the fact that she had tripped him. I did not see how she managed it the third time, but Portagee stumbled again, and his fall could only have been caused by her, for she stood almost over him. He grabbed at her leg, but she leaped back quickly and screamed as she darted, quick as a fox, across the high plain.

Portagee jumped up and raced after her. She had a good lead on him, but as we watched, we saw that with his long strides he would soon catch her. There was a great tumble of rocks on the edge of the plain that led to a twisted path up into the hills, and reaching them first, Panee scrambled upward over them, moving with the swift sureness of an animal. Portagee, though, like the other strangers, did not know how to run quickly over rough ground, and he climbed badly. He was only halfway up the first terrace of rock when she reached the second small plateau. We saw her look back at him, and it seemed to me that she waited for him, but when he reached the plateau, she was already running, although more slowly this time. He almost caught her, but she turned and ran into the soft mossy place surrounded by big boulders. We saw him lunge in after her.

Some children started to follow them across the plain, but their mothers and older sisters called them back, and the game continued. Everyone played recklessly without rules or sides, and the women looked at each other and laughed a lot, for they knew that Panee was the first to catch a stranger.

Soon Panee emerged by herself from the hiding place between the boulders. She walked slowly across the high plateau and made her way down through the tumbled stones. At first she seemed not to notice us at all as she caught her loose black hair together into a knot and hid it in her parka. Then, seeing that the game had stopped and we were all watching her, she glanced back at the hiding place and started to run toward us. She ran slowly, solidly, like a married woman. When she reached the others, she laughed and gave the ball a kick. This started the game again.

Portagee came down through the boulders carelessly, his short black jacket flung over his shoulder. At first he kept his head bowed, so that I could not see his dark handsome face. He sat down near me and would not play in the game again, though the children pulled at him, urging him to get up and kick the ball. When Pilee laughed and spoke to him, I noticed that Portagee did not answer. He kept his eyes on Panee, watching every move she made.

Woman's Ivory Comb

10

With the waning of the egg-gathering moon the tides swelled and carried away the last ice that clung to the shores. The sea was open. Sarkak sent Yaw and four other young men to bring the boats we had left at the winter camp, and after walking across the mountains stretching between our fishing place and our winter camp, they returned three days later, singing as they rowed the big skin women's boat. They had three kayaks lashed across her gunwales and five more towed behind.

There was great excitement when the kayaks and the umiak arrived, for everyone had grown tired of eating fish and birds and eggs, and we all longed for the taste of some dark-red seal meat. Out on the fiord the returning kayakmen had seen seals along the edge of the drifting ice, and we were eager to have them. But first we had to suffer four days of wind. Kayakmen hate wind above all other things, for any breeze ruffles up the smoothness of water, and in the short chop of waves, seals surface and breathe and disappear again without being seen.

The umiak belonged to Sarkak, and every kayak belonged to some particular person. Every young man knew someone well enough to borrow a kayak when it was not being used. This was our way, for we share everything. Nuna's mother owned a kayak. It had belonged to her dead husband, and she had brought it with her to our household. Being a woman, she could not use it herself, but because I often did favors for her and sometimes brought her a seal to share with others, she let me use the kayak whenever I wanted. She even patched it for me so that it no longer took in water.

By now the mosquitoes were rising off the ponds and coming to us, weakly at first, in softly singing hordes, but we knew they would grow stronger as the sun warmed their wings. Four days after the kayaks returned, the water became smooth and calm again, and I could scarcely wait to leave the shore and the mosquitoes far behind me.

Kangiak and Kakuktak helped me rig the hunting gear on the widow's kayak, and they held it steady as I slipped my crippled legs beneath the long slim deck. Kangiak then climbed into Sarkak's kayak, showing Kakuktak how to do it without upsetting the delicate craft. One after the other they pushed away from the shore and followed me down the long stillness of the fiord. Our long double-bladed paddles left twin circles on the water, like the legs of giant water bugs. Ahead of us, we knew there must be seals hiding in the loose scatter of ice.

For me it was a dreamlike sensation to be afloat once more, to peer down into the deep clear water and watch the great fronds of seaweed move with the tide. On the water my crip-pledness was gone, and my arms seemed to sing with strength.

When we returned after being out all day, the night sun had come down to walk on the edges of the hills before it would rise into the sky again and become a new day. All the women and children were down at the landing rock, trying to gauge the amount of meat each kayak carried. Everyone was delighted at the thought of the feast to come, for the three of us had shared in the killing of a great bearded seal.

Although it was Kangiak's harpoon that had caught the great seal for us, it seemed to me that this sea beast had in some way come to us at Kakuktak's bidding. It was indeed as people had said. Kakuktak was a fortunate hunter. The first time he sat in a kayak he was able to share in a great kill. He was so fortunate that he was able to let his luck run over onto other people as well.

I was tired from the day in the kayak and trembling after my climb from the beach, and I was glad to be helped by Kangiak and to lie down in our tent in my humble place at the far edge of the bed. I ate little and slept soundly until a small noise woke me in the middle of the white night. I came fully awake and heard two girls hurry past our tent, whispering softly. I removed the small bird-skin plug from the peek hole by my head and saw these girls walk up and stand boldly be-side the entrance to the strangers' tent.

One of them was Panee. She reached out cautiously with one hand and scratched the seaskin flap. With the other hand she waved away the clouds of mosquitoes that crowded around the opening of her parka hood. I could see now that the other girl was Evaloo. She was Sowniapik's daughter, who had long ago been promised by her father to Atkak for his son. I had always thought of her as a stupid girl, but she was young and red-cheeked and had a smooth close-kneed way of walking that excited me.

Panee reached out again and shook the entrance flap. This

time Portagee thrust his head out of the entrance and looked at the two girls, smiled and then quickly drew his head inside. The girls continued to stand there, giggling nervously as they fought off the mosquitoes.

In a few moments Portagee reappeared, fully dressed, followed by Pilee, who pulled his short black jacket over his pale naked shoulders as he left the tent. The two men walked quickly away from the tent and turned toward the path that led into the hills beside the river. They beckoned to the girls. But the girls hung back and would not follow the strangers. The two young women did a violent pantomime of fighting off mosquitoes, and then they turned quickly and darted inside the sealskin tent, where Kakuktak still lay. Pilee and Portagee whispered together for a moment, and then they, too, ran back and plunged inside the tent, drawing the flap tight against the starving hordes of mosquitoes.

I replaced the piece of bird skin in the peek hole beside my head and rolled over onto my back. Many thoughts raced through my mind before I fell asleep. Portagee and Panee had lain together up on the hill, and now, so soon, she was back for more, this time bringing a friend with her. Pilee must at that moment have begun for the first time his coupling with Evaloo. Now of the three only Kakuktak had not had a girl, but perhaps before they left the tent, he, too, would have bent one of these girls double beneath him. Perhaps he would bend both of them, for I could tell that they were wildly willing, just at the age when girls are in a hurry to become women. I did not know anything about the strange coupling habits of the foreigners at that time, although there was already much talk about this and some speculation about the powerful Portagee. I had noticed from the day Pilee started to get well that all three strangers were excited by our women. Such feelings are probably shared by men everywhere. Yes, and women and animals, too. We are none of us so different when it comes to the thrill of mating.

But it was all wrong. I felt that strange uneasiness again,

as if something evil were slowly creeping toward us. These girls had found it easy to cross the short distance that separated Sarkak's tents from the tents of their fathers. It was exciting for them to kneel down on the bed and bend themselves under the thrusting weight of these exotic strangers. These girls were like wild children playing, but if they continued to lie with the strangers, they would gain power over them. They would learn to speak to them and advise them. I wished that these thoughtless young girls were full-blown women and as wise as Ikuma. She would know how to handle the strangers and still hold our whole camp together.

This secret meeting was Sarkak's fault. It should never have been allowed to happen. As he had given the strangers meat for their hunger, boots to wear and a bed to sleep in, so should he have lent them women, real women, hunters' wives, who would have known how to satisfy these strangers and then returned to their husbands and families without harm. This is the usual way in our camp. He should not have let the strangers become starved for women. Now, instead, these young girls were running in and out of the strangers' tent at night, and Sarkak knew nothing of it. As for young people coupling together, Sarkak thought no more of it than the casual mating of dogs in his team. But because the hunters' daughters were secretly lying with the three giants, those warriors who, Sarkak thought, belonged to him, it was dangerous. It could cause him to lose control over the foreigners, and if that happened, the split in the camp would widen into three groups. Everyone would suffer for it.

I was tired after my night of wakefulness, for the girls had stayed with the strangers all night, and I could not help but hear their smothered laughter. The foreigners in the morning seemed half dead after their orgy in the tent, and Sarkak, for some reason of his own, was in a surly mood.

Pilee, having nothing better to do, picked up a dog whip, and holding it the wrong way, tried helplessly to flick the long lash out before him in imitation of a dog-team driver. Portagee lay beside the entrance of the tent, laughing at Pilee but too tired to rise and try it himself.

"Go and wet the dog lash for them," Sarkak told me. "They'll never make it crack that way."

I hobbled over to Pilee, led him to the fresh-water pool and showed him how to soak the braided sealskin lash. Pilee tried again, bending his elbow without rhythm, trying to move too fast. The long lash curled once more around his feet.

Sarkak, watching him, said, "He can't crack that whip. He entangles himself like a woman."

Pilee glanced at Sarkak and with disgust flung the dog whip onto the ground near the entrance to the tent. He bent over, picked it up again and drove the heavy whip handle between two big stones that weighted down one side of the entrance to the tent. Walking across the stony beach, he stretched the wet lash straight down toward the sea and placed a stone upon the tip of the lash.

"What is that supposed to do?" said Sarkak.

I had no answer for him, and Pilee could not understand his words. Pretending that he had not even heard Sarkak, Pilee, for no reason known to us, started to throw loose rocks over the long straight line of the whiplash.

"What is he doing now?" Sarkak asked me. But I still had no answer. I could only stare at the angry stiff-legged stranger as he flung the stones faster and faster.

Pilee stopped only briefly to straighten up and call, "Portagee!" and the big brown man rose slowly and ambled down over the stones, with his loose bearlike way of walking. Pilee said something quickly to him in their own language, and they both glanced at Sarkak and began working together. Slowly, where the stones had been removed, we could see a straight line of clay appearing along the edge of the stretched whip.

Then Pilee walked up to the tent and got a harpoon line. He fastened it to the big stone on the other side of the tent entrance and drew it straight down toward the sea. He did this with great care, so that between the harpoon line and the whiplash there was exactly enough space for two men to walk side by side.

Now the strangers bent to their task in earnest, hurling the stones away from between the lines with surprising force.

"Look at them. Those two, they eat like four men and play like children." said Sarkak. "Son of mine," he called out to Kangiak, who was coming up with Kakuktak from the river, "come and see this. Come and take a look at these two using so much energy to destroy the land."

As he neared us, we were surprised to see Kakuktak strip off his parka and hurry to join the other two men flinging stones. After some time, when they had cleared all the skull-shaped stones from between the whiplash and the harpoon line, the men threw themselves on the ground, panting for breath. Yet they seemed proud of their work and called, "*Peeyuk? Peeyuk?*" to Sarkak, hoping he would agree that this removing of stones was good.

But Sarkak only answered, "*Shunukiak?* What is it?"

The strangers rose and once more stretched the two lines from the point where they had stopped clearing the stones to farther points down toward the sea. Between the newly stretched lines I could see a large pointed boulder. I believed they would have to go around it, for it was buried deep in the hard clay and would take many men to move it. But when they reached the stone, Portagee went behind their tent and returned with a heavy, curved walrus tusk and a short, strong length of driftwood. Together the three dug and heaved and fought against the rock. Many of us gathered near them, but they turned their backs on us and did not seem to want our help.

"I'm hungry," said Sarkak. "Let us go and leave these children to their play."

Ikuma and Nuna hurried up to the tent, and all the rest of us turned away and left the foreigners to their senseless wrestling with the rock. We ate quickly, without much talking, and went to sleep.

Early in the morning the old widow whispered to me, "What's that sound?"

Dimly I came awake and heard the unfamiliar clicking of stones falling against stones. Because it was the warmest time of year and I had no woman, I had slept fully dressed on top of the sleeping skins and could leave the tent quickly. I hobbled outside, and although the whole fiord was white with early-morning mist, I could see the outlines of the three *kalunait*, who were already up and eagerly clearing their path that now stretched more than halfway to the sea.

Kangiak and Sowniapik joined me beside the new path.

"They got it out," said Sowniapik.

"Without any help from us," said Kangiak, staring into the huge wet hole where the boulder had been. "They must have worked most of the night."

When we walked near the strangers, we could see that they were tired of their work, and now they welcomed any help we would give them. Some kayakmen and their sons and daughters joined us, and we ourselves began clearing that crazy path. Slowly, as the morning wore on, the *kalunait* stopped working and became our masters. Pilee shouted harshly at the young people, and when they slackened their work, Portagee strode toward them with anger on his face, as though he might strike them.

The work was not completed until evening, when heavy sealskin bags of gravel carried by the women had been spread along the whole length of the path and a neat border of stones had been placed along both sides, from the entrance of the strangers' tent to the sea.

"*Peeyuk. Peeyuk.* Good. Good," the strangers cried excitedly.

Pilee was the first to step into the finished path, and he caught Kakuktak by the arm. Together, smiling and nodding, they walked like white-faced gods down to the sea and back. The brown man followed a few paces behind them, and in this way the three strangers seemed to possess the path for themselves.

None of us, not even Sarkak, ever walked on that path. It is still there for you to see, although the ice and tides have destroyed the lower half and our tents are long gone from that place. The geese do not come to nest in that part of the land any more, and the caribou do not pass there in autumn. Some people say the animals see that straight path and flee from it in fear, for they know that it was built by men.

Sealskin Kayak

11

From the first day we brought the strangers to the village, everything started to change for us. We began to look at our own lives through their eyes. For the first time we started to see ourselves. Without a common language to speak together, we had to observe each other carefully. Perhaps this was not a bad thing, for in watching a man, his face, his hands, his movements, waking and sleeping, and in listening to the tone of his voice, you may come to know him better than he could ever know himself.

By the middle of summer the foreigners had begun to relax. They slept in our beds, laughed often and seemed to feel as safe as children among us. They were learning to live freely as we did, enjoying each day, not caring about tomorrow. They ate huge quantities of food. They wolfed down the seal meat we gave them and devoured countless eggs that the women and children gathered. They grew heavier. More and more they tried to make themselves understood by talking. The children seemed to understand them best and would often tell us what they said, and we would find that they were right. Children are not supposed to know much, but they have good memories and a quick ear for strange languages. The foreigners were no longer shy. They wanted us to know them, and they sometimes seemed to compete among themselves for our attention.

One day I remember the strangers talking excitedly together, sometimes laughing, uttering their flat shallow-sounding words, piling them one on top of the other, like skipping stones. Toward evening they walked together up into a narrow ravine in the hills. Later they came back down and took three driftwood poles out of their tent, leaving it sagging and almost collapsed. Then they returned to the top of the path and started shouting, "Aa-hoy! Aa-hoy! Aa-hoy!" while waving the long poles above their heads.

Everyone hurried outside the tents to watch them, and we heard Kakuktak calling, *"Kilee, kilee, kilee,"* half-magic words we call sometimes when we want a seal to come to the harpoon of the kayakmen.

Sarkak went up the path first, of course, followed by the hunters, their women and the old people. The children scrambled wildly upward through the rocks. I dragged myself up, too, helped by the dear bitch Lao, and when I got there I saw everyone standing or squatting on their heels in a big circle around a newly formed outline of stones. It was almost as large as a women's boat but slim and pointed at both ends like a hunter's kayak.

When we were silent, Pilee walked stiffly back and forth, as though he did not see us, his eyes searching the hills. Then suddenly he shouted, *"Tuga, tuga, tuga,"* the words we call out when a sea beast is sighted.

Quickly Portagee and Kakuktak snatched up their long poles, and with Pilee they ran to the stone outline of the boat.

73

They pretended to climb over its imaginary gunwale and knelt down inside. Pilee sat on a high stone at the stern of the boat, guiding it by holding his pole like a long steering oar. Kakuktak was in the middle of the boat, facing Pilee, and moving his pole back and forth with a long steady stroke like a kayakman sitting backward. In the front of the boat Portagee rose up and extended his arm, pointing forward with the first finger of his right hand at the imaginary whale. Kakuktak moved and sat down. After stroking briefly, he moved again and again sat down. In all he sat in four places, and in each position he rowed hard with the long pole. Twice he placed it out on one side of the boat and twice out of the other. In this way we could easily see that it required four men to row the boat and that Pilee was the one who steered it, the one who commanded it.

Now Portagee pointed his long arm forward again and picked up the pole. He held it lightly balanced in both hands, aiming it forward like a huge harpoon. Kakuktak pretended to row hard, springing his back and straining his legs, so that we knew he was used to working hard in this way. Pilee bent against his steering oar and started calling out to Kakuktak, loudly at first and then more softly, until he almost whispered. From the tenseness of his voice I could imagine that they drew close to the whale. He called out a long stream of words, speaking very rapidly. The words sounded like singing, for they had a rhythm and excitement in them that somehow set the pace of the swift strokes of Kakuktak's oar. I heard a murmur of excitement run through the women watching.

Leaning forward over the bow of the boat, Portagee gazed intently beneath the surface of the imaginary water. Then he seemed to see something, for he swayed back fast and held tight to the long pole. Kakuktak raised his oar in the air but did not turn his head to look at the surfacing whale. Suddenly it rose, its back almost touching the boat, and I believed that at that moment I could almost see it, too. Portagee blew out his breath noisily in imitation of its breathing. Then he reared

74

back, taking careful aim along the rough pole, and drove his harpoon forward and downward, deep into the whale's back. He knelt down quickly, leaning sideways to avoid the imaginary harpoon line as it whipped over the bow, and he looked down to see how deep the whale would sound. From an imaginary bucket he dipped up water and poured it over the hot smoking line to keep it cool as it ran around a turnpost. Then they all three held onto the sides of the boat and swayed back and forth as the whale rose to the surface and dragged them at great speed through the water.

I could scarcely believe my eyes, for all of this was like our own sea hunting, but the strangers were using their boat as we would use a sealskin float. They allowed the whale to drag them while he was still full of life.

We watched as they slowly hauled in the imaginary line and let it run out again, and in their clever pantomime we saw the whale surface three times. As he rose again to breathe, they were almost on top of him. Portagee, his muscles bulging, picked up the pole once more. This time he made us believe that it was a killing lance, and he drove the blade in and out of the great beast, giving each thrust that skillful bloodletting twist we knew so well. Again the foreigners pretended to hold the gunwales, as the whale, in its dying, thrashed and rolled over and over as the spirit ran out of it and hid beneath the reddening sea.

Kakuktak leaned over the side of the boat and caught the imaginary fin of the whale and held it fast while Portagee stepped boldly out onto its great yielding belly. With his knife Portagee slashed a short double vent in its thick skin and fastened a pair of lines to it. In this way they towed the floating carcass, tail first, back to their great ship, all three of them rowing and singing, straining with every stroke. Finally they lifted their oars high and signaled their ship to come to them.

Suddenly they jumped up, stepped out of their stone boat and, smiling, bowed before us. Their pantomime had ended. People blew out their breaths in surprise and pleasure, for we had all understood perfectly this hunt of the whale. Now we knew much more about these strangers, for we saw that they had a real hunting skill of their own.

Looking at these three men and remembering their dead companion we had found frozen in the valley, my count made four. Where were the other two men, I wondered, the missing ones? Our minds must all have worked together, for Sarkak walked up to Pilee and pointed to his place in the boat, then to Kakuktak and Portagee and their places, and then he pointed to the three empty places.

Pilee nodded his head. He walked away from the stone outline of the imaginary boat and started slipping on the tundra, as though he stood on ice. He walked cautiously, looking around himself. Then he fell. As he went down, he grasped for the hand of another imaginary man, and, struggling, they both appeared to slip into the water. Pilee lay thrashing on the tundra for a moment and then relaxed and became still. We all knew that he had acted out the drowning of the two missing men.

Thus it was that we discovered how these strangers had come to us and how their companions had died on the way.

Whaler's Harpoon

12

For the two and one half moons of summer the entire world seemed full of the river's singing, and the sky knew no darkness. Children usually played throughout the long white nights and slept soundly in the midday. In the mornings mist drifted in from the sea and wound its way among our sealskin tents. It crept low between the black hills and seeped like white smoke over the tundra, hiding the vast inland from view. Out in the fog beyond the camp, it seemed like an unreal dreamworld. One could hear geese calling, young people laughing and dogs howling. The sounds they made were all strangely the same, as they mixed and blended together.

Since I was a small boy, I have always heard that fog in summer is caused by young people carelessly coupling with each other as they lie out on the open tundra. Young people should be more careful what they do under the open sky, since fog never fails to spoil the summer hunting. Fogs do not come to us, they say, when people lie together properly inside the tents or snowhouses.

So careless were our young people and the strangers, too, that heavy fog came to us for five days. It was so thick at first that the kayakmen stayed inside the tents. We all slept too much, and people grew bored. Sarkak became restless and bad-tempered. Then the rain came, with strong winds driving heavily against the tents, night and day, with a violent whipping sound. When the rain stopped for a while, men hurried outside to search the sky, hoping to see some sign of lightness between the clouds, some break in the weather. They straightened the tent poles, piled heavier rocks around the bottoms of the tents and shook their weather amulets at the sky. But the rain came again and again, for five more days, lashing the river and the tents, melting the last gray patches of snow, turning the hills into black dripping monsters.

With so many people crowded into the beds, it was hard to live in the tents. At first it was comfortable enough. We slept a lot, talked together and listened to old stories. But too much sleep makes the head ache, and one's thoughts grow heavy. Someone coughs and spits and coughs again, always in the same way, and everyone grows nervous.

Once during the storm we heard Pilee and Portagee shouting at each other in the little tent next to ours. Pilee rushed cursing from the tent, in spite of the driving rain, and many eyes watched him stamping along the high bank of the swollen river. When I thought of the three strangers, it was with pleasure and yet with misgivings, for although it was exciting to have them among us, I could see that the whole life of the camp was changing.

When we had all had more of this cold dampness and confinement than we could stand, the old widow, Nuna's mother, started that crazy singing of hers. I heard the same words flow out of her over and over again, a widow's song, a song her husband never heard her sing before he disappeared:

> *"Ayii, ayii,*
> *I must not live out all my days visiting*
> *I must find my way home*
> *I must fly, fly, fly, to my home."*

Again and again she sang it, slowly at first, just humming the rhythm, "Ayii, Ayii." Then louder and louder and louder she sang until she was almost screaming the words as she waved her arms in the air and cried out, "Fly, fly, fly, to my home."

Sarkak allowed her to continue, because we all respected our old people and because we were always afraid of a person gone crazy. Sarkak also believed that he might be hearing the soul of her dead husband, singing words of advice to us through the mouth of his widow. In the next tent I heard Portagee imitate the sound of the widow's singing, and Pilee laughed, so that I knew their anger was gone.

I wanted more than anything to run outside the tent and go away from the awful singing. Yet I could not risk it, for I had only the clothes I wore on my back. If I got wet in such a foolish way, people would laugh at me and think me a nervous fool. I tried to put the singing out of my mind by looking at the far side of the tent where Ikuma sat calmly beside her seal-oil lamp, with her loon-skin sewing bag across her knee. I watched her as she slowly dampened the long caribou sinew by holding it in her mouth. Then, squinting her eyes, she

78

threaded her precious copper needle and sewed the fine stitches that would make Sarkak's boots waterproof.

Next to Ikuma Sarkak lay on his belly, propped on his elbows, naked, with the caribou sleeping robes flung carelessly across his back. He stared at the gravel floor in front of the bed but saw nothing. He had closed his ears to the high-pitched singing and was wandering with his mind through some distant land of his youth.

On the other side of Sarkak lay Nuna, also on her stomach, her shoulders the color of smooth sand. Her long hair, spread across her back like a cape, shone blue-black in the lamplight. She sometimes glanced at her mother when the old woman's voice broke as she gasped for breath to continue singing. But Nuna seemed indifferent to the song. She had a length of braided caribou thread stretched between her fingers, and she had formed a complicated string figure of two caribou. But try as she would, she could not make them move. Ikuma, who had taught her the figure, leaned over, smiling, twisted Nuna's wrists and moved her fingers in the proper way, but still Nuna could not make the caribou figures walk across the strings.

During most of the long rainstorm Kakuktak also lay in our bed. At this time he seemed to prefer our company to that of Pilee and Portagee, who had almost nightly visits from Evaloo and Panee. Kakuktak lay flat on his back, staring at the bright dripping holes in the roof of the tent. He sometimes wore his hat in bed, which I always thought strange. He also wore his black jacket buttoned to the neck, for he was often cold, but I knew he wore no pants or boots. He always rolled them together to form a pillow beneath his head.

Next to Kakuktak lay Kangiak, who had become his best friend and adviser about our ways. During the bad weather Kangiak talked a great deal, but he spoke slowly and simply so that Kakuktak could follow. In this way we believed Kakuktak would come to understand our language.

On the other side of Kangiak, our brother Yaw was fast asleep, with the covers over his head so that he could not hear the widow's wailing. The widow's place for sleeping was next to me, against the damp wall of the tent, beside the second lamp, which I had to tend when her soul went flying.

We all slept with our heads toward the entrance, as was our custom, so that the men could slip out of bed quickly if they heard a strange noise, such as narwhals blowing in the fiord or dogs fighting so hard that they might kill each other. I usually liked living in the tent, for it was a warm and dark and secret place, and the soft yellow light of the lamp cast shadows everywhere in strange patterns. But during this long summer storm it was torture to lie staring at the brimming stone urine pots and watching the curving rivulets of sweat run down the inside walls while the crazy widow sang and sang.

Finally Kakuktak could stand the sound no longer and went and walked beside the swollen river until he was soaking wet. He returned, his wet boots squishing on the sodden tundra, to lie shivering naked in the bed, the steam rising from his wet hair.

Slowly a lull came in the storm. The wind shifted and breathed gently out of the north, opening the sky once more. Like magic the bright sun and wind dried the land for us. The water in the fiord turned bright blue and glittered as though it were filled with hidden lights. A new feeling of joy came to me, a feeling of excitement that would not let me sleep.

We could see that with the coming of the foreigners our possessions had increased. We needed still another boat. The frame of an old wooden umiak lay on the high beach, and Sarkak sent two men with strong skin line to relash its gunwales to its ribs. Women followed, carrying huge soaked sealskins, which they flung over the upturned frame and sewed with double lapping seams. Slowly the skins dried in the sun and drew tight against the frame. The big boat became like a smooth and mottled whale. It was a women's boat, one that they would row themselves, to transport tents and meat and dogs and children.

13

On the last two days of the rain Pilee had gone to sleep in Sowniapik's tent, because he could no longer stand either the company of Portagee in the little tent or the crazy singing of the widow that drifted out of Sarkak's tent. They say that to fill the boring time between waking and sleeping, Pilee took a flat stone, and spitting on it, ground the point of his sea knife until it was deadly sharp. He took a long time to do this. He lay belly-down on the bed, slowly honing the shining metal against the stone, testing the blade many times against his thumb and occasionally cutting away some of the hair that grew on his face. He seemed to enjoy the knife's new sharpness. It was as though he and the knife were companions, and he glanced only slyly at the other people in the bed.

When the rainstorm ended, Pilee discovered that Sowniapik had a flat piece of driftwood behind his tent. This wood was almost as long as a man and as thick as his leg. It was nicely squared, with nail holes in it, and must have come from some large foreign ship that had been wrecked far away. Wind and tide had carried it to our coast.

Pilee knew a game that he began to play with his sea knife. He would stick the knife lightly in one end of the long piece of wood, and then, using his two forefingers, one held before the tip and the other behind the hilt, he would flip the knife. It would whirl three times through the air and land point-first, quivering in the wood near the other end of the plank. He made a small mark on the far end of the wood, and he could almost always strike the mark or come close.

Pilee allowed me to practice the game with his knife, and Sowniapik practiced, too. Slowly we gained skill until we could always make the knife flip and stick in the board and sometimes even hit the mark. Some of the other kayakmen and even Sarkak tried it a few times, but we were too far ahead of them, so they usually stood by and watched us play this new game.

One evening Pilee and I went to Sowniapik's tent, and the three of us started to play the knife game. We took our turns proudly with the shining blade, and imitating Pilee, Sowniapik and I groaned whenever our opponent's knife point hit the mark. After we had played for some time and the others had gathered to watch, Pilee held up his hands to draw everyone's attention. Then he took the knife and carefully cut a white button from the top of his pants. He held the precious button up between his thumb and forefinger for all to see and then placed it in the center of the long piece of wood. Looking around, he saw a pair of short summer mitts belonging to Sowniapik. They were new sealskin mitts, with a thin dog-skin trim at the wrists. Pilee pointed to them and got Sowniapik to pick them up and hold them over his head for all to see. Then Pilee had him place them beside the button.

Pilee stabbed a new small knife mark on the board, and using an imaginary knife, he showed us with his hands that if his point struck closer to the new mark than Sowniapik's, he would win the mitts, but if Sowniapik's knife flip came closer, then Sowniapik would have the button.

This was a whole new idea to us, and no one fully understood what Pilee meant. Seeing this, Pilee took up two pebbles from the floor of the tent, and he gave one to Sowniapik and kept one himself. He placed his pebble on the board and got Sowniapik to place his there also. Pilee then flipped the knife, and Sowniapik flipped the knife. Pilee's blade was closer to the mark, and he picked up both pebbles. In this way we came to understand this kind of gambling for the first time. It was a very exciting idea.

Sowniapik was delighted to flip the knife for the button, and we all gasped with wonder to see that he won it from Pilee and still retained his sealskin mitts. Because he was bursting with pride at his good fortune, Sowniapik jerked off his parka, and in a moment his wife had sewn the button onto the very center of it. When he drew it on again, the button seemed to wink magically in the flickering light of the lamp like a white third eye.

Sowniapik looked around wildly, trying to see some possession of his that he could bet against Pilee. Remembering one, he quickly put his hand down beneath the covers and drew out the bound cluster of little ivory knives, the amulet he used to rattle when he wanted to cut the weather. They were yellow with age, for they had come down to him from his ancestors.

Pilee looked at the little knives with disdain. He thought that they were a child's toy and did not know that they would sometimes cut away bad weather or calm a stormy sea. We had no words to tell him this. To keep the game going, though, Pilee accepted the little ivory knives and reluctantly cut away another white button from the top of his trousers. Pilee also showed us two more he had at the back of his pants, and we grinned slyly, for we thought Sowniapik would soon enough win those, too. Then Pilee did a pantomime of how his pants would fall down if he lost all his buttons, and we laughed aloud, for we were delighted with this humor.

After the second button and the cluster of little knives were laid in the center of the board, Pilee flipped his iron knife close to the mark. But Sowniapik flipped the knife closer, and he won again. Then Pilee bet another button and this time won. The game went back and forth between them, with the buttons, the mitts and the clump of ivory knives, until Sowniapik had won all four of Pilee's buttons. His wife sewed them all onto the chest of his parka triumphantly, and they seemed to wink in the light like the eyes of two staring foxes.

The tent was hot and steaming wet, crowded with people. We were excited by this great new game. I was the third player, but I had been forgotten in this contest between the two men. Everybody was looking at Pilee and Sowniapik. With a gesture I shall never forget, Pilee held the knife itself aloft and pointed to it. People gasped, for they knew that he offered it instead of a button. Sowniapik's eyes narrowed as he watched Pilee's face, for he wanted the iron knife more than anything he had ever hoped to possess. Slowly he began to take off his parka with the four buttons on it, but Pilee reached out and stopped him. Then Pilee took Sowniapik's hand and placed it on his daughter Evaloo's wrist, lifting their hands together. At the same time, in his other hand he lifted the knife.

It took us all some moments to realize that Pilee wanted Sowniapik to offer his daughter as a bet against the knife. When Sowniapik understood at last what Pilee wanted in the game, he glanced at his wife. He did not like what he saw in her eyes and started to release Evaloo's hand, but his hunting companions groaned with disappointment, so he jerked her hand upward again. The girl was trembling with excitement. For the first time in her life she was the center of everyone's attention. So the bet was made and understood by all.

Pilee stabbed the board hard, making a clean new mark, and offered the knife to Sowniapik first. Sowniapik crouched, aimed and spun the knife with all his skill, and it landed right beside the mark. Everyone blew out their breath, believing that he had won the knife. But Pilee moved into place. Slowly and carefully he gauged the distance with his eye, held his tongue between his teeth and flipped the knife. It flashed down the board and buried itself into the very center of the mark.

We drew in our breaths sharply. Pilee clenched his teeth in a half smile as he reached out and reclaimed his precious knife. Then, with his left hand, he stretched across Sowniapik, grasped Evaloo's wrist and hauled her roughly over to his side. He dug his knee into my hip, and I moved sideways to make room for Evaloo. Pilee forced her to sit beside him, and because she tried to draw away, he put his arm around her neck and dug his hand down the front of her parka between her breasts. He seemed to stare at us all in defiance. The thought came to me again that he and the other two foreigners were one thing, and we were another, and perhaps we could never really be together, never understand each other.

Pilee looked at Sowniapik's wife, and I followed his eyes to her face. It was like a death mask made for the dance house. She seemed without blood, without life, her eyes drawn into sharp slits that let out no light. Pilee quickly let go of the girl, stuck the knife in the board again and lay back on the bed so that we could not see his face, hoping we would not see that he was trembling.

Everyone started coughing, which is our way of easing a tense situation. The tent was thus filled with a sound that was neither laughing nor crying, yet no one had to speak. I was glad that I was not Sowniapik, even though he had the four wonderful buttons on his chest. He would somehow have to settle with his wife for the daughter he had just lost.

When I looked around again, I could scarcely believe my eyes, for Sowniapik had reached back and was holding up the hand of his other daughter, Mia. No one was as surprised as Pilee, who sat up quickly and looked hungrily at the second girl and then at Sowniapik. Pilee drew the knife from the board and held it above his head. This time Sowniapik reached out, and taking Pilee's knife hand, he drove it down with force until the knife stuck in the board. Then he took Pilee's hand and made him grasp the wrist of his first daughter, Evaloo, and made him raise it again. So Sowniapik's first daughter was bet against his second daughter. I thought to look into Sowniapik's wife's face, but I did not have the courage, fearing that it would be more terrible than before.

Pilee's face was deadly white and sweating. I believe that our closeness suddenly terrified him. I saw him look around at the cold eyes of the kayakmen, trying to guess what they were thinking. Then he forced the knife up out of the board and offered it to Sowniapik. But Sowniapik did not accept the knife or move or even change the expression on his face. His gaze seemed to bore straight through the brown-haired stranger.

Pilee made a new mark, knelt down and quickly spun the knife into the very heart of the target. He drew the blade out of the wood and handed it to Sowniapik, who, like a man in a trance, spun the knife without hope or skill. It landed on the very edge of the board, far from the mark.

This time Pilee did not reach for the daughter, Mia, but simply sat in his place. A moment of silence passed before Sowniapik, without looking, reached back and grasped his daughter by the neck of her parka. He hauled her forward and flung her roughly at Pilee. Those of us who had been sitting on the bed moved away. We wanted to be in some other place.

Pilee sat alone on the bed, holding his precious knife. Both of Sowniapik's daughters cowered in fright on either side of him. Pilee must have known that every eye and every hand in the tent was against him, for with a sudden gesture he leaned forward and handed Sowniapik his knife. Pilee handed it to him backward, with the handle out and the blade pointed toward himself. This has a special significance to us: It is a sign of surrender, a sign of giving.

We all started coughing again, and the terrible tension in the tent was broken. Now Sowniapik had the precious knife, and Pilee had the two daughters. We all knew that Pilee could do nothing with the girls except to lie with them, which, after all, would not hurt them. They were said to be good at lying with men, for the young men in our camp had given them a lot of practice. If Pilee hurt either of them, some relative would soon seek revenge upon him. If he could feed them and truly call them his own, we would be very surprised. Sowniapik had really won, for he now owned the precious shining knife. He had only his wife's feelings to worry him, though that was bad enough. Later I heard Ikuma say that Sowniapik's wife went to bed holding a needle in her hand for several moons, and he was afraid to go near her, fearing that she would stab him in the groin. But she let Pilee sleep between her daughters in their tent whenever he wished, and she even came to like him and to admire openly his hot thrashings in the bed. She, like several other women, made new boots for him and chewed them soft while they were drying. Pilee was always able to work a kind of magic on any of the women who came near him. It did not matter to them that he was often bad-tempered, slept through the mornings and could not make a seal come to him during the rare times he did go hunting. They recognized his other strength that had nothing to do with food gathering.

Cutting Tool

14

Sleeping places for the foreigners were settled by the middle of summer, as settled, that is, as we would ever care to have them, for it was our custom to have visitors we liked sleep in any tent or igloo. This was good, for the changing of sleeping places among all villagers and visitors truly joined us together into one great family.

Kakuktak slept with us in Sarkak's tent. Portagee slept by himself or with Panee when she came to visit him in the little tent, and Pilee ate and slept with Mia and Evaloo in Sowniapik's tent. This occurred, I believe, because the three strangers had become secretive with each other. They had arrived together, but now we could see that they were breaking apart. Because of his strange hat and the bright metal buttons on his jacket, his strong way of talking and his position as boat steerer, we were made aware that Pilee was somehow above the other two men. Portagee, with his huge strength, his smooth-muscled brownness and his booming laughter, was no brother to these two pale men, and sometimes I could see that he wished to break away from them. Kakuktak, even though he had yellow hair, was most like ourselves. We knew that he would soon be able to speak fully with us. He learned all our ways from us and melted into our lives. Kakuktak had the gift of understanding our language much more than the other strangers. Perhaps this was somehow connected with the marks and scratchings he made in the flat bundle of thin white skins.

With each passing day it was easy to tell that Sarkak had become very fond of Kakuktak. Sarkak showed his feelings in a dozen ways, and it must have left his sons and relatives and even some of the kayakmen with a feeling of jealousy toward Kakuktak. But still they also could not help but like him, for he had a way of listening and smiling that was much admired. Every child, and all of the old people in the camp, had become his friends.

In the mornings Sarkak would often lie and watch Kakuktak until he saw that he was awake, and then he would ask him some simple question, choosing easy words he knew Kakuktak had written down. If Kakuktak understood him and answered him, Sarkak beamed with pleasure. When they were up and out of the tent, or just sitting on the edge of the wide bed, Sarkak liked to sit between Kakuktak and his favorite son, Kangiak, and talk to both of them. Tugak and Yaw could not have liked this, but they were slow to take offense at anything. At this time in midsummer the split in the camp seemed to be mending itself. We all relaxed in the abundance of food and good weather and the excitement of having strangers among us. It was a pleasure for all of us to have Sarkak in such an expansive mood, for there were times when this had not been so, when his black moods had frightened and depressed us all and destroyed every happiness. Some of us dared to believe that this good life would stay with us forever.

Kangiak and Kakuktak became good friends. They tried talking to each other constantly and shared jokes together. They could wrestle and skip flat stones across the water with about the same degree of skill. I saw them sometimes running together up on the inland plain near the lake, and I wished that I could run with them, for the whole plain was covered with a bright blanket of yellow poppies and soft red fireweed.

Sarkak was never far away from Kakuktak and Kangiak that summer. Sometimes I heard him call out, "Sons of mine, come to me." In these words one could tell that he desired to have Kakuktak as a son, that he already thought of him as his adopted child. Often Sarkak would sit inside the tent and boast to us about how clever Kakuktak was. He would speak of how quick and skillful Kakuktak was becoming with a bird dart and how splendid his drawings were in the brown-covered bundle of white skins. He would remark how wise Kakuktak was to remember the words he had heard the day before. Sometimes I had heard Kakuktak say these very words, haltingly like a child. Then Sarkak would repeat them to us quickly and smoothly so that they sounded correct and adult and made everyone pleased with Kakuktak's knowledge.

At this time Sarkak spent little time with his wives. He seemed entirely bent on teaching Kangiak and Kakuktak the many skills he possessed. I knew of his great ability with a throwing board and the three-pronged bird spear. I knew that he could make fire not only by whirling a bow drill, but by striking two flints together as well. I found that he remembered ancient skills from the past that we had never witnessed before. One day I saw him kneel and lure a quick and nervous weasel out of the rocks. He deceived it into coming to him, and then he snapped its neck as quick as lightning in a way I had not thought possible.

Kakuktak had a great fondness for the bow, and he and Kangiak practiced together endlessly, as though they played a game. Sarkak had lost much of his real skill as an archer, for he had not hunted in years. He asked Okalikjuak to come and teach these sons of his how to make and use a bow.

Okalikjuak was a lean, quiet man, with a narrow face baked brown from wind and sun. When he was young, he had been carried north in his mother's hood and had grown up among the caribou people. These wild inlanders had made two slits on either side of his lower lip and had forced a pair of round antler buttons through these holes. After he returned to us, he continued to wear them. I could not think why, for these bone ornaments gave him a wild inhuman look.

That summer Okalikjuak taught Kakuktak and Kangiak the archer's skill. He showed them how to crawl across the open plain, holding bow and arrows in their mouths. He showed them how to deceive animals and how to wait, crouching, holding the bow flat, horizontal to the ground, while driving arrows swiftly and silently into the mark.

Kakuktak gained skill with the bow as quickly as he had with other weapons. He was indeed material for a son.

One evening when Kangiak and Kakuktak had gone hunting, Sarkak returned to the tent to lie down between his wives. He was warm and expansive with me and with the women and spoke of the young men gathering skills. He asked Ikuma about the boots he had ordered her to make for Kakuktak, and she drew them out from beneath her sleeping skin. Sarkak inspected them with as much care as he would his own, for he knew that Kakuktak had no way to judge well-sewn boots.

Nuna took one up, examined it and sighed, for she doubted that she would ever be able to sew such a masterpiece of a boot, one that would allow a hunter to stand in the freezing sea for half a day without getting his feet wet. Nuna spoke in a false way, but she was careful to offend neither Sarkak nor his older wife.

"Now Kakuktak has beautiful new boots, and all the children in this camp act as though they were his children. Kakuktak does not need a wife."

Sarkak sat up quickly, for he had not thought about the idea of a wife for Kakuktak. He let his mind dwell on this thought, and I could see the excitement rising in him. His women were always clever at planting ideas in his mind just at the right moment. He swiftly drew on his boots and light parka and left the tent. We heard him pause outside the entrance flap, then slowly move away.

Ikuma rose quickly from her place on the bed and stepped

quietly over to the flap of the tent. Nuna glanced at her mother, and I turned to see the old widow. She was poised silently, as still as a hunting fox, her eyes narrow and alert. Her usual mindless nodding and humming had disappeared. She looked at her daughter and drew in her breath with approval, for she was fully aware of the sly power of women.

Nuna followed Ikuma to the entrance. I could not bear to wait and then ask these women where Sarkak had gone. I felt I had to know, so I eased myself off the bed and hobbled over and stood with them, peeking out of the tent flap.

We saw Sarkak in the middle of the camp, standing fat and bold, his head thrown back, looking at all of the tents. He hesitated for a long time.

"He will go to Poota's tent and ask him for his daughter Neevee," said Ikuma. "In all this camp she is the young girl Sarkak desires most for himself. He will have her now for Kakuktak."

As though her words propelled him magically, we saw Sarkak turn and make his way grandly to the entrance of Poota's tent. There he stopped and coughed several times to warn the family of his presence.

Nuna flung her arm affectionately over the shoulder of Ikuma. They held their heads together and clasped their hands over each other's mouth, fearing that they might be heard. They jumped back into the bed and covered their heads with the thick sleeping skins, but even then I could hear their wild unruly laughing. It is not right for women, especially a man's own wives, to make light of him in this way, and I should not have heard them. But because I was a cripple and often had to remain with the women, they had grown used to me and did not hesitate to act out any rudeness before me. They also often said and did very private female things. Later I will tell you more of their strength in this household, and of their trickery and power over men. Some say that men rule the women in this land, but I am not one who would say that is so, for I have heard the women softly whispering to their husbands in the bed at night, yes, even about hunting plans. In the morning the hunters all too often follow the women's advice, although no man would admit this.

Of all the girls in our camp I liked Neevee best. She had been born perhaps fifteen winters ago, and she carried the name and wise spirit of her grandmother, her father's mother. There was a gentleness and yet a feeling of strength hidden within her. She had a wide beautiful face, with cheeks glowing softly red like the belly of a sea trout, a high and smoothly rounded forehead, with clear tanned skin drawn tightly over it. Her teeth were strong and white and even, and her nose was small and so delicately flat at the bridge that if you looked at her sideways across her clear profile, you could see both shining pupils of her dark slanting eyes. Her hair was long and of that kind of black that appears blue in the sunlight. If you touched her hand, it felt warm and smooth as goose down. She was shy with men, which becomes a young girl, but because I was crippled and different from the others, she would often talk to me. It was a joyful thing to hear her laugh, and whenever our conversations ended, I would watch with longing as she hurried back to her family's tent. She moved over the rough ground like smoothly flowing liquid, in that skillful woman's way of walking that looks so effortless.

Sarkak remained for a very long time in Poota's tent. He stayed so long that while I lay spying on him through the tent flap, I fell asleep. Kakuktak and Kangiak must have stepped over me on their way into the tent, for when I awoke, they both lay sleeping on the wide bed. The morning sun was strong, and the air inside the tent had grown thick and hot in a way that makes one wish summer would last forever.

I sat up when I heard Sarkak's footsteps on the gravel. He walked slowly to the stream, and taking up the bone ladle, bent down and drank. Poota stepped out of his tent, followed closely by his wife. They watched Sarkak's back as he came toward our tent, and I guessed that Poota's wife was very excited, for she was talking fast in a low voice and pointing both at Sarkak and inside their tent.

Just before Sarkak reached the entrance to our tent, I crawled back into bed and pretended to be asleep. I heard him pull off his parka, pants and boots and flop down between his wives. I heard Ikuma whispering to him, cautiously asking him about the marriage arrangements, but he only grunted in reply, and stretched and sighed and fell asleep.

That afternoon, when we awoke, it was bright and windy. Kakuktak and Kangiak, following Sarkak's advice, took the kayaks and hunted in the near bays, trying to spear the almost flightless young eider ducks that swam near the shore. I sat outside the tent and carved a soft piece of potstone into the shape of a sea bird to see if it would bring them luck. Sarkak slept almost the whole day and toward evening sent Ikuma walking while he and Nuna remained in the tent alone.

Kangiak and Kakuktak returned just as the sun touched the hilltops, flooding the whole tundra plain with its sharp golden light. The wind had died, and both men carried big bunches of fat eider ducks. Up the gravel beach toward the tents children ran beside them, boldly trying to count the number of birds they held. Sarkak, Nuna and Ikuma were out to greet them, and Kangiak and Kakuktak proudly flung the plump birds down at the women's feet.

The water above the lamp was boiling, and in a moment the women skinned the feathers from eight of the birds and crammed them into the stone pot. They called children into the tent and gave them some of the other birds, with careful instructions as to whom they should be given. The two young men lay on the bed, savoring their hunger as they told Sarkak about the hunt and waited for the ducks to warm and soften. The fat from the birds and the gelatin from the broad beaks and webbed feet melted into the water and thickened it into a rich yellow broth that steamed and glistened, filling the whole tent with its delicious odor.

Sarkak reached into the pot and selected the two largest ducks. One he kept for himself, and the other he offered to Kakuktak. Everyone else then took a bird, and with their fingers they stripped the steaming meat from the carcasses, holding them with gentle dignity, eating swiftly, with skill and politeness. At first Kakuktak gnawed at the bird carcass with his teeth in a savage way, and we could scarcely bring ourselves to look at him. But then he remembered our way of eating, and minding his manners, he began delicately stripping away the soft meat.

When he was finished, Sarkak belched with pleasure and spoke softly. "Wife of mine, take those others," he said, pointing with his foot at the big pile of feathered birds that remained, "and carry them to the tent of Poota. Give all of them to that family, saying that they come from Kakuktak, that he sends the birds to them."

Ikuma was surprised, for she herself had not carried birds to another family for years. She had grown accustomed to sending them with children. But understanding Sarkak's intentions, she immediately rose from her place, gathered up the big cluster of soft brown birds and with them left the tent. It was not long before she returned. I wondered what Poota and his wife must be thinking of this simple gift of food delivered with such care.

After drinking the yellow broth that remained in the pot, we lay back on the fur-covered bed for a while and enjoyed feeling the rich duck fat spreading through our bodies. Suddenly Sarkak said to me, "Go to Poota's tent, and say to my dear hunting companion that Kakuktak, the one who is like a son to me, wishes to come to their tent to sleep. You will also stay in Poota's tent and sleep on his bed and in the morning tell me how it goes with all of them."

Like Ikuma, I arose and made my way to Poota's tent. He and his wife, Mikigak, and their small children and Neevee sat in a straight row along the front of the low bed. On the edge also sat Mikigak's old mother, Ningiuk, and Ningiuk's other daughter, who was the same age as Neevee. She had not been chosen to be a wife, for she was shy and unimportant.

I could tell that they were nervous and unsure of themselves because of the messengers hurrying from our tent to theirs. They did not know at this moment what they should do except to make room for me on the bed. Neevee's younger sister ran out of the tent, and I knew she would find a place to sleep in a neighbor's bed.

We sat and spoke not one word at first. Then Poota pointed toward the pot and said, "Some ducks have given themselves to Kakuktak."

"Yes. In a little while he may arrive," I answered.

No one moved or spoke. Outside I could hear a loon calling to us, laughing at us far down on the fiord. We sat silently for some time, and then we heard footsteps on the gravel bank. Two persons came and stopped by the entrance, but for a moment they made not a sound. Then there was coughing outside, and Poota coughed inside. The flap was thrust aside, and Kakuktak bent low and entered the tent. Behind him, squatting in the entrance, was Sarkak, smiling, nodding, balancing his big bulk delicately on the slim toes of his beautiful sealskin boots.

"Visit us," called Poota. "Come in and visit."

But Sarkak only smiled and nodded, then dropped the tent flap, and we heard him walk away.

Poota's third child, a young boy, shoved hard against me as he made room for Kakuktak on the bed. He did not intend to leave the tent and miss any of the exciting things that he hoped might take place between this yellow-headed foreigner and his sister Neevee. Poota waved toward the empty place on the bed, and Kakuktak sat down cautiously between Neevee and her father. Her young brother blew out his breath in noisy delight, and Neevee, without looking at him, dug her elbow into his ribs to silence him.

The ducks were quickly skinned and shoved whole into the pot, and the feeling of tension went out of the house. Poota's wife showed Kakuktak a complicated string game we call the flying owl, and soon Neevee showed him a simpler one. She patiently tried to teach him the game, but he seemed excited and could not make it work.

After a while, when Neevee's brother asked him, Kakuktak took out his marking stick and bundle of white skins and made drawings of strange animals that we had never seen. Some animals had long tails that they curled around sticks when they hung upside down. Other animals had noses longer than their tails, big flat ears almost as long as their heads and long curved tusks like walrus. When he was drawing, Kakuktak told how these strange beasts bellowed, roared and jabbered, and as he imitated their sounds, he laughed with delight, and everyone in the household shouted with laughter as they tried to imitate him. To see his drawings, they crowded around him, and Kakuktak felt them press against him, encouraging his storytelling that he performed with so few words. Kakuktak leaned back among them, feeling all the warmth of Poota's family, their flesh, their fur-clad bodies. Their dark shining eyes possessed him. He seemed to feel himself a part of them and they a part of him. Neevee and her younger brother and the old woman, Ningiuk, had pushed me into the warm circle as though I, too, belonged within this family, and my soul wished that it could have been so.

Kakuktak paused in his drawing and looked at me. His eyes were shining, and his face was flushed with pleasure, for he could see that all the formality our people use outside the house was gone. But it was something more than that. On this first evening in Poota's tent, seated on the edge of the wide bed, I felt that Kakuktak had found a warm place that he could call his home.

Sarkak's tent could never be like this. Sarkak was too clever, too restless, too powerful, too ambitious, to permit his household to know this kind of relaxed pleasure. His restlessness crept into our souls. When Sarkak spoke, we jumped to do as he asked. We ran for him. We hunted for him. We all lived for him. His wives sewed for him and cared for his children, and although he was never harsh with them, they feared him, for they best knew the power he held over others. He had gathered together the biggest hunting camp that had ever been known, but he could never make a real home where people ate and slept and laughed and lived as if only that very moment counted. Sarkak lived only for the future. It was as though "now" never existed for him. He could invite people from neighboring camps and give immense parties that would last from one moon to another before we would use all of the meat we had gathered. But when it came to simple pleasures —the rewards that come after hunting and waiting on the frozen sea, the relaxed visiting, storytelling and later the playing in bed—those true delights Sarkak and even the people in his household would never fully enjoy.

Poota's wife moved the thin stone pot from its place above the lamp and placed it on the gravel floor before us. We each removed a duck, carefully, for they were steaming hot, and the meat was almost falling from the bones. Poota ate from the pot first, then Kakuktak, then I, Avinga, then the women and the young son. But there was plenty and still more for all of us. In the end we passed the pot, each tipping it up, gauging his share and drinking off the rich yellow broth. When it was finished, we laughed and wiped our hands and mouths with the soft skin of a big white hare.

Poota, Kakuktak, the young boy and I went outside the tent. Each made his own steaming design in urine on the rocks. It was almost dark outside, for the summer was passing, and the sky was a deep icy blue. We looked for a star among the scudding clouds and felt the first cold darkness of autumn. The lamp in each tent glowed faintly in the new coming of night. Behind us we could hear the soft laughing and the whispering voices of Neevee and her mother. I shuddered at the thought of the coming blizzards and could hardly wait to be inside once more.

We lay back on the warm skins, and I could smell the sweet

heather thickly spread beneath the bed. I watched Neevee's brother trying desperately to stay awake, but his head nodded and his eyes closed, and finally the old woman, Ningiuk, covered him with a soft caribou skin as he drifted away from us. Ningiuk's younger daughter also slept. Poota soon slept heavily, and his deep rhythmic breathing was heard and felt across the whole width of the bed. Then the old woman slept. Poota's wife slowly trimmed her lamp, lay down and listened. I watched and waited in the half darkness of the tent. I was so excited that I could not sleep.

For a long time Neevee did not move, but her eyes remained open, staring up into the dark shadows of the tent. Kakuktak sat up beside her and drew off his parka, slowly exposing his shocking smooth white torso. He rolled the parka into a soft pillow for his head and lay down again beside Neevee. I saw him draw slightly toward her, away from the touch of her father's back. Neevee waited for some time, then sat up. She turned from Kakuktak and, facing me, slowly undid the long braids that held her hair. In one smooth movement she drew off her parka and shook out her hair, allowing it to spread over her naked shoulders. Then, without looking at Kakuktak, she slid quietly down beside him under the skins that covered all of us.

I could hear them moving and breathing and knew that they were feeling the heat of each other's naked body. They did not care about the father's back on one side or the young brother on the other. Neevee showed Kakuktak how to place his nose beside hers and sniff tenderly, a custom of our people. I saw them do this and heard their soft laughter muffled beneath the covers as they felt the thrill of being together.

Then I saw for the first time in my life the thing the foreigners do with women. I saw Kakuktak raise his head above Neevee's, then bend down and place his whole mouth over her mouth. I thought he was biting her, and she must have thought so, too, for she struggled desperately. I thought to grab his sea knife and stab him in the kidney, for his whole white back lay exposed to me. I might have done this, but in her struggling I saw Neevee's arms encircle him and her fingers hook against his skin, drawing downward, leaving long pink marks along his back. She held him, pressing him tightly to her, and when they parted for breath, they looked at each other, and then they placed their mouths together again in that unbelievable act of wildness. So shy were they that they had moved very little. Their hot animal feelings came to them and went and came again without being satisfied. It was like a long delicious game for them that seemed never to end. They lay as safe as young children playing in the wide warmth of their family bed.

I must have grown weary with watching, for I fell asleep and dreamed that I saw Kakuktak as an old, old man with long white hair and a long white beard. His clothes were white and around him ran countless children who had yellow hair and pale skins, but when I knelt among them, I could see that they had the dark quick eyes of our people and the big jaw muscles that make our faces wide and draw our skin so smooth and tight. Were these dog children? I wondered, for they did not seem better or worse than any others. I remember that a white bear came in the dream and stood silently among us, and we were not afraid of him.

When I awoke, I was trembling, knowing that because of such a bear dream, I should quickly lie with a woman. I thought that if I even touched a woman, it might be enough, so I reached out for Ningiuk's daughter, who slept near me. But it was morning, and she was gone. I looked up and saw that Poota and the boy were also gone. Poota's wife knelt sewing in her place by the lamp. Only Kakuktak and Neevee still lay in the bed, curled together, sleeping.

I sat up, pulled on my parka, and using a broken harpoon shaft as a kind of crutch, made my way out of the tent. I looked up at the sky and down toward the sea. The gray bitch came up to me, and I leaned against her and touched her as though she were a woman, hoping that this would fulfill the dream of the white bear. Then I hobbled off to Sarkak's tent to report to him all that I had seen.

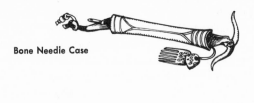

Bone Needle Case

15

When our brief summer was almost gone, I awoke one night and heard Tugak talking excitedly with Sarkak.

"The fish have returned," he said. "If you come now, you can see them from the high bank." He ran out of the tent. His soft boots sent the gravel flying.

Everyone left the bed, drawing on pants and parkas, and hurried to the river below the falls. I called to the gray bitch, Lao, for I knew that she lay waiting near the tent, ready to help me.

Others were already at the riverbank, watching in the twilight. I knelt by the bitch and peered down into the water. Below me the river swept smoothly toward the sea in a broad path of blackness, the water sometimes swirling up in dark swift eddies that could drag a man down to his death in an instant. The pale light did not seem to touch the river below the roaring white water of the falls. I watched school after school of bright sea trout flash their red and silver sides in the darkness of the racing river as they fought their way upstream. Fish beyond my counting steadied themselves in this rushing force, struggling to hold their position, letting the freezing waters slip past their ice-smooth sides. Now that the last moon of summer was full, the fish goddess had returned to the river. Like magic arrows, the fish darted back from the vastness of the sea, and carefully the goddess lifted them on the huge tides and guided them up the river to leap the falls and make their way back into the quiet depths of the lake that would be their winter home.

"See that no child of this camp throws stones toward the river," said Sarkak. "See that no one does anything that might offend the fish. Clear the openings to the stone trap, and watch it very carefully. When the tide turns, call me and we will roll the stones back into place and close the trap."

I lay on the soft moss of the tunda and watched the river and the sky. Five falling stars raced through the pale night before dawn came and with it a coldness that numbed the mosquitoes. Slowly the river rose with the tide until it flooded its stony banks and the silver hordes of sea trout were carried upstream on their journey home. As the incoming power of the salt sea met and mingled with the fresh-water force of the river, I saw the water go slack. The falls ceased to roar, and the fish surged forward in the icy silence. Our people long before us had built a false channel in the river, and into this slipped whole schools of shining fish.

On a signal from Sarkak four spearmen waded out quickly into the rushing water and heaved the heavy stones back into place, closing off the narrow entrance so that the fish could not escape our trap. When this was done, everyone shouted with delight as the fish flashed through the shallow knee-deep waters. I saw Kakuktak hurrying down from Poota's tent to join the crowd. He was followed by Portagee and Pilee, as even they had left their girls.

The fishermen tested the lashings on their double-pronged fish spears, and Sarkak, taking one of these, walked carefully out into the weir, for the rocks beneath his feet were smooth and slippery. When the water reached the top of his sealskin boots, he stopped and stood quietly, his eyes adjusting to the strong sunlight that flashed across the water. He held the spear lightly poised in his right hand and waited, motionless. Then he struck downward with a thrust so swift that I could not see it, and when he raised the spear again, it held a huge thrashing sea trout, pierced through the back and firmly held between the two springing jaws of bone. Blood ran down the silver sides of the fish, and Sarkak laughed with joy, for this was what every man lived for. Here he was with a whole camp of men, women, children and dogs to feed, and because we lived like true people, offending neither men nor spirits, the fish had come once more to give themselves to us.

Sarkak, not caring now about water seeping in over the tops of his boots, splashed back to the edge of the bank. The three strangers crowded around him. He placed the shaft of the spear under his right arm, and holding the big fish firmly by the gills, he forced open the spear's prongs. Carefully he handed the gasping fish to the mother of Poota's wife, Ningiuk, the oldest woman in the camp.

Crooning to the fish, Ningiuk walked a few paces upstream beyond everyone, and, kneeling down, she took her woman's knife from the hood of her parka. She held the powerful fish firmly and slit it open. Removing one eye and some secret parts of its entrails, she cast these out onto the water beyond the weir and cried out, "Swim, soul, swim. Swim back to your dear father's house."

Then, as she turned back to the crowd, men began to laugh and pull off their pants, tossing them to their wives or to young girls whom they admired. Some men removed their boots and turned up their parkas as well, before they eased their half-naked bodies into the freezing water. It was deadly cold, and the rocks on the river bottom were as slippery as ice, but the spearmen dared not flinch before this gathering of old people and women and children. They thought only of the fish. Kakuktak and Portagee also entered the trap with them after some urging from Kangiak and the others. Pilee only watched. Although the sun still stood high and filled the river valley with light, it no longer shed its warmth upon us, and a breeze blew the shining mist from the falls down upon us, and the dampness set us shuddering.

Poota speared the second fish and Sowniapik the third. Then everyone seemed to have a shining sea trout on the end of his spear. Quickly the men released the big fish from the jaws of their spears and flung them with wild abandon into the waiting crowd. The women and children leaped back, laughing, then lunged at the big cold slippery fish before they could flip back into the water. When anyone on the bank caught hold of one, they carried it back to the hollow stone cairn, where the fish lay in a mounting pile of shining silver bodies, eyes staring, gills gasping. The men, their legs swollen and blue with the cold, did not leave the river until after most of the trout in the weir had been caught. Then many of the women removed their own boots and pants, and entering the water with the older children speared all of the remaining fish.

That evening we slit open and ate the beautiful cold pink flesh of the sea trout until we were filled and could eat no more. Next day the women slashed open all the fish we had not eaten. They cut out their spines, flung the entrails to the waiting pack of dogs and hung the bright winglike forms on long lines between the tents to dry and darken in the wind and sun. The dogs had eaten until they were almost bursting and could sleep beneath the long lines of drying fish without even looking up.

The three strangers had taken only a small part in the day's fishing, for they had no real skill with the spears, and they hated the icy cold of the water. But on that first night of the fish feasting they were anxious to share with us. Pilee and Portagee found a huge flat stone in a hollow place in the rocks, carried fire from Ikuma's lamp and there lighted some dry tundra moss and some driftwood twigs from the beach. When the flat rock grew hot, they laughed like children as they split open several of our fish and laid them on the stone. The heat first turned the delicate meat from pink to white and then burned black. They urged Kakuktak to join them, and with a great show of pleasure the three foreigners took up the hot crumbling flesh and ate it. We knew how to do this, of course, but we thought it a disgusting way to spoil meat, and the smell and the evil greasy smoke that rose from the fish was offensive to us. We turned our heads away so that we would not have to see them disgracing themselves by eating this ruined flesh.

Next day we watched the tides and waited patiently. But the fish in numbers did not come to us again. Something must have offended them. Perhaps the fish did not like to have their flesh burned black; perhaps some child or one of the foreigners had thrown a stone toward the river and angered them. When the huge tides did come, the river went mad, and we were drenched with a deluge of rain. The wind rose and blew violently out of the south. Most of the fish lines fell in the night, and the dogs devoured the catch. Too much of the high tidewater was forced into the narrow river, and it overran its banks, flooding over the top of our stone weir, which disappeared entirely beneath the surface of the rushing water. No fish were held during that vital time. They all passed over our trap and up the river to hide from us in the depths of the lake. There they would remain, locked beneath the oncoming winter's ice. Nine freezing moons would pass before summer would drive the fish to the sea again.

It was a terrible thing to lose the fish, to go into winter with our river caches empty. The strangers did not fully understand our misfortune, but they would suffer for it later. If the fish caches are empty and winter hunting goes badly, people often die during the broken ice of early spring when hunting is impossible. We knew whole camps that had starved to death, slowly, miserably, because the summer fishing had failed them. It was just as well that our three visitors did not know this, for we believed that there was no way to change the bad things that were coming to them or to the rest of us.

What people said about these *kalunait* was true. Whenever we tried to like them, they would do something offensive, something disgusting, to remind us that they were foreigners, after all. They had been born in some far-off outlandish place, and perhaps they could never be one with us.

Fish Spear

16

Sometimes I wondered if the three foreigners, each one so different from the others, could have been born in the same place. Portagee was so much bigger than the other two, and stronger, yes, and better-looking, with his dark eyes, his smooth beardless face, his square white teeth and his wild black hair. Some people started to call him Kayuk, meaning wood-colored brown man, but that name did not last. He had a loose, sinuous way of moving, like a bear on ice, and yet with all his height and lean-muscled weight he could take a run and jump across the stream as though he soared on the wings of a hawk. He would spread his arms and shout when he jumped and laugh so hard when he landed that you would think he was going to fall down. Portagee was unbelievably good at the dancing and singing, but he was good in his own special style and was not like any of us. He had other strange ways, too, that seemed to us both good and bad. I will tell you more about him later.

Pilee was not at all like Portagee. Yes, he was also good at dancing, but in a different manner. He was light on his feet and nervous as a shore bird running from the waves. He did not bother with the rhythm and beat of our big drum. If Portagee or anyone else teased Pilee, or if he failed to understand

105

us, he grew red in the face, and you could see the hot blood rise up in him. Then he would start shouting or grow deadly pale and silent.

Pilee had a natural craving for women of all ages: little girls he played with, young girls and borrowed wives he lay with and old women he wooed and teased into sewing for him and doing his chores. He liked to use women, and it seemed to me that they encouraged this, for women liked him, too. Pilee always paid attention to them. You could easily see that most men disliked him, even the other two *kalunait*, but he cared not at all about that.

Of the three strangers we feared Pilee the most. He was weak compared to the big brown man and not at all clever in understanding our ways like Kakuktak. He seemed to be someone we could never really know or trust. Once, I held a young wolf just taken from its mother's den. I forced its head between my knees and tried to look into its eyes, but it was impossible. The wolf would shift its gaze and never look straight at me. Pilee, with his curly hair and quick temper, was like that. He would never really look at you. He had the eyes and the soul of a wolf.

Kakuktak? You ask me what he was like? Well, he was like ourselves, although his goodness may have been the goodness that he so quickly learned from us. I will tell you a great deal about him after I have told you about Neevee and about the things that happened between those two. After all, she knew him much better than anyone. She taught him our ways with her soft voice and with her body as they lay together naked in the night. She came to think of his smooth white skin and yellow hair as something beautiful. She teased him about the ugly wisps of hair that grew on his jaws and beneath his nose, for we rarely grow beards, and our women find rough hair on men's faces offensive. To please Neevee, Kakuktak honed his sea knife into deadly sharpness, rubbed seal oil over his beard and shaved his face until it was as smooth and clean as any one of our young men's.

106

Those two, Neevee and Kakuktak, would lie surrounded in the wide bed, and yet they often seemed to be utterly alone with each other. For a while, during the early moons of winter, I slept next to them and heard some of their quiet laughing and their whispering. Those were the times in my life when I wished most desperately that I could have been a whole man, with a woman of my own to talk to and to laugh with and to hold in the quiet of the night.

Goose-Wing Brush

17

Poota's son saw them first and ran to his father's tent. In a moment everyone in the camp was out, watching as two men approached from the inland along the curving bank of the river. They plodded slowly, heavily, bent beneath the great weights they carried on their backs. Beside them staggered three dogs, each burdened with bulging twin packs tied across their shoulders. Sarkak's eyes were not so good as they had once been, and he waited until the two men drew closer before he recognized them.

"My cousin Tunu and his son Nukinga arrive?" Sarkak said.

"*Eeee, eeee*. Yes, yes," answered the others.

"They arrive loaded down with caribou meat. Look at the size of the pack that Nukinga carries," said Okalikjuak. "There is no one else in this whole country who could travel with a weight like that."

"Look how easily he walks, as though he carried feathers, and see the dogs bending bowlegged under their loads. They have a lot of meat," said Poota. "See the dear old Tunu. He is almost finished carrying for today. He must be glad to see this camp. Tunu is a good man, generous with meat. He is fond of certain women in this camp, but I do not think that he will bother them tonight. When we take that huge weight from his shoulders, he will float up into the air."

Sarkak could have sent a young man to help Tunu with his heavy burden, but it was not the custom. It would have been an insult, suggesting that Tunu could not carry such a load. It also would have made Sarkak appear too anxious to get his teeth into some of the fresh caribou meat. Sarkak must have felt his mouth fill with water, as I did, just thinking of the tender red haunches.

Poota's wife turned and went into their tent, and Poota darted in after her. I did not need to listen to them speak to know that he was asking if Tunu could sleep in their tent, sleep with her. She could easily have refused him by not answering. By her saying nothing, he would not dare invite Tunu. That would make her bad-tempered and angry at him for who knows how many moons. Women have long memories for such things as that. If she agreed to have Tunu sleep in the tent, to sleep beside her, she would answer him politely, saying, "*Isumuminipalook*. It's only up to you." This she must have said, for I saw Poota come quickly out of the tent with a look of pleasure as he went to stand beside Sarkak.

Tunu walked up and stood before them, smiling warmly, his face wrinkling into countless creases, his eyes twinkling with delight.

"*Tikiposi*. You arrive," said Sarkak formally.

"*Eeee. Tikipoguk*. I arrive," answered Tunu in his deep rasping voice.

Nukinga, his great hulking son, stood respectfully behind his father, watching all of them, forgetting that he carried a pack that weighed almost as much as two men.

"*Oomitualook*. It's heavy," said Tunu, and with a sigh he eased the big pack of meat off his back and dropped it carelessly to the ground. He then removed the short bow and closed quiver of arrows from around his neck, and his son did the same. Many hands helped to unload the three dogs that lay panting on the ground and take the meat to the safety of the high stone racks.

At this moment Tunu looked up and saw the three foreigners standing alone in front of our big tent. He quickly reached out and touched his son's hand. Together they stared in horror and disbelief at the tall gaunt strangers. We had come to know them so well that we had almost forgotten the unreal appearance of the *kalunait*. With delight we now discovered that they would create an unending source of wonder to visitors when they saw them for the first time.

"Come, sleep in my tent," invited Poota.

Tunu answered with a long low cry of pleasure: *"Eeee!"* for he and Poota had grown up together near the mountain with the ice window, and they loved to talk together about their early life in that camp.

It was as Poota had said. Tunu and his son did not immediately bother the women but slept and ate and slept again, regaining their strength after their summer journey inland for caribou. They had come to us after the kill because our camp was closer than their own, and they knew we would gladly load their meat into one of our kayaks and send it to their camp, which was only three days eastward along the coast. They gave a generous portion of caribou meat to Sarkak and to every other household in our camp during a whole day of formal visiting.

On the following day Poota went seal hunting and was gone all night. Tunu lay in his place. Kakuktak was very nervous seeing this, and I think he feared trouble. Neevee and I laughed and tried to calm him, telling him again and again that it was all right, that it had been agreed upon. It was *peeusinga*, our custom, as we say.

On the third day after the newcomers had arrived, almost all the young people gathered on the big rocks beside the soft sandy place at the end of the beach, and slowly the men went and joined them. Tunu and his son were almost the last to arrive, and they sat shyly on the edge of the crowd. Kakuktak stood with me beside the rock, and I saw him looking at Nukinga. I wondered what he was thinking. Nukinga's shoulders were as wide as that of two men, and he had a neck almost as big around as my waist. His arms were short and powerful, and his square hands bulged with muscles. His wide face was brown and bony, with eyes set high and far apart. His mouth seemed to be curved up at the corners into a permanent smile. We wished that he belonged in our camp, for he was known to be good-natured, and there was no strength like his anywhere in our whole world. When he walked through the camp, he swayed carelessly, like a bull walrus, but some had seen him on thin ice, and they said that he could move as lightly as a fox when he sensed danger.

Two young boys stepped forward into the sandy circle, shuffled for a moment, then started cautiously circling each other. They were of equal size. But when one darted in and grasped the other around the waist, he gave a clever lift, leaned sideways, and the other boy lost his balance briefly. Although he regained his footing immediately, the match was over. The wrestling match had been won. Two other young men took their places on the sand, grasped each other and swayed for a moment. The instant that one lost his balance he was released, and the other man had won.

To everyone's delight four others played the game, and then the men turned and called to Nukinga, who just sat smiling, looking at the ground between his knees. Though Nukinga was big and immensely strong, he was young and not really clever at the wrestling game.

Our camp had Atkak, the best wrestler in the whole country. It was said that no one had beaten him during my whole lifetime. For all his quick strength and cleverness Atkak was a shy and quiet man, but he stood up and pulled off his parka and walked out onto the sand. He smiled at Nukinga and

110

raised his eyebrows at him, meaning "Yes, yes," urging him on affectionately, the way one does a younger brother.

"*Namunilunga*," said Nukinga. "I'm not enough for him."

"*Ataii. Ataii*," called the watchers, and Nukinga got up slowly and stripped off his parka. His smooth torso did not at first reveal all his strength. You had to look at the way his back muscles curved in as deep as a man's hand to meet his spine. You had to see the great neck muscles that rose smoothly from the place where his shoulders joined his body, running almost to his ears in a long slanting line.

The two wrestlers stood before each other, legs slightly spread, arms raised, fingers cupped, smiling yet alert, staring into each other's eyes. Atkak moved like lightning. His arms slipped around the boy's waist, and he heaved to force him off balance. But Nukinga seemed rooted to the sand. He locked his arms slowly around Atkak's back and twisted only a hand's breadth to the right, but we saw Atkak lose his balance. Instantly Nukinga released him. It was over. Atkak had lost in the wrestling for the first time since his boyhood. The boy Nukinga had won. The onlookers gasped with disbelief.

Both wrestlers, smiling, started to leave the sand together, but I heard a murmuring and turned around. There was Pilee standing up on a stone, urging the big Portagee to pull off his parka. Why hadn't we thought of this before? I wondered. Of course, it would be a wonderful thing to see Nukinga and Portagee play the wrestling game together.

"*Eeee. Eeee*," cried all the men. "*Ataii*."

Glancing toward the tents, I saw all the women looking down at the wrestlers, as excited as we were. Kakuktak stood up quickly, but his face showed no pleasure, and his hands were jammed into his pockets. I saw that he was nervous, and I remembered that we did not always play games in the same way.

Young Nukinga turned and walked back to the center of the sandy place and stood smiling, waiting. Portagee leaped into the circle, crouching, ready, his legs spread wide apart, his arms outstretched, his fingers wide and hooked like claws. Even bent down in this position his head was still above Nukinga's. Portagee waited not an instant. He lunged in at Nukinga, who seemed to be standing unprepared for the attack. But Nukinga's arms shot out and clasped low around Portagee's back. I saw Nukinga's wide back arch mightily, and Portagee went over, losing his balance. He would have fallen to the sand if Nukinga had not saved him.

Nukinga smiled at Portagee politely, and to everyone he said, "He is very strong. He is like a giant." Then he turned and started to walk away. For him the match was over; he had won. But Pilee ran out and pointed, too excited to speak, and seeing him, Portagee sprang quickly after Nukinga and tapped him hard on the shoulder.

It is not our custom for adults to wrestle many times together; only young children do that. Nukinga had won, and that should have been the end of it, but the big brown man, not smiling, demanded to try again. Nukinga looked at his father and at Sarkak and then turned and stepped back onto the sand.

Nukinga seemed to wait unthinkingly for the attack, but when it came, we could see how ready he was, for this time his huge arms whipped beneath Portagee's grasp and locked like bear's paws around the sinuous waist of the big stranger. I saw him shift his weight backward with his right hip, then drive his weight forward and to the left, carrying Portagee off balance. Again he held Portagee so that he would not fall. Only when the brown man had regained his balance did Nukinga release him. He had won again.

Nukinga turned away once more, but to my astonishment Portagee shot his arm out and locked it tightly around Nukinga's throat, grasping his one hand with the other, cutting off Nukinga's wind. It was an attack such as one might make before a killing. Portagee then quickly placed his long leg behind Nukinga's, and with a sharp twisting motion he upset his balance and flung Nukinga to the ground, falling heavily on top of him. Nukinga fought back, for he must have known terrible fear. He must have thought that Portagee had lost his mind, had gone mad, for such a violent attack could not come from a sane man. Portagee hung above Nukinga, his knees on either side of his body, his arms pinning Nukinga to the ground. Portagee's eyes bulged, and he bared his teeth like an animal fighting.

Kakuktak and Kangiak and Tugak and Yaw ran out onto the sand, and together they pulled Portagee off Nukinga. Both wrestlers were panting and wet with sweat.

Nukinga leaped up and stood looking first at Portagee and then at his father. "Someone should open him up with a knife," said Nukinga, "and look inside to see what kind of a soul he has that makes him play a game like that. I think that man has lost his soul."

But Sarkak and Atkak and Poota crowded up to him and said, "No, no. Do not say that. These strangers do not know how to play our games. They do everything wrong. They surprise us every day by their differences. See, look how the big one is laughing now and playing with the children, showing them the ring in his ear. Look how he is smiling and nodding his head at you. That means he likes you, because you are strong and he is strong. It is the *kalunait*'s way of playing. After all, you must remember that these foreigners know very little about life. They are violent, savage people."

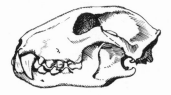

Bear Skull

113

18

On the day following the wrestling Tunu and his son left the camp, and the first pale edge of the autumn moon appeared. Sarkak stood outside the tent, staring at the flatness of the sea and fumbling with the drawstring at the top of his sealskin pants. The big brown dog, Pasti, came too close, and Sarkak kicked him hard in the ribs.

"*Unalook*," Sarkak shouted, and I saw Kakuktak and Pilee turn and stare at him.

You could tell by the power in his voice that Sarkak was in a good mood, a mood to expand, to travel, and he gave the familiar cry that is heard in every camp: "Wives," he called. "Are the boots finished?"

"*Eeee*," they answered in chorus from inside the tent. "The boots are finished."

"We shall go, then," he called to them, and walked slowly down toward the beach. He stood there for a while, staring out at the leaden sea, watching the tide rise, allowing the idea of leaving to spread through his mind, spread through the whole camp, for others in their tents had surely heard him, and it would take only a moment for everyone to grasp his thought of leaving. At the end of the long fiord silver-gray clouds drifted like a herd of migrating caribou across the horizon. Under them wavering white fingers of snow reached down to the sea. One did not have to look twice to see that the sky would soon be full of whirling flakes.

When Sarkak turned around and looked back, almost every tent was down or half collapsed. Small bundles of clothing lay scattered on the ground, along with heaps of sleeping skins, lamps and pots, and dogs. Everyone, including the children, helped to roll up the tents and carry the few possessions down to the shore. Our people are used to moving. We believe in moving. It is for us like searching for a new life. We always believe that each new place will be crowded with land animals, birds and sea beasts waiting to give themselves to us. The very thought of moving fills us with hope.

Men and women, as many as I have fingers and toes, grasped the long wooden gunwales of the two big umiaks and carried the boats carefully over the rocky beach into knee-deep water, for they did not wish the skin bottoms to be torn. One man climbed into each umiak, and with Sarkak calling out to them, they carefully loaded the boats. On the bottom they folded the soft skin tents, then placed stone lamps and pots, sleeping skins and clothing bundles on top. Above this they placed two long sleds, the harpoons, all that remained of our dried fish and our few last pieces of seal meat. Then the pups were tossed into the boats, and the children. Several bad-tempered dogs had their mouths tied shut. We left the other sleds behind, to be picked up by the young men when the snows came.

I prepared the old widow's kayak for the journey and joined the seven other kayakmen. I think that Kakuktak and Porta-gee would have preferred to be in kayaks, too, but they, like the women, had to sit in the umiak Sarkak was steering. Only Pilee seemed content to lie back on the rolls of fur bedding in the other umiak, resting between his girls, Mia and Evaloo, letting the women row him to some new place.

Sarkak and Sowniapik, who was steering the other umiak, took their positions at the stern of each boat, seated high on the softest bundles, resting their weight grandly on the broad steering oar. The strongest women took up the heavy oars in each boat, and two by two they stroked the big umiaks away from the land. They laughed and groaned with pride at the heaviness of the load, the great weight of their possessions, their children, their dogs. They did not believe that any other people in the world could possess such riches. Although no one saw us leaving with our two heavily loaded boats and the fleet of slim kayaks, the women tried to imagine what their humble neighbors living north and east of them would think if

115

they could only see this tremendous display of wealth and power on the move. All thoughts of starving fell away from us, for were we not traveling to some distant place of plenty? Was Sarkak not taking us to the sea beasts that waited somewhere on this coast, waited for our coming?

The kayaks and our two heavily loaded sealskin umiaks moved slowly southward down the long fiord, and as we left the land, a light snow squall blew over the mountains. Instead of returning directly to our winter camp, Sarkak had decided that we should travel along the coast to hunt for seals or walrus and to search for any dead whale that might have washed onto the shore, for a dead whale can provide a whole camp with food for a winter.

The kayakmen led the way, spread out like water bugs over the green water, carefully searching every bay for food. When the wind blew and whipped the water into waves, we could not see the seals. On those days we pulled into the shelter of the shore, upturned the boats and huddled under them to get out of the wind while the hungry bowmen went walking, searching for any kind of small bird or animal. But they did not find enough to feed the children. Our small supply of fish was almost gone, and still no seals came to us. We began to wonder what fate the future would bring.

One morning, after ten days of traveling, when the wind was down and my hunger would not let me sleep, I left our camp early and paddled for the whole day along the coast without seeing a single seal. I had the uneasy feeling that some hidden spirit was trying to hold the sea beasts back from us. For the first time since spring I thought of the squares of dried food and the black specks the foreigners had brought with them when they arrived among us. I supposed that they had been quickly eaten or thrown away. Certainly no one had bothered to share them with me.

The skin bags of fish we carried were empty, licked clean by the children, and there was nothing left to eat. Slowly I came to realize how greatly the three strangers dreaded the coming of winter. Now, with the first hint of hunger, you could see how much they feared that we would all lose our lives. Each day the big brown man and Pilee and Kakuktak seemed to grow more gaunt and nervous. It was hard sometimes to think of them as friends. They did not seem to join with us any more, as they had in summer. I often watched them as they stood and spoke together in whispers, their faces drawn tight, their eyes grown sharp with hunger. I saw them searching secretly through the bundles in the umiaks, unable to believe that all of our food was gone. Now only the smallest children were nourished by suckling at their mothers' breasts. This they did fiercely, like young wolves, as though they, too, could sense the coming famine. We had nothing now, no meat or fish. If this continued, our old people would never see the end of winter.

At dawn the next morning, during the low tide, I saw the three strangers dressed in their black clothes, walking along the empty stone beach, bending and searching like ravens for small dead things. Women following them found *kawanik* in the tide pools, a coarse seaweed one could eat. When they showed this to the strangers, the three men wolfed down great quantities of the slimy roots, trying to fill the terrible emptiness in their bellies. We knew that this seaweed would help a little, but it was not meat. It would not heat their bodies or drive away their hunger.

For the next five days the wind blew, and if seals rose to breathe, they hid themselves in the watery valleys between the waves. Slowly we felt the strength ebbing out of our bodies. We traveled painfully, silently, without speaking. Our heads ached, and our tempers grew short. The length of time between plenty and hunger is very brief. We traveled on like ghosts to the place called Tikirak, a rocky peninsula pointing like a stone finger far out into the sea. Wearily we paddled along its full length, and near the very tip we entered a small cove. From this place, Sarkak said, we would travel no more. The choice was no longer ours, he said; we would live or die

117

here. Many thought this would be the end of our journey. We slowly pitched our tents, turned the big boats upside down to form shelters and built clumsy stone walls around them. Sitting silently, we watched the gray sea heave and listened to the hungry children crying. Rain and sudden squalls of snow played endlessly across the sea's face. For three days we watched and waited. Then one night, in the fullness of the moon, the huge tide rose and flooded the cove almost to the entrance of our tents. There it paused before receding slowly along the shining path of the moon, exposing a vast plain of slippery boulders and long twisted ropes of bitter useless seaweed.

Before the first light of dawn the women hurried out over the tidal flats, searching for wet beds of sandy clay. There, beside shallow pools, they found tiny breathing holes, and digging with their powerful fingers and sharp pieces of bone, they gathered delicious long-necked clams. The clams were large and strong and hard to catch. The women had to work fast, taking advantage of this big tide, which would occur only on this day. All their efforts gave the camp just one good feeding, but it brought back the hope of life to all of us.

For five more days gray fog and freezing rain swept in from the sea. The long stone arm on which we lived stayed wet and shiny black. Icy whiteness appeared along the water line where the salt sea licked the rocks with frost. Babies grew feverish and whimpered endlessly. The mothers jogged them up and down in their hoods, humming wordless songs to them, trying to make the children and themselves forget their hunger.

That morning a lean black raven flew over our rock, and I heard the old widow singing to it in her harsh cracked voice:

> *"On this rock the wind has wings,*
> *Winter and summer.*
> *On this rock the nights are long*
> *And spirits roam.*

I've seen their faces, seen their eyes,
Like ravens hovering.
Their dark wings form long shadows,
We must fear them.
Ayii, ayii."

The three strangers were restless, sometimes moving from the tents to sleep out under the big skin boats and then back into the tents again. They were gaunt with hunger and talked to no one except the girls they slept with. Pilee and Portagee each wore caribou skins wrapped around their shoulders to fight away the cold. It gave them the appearance of imitating women. Kakuktak wore a wolf skin over his black jacket. He wore it in a new way, with armholes cut in the sides and lashings across the chest. With his round eyes and long tangled yellow hair he looked like a strange animal.

Each morning at dawn and again at noon and in the evening before darkness came, two kayakmen would climb to the highest place behind the camp and search the sea for any sign of life. Barely visible in the distance was a small island of rock. When the surf was running, the rock was difficult to see, for it was worn smooth and shiny black. It almost disappeared at high tide, but even then we could see and sometimes hear the waves breaking with a heavy sucking sound over the far edge of the rock. It is said that around this rock beneath the sea lie great beds of clams, and the walrus sometimes come here during the autumn moon to dig with their tusks and fill their bellies with the soft rich meat.

The kayakmen could do nothing, for this was not a seal-hunting place. They sat huddled together under the big upturned boats or in the darkness of the skin tents. When their harpoon points had been honed to deadly sharpness and the skin lines dampened and carefully coiled again and again, they slept until their teeth grew furry. Then they sat up on their beds, and taking soft pieces of bone or small pieces of potstone, they carved the likenesses of walrus. This they did

119

with painstaking care, saying nothing, trying to use up time as they slowly scraped and smoothed the little carvings and rubbed them with oil.

The three strangers lay and watched us sharpening our harpoons. Sometimes they examined the small figures we so carefully carved, and they curled their lips and laughed at us, as though we were stupid children, and pointed out to sea and made motions as though we should paddle and hunt from kayaks. But we knew there was nothing out there. We could only sit and try to forget their sneering.

During the carving the kayakmen spoke together of walrus, of their huge bulk, their agility, their tremendous strength and their gleaming ivory tusks. They thought of their immense bellies full of warm clams, enough to feed a dozen hungry men. Every word they spoke was carefully chosen, for some walrus spirit might be near and listening.

I remember Sarkak on the fifth night of the waning moon. He was as restless as a fox caught in a stone pit, and it seemed to me that much of his fatness had faded from him. In the darkness of the skin tent he crouched between his women. He was not used to hunger in the camp. He hated it as he would an insult flung at him in a song fest. He said aloud that someone had broken a taboo, but I know that he blamed himself for our hunger. He considered it to be the result of his own bad planning. He knew now that he should have left the summer camp as soon as the fish had failed us.

Twice I saw him angrily heave himself up off the bed and push himself out into the night wind. There he stood alone, listening in the fog. Both times he returned to us without a word. On his third leaving he remained standing just beyond the tents for a long time. Then he came near the tent flap and called softly to us. Kangiak, Tugak and Yaw went out quickly, and I hobbled after them. The freezing dampness whipped in from the sea, touching our spines with chilling hands. Each man stood listening, waiting, in the womblike blackness of the night. We saw and heard nothing save the sad moaning of the wind.

"*Ivik*. Walrus," he whispered. "Smell them. Smell the fat. Smell the meat. They have come to us now. In the darkness they have come to the rock."

I sniffed the salt air, and at first I smelled nothing. Then a faintly pungent animal odor drifted in to me from the sea. As we stood there, the walrus scent grew stronger. I breathed it in with ecstasy, feeding my nostrils. In my throat once more was the rich smell of meat, meat enough for the long winter. The smell also carried the promise of oil for our lamps and food for our dogs and sleek ivory tusks to carve into harpoon heads and snow knives and sled runners. For us it was the smell of life. In an instant the heavy animal odor drove away our darkest fears of starvation and death.

I looked around, trying to see Sarkak's eyes and the eyes of all my brothers, for I wanted the pleasure of seeing them at the very moment when the stark masks of hunger fell from their faces.

Other kayakmen came from the tents and stood with us. We said not one word to each other, for there was no need to speak as we let the thick heavy scent of walrus fill our nostrils. Kakuktak and Portagee came and stood with us. I know now that they did not recognize the smell of the great beasts, nor did they guess why all the hunters of the camp stood outside the tents in the wet blackness. How could we tell them that with one breath of wind everything had changed for all of us? Our kayakmen needed only to smell the walrus to know that animals that close could be taken. Around me in the darkness I heard a clicking of the little ivory knives that men shake to try to cut the weather.

In the tents we did not openly speak of this to the women, of course, but they, like all our women, had a secret way of knowing such things. We could tell they knew that walrus were near us. Their eyes were shining. They hugged their children, licked their faces and whispered in their ears. You could tell by the way the children stared at their fathers and clung to their mothers and shivered with expectation that they, too, knew something was about to happen.

I went to sleep with all the others. I slept more soundly than I had since the first night that the moon had been reborn, which proves that it is not hunger so much as fear that drives away sleep and makes a man's belly bloat and rumble.

Ivory Knife Charm

19

In the morning I awoke before dawn and heard people hacking and coughing. Men and women from the camp were stirring in the darkness of the tents, crawling from beneath the two big boats. Outside, the black rocks were slick with ice, but the wind was down, and the cold sea heaved smoothly with a long gray swell as though some monstrous beast lay beneath the surface, gasping, sighing, slowly expanding and contracting its great rib cage, causing the sea to ebb and flow endlessly against the long black arm of rock.

Men and women carried the hunting gear out quietly and laid it down beside the upturned kayaks. Out in the darkness of the heaving sea the low smooth rock lay wrapped in mist, hidden from us, waiting for our arrival. Dawn came slowly, gently unfolding its pale wings across the eastern sky. At first light men lifted their thin-skinned kayaks over their heads, carefully carried them down through the rocks and placed them cautiously in the water. I saw Poota and Sowniapik slip quickly into their long slim craft and push out into the powerful swell that bounded dangerously back from the rock face. Then Kangiak and the four others pushed away from the land and formed together like a loose wedge of geese. The women and children stood silently in front of the tents, watching the kayakmen stroke their way out steadily toward the rock.

With one hand the men arranged their gear around them. Each hunter placed his harpoon in the ivory rest on the right side of the slender deck and his killing spear on the left, and neatly coiled the harpoon line in the shallow drum that rested in the center of the narrow skin deck. Behind each kayakman on the back deck lay an airtight sealskin float, which was half inflated and attached by a long line to the harpoon.

As the others moved out, I followed behind them in the old widow's kayak. I could feel my throat go dry and my shoulders hunch as the strength ran tingling down through my arms. With the long, narrow double-bladed paddle I forced the slim craft forward until I reached the center of the wedge of kayaks and heard the soft slap of water on their sides.

When I looked back at the tents, I saw Sarkak's figure standing motionless and alone, down at the very edge of the water. On the highest boulder halfway between the women and the sea, I saw the three foreigners standing together. They must only now have become aware that a hunt was taking place, aware that something important was about to happen to us all.

The breeze shifted slightly, gaining strength with the coming of morning, and the smell of the walrus came to me again. It was overpowering this time, laden with the heavy night smell of rut and excrement. A light gust of wind opened the fog, and for a brief moment I could see the rock. It was covered with a solid living mass of walrus. All the kayakmen moved forward into the wind, confident that the weak-eyed animals could not see or smell them. Perhaps none of these sea beasts had ever seen a man before, yet we and the killer whales that ranged beyond the ice were their only true enemies. I felt my heart pounding as I saw the big muscular brown bodies humping forward in a rhythmic flow as they pressed tightly one against the other to allow more and more walrus to leave the sea and crowd up onto the smooth black rock, their breaths steaming white in the morning stillness.

As we paddled forward, I could feel the silence. Then suddenly the air filled with a strange wild tenseness. The whole herd had become aware of us. Suddenly the walrus stopped their endless swaying and became motionless. They became like an island of carved brown stones. Every head turned in our direction, the thin-tusked females listening, the big bulls holding their heads high, their heavy white tusks curving down dangerously like knives as they peered, weak-eyed and wary, into the fog.

Then we heard the first challenge, a deep-throated, grunting roar. Four times it rumbled up to us from the belly of a huge bull walrus weighing twenty times more than one of the men who hunted him. This big bull proclaimed himself the leader, the fighter, the strongest on the rock. He could smell us now and see us. He roared again, and shouldering the younger males and females aside, he violently heaved his great bulk down off the rock with a series of powerful thrusts on his short wide-webbed flippers. Out of the water he was battle-scarred and clumsy, but when he slipped his huge brown bulk into the sea, he seemed as sleek and graceful as a salmon disappearing smoothly beneath the surface. All of us eased our harpoons from their ivory rests and waited.

Our eight kayaks were strung out in a long curved line, waiting to see what would happen. Suddenly this great walrus rose out of the water, roaring, thrashing, red eyes rolling, warning us away from his females. He caught sight of Nowya's kayak first and lunged toward it. Nowya snatched up his harpoon. He swung his right arm smoothly backward and then darted it forward. The harpoon slipped through the air, flat above the water, the line whipping after it, uncoiling like a living entrail. Its sleek point drove deep into the thick leather that protected the bull walrus' neck. The whole harpoon head was buried, and the harpoon's heavy driftwood shaft collapsed, as it should, into three pieces loosely tied together. If it had remained stiff, it would have torn loose when the big beast thrashed in the sea.

The bull walrus dove, and Nowya swept his hand across the back deck of his kayak, knocking free the air-filled sealskin float. It flipped upright, danced on the water, then disappeared beneath the surface as the great bull lunged into the depths of the sea. In doing this the walrus snapped the sharpened harpoon head sideways, and it cut into the thick layer of blubber that lay beneath the tough brown leather of his skin. The point was now embedded forever. It would not come free until some human cut it from him with a knife. But this battle had only begun.

I was near Nowya and saw him as he turned his head sideways and gestured to us, so wild was he with the excitement of the hunt. He had been the first to set the point of his harpoon into this great prize. But he should not have turned his head or taken his thoughts from that enormous sea beast. As I watched him, I saw his body and then his whole kayak thrust violently upward out of the water. It seemed to pause for a moment, balanced on top of the great thrashing walrus head. Then the long thin kayak bent and skidded in the air as it turned over. I heard the sealskin tearing and the ribs breaking. Nowya was upside down. He was only half out of his broken kayak when he struck the freezing water. I saw his head snap back sickeningly as he disappeared and as the walrus' bulk seemed to crash down on top of him. The sea turned pink in a tangle of wreckage amid coils of skin line and a float that danced like a living thing. The empty broken kayak filled with water and began to sink beneath the surface. All we ever saw of Nowya was one black boot as it raised above the water, twitched and sank as he slipped away from us forever.

The big bull sulked beneath the surface of the sea until his lungs were almost bursting. Once more he flung himself boldly upward into our midst, gasping for air. Two harpoons flew out and struck him before he could draw his second breath, and we shouted at him in our anguish and hit the water with the flat sides of our double-bladed paddles. His instincts caused him to duck beneath the surface again, this time without enough air. We watched the three floats and drew near the place where he would have to surface again.

From the corner of my eye I could see and hear the whole herd on the rock, swaying with excitement, roaring in fear and confusion, bellowing their defiance as they started to lunge into the safety of the sea.

Suddenly this killer of Nowya reappeared among us, head flung back, red-eyed and roaring, lungs heaving, white tusks deadly. I do not think he even saw us. Sowniapik drove his paddle into the water with force, making his kayak slip forward and swing to the left, and instantly he snatched up his killing spear and drove it in and out of the bull's throat three times. Then, with his paddle in his left hand, he quickly drew back out of danger. The big bull coughed deeply, and pink blood came frothing up from his lungs. When he next rolled to dive, the water turned red, then almost black, as his heart pumped dark rich blood into the coldness of the sea. We turned away from him, for we knew that he was dying now and that all his meat was ours, safely held with three harpoons and floats.

With Kangiak beside me we turned our kayaks and went toward the rock. It was almost clear of walrus now, save one young bull who waited there, nervously holding back, roaring fiercely at some frightened females just below him in the water. All memory of Nowya's drowning faded from my mind as I thought of the huge abundance of meat swimming live before me, grunting and blowing and surging through the deep clear water.

I followed the young bull, who jealously herded a dozen females ahead of him, roaring and threatening them with his tusks when they panicked and tried to break away from him. I pressed in upon him, and he turned and lunged toward me across the surface of the water. My harpoon struck him in the fold of the neck, and as he dove, I used his great rolling body like a rock to shove my thin-skinned kayak away from him. As I waited for him to surface again, I peered nervously down into the water, not only for the young bull, but because the sea around me was full of frightened females scattered from the herd and swimming for their lives. When they rose for air or to search for the herd, they could easily turn over a kayak. Many men have drowned in this way.

Every kayakman seemed to have a walrus harpooned and fighting hard against a float. Their killing spears darted in their hands. My heart sang, and my hands trembled with joy, and gas thundered out of me and drummed against the boat bottom as I saw this great weight of meat around me. For in these few moments our whole camp had been allowed to push death away and return to life. I was shaking so in my excitement that it took several thrusts with the killing spear before the young bull ceased his thrashing and floated peacefully beside me. He left a shining trail of oil on the surface of the freezing water, reflecting like a rainbow of light as the new dawn filled the sky.

Far away on the long arm of rocky land I heard the faint screaming of the women, birdlike in their chorus of delight, and then for the first time that day I saw the umiak. Standing up in the bow was the big Portagee, and rowing hard behind him stood Kakuktak and Pilee. In the stern of the boat on the heavy gunwale sat Sarkak, short and squat in his bulky dog-skin parka, his hood flung back, his long hair blowing out in the wind, as he worked the stern oar with all the cleverness that he possessed.

I caught the harpoon line attached to my upturned floating walrus and pulled my kayak to him. Carefully I cut a hole in his thick upper lip beside his tusks and passed a strong line through it. Then, like the others, I started to paddle against the tide that was starting to run out with increasing force. I used all the strength of my arms, and yet I scarcely moved the kayak or the walrus, so great was the dead weight of that dear sea beast.

When I rested, I looked up and saw the big clumsy umiak approaching me, moving fast through the water. It was rowed by Kakuktak, Pilee and three of the strongest boys. They stood up facing the bow, pushing on the heavy oars. Sarkak sat high on the rear thwart, steering with the heavy stern sweep. In the bow stood Portagee, rigid as a stone carving. Everything about him seemed familiar to me, for was this not exactly as he had stood in the pantomime of the whaling boat up on the hill behind the camp?

He held the harpoon in a strange manner. His right hand cupped the butt and held it stiffly above his head; his left arm, straight before him, aimed the point at the water dead ahead of him. He stared down into the sea and waited.

A bull walrus rose before him, and I saw the oarsmen working desperately to close the gap. It dove, but when it rose again, Portagee was close enough. He swayed back stiffly and then smoothly sprung his whole body forward as he released the harpoon. I saw the point drive deeply into the swimming animal's back. A shout went up from Sarkak and the oarsmen in the boat.

Portagee should have flung the big sealskin float out of the thin-skinned boat, but instead he snubbed the skin line around the front thwart as he had done in their pantomime. The big bull walrus plunged deep into the sea, and I saw with horror that the line went tight, stretching like wet gut. Just before the taut line could tip the boat, the big brown foreigner paid out the line, a little at a time, grudgingly, as he desperately held onto this immense prize of food. I saw the old umiak stop and shudder, with its bow forced down almost to the water line. The stern, where Sarkak sat, rose up and trembled in the air. I was amazed at the strength of the new sealskin line. Imagine this crazy man trying to hold a full-grown male walrus tied to a thin-skinned boat. It was all madness, and I believed they would die together in the freezing water.

As the bull turned in his mad attempt to escape under the water, the boat stern slammed down into the waves, and the clumsy umiak jerked forward once more and raced through the water, pulled by this hidden force. I could not believe that Portagee would ignore Sarkak's angry shouting at him, that he would not throw the big sealskin float into the water. But that is exactly what he did. Kakuktak and Pilee were holding the sides of the boat, shouting with laughter as the old skin boat swayed and skidded across the reddened sea.

Portagee had no time to laugh. He worked like a wild man, head down, back humped, his muscles straining as he skillfully drew the line in, snubbed it, waited, then shortened it again, slowly closing the gap between the walrus and the boat. When the line was dangerously short, the walrus suddenly dove again, and the boat lunged crazily sideways. I started to paddle hard toward them, wondering if I could save one of them from the freezing sea. The line snapped downward, and the boat shuddered. Portagee still held fast, scarcely paying out an arm's length of line. The strain on the boat was immense as the beast fought to gain depth beneath the sea.

But slowly his muscles and his huge lungs failed him, and I could see that we had won. The walrus, mouth open, fighting for air, rose almost beneath the bow, and Portagee lanced him with the sharp point of the killing spear. Three times I saw him dart it into the big bull's throat between the great tusks. He did this neatly and swiftly, in a way I had never seen before. The walrus surfaced again, spinning crazily in the water, something that usually happens when the spirit is flying out of a sea beast. Then it was over, and the great weight of the walrus rolled belly up and floated peacefully just beneath the surface, with only the tusks rising above the red water, pointing upward like the curved white horns of some demon from beneath the sea.

The three *kalunait* roared, and Portagee slapped his own buttocks loudly. I was shocked to hear such laughing and shouting from a boat with a newly dead sea beast attached, and surprised that our young boys were so quick to call out and laugh in shameless imitation of the foreigners. Sarkak sat alone, an old man, gaunt and silent in the stern, for he, the great hunter and planner for us all, had acted only like a servant to these strange men.

Now Portagee flung the sealskin float out of the boat to mark the dead walrus, and they pursued two female walrus, managing to harpoon one of these in almost the same manner. They also lanced one young walrus with the killing spear alone and hauled it up bodily into the boat.

Portagee, not Sarkak, took command and gave the order to return to land. I watched them begin rowing, still shouting irreverently as they towed their great burden of meat back to the long black point of land. There the hungry women stood screaming with delight, and the babies wailed in terror. Each kayakman also paddled toward the camp, not caring about the walrus that swam quickly past, moving out and disappearing with the great ebbing tide. We stroked hard toward the women on the shore, each boat drawing a great floating prize.

Portagee and Kakuktak and Pilee now forced the big oars through the water, and as they did so they sang out some song that exactly matched the rhythm of their strokes. I wished I could have understood the words of their song, even though it was wrong of them to sing out there on the sea right after such a great killing. We knew that the waters must have been swarming with the souls of dead walrus, and at this time it was important that we show them respect, not triumph. For had they not come to us from some distant place and given their flesh to us so that we might live? Still, even with the foreigners rudely singing, we managed to reach the shore without another mishap, which made me think again that these three round-eyed people lived by other rules and perhaps would not be hurt by disobeying our taboos.

20

When we reached the shallow water, we waited, and soon we heard the long formal wailing of the women as they drew their hoods over their faces and mourned the death of Nowya and comforted his wife and children. But on this day when we had all been given life again, we could not force our thoughts to rest for long with the dead.

One by one we eased our kayaks in to the shore. Stepping out, we passed the harpoon lines to the gathering of women. There was no longer a heavy strain on the lines, for the ebbing tide had grounded all the walrus, and by the time we had placed the umiak and the kayaks safely up on the rocks, the walrus lay almost fully exposed on the rock-strewn beach.

Sarkak walked down to the big bull walrus that they had killed in the umiak and called to the three foreigners. They followed him. Borrowing Portagee's knife, he reached down and cut the huge right-front flipper with a circular motion, exposing the thick hide, the rich fat and the dark-red meat against the whiteness of the bone. Quickly Sarkak drove the point of the knife between the joint and cleverly severed the tendons. The huge handlike flipper easily parted from the body.

"*Nuliunga.* Wife of mine," he shouted. Ikuma came forward, and he handed her the choice flipper. It was so heavy that she had to lean sideways to balance the weight as she walked proudly back among the starving women.

Sarkak then cut away the other flippers and gave one to each of the foreigners. Pilee was the first who thought he recognized the meaning of this giving away of meat, and he called out to his two girls. Pushed from behind by others, they moved shyly forward. Pilee slashed two handholds in the huge rear flipper, and together the girls carried it up the beach. Everyone knew that it was wrong of him to do this. He should have given the meat to the girls' mother, for in our eyes he did not own these girls he slept with and had won with the knife. They were only on loan to him from that family. But Pilee knew nothing of this. He thought he owned them.

By now we had almost grown used to these foreigners. We no longer expected them to do things in our way. When they did, we all looked upon them with pride like small children of our own who were learning our customs.

Portagee did not hesitate but called Panee, the daughter of Atkak. This, too, was wrong, but some of our foolish women beamed with pleasure, and even the father of the girl did not say one word against it, for Portagee was himself such an incredible prize for that girl to win.

When it was Kakuktak's turn, he stood shyly looking at the slippery stones beneath his feet, awkwardly holding the great slab of meat in his right hand. Without raising his head, he called Neevee's name softly. Although she was very shy, she stepped forward and accepted the meat. This new style of doing things, this ignoring of the parents and giving gifts directly to the girls, probably shocked the old and pleased the young. Our girls seem shy, but they are sometimes shameless. Certainly this new way of doing things would never have come about except for the foreigners.

All of the kayakmen cut flippers from the walrus and called to their wives. I had no wife to call to, no one to give meat to. If I had been free, like the foreigners, I would have called to Neevee and given her the first meat, but I was too shy to do that, and so I called no one.

When this formality was completed, we drew out our short knives and borrowed the long iron knives of the foreigners and cut into the thick leather hides. The kayakmen sliced neatly through the huge animals, opening them up, exposing their beautiful entrails to the sky. Quickly and cleverly they cut downward, separating the giant ribs. Finding the vital cords between the vertebrae, they severed them and divided the huge spine into many sections, each small enough for a man to

132

carry. During the cutting the men ate a few thin strips of the rich warm meat, but only a little, for they worked desperately to finish their task before the tide returned.

All of the men and women and children and the three foreigners, red-handed like the rest, carried or dragged the great sections of meat up onto the rocks above the highest line of tide. Of all the people only Sarkak did not engage himself in the cutting and hauling of the meat. He sat alone on a high flat rock, with a soft caribou skin folded beneath him and directed the piling of the meat and fat in growing mounds. A dozen severed heads with gleaming ivory tusks stared blindly out to sea. Some of the entrails were flung to the dogs. Parts such as the heart and liver were saved as delicacies, and the long intestines were washed and cleaned and braided for drying.

When the rising tide reached up and touched the reddened boots of our exhausted butchers, it found only oily blood-stained rocks, for all the meat was safely ours. The sun had not reached its highest place in the sky, and yet we trembled with exhaustion and cold and a hunger that could not be banished by a few strips of meat. We knew that if we tried to eat a lot, our shrunken stomachs could rebel against us and fling the food back onto the stones.

Men washed their boots in the salt pools and carefully removed any drop of blood that might have touched their clothing, for it is not right to have the life of animals upon you. We laugh at the wild ignorant people living north of our land, for we are told that they cut holes in the great blankets of walrus fat and stick their heads through and carry this oily mess over their shoulders in a disgusting way. They are worse than wolves and care nothing about blood and oil on their clothing or their boots. That is why we rarely take wives from among them. It is far better to marry your own cousin and live within the good house of your uncle rather than sleep in the same bed with those lice catchers.

One thing I will say for the strangers: They, like ourselves, hated blood on their hands and boots and clothing, and I saw them bending by the tide pools scrubbing themselves clean.

I crawled into our tent, stripped off my clothes and rolled into the caribou sleeping skins, as did all the others. We went to sleep, leaving all that richness of meat exposed to the dogs, but so full of blubber and entrails were they that their scrawny sides were stretched to bursting, and we knew they could eat no more.

Sharp pangs of hunger awakened me. At first I thought that the whole walrus hunt might have been a dream. But as I hobbled out of the tent in the long autumn light that comes before evening, I could see the severed heads lined up along the rocks and the heavy piles of meat beyond. This time of plenty had truly come to us.

I heard two women talking and laughing beneath the big upturned umiak, and then I saw Sowniapik emerge and stretch himself and hunch his shoulders, drawing his bare hands up into the sleeves of his parka. The sun was slipping smoothly down the western sky to hide beyond the flat edge of the world. The wind had died with the day, leaving the water oily, slick and shining, reflecting the pale sky like a field of thin new ice. One by one, people came out quietly from their sleeping places and were caught by the quiet magic of the evening. Kakuktak, Portagee and Pilee stood together near Sarkak and like all of us watched the sea that had thrashed with great roaring beasts in the morning, had turned red in the afternoon tide and now lay silent once more, having given us its riches.

"*Kakpunga*," shouted Sarkak.

Knowing the word meant "I'm hungry," Portagee shouted it up to the sky. Three times he bellowed, and others laughed and echoed, "*Kakpunga!*"

Sarkak directed that the meat of the young walrus be brought to him and ordered that it be divided into four portions, one for himself, and one for each of the three foreigners. Pilee immediately arranged some flat stones, borrowed fire from Ikuma's lamp and lighted heather from his bedding. When the heather burned, he carefully fed it chunks of walrus fat that flared up with a hot white flame. Soon the smooth flat rock was hot, and the three of them placed this tender young meat on the rock and burned it black.

Portagee and Kakuktak and Pilee roared with delight, and catching the sizzling pieces of meat on the points of their knives, they waved them in the chill of the evening air and then devoured them. They crouched together as they ate like starved wolves. But no one spoke or even noticed them, so silent and intent was everyone with the great joy of eating.

The strangers liked the open fire, and Pilee kept feeding chunks of fat into it. No one cared if he used the fat, for it seemed to us that we could forever waste all the food and fuel we wished. Now our supply seemed endless, and if we ran short again, we would surely be given more. The children ate, of course, until they were sick, and we laughed and offered them more, and they ate more and were sick again. I filled my stomach slowly and watched the first stars come out and the crescent moon lie on her back, with her feet in the air like a white bitch pretending to be afraid of the dog star. The first pale-green lights of winter wavered in the sky, and some men whistled at the lights and waved their arms and seemed to cause the lights to ebb and flow. We laughed with joy at the sky, and the *kalunait* must have thought we were crazy.

Portagee stood beside the upturned umiak, and I saw him run his hand over the tight sealskin cover. He struck the bottom sharply, and it resounded in the darkness like a huge drum. He struck it again and then again, and every head turned and listened to him. He smiled and spread his arms wide in the air, and then he hammered with both hands on the tight skin and sang out wild words we could not understand, nor could we follow the quick rhythm of his drumming. Frantically he flung his head forward on his chest and then snapped it up again, faster, faster, shaking his mass of tightly curled black hair. The gold ring glistened in his ear, and the white of his eyes and his teeth shone against his beautiful dark skin.

The sounds he made excited us all, both the strange pounding rhythms and his wild singing. But we could not understand any of it, for it was too different from our way of drumming, our way of singing. Yet even now on some evenings in autumn, when the sun has disappeared and the sea is still, I imagine that I can hear and feel that savage booming off the skin of the upturned boat. Imagine, a sound so strong that it has remained with me, haunting me through all these countless seasons.

Some of the women and young girls tried to set up a chorus to answer Portagee's drumming, but it was too fast for them, too difficult. In the end they laughed at themselves because they could not follow. Portagee urged them to try again, but they all laughed so much that the drumming and the singing ended.

Portagee in his excitement still whirled among the women's chorus, grabbing at some of them. Then spinning round and round, he returned to the great boat drum and flung himself beneath it. A number of young girls scrambled quickly under the umiak to join him there, without secrecy. The older people laughed, looked at each other and blew out their breaths. They could scarcely believe all the wild new ways that were coming to them through these foreigners, these big children who knew so little and yet who had changed our lives so much.

Suddenly Sarkak was gone. He was alone in our tent. Without seeing his face, I knew that he hated this new lack of control, for it was not his way. He had gained no real command over these *kalunait* and could no longer prevent the things that were happening in his own camp.

That night we slept more soundly than we had since the new moon had come to us, and in the morning we hauled the meat to safer places and covered it with huge stones. The stones were rammed tightly over the meat so that they could not be moved by dogs or bears, and only the cleverness of a man could understand the drawing of the key stone to release the cache.

On the following day we filled the umiaks and the kayaks with as much walrus meat as we could carry and set out at dawn. We paddled for three days, sleeping each night along the coast, scarcely bothering to hunt the seals that had reappeared in great numbers. Around us the whole sea lay smooth as ice. The air was cold, and great flocks of sea birds darkened the southern horizon.

Finally we saw the sight we longed for: the two tall man-shaped images built of stone that marked the narrow entrance to the bay of our winter camp.

Harpoon Head

21

As my kayak touched the shore, I wondered at how desolate, how unused, our campground seemed. This place where I had been born should have shown some marks of our laughing and dancing, but only the empty boat racks and high stone graves still stood to remind us that we had once before lived here.

When we were ashore and the boats were unloaded, I helped Kakuktak, Portagee and Pilee put up their own small tent, although we all knew that only Portagee and Panee would sleep in it. Everyone arranged his tent near the north hill to find shelter from the autumn winds until the real snows needed to build our igloos came again. Our hunters dragged half-frozen walrus meat up to the caches, and women cracked holes in the thin ice on the drinking pond. Our autumn camp started to come to life again. From the time I was a small boy, we had always waited for winter in this place.

Each morning when I awoke, I could see the breaths of all the family rising in white plumes inside the cold darkness of the tent, and a thick scum of ice had always formed on the stone pots. Above the tent, in the first light of dawn, I could hear the last flocks of snow geese calling to each other as they rose up from their frost-whitened resting places in the valley behind our camp, heading south across the great expanse of gray water that lay beyond our small protected bay.

The weather had turned cold, and the foreigners shivered in their dark, thin clothing. Sarkak decided to have the women make parkas for them. Of course, Ikuma made Kakuktak's parka, and she was helped by Nuna. But it was Sarkak who selected the sealskins and decided on the design. Kakuktak's parka was slit up the front, to permit easy running, and had a deep warm hood that tapered into a tall point of pride. Sarkak chose a handsome marrying of narrow sealskin strips, light and dark, to be sewn together at the hem, wrists and hood, to strengthen the garment and to make it beautiful. Such a distinctive design would allow us to recognize the wearer, even at some distance.

Pilee's parka was made by Sowniapik's wife. It was neat and simple, and it fitted him perfectly, but it had almost no point of pride on the hood, which told us much. But the strangers did not seem to notice.

Atkak's wife made Portagee's parka and a pair of pants for him as well. Both were much too large at first, for she had an exaggerated idea of the hugeness of the brown man. When he tried them on, the three foreigners roared with laughter, and we laughed with them, like people related to each other, like people belonging to the same family. Then Atkak's wife cut the garments down for him and altered them to fit. But whenever Portagee pulled his parka on over his head, people still laughed, and Portagee laughed, remembering the first fitting.

During the second moon of autumn, after the new snows

had come and disappeared, the tundra moss turned softly red. On the driest days the women went out with the children and gathered great bundles of the soft sweet-smelling heather to place beneath the sleeping skins of our beds. Sharp-eyed children made a game of finding the few red low-bush cranberries and frost-bitten crowberries that lay hidden in the tundra, for there were many more than usual that autumn. At first these berries went from their hands into their mouths. But when they grew tired of eating, they filled their parka hoods with berries as a gift for some favorite person in the camp.

When the women and children returned after the first day of the heather gathering, they shook out their parka hoods and were amazed to see Portagee and Pilee and even Kakuktak wolf down the bright berries as though they were the only food in the world. The children laughed with delight, for they did not really like the berries and almost never ate them after the first day's gathering.

On the following morning more children went out with the women, and this time they did not eat the red and black berries they found but made a game of loading three large sealskin buckets. When they returned in the freezing darkness of late afternoon, they brought the buckets to the strangers as a gift. Pilee, Kakuktak and Portagee ate a few handfuls of the berries but decided among themselves to save most of them so that they could eat some each day while they lasted. Knowing that the dogs would not touch them, they carelessly left the berries outside their tent. That evening the air grew warm, and my legs ached. I knew that we would soon have snow, and during the night I heard the sharp rattling of wind and rain against the side of the tent. I slept again, and when I later heard the sound, it was muffled and soft and heavy. I knew without looking that our first heavy snow was falling. About midday I dressed and went outside. The whole world was covered with a blinding whiteness. Only a few wet rocks jutted out through the new snow, like sleek black ravens. Big wet flakes whirled in toward me, driven by the wind.

I saw Sarkak outside, walking through the snow, stiff-legged with pleasure, and Poota and Okalikjuak hurried after him and laughed and pushed each other like children, so glad were they to see our winter come again. With this coming of the freezing moon, the whole land would change to glaring whiteness, and the ice pans in the sea would join together and freeze into a huge new hunting ground. Then the whole white world would be ours once more to drive our dog teams where we pleased. We would be free to go, to travel. The snow would be hard and fast, and animals would leave fresh tracks to follow. On the sea the seals would make their breathing places in the ice, showing us where they were, so that we could stand and hunt them.

But that autumn the true cold did not come to us at once. First the clouds came down and covered all the hills, and then the killing winds reared in over the blackened seas, bringing us freezing rain that turned into white sleet. The night cold turned the tents to ice, and their shaking sounded like boats smashing against rocks. For many days the women and children and most of the men stayed in bed to keep warm, but even then two young children of our camp caught chills and died of fever. I remember being half afraid to look at the two small stone graves that their parents built for them. They stood piled above the ground in rocky silence, slowly turning white. Many women wore their oldest clothes and hid their faces deep in their hoods. They moaned and clung to their children and spoke of death. I thought of how life had some boundless moments of joy out on the hunting grounds at dawn and in the dance house and in the bed at night. But beside these times there was sickness and hunger and loneliness and fear.

Finally the big snow we waited for did come, and the white giants hiding in the blizzard whistled and screamed and whipped our frozen tents for four days and four nights, and no one could go outside. On the fifth morning there was deathlike silence, and I looked out on a new white world that was utterly changed. Everywhere great wind-packed drifts were carved into strange shapes, driven in long hard curves against the hills. The sun did not come to us that day, and the clouds scudded dark and low just above our heads.

I saw Portagee with Pilee, bundled up with a mixture of their clothing and our own, out searching though the snow around the little tent. They kicked the hard drifts with their feet and stamped around the edges of the tent. Because I was curious, I went to help them, and a few women and children also joined the search. The strangers outlined the shape of the three skin buckets with their hands and pointed into their mouths, cramming in imaginary berries. We did not understand them, for we believed that they had eaten the berries during the storm and that now perhaps they were foolishly looking for more berries in the snowdrifts around their tent. Some thought that the strangers were mad, and some thought that they were joking with us, and so we imitated them, stamping our feet and swallowing imaginary berries, making it into a game.

But the two foreigners did not smile, and suddenly Pilee jerked off his mitt and pointed his finger at us and shouted, "You steal. You steal."

We did not know what those words meant, but we joined in the game, and all pointed at them and answered, "Oooo steeel. Oooo steeel!"

Portagee stood still and stared at us, and Pilee grew red in the face. He shouted at us, "Bastards. Bastards," and he kicked the top off a hard snowdrift. Picking up a chunk of snow in each hand, he flung them violently at the children. We did not laugh, for this was a hostile thing, a thing we never do.

They both turned away in rage, and Pilee was still loudly mumbling when they stamped back inside the tent. We did not call them "Pastars," for the word was hard to say. We did not know the word, but by looking at their narrowed eyes and the curl of their lips, we knew it had a bad meaning.

141

That afternoon Sarkak and the hunters took their long thin probes and their snow knives and walked across the wind-packed drifts. So hard was the new snow that it squealed like small animals beneath their feet and took no footprints. They carefully drove their probes downward to test the snow, and in this way they selected the best places to build each igloo. The men worked in groups. Cutting straight down into the snow with their long knives, they freed and lifted big blocks and stood them upright one against the other in a ring. Slowly six houses rose in coiling spirals, each snow block cleverly cut to fit against the next. The builder inside each new house never stepped outside. He constructed the entire house using only the blocks he had taken from the snow floor inside the igloo. The waist-deep hole he first stood in became the new floor of the snowhouse. Finally, the wedge-shaped key block was carefully lifted and fitted into place in the top of the dome, immediately giving the house enough strength to bear a man's weight.

Outside each snowhouse the women chinked the cracks between the blocks with fine snow, and a man built a meat porch and a long twisting entrance tunnel, sloping down from porch to house, to keep out the wind and cold. Finally a fist-sized hole was cut in a short snow chimney for ventilation, and a large clear sheet of fresh-water lake ice, the thickness of a man's wrist, was placed in the sloping wall above the entrance passage to allow light to enter the house.

The strangers could not help us, for, of course, they did not know how to build a snowhouse. Even our young men cannot build a good one. Pilee never even came out of the tent but lay in the warm darkness between his two girls and waited for others to complete the work. Kakuktak watched for a while but went off hunting with Yaw after a flight of ptarmigan. Of the three foreigners Portagee was the only one who tried to help in the building, and finally seeing how difficult it was, he knelt and joked with the women and tried to help them fill the cracks between the blocks. The work made him warm for the first time since we had arrived at the winter camp.

When the new igloos were finished, the women carried bundles of dried heather from the tents and spread it out over the snow sleeping bench that stretched across the entire back half of each house. Over the heather they placed white bear-skins and sealskins, with the hair side down toward the snow, and on top of them they spread the soft winter caribou skins with the thick hair facing up. Over these skins on which we would lie, they placed the caribou robes with the hair turned inward, to make a warm nest for naked sleepers.

At this time two new side igloos appeared in our village. One for Nowya's young widow was attached by a snow tunnel to the side of Okalikjuak's house. Living beside her brother and sewing for him gave her his protection. Visitors to the camp would have to ask Okalikjuak's permission to sleep with her, and this he would give only with her consent. In any camp a young widow living without the protection of some man is in danger, for if she does not agree to lie with a trav-eler, he can simply rape her without fear of reprisal.

The other side igloo was attached to Sarkak's big snow-house. It was made for the three foreigners, but they never really used it for sleeping, so great was the warmth and hospi-tality of parents and of our young women, too. They were not always content to lie only with their families.

At this time in the early winter Sarkak wished to have Kakuktak living with him in his snowhouse. I do not know what special arrangement he must have made with Poota, but one night Neevee appeared in Sarkak's igloo, and a place was made for her in the bed. Kakuktak came without complaining and brought back his extra boots and sleeping skin from Poota's house, and for a time he slept with Neevee in our big igloo. They both must have missed the warmth of Poota's family as much as I did.

Ivory Snow Knife

22

Ikuma and Nuna knelt beside each other, quietly sewing in the warm light of the well-trimmed lamp. Nuna hummed softly, but she did not speak, for she knew that Ikuma had her mouth full of sinew that she was softening to use as thread for the boot vamp. It was late, and in the darkness of early winter all the children in the camp slept, and every man was seal hunting out on the ice; every man, that is, except me, Avinga. I was used to staying in the camp with the women. I didn't count. When the freezing wind blew in over the open water of the sea, my legs pained me so that some days they could scarcely bear my weight. I lay beside Nuna's mother, on the far side of the wide bed, drawing useless circles on the soft fur and watching the guard hairs straighten and make the marks disappear.

Sarkak had not hunted for years, and yet somehow the coming of the foreigners had charged him with excitement. He was so anxious to teach them our ways that he, himself, had taken to hunting again as eager as a young boy.

Nuna stopped humming, and I looked up and saw both women raise their heads and listen. I could hear the soft creak of footsteps coming toward the house.

"It's the widow Akigik," said Ikuma.

Nuna raised her eyebrows in agreement, and they looked at each other and waited.

The footsteps stopped outside for a moment. Then in through the long passage came the small, broad-hipped woman Akigik, with a heavy baby on her back. She pushed aside the sealskin hanging and ducked through the entrance. She coughed nervously, shoving her square, reddened hands deep into the opposite sleeves, and bounced softly to quiet the infant hidden in the soft pouch of her parka.

To recognize their visitor, Ikuma and Nuna, kneeling on

the bed, made a small sound of pleasure. "*Eeee*," they called to her softly, and made a place for her to sit by them on the bed. Nuna's old mother simply coughed and sat staring at the visitor.

Ikuma and Nuna spoke the few words needed for politeness, and then both women made their needles fly. This widowed sister of Sowniapik's was a great talker. Her gossip did not usually interest them, but she was always truthful, and since she came from the house where Pilee now lived, all her words were worth hearing. They listened carefully.

Akigik spoke for a while about being short of sewing sinew, and Ikuma gave her a small sheath of leg tendons. While she tucked the gift safely away in a corner of her parka hood, she was silent for a moment, and then she spoke.

"*Kalunait* are really very different from ourselves," she said. "You know that Pilee really did buy those two young girls with the knife. Well, I should say he borrowed the girls. He could never feed them. He can't even feed himself. My brother Sowniapik gets the food for all of them, and he has the knife. But it is the women in our house who want to have Pilee there. He likes women. He is always trying to talk with them, touch them, fool with them. Our men are too shy for that when they are young, and too full of themselves when they grow older.

"Just to be near our bed at night is a pleasure, and no woman in our house would miss it. Sometimes our neighbors' wives and daughters crowd in to watch Pilee and his two girls go to bed. You two would be more than welcome to come over and watch them any night you wish.

"Pilee likes to eat and get into bed early, and then he arranges my nieces in this way or that way, according to his desires. The girls used to be very shy about this, but the older women have teased them and urged them on so much that the foolish little things have grown to like their audience and perform quite freely now. Pilee makes a lot of noise when he is in bed between his girls and thrashes around under them, over

145

them and beside them. He does all of this best when the men are away hunting. He is a little shy when they are around. But, as I said, he doesn't mind women being near him at all. He likes them all, young and old.

"He always has trouble with his feet being cold, and in the night he usually leaves his inner boots on when he thrashes naked in the bed. All hair and tattoos he is. He often gets himself tangled up and turned around. Last night his one boot was hanging out over the front of the bed, and he poked his head out from underneath the fur covers and pointed at the old woman, Ningiuk, who had made the boots for him and who was standing there with the other women, watching. He pointed at the boots, and he pointed at her and said, '*Kumik-chiak, kumikchiak.* Beautiful boots, beautiful boots.' Then he ducked under the covers again and made the girls scream with his tickling and grabbing, yes, and his biting, too, I am told."

Through this whole long tale Akigik's dark eyes glowed brightly, and her mouth worked hard over the long rhythmic words she constructed, building one upon another, breathlessly, endlessly. She paused and dipped the wide horn ladle into the ice water in the pot and drank slowly. The water cooled her thoughts of the exciting nightly struggles, and she was able to continue.

"One would think those useless nieces of mine would learn to sew watertight boots if they want attention, but they do not. They have become proud performers in the bed like strong men in the wrestling games, and when Pilee actually bends Evaloo under him, she sometimes slyly draws back the covers so that you can share her good fortune with her.

"I tell you, the young girls today have changed. There was nothing like this when I was young. One ran and hid in the hills to do such things. But, of course, we did not have foreigners with us then."

Both Ikuma and Nuna raised their eyebrows in agreement with her. Indeed, our village was changing. The coming of these foreigners had altered everything for us in the camp.

"If you think that is strange," said Ikuma, "I have a story to tell you of what I have heard about Portagee and have seen with my own eyes."

The widow Akigik made a sweeping gesture with her hands, but she stopped quickly and made a face. Lunging back with her two hands over her head, she jerked a naked baby boy out from beneath her hood and held him at arm's length as his thin yellow stream arched against the snowhouse wall, steaming in the frosty air. When he was finished, she shook him and licked his face with tenderness and said, "Almost washed your mother's back, did you?" She then leaned forward and flung him gently over her shoulder and in straightening up let him slip down into the warmth of her fur pouch.

The howling of the dogs and the crunching of snow told us that the men had returned, and I, myself, never heard Ikuma's story of Portagee. Akigik rushed out of the snowhouse, and Sarkak's two wives pulled on their long-tailed outer parkas and hurried out to greet their husband and the other hunters.

I lay in the big house, with my back to the old widow, and tried to imagine what form Portagee's sexual prowess would take. I would listen carefully from now on, for I was anxious to hear more about him and also about Kakuktak. I wished to understand everything I could about these strangers, these dog children, who had come so weakly among us and had somehow gained enough strength to change our lives.

Horn Cup

23

One midday during the short gray twilight that comes to us at the end of the first moon of winter, I heard the short cry people give to alert other villagers that a dog team is approaching. Climbing up out of the igloo passage, I saw two sleds coming toward us over the snow-covered ice of the bay. The closest sled was little more than a dot, but still we could make out the three dogs and the lone driver. We all knew it must be Atkak returning from the big lake near the summer camp, for he had gone there to catch a fish to feed to his father, who was very sick. A fish was the only thing we knew of that would help to make the old man well again. The other sled would be that of his oldest son, whom Atkak had sent east to bring the shaman from his camp.

Atkak's father had fallen in front of their snowhouse six days before. It was as though some evil thing had entered into him and remained pounding wildly within his chest. Since then the old man had lain on the bed, eating nothing, scarcely moving, breathing badly. The older women crowded around him, assuring him again and again that he was going to die. To them death was interesting and only a little frightening. But I believe that the strangers feared the coming of death, for I noticed that when the old man was sick, Portagee quickly moved out of Atkak's snowhouse and chose once more to sleep in our side igloo.

At first we could only guess about the distant dog team, but as it slowly approached, I heard the hunter with the sharpest eyes saying that it was the sled driven by Atkak's son.

"Yes," said Sowniapik, "and someone is with him."

"Two others arrive with him," added Okalikjuak, "one large and one small. The big man lies on the sled, not helping through the rough ice. It is a sick man or perhaps the shaman."

148

Others answered, "Yes, it must be the shaman."

Kangiak looked at me in that strange way of his, not smiling, not scowling, and said, "He is saving his strength to wrestle the stones in which the spirits live."

I emptied the stone urine pot, slung the bones and bird skins to the dogs and went back down into the snowhouse to finish scraping a little bone carving, for I knew that it would be a long time before the sleds would arrive. When I went up again, it was because I heard our dogs howling with excitement. It was dark, and an icy wind moaned around the passage as I stepped outside. A half-moon raced through the thin clouds, and the hard-packed snow caught the light of the moon and drew it straight to my eyes in a wide river of silver. Men and dogs looked like a part of their own sharp shadows moving fast against the biting cold.

Atkak halted his team near the center of the camp and left the sled, carrying a big frozen fish by the tail. It was as stiff as ice, and he carried it like a club as he headed toward the entrance of his igloo. His family stood there waiting for him. He stopped as his wife spoke to him, and she must have told him of his father's death. He stood quietly for a moment, then spun around and flung the precious fish at the dogs. It was a crazy thing to do, for his team was still harnessed and half starved after three days of traveling. They fought savagely, in a wild tangle of lines, and Atkak stood rigidly, doing nothing, as though he did not see or hear the bloody battle. Atkak had traveled and worked for three days in the freezing cold to catch that one fish for his father, and now he had cast it away and could not even enter his own house.

While we all stood shivering in the stinging wind, watching Atkak, the second team came up through the barrier ice, guided by his son. It was easy for me to recognize the shaman who rode on it. He was short and very heavy, and he clung to the sled like a favored wife, waiting for it to halt completely in front of the igloo. I could not tell, at first, who the shaman had with him.

Kakuktak and the big Portagee came out of the snowhouse and stood beside me, their hoods drawn forward against the cold.

"*Keena? Keenaoona?*" said Kakuktak. "Who? Who is this?"

"*Angokok*," I answered, pointing at the shaman. But I knew he would not understand our name for this magic man, this healer, with the skin line tied above his ears and the cluster of fox teeth dangling down over his forehead. He wore a strange parka, styled almost like a woman's, that bulged over his belly as though he were pregnant.

Ikuma next hurried up out of the entrance passage, and helping myself with a harpoon shaft, I followed her over to the newly arrived sled. Ikuma was just like me: We two were always curious about the ordinary life of the shaman. We often used to speak about him, wondering how he managed to live without hunting and yet keep his belly so beautifully fat.

During our lives Sarkak and the shaman had always been the two most important people in the land. They both knew this, and because of it they competed with each other, the one using his religious magic, and the other his immense wealth of food.

The shaman had with him a dirty boy dressed in tattered clothing. As I drew closer, I could see that he was that useless son of Anaktok, a boy who could only play with himself and look at his feet and mumble. Someone had roughly hacked his hair short with a knife, leaving only his forelock that hung down to his shoulder. A hunter traveling westward had told us that this boy had fallen down in a fit during the first spring moon and that this was why the shaman had chosen him as an assistant.

Now many people gathered around the two of them, standing in a circle, their hoods hiding all their faces in shadow. At first no one spoke, and I watched and waited to see what would happen, for the shaman and most of the people did not know that the old man was dead. Finally Atkak told everyone.

Then, turning, he started to lead them all toward the igloo.

The shaman spread his arms and called out, "*Owka, owka.* No, no," in his high unnatural voice. Then he called for a snow knife and clumsily cut a big block of snow. Sneaking forward, he placed it in the entrance to the porch, carefully sealing up the house. He then stepped back, and with a great show of ceremony he urinated in the form of a cross against the blocked door. He called to the dirty boy, and he, too, urinated there. He then urged the people back, and we watched as the biggest dog ran up and sniffed and yellowed the door. Many other dogs followed.

The three strangers laughed at this, for they did not understand that the shaman was disguising the entrance way, cleverly hiding it from the ghost of the dead man. I shuddered with cold and with fear at the very thought of that house, for it had been full of singing and laughing and storytelling only a few days before, and now it lay bleak and haunted, a place of horror, with its oil lamp sputtering unattended, casting its last trembling light through the ice window above the entrance before it, too, died in the cold.

The shaman turned away from the sealed entrance and looked around him. I had the feeling that his eyes searched for Sarkak, for he had not seen him in the crowd of people. He looked toward our snowhouse, and there he saw Sarkak standing in the starlight, making no movement to come and greet him. Behind him stood all three strangers, like giants in their new fur parkas.

Turning like a woman searching for some lost thing, the shaman hurried toward the first snowhouse in his path. Without waiting for an invitation from the owners, he ducked inside the passage, followed by the dirty boy. It was Okalikjuak's house.

Atkak and his sons unlashed the shaman's bag of clothing and his sleeping skins and carried them after him, down into Okalikjuak's igloo, where he would stay the length of his visit.

Atkak and his family were now without a place to sleep. Everyone crowded around them, and they were led down into the warmth of Tungilik's snowhouse.

When we returned to our house, Sarkak had already gone inside, and the three foreigners had made their way down into their small igloo that was attached to the side of our big entrance porch. Portagee had brought Panee with him, since Tungilik's snowhouse was now crowded by Atkak's family. I paused and looked in on them, and I cannot tell you how much I wished that I might have had the power to speak to these *kalunait*. They did not understand who the shaman was or why he had come to our camp. They may not even have known that Atkak's father was dead, though I said that in a simple way to Kakuktak several times. I repeated "*Ittok toko-vok.*" But I worried that I had no clear words to warn them that there were old jealousies between Sarkak and the shaman. They all three looked at me from their places on the bed and shook their heads in that strangest of all their gestures, and we laughed together in our common ignorance.

I said, "*Ionamut,*" meaning there is no help for it, no help against death.

Kakuktak seemed to understand me and answered, "*Iona-mut.*"

The next day was without wind, but I pulled on my extra caribou-skin stockings and eased my feet into my sealskin boots, for I knew that it would be freezing cold outside, and I did not want cold feet to cause me to miss any of the events. It would be something worth seeing, to witness this fat shaman break the dead man's spells and guard the village against his roving ghost.

I spoke loudly, calling out quickly to Kangiak. I knew that the sound would excite the strangers and get them out of bed. Pilee was not in the small igloo. He must have been sleeping with Evaloo and Mia in Sowniapik's bed. But Portagee and Kakuktak hurried outside after us. Since I could not tell them about the shaman, they would have to see for themselves how he worked his magic.

On this morning the village lay half buried in winter. The domes of our igloos were almost lost in snow. The blue shadows of entrance porches, wandering dogs, upturned sleds and kayaks, urine stains and shallow footprints were our only marks floating on a world of whiteness.

When we reached Atkak's snowhouse, many people had gathered there already, and the fat shaman moved around importantly. He seemed to be measuring the stricken snowhouse that held the dead man. He had never seen Kakuktak or the big brown man near him in the light of day, and yet, as we approached, he in no way acknowledged the fact that he saw them or that they were in any way different from ordinary people. I had expected him to act like this, for it was his way. What was about to happen was to be his own performance, and he did not want it spoiled by any foreigners.

He called out sharply to the dirty boy, who stood gawking in horror at the giant Portagee and the white, pale-eyed Kakuktak walking with me across the hard snowdrifts. The shaman made the boy go and cut a small hole in the urine-stained block that covered the entrance, and he told him how to cough loudly and call certain familiar words into the passage to attract the spirit. The boy did this repeatedly while the shaman took a long-bladed ivory snow knife and licked it carefully with his wide tongue until its blade was smoothly coated with ice. Then he crept around to the side of the house, plunged the blade into the wall of the igloo, and, using both hands, cut violently in one huge circular motion. He lightly kicked the outlined circle, and the wall crumbled, forming a large opening for him to enter. Our people drew back in fear, not wishing to be in line with the new entrance. But Kakuktak and Portagee, unafraid, crowded forward for a closer view of the silent form of the dead man lying inside on the sleeping platform.

The shaman led the way, striding boldly into the igloo, peering all around him, holding out his hands as if to feel for any unseen spirits. He stepped up onto the sleeping platform and bent down stiffly to look into the dead man's face. Then he called to Atkak and his sons and other relatives and instructed them to take the corners of the caribou skin on which the old man's body lay. They carried him outside. He was frozen stiff and pale as a bleached bone, and although I could see his features, he no longer looked like the real man I had always known. That real man, the good dancer and singer, the storyteller, had flown out of him.

They carried his body some distance from the camp, to a hilly place where there were other scattered graves. Slowly we all trailed up the hill, walking carefully in each other's steps, tramping a narrow path in the snow. The men found a place where the wind had almost swept the black rocks free of snow, and there they laid him carefully on his side, facing the frozen bay. Atkak laid the old man's short knife, his bow and a bone drinking cup beside him. The other men gathered many skull-sized stones and placed them around his form, then quickly covered his body with heavy stones, piling one upon another until they formed a black mound as high as a man's waist.

The shaman came and placed the last large stone on top of the grave, and he did it in such a way that I felt he was weighting down the body so that its ghost could not rise and walk at night, although as a child I believed that the stones on a grave were placed there to protect the dead from dogs and wild animals, even after the spirit had flown away.

While we were all gathered near the new grave, the shaman called out to us, "Beware, for with the coming moons others will die in this place. Be careful, for great harm may come to all of you." Then he shouted harshly to the dirty boy, ordering him back to the snowhouses. The boy, who had been staring for a long time at Kakuktak and the tall dark Portagee, turned and then jumped in fright, for he faced the wild-eyed Pilee striding up the hill toward us.

The next morning it was as though nothing had happened in the village. Atkak and his wife were out early starting to build their new snowhouse, and many neighbors came to help them. There was much joking about the increased size of the house, since it was both a wider and a taller house, built that way, everyone said, to accommodate the tall Portagee, along with Atkak's daughter, Panee.

The shaman and the dirty boy stayed on for half a moon to eat our food and in this way collect their payment for protecting the village against the old man's ghost. The shaman only talked and ate and slept and kept the dirty boy close by his side. We rarely saw either of them leave Okalikjuak's snowhouse.

The foreigners' little side igloo off Sarkak's house was almost always vacant. I let the gray bitch sleep in there on some cold nights, and no one seemed to notice.

Stone Grave

24

When half a moon had passed after we had put the stones on the old man's grave, a huge white bear came to us one morning, moving upwind, off the darkened ice of the sea. The bear must have been hungry, for he quietly killed and ate two of our dogs without disturbing the others, which seemed almost like a miracle to me. Of all the animals a white bear is most like a man. Sometimes a bear will play like a shambling fool and at other times act with great wisdom and cunning. Bears do not know men or fear them, for when a bear meets a man, it is almost always a moment of death.

Ikuma was the first to hear the bear rubbing its side against our entrance passage and woke Sarkak. Everyone was alert in an instant, and we heard the dogs start their low moaning, a sound they make only for a bear. Kangiak and Yaw jumped up from the bed. Kakuktak was right after them. Outside we heard the big dog Pasti snarling as he rushed in at the bear. The bear bumped hard against the side of the snowhouse as Pasti leaped at him, and with one sweeping motion of his ripping claws we heard him disembowel the dog. Then we heard the snow squealing as the bear shambled off toward the jagged pressure ice heaved up at the edge of the frozen sea.

We rushed out and saw the running bear with twenty dogs around him. Just then he stopped and turned to fight them. He had chosen a great slab of sea ice to be at his back for protection. Two dogs rushed boldly in at him, and with one smooth motion he killed the first dog and hamstrung the second, allowing it to drag itself away, leaving a dark-red trail across the snow. All the dogs in the camp stood grouped around the bear, each waiting for its chance. They seemed to understand all the danger that waited for them in the beast's heavy curved claws and the half-open mouth. The bear's narrow head swayed slowly from side to side on his long sinuous neck.

All of us, still pulling clothes on, hurried halfway to the ring of dogs, then stopped cautiously, for we knew bears to be very dangerous at times like these. Kangiak carried a light killing spear, and Okalikjuak his bow-and-arrow case. But Sarkak was anxious to end the bear's life himself before too many dogs were killed. He called for his long ice chisel, and when it was brought to him, he drew the iron knife from his boot and quickly bound it to the end of the shaft with a length of sealskin line. He borrowed Kakuktak's knife and stuck it in his boot tip, and waving the others back, started out alone across the hard-packed snow toward the bear.

Sarkak began to run lightly on his toes, not at the bear, but to the left, and as he went he gave a call imitating a wounded raven: "Cauk, cauk, cauk!" It is a call that dog drivers sometimes use when they wish to excite their teams into running. Instantly the dogs started yelping and darting quickly in and out, feinting at the bear.

"Cauk, cauk, cauk," Sarkak called again as he turned sharply and ran in among the dogs.

The bear's head stopped weaving, and his black eyes watched the running figure. The bear was panting heavily, with his blue tongue lolling between great yellow teeth, and his breath steaming white in the freezing air.

"Haar, haar, haar," called Sarkak, and our lead dog, followed by my brave foolish bitch, rushed in at the bear. As the bear reached out to kill her, I saw Sarkak step forward within arm's reach of the bear and drive the iron knife into its side once, twice. As he tried for a third strike, the bear turned, dropped onto all four feet and came at him fast. It was the moment the dogs had waited for, and in an instant they swarmed in upon the bear, tearing mouthfuls of skin and hair from his back and sides. The bear whirled on them, and I could see a great red patch spreading over his white side. Sarkak struck again, his feet planted wide apart, his big shoulders driving all his weight behind the spear. He must have cut the big artery to the heart, for the bear stumbled and fell. The dogs leaped at him again.

I have never heard a man utter a sound as terrible as that which Sarkak then forced up from the depth of his belly. It was a roaring noise like a torrent of angry water forced between boulders, and it had in it the sharp cracking of whips and the breaking of bones. It was a sound of death. Every dog heard it clearly, and it drove fear into them and broke their bloody passion for the bear. They no longer acted like a wolf pack; they drew back and made room for Sarkak to walk through them. He touched the staring eye of the bear with swiftness and with caution, wanting to be sure that its soul had flown away.

As Sarkak straightened up, I hurried down with all the others to look with wonder upon this huge white dog killer

157

that had come to us like a gift in the darkness of morning. Ikuma and Nuna skinned the bear quickly while it steamed hot in the morning air. Its great hide slipped off as easily as a parka. This white fur robe, of course, belonged to Sarkak alone, but the sweet meat was cut up and divided fairly among all the people in the camp, for bear meat is well known for giving strength and power in the hunt and in the bed. Everyone was eager to have his share.

The killing of a white bear within a camp was no little thing, and the shaman came out to see if there might be any magic attached to this silent dog killer. As the shaman bent to examine the genitals of the bear, he found himself standing beside Sarkak.

The conversation between them started slowly at first, while they watched the bear being skinned and waited to study his entrails for any unusual signs. The people drew away from them and pretended not to notice that they had started to speak together. At first they each mumbled only a word or two. Sarkak began, and the shaman merely grunted his acknowledgment. But gradually the conversation grew and fattened, and these two powerful men of influence, who had known each other all their lives, began to relax once more as they were caught up in the pleasure of words.

Their desire to exchange ideas was boundless, for each of them loved best of all to talk. The long separations that they experienced never failed to fill them both with strong feelings of jealousy and mistrust. Nevertheless, they were a perfect conversational match for each other, and they both knew it well.

Sarkak began by mentioning the elaborate plaiting of a new dog whip he had been given, and after he had divided the bear meat, he led the shaman to the entrance of his igloo to examine the work. Of course, neither of them was really interested in the craftsmanship of the whip, but it gave them both the excuse to go together to the entrance of Sarkak's igloo. Sarkak's wives darted past them into the entrance passage so that they could be in their proper places to greet the guest. Then Sarkak easily led the shaman into the house by asking a question, knowing that the shaman would have to follow to answer.

Ikuma and Nuna called out, "*Taktualuk, taktualuk*. It's dark, it's dark."

And the shaman twice called out, "*Koumajualuk*. It's light here. It's light."

With this first formality completed, Sarkak heaved himself onto the sleeping platform. Sure of this small victory, he did not indicate, as he should have, where his guest should sit. This was the second move in their complicated game. The shaman had expected something like this, for it was not like Sarkak to be so outgoing. Sarkak would have to show some rudeness somewhere. Sarkak should have offered the shaman the warm place of honor in the very center of the wide bed, which would, of course, give him the privilege of sleeping there later. But he did not. The shaman, without hesitation, heaved himself into the place of honor and then with a grunt rolled himself slightly sideways, away from center and away from Sarkak, in a subtle gesture of disdain. They stared at each other with cold admiration, for each had given and taken a powerful unseen blow. Each knew and reveled in the fact that he would never find such a worthy adversary again.

It was time for their long conversation to begin, for it would take at least all of one day and a night to be completed. First they talked of the hunting and of the people living north and east of Sarkak's camp. The shaman was an endless traveler by necessity, for he lived entirely on the food of other hunters. Even with his bright skill of magic he could wear out his welcome very quickly. He had no dogs of his own, for other people carried him wherever he wished to go. Some did it because of fear, and others did it out of respect, for it was widely known that he possessed great powers. He could break a spell of sickness or choke an unborn son with the child's own umbilical cord. He had sometimes caused the winds to guide the caribou toward the hunter, and it was said that he could send his soul walking on the moon.

As the conversation wore on, Sarkak and the shaman started slowly to flatter each other while belittling their own power. In this way each boldly showed his own self-confidence. In this way each one asserted his own strength and importance.

Sarkak said, "Without your help last year all the people in this camp would have starved to death, for we have so little skill and only a few miserable useless dogs. Our kayaks are falling into pieces, and there is never any organization here. Three great new bellies have I to feed when we here can scarcely feed ourselves."

"Everyone knows that it was not I who helped this camp," said the shaman. "I am only a poor man, a shabby starving begger, helped by others. Sometimes, in my hunger, I do have a kind of wakeful sleeping in which a power from beneath me enters my body and speaks out to the people through me. I, myself, am a poor man, a miserable man, knowing nothing."

They both went on in this humble vein, gradually turning their voices to a singsong so that the listeners would understand that they meant not one word of what they said.

The dirty boy had slyly entered the snowhouse and squatted silently beside the great quarters of bear meat. He was wildly hungry and did not intend to let any offer of food escape him.

Sarkak, surrounded by his huge meat caches of walrus and seal meat and secure in his wisdom, continued to lament the fate of the good men, the hunters, who had been ill-advised enough to gather into this poor camp of his, running the grave risk of starvation because of his poor leadership. Then Sarkak called for food, and Ikuma dragged forth a rich red haunch of bear meat and placed it on a clean sealskin, watching the shaman's eyes to see whether putting parts of these two animals together was breaking a taboo. But he did not seem to notice, so hungry was he for the sweet taste of bear meat.

The two men got up off the bed and squatted with their backs toward the others, as was polite. Sarkak proudly displayed the dead man's sea knife and cleverly sheared thin steaks from the half-frozen quarter. One of these he carelessly pushed toward the shaman. With the heavy iron knife Sarkak chopped down swiftly, shearing away thin morsels of meat still glistening with frost. When he had enough for the first helping, he passed the wonderfully sharp sea knife to the shaman, who did not pause to admire it, but quickly set to chopping his own meat into thin succulent slices. Without speaking, they ate the cold delicious meat, and cutting more, ate again and yet again. The women watched the wide backs of the two men and nodded in wonder, for it was a time of plenty, a time for feasting, and they knew that they would never again see such a pair of eaters. In our whole world there were no two men such as these.

Portagee's huge frame darkened the entrance passage, followed by Pilee. Knowing who they were, the shaman, his mouth stuffed with meat, did not look up. Then, slowly, he raised his head and stared at them, wiped the grease from his mouth, spat a piece of gristle on the floor at their feet and went on eating, as though they did not exist. The two strangers looked at Sarkak, and seeing nothing in his face, they turned and left.

When Sarkak and the shaman had finished the heaviest part of the eating, they returned to their places on the wide bed and lay down. Sarkak pulled off his parka, for eating the rich bear meat had made him hot and sleepy. He sat stripped to the waist, staring at the lamp, half drugged with food, his black hair hanging loosely over his shoulders.

The shaman rose with a grunt and called to the boy, who now squatted, eating with the women. The boy supported the shaman out of the entrance passage, and we could hear him urinating and vomiting. With dignity the shaman then returned, and the boy helped him remove his greasy parka before he reclaimed his place almost in the center of the bed.

Ikuma cut more meat and handed it to the young wife, Nuna, who sat beside Sarkak's head. She laughed softly and gently stuffed choice pieces into his mouth. The dirty boy cradled the shaman's head in his lap and fed him, as was their custom. I noticed that whenever the shaman's eyes were closed, the boy slyly stuffed his own mouth full, and his small slanting eyes never left the shiny iron knife that lay beside the meat on the snowhouse floor.

Sarkak and the shaman slept like dead men, and all the others found their places on the long bed and slept until the gray dawn of midday came once more. Then, seeing that Okalikjuak and three young men were going caribou hunting, the shaman quickly decided that he would have them deliver him back to his camp. He was anxious to leave Sarkak's house now while they were both on good terms with each other. It had not been like this for ten winters, and he knew that if he stayed for even one more sleep, it might all be spoiled, for they had that jealous uncertain kind of relationship.

Sarkak was so pleased to see the shaman leaving that he gave him a slab of walrus meat that outweighed him. Sarkak even stood outside with the young men and the foreigners to watch him depart.

Bone Scraper

25

I like to think now of the daily life we lived that winter with the foreigners. Many small things happened that did not seem important at the time, but now I see that they were all in some way a part of what was to happen.

One evening I remember Neevee kneeling on the bed, folding and cutting intricate patterns out of a scraped sealskin. Kakuktak lay beside her. As she worked, I watched his face and saw an idea come to him. He sat up quickly, and with his knife he scratched a light outline on the dark skin. In a moment he had made a clear image of a bird. Neevee, seeing this, cleverly cut it out of the sealskin and held it up for all of us to admire. Kakuktak took it from her, and reaching upward, held the dark silhouette against the side of the igloo. He was so pleased with this black image against the white snow that he made a pounding motion with his fist as though he wished to peg it to the wall. Neevee, laughing, made him give it back to her, and licking it carefully, she returned it to him. Understanding her, he held it against the igloo wall until it was frozen into place.

This started a new style in our village, and to amuse themselves all three *kalunait* and the girls they slept with made fancy cutouts and froze them to the walls. Soon many foolish women copied them. The foreigners mostly made ships and whales and big-breasted women who were half fish and strange animals and running men. It gave the insides of the igloos a crazy foreign look, as though they no longer belonged to Sarkak or to us.

More than half a moon passed before the caribou hunters returned to our village. A man and a young boy from the nearest camp came ahead of them to announce that our hunters were there visiting and resting, and if the weather allowed them, should arrive back in our camp within the next few days. Our hunters would have to travel slowly, they said, only walking. They could not ride because their two sleds were piled so high with fresh caribou meat. This advanced word of their success and their time of arrival caused great excitement in the camp.

These two visitors said that they had heard of the foreigners who had come into our camp and that they were anxious to

163

examine them and hear them speak as dogs howl: from the fronts of their mouths. Indeed, by this time we were proud to show off our three exotic *kalunait*.

The next evening Sarkak's igloo filled with young people, and with their urging Kakuktak took out his precious bundle of white skins and made a drawing. He drew a great toothed whale with terrible jaws, biting in half a boat full of six men. We all cried out in amazement, for here we do not know that strange kind of monster.

When Kakuktak put the skins away, everyone sighed with wonder and said he must show the drawing to the hunters who were to arrive soon. Then they said, "What shall we do to show we are glad? What shall we do to welcome the hunters?"

Tugak, who loved both dancing and women, said to his father, "Should we dance?" And then he said again for all to hear, "I shall ask my father if we should dance."

Sarkak rolled over in the bed and saw all the young faces and the red cheeks of the girls, their eyes shining black with excitement, and he said, "Dance? Yes, dance. Build a big house, and dance until it falls down from the heat of your dear thighs. Dance!"

The young people rushed noisily out of the house to begin their work. They ran toward the igloos of Okalikjuak, Sowniapik, Poota and Tungilik. The four snowhouses, forming a square, had purposely been built into the huge drift that swept upward to the hills, and each had been placed about ten paces from the center of the square.

In the beginning Portagee and Pilee stood and watched with wonder as a big circle was paced out, its arcs touching the four igloos, and as Tungilik, the most skillful snowhouse builder, stood at the central point between the four houses and took command. Wielding his snow knife swiftly and cleverly, he hued big blocks out of the snow, and the young men carried them to the edge of the circle and set them one against the other in their place. They curved the blocks neatly against the four snowhouses, and when the walls spiraled upward beyond the height of a man's arms, they used the long sleds as ladders, and climbing these, they cleverly put the roof blocks in place. The women and young girls chinked the outer cracks, and so well was the big dome built that they could safely climb on its sides before the key block was set in place in the top of the dome.

Long before morning the big dance house was finished, and the strong skin line for the acrobats had been anchored into place across the dome. Then, with a cry of delight, the builders made four entrances to the dance house by cutting through the side wall of each of the four houses so that the heat from their lamps could warm the space beneath the big snow dome. Exhausted, everyone made his way to his own igloo through the gray gloom of midmorning. They did not touch the rich seal meat that lay in every snowhouse in the village, for they knew that one must treasure hunger before a feast.

In the late morning I awoke and heard the calling of men driving dogs: "Haar, haar, haar!" I also heard voices outside the snowhouse, and, getting up, I went out with the others. Okalikjuak was guiding two sleds toward us through the barrier ice, and it was just as we had been told. Our caribou hunters were proudly walking, so heavy was their load of meat. The dogs' sides bulged with overfeeding, and they did not work well. The men, too, seemed fat and contented and not interested in hard work. They had that air about them of great hunters, and yet I knew we would not chide them, for they had brought us an abundance of meat.

The older women ran to the sleds and saw the bundles of caribou legs lashed to the loads, and they were pleased to think of the long strong sinews that they would have for sewing. They passed their hands over the huge rolled bundles of thick winter sleeping skins and sighed with pleasure. Only later would they grow critical and complain about the quality of each skin.

The hunters were tired from their long journey, and they slept through the faint twilight of midday and into the long silent darkness of the afternoon. But by early evening the young girls were up again, whistling in their excitement at the star-filled sky and rushing into each snowhouse, calling out to everyone, reminding them that there would soon be dancing. These girls ran boldly, searching for the three foreigners. When Tungilik's daughter found Portagee sleeping, she shook him and called him to the dance. The big brown man grabbed her and held her to him, laughing and squealing, until she bit him and he let her go.

The three *kalunait* were as fascinated and excited as the rest. They hurried out into the night, and when they saw the new dance house completed and glowing with light, they ran to their small igloo, where they kept their clothes. Using chunks of seal fat and their sharp knives, they shaved the shaggy beards off their cheeks and jaws and washed their faces in melted snow. They rinsed out their mouths with ice water and with their forefingers rubbed the furriness from their teeth. After taking off their inner parkas, they pulled on their high-necked sea sweaters and their black pea jackets. Pilee polished his jacket buttons with spit and a piece of caribou skin and put on his neat little short-brimmed hat. Over their trousers they drew on their high fur stockings and tight black sealskin boots. Then they were ready. They flung their warm outer fur parkas across their shoulders, with the arms tucked under their belts, and swaggered out. We soon discovered that no one of our people loved the excitement of a dance more than they did.

Inside the big house everyone was shy at first, and the three *kalunait* stood wondering at the immenseness of the glistening white dome that had sprung up while they had slept. Kakuktak walked around it, measuring it in wonder. It took him eight full strides to cross the room. The dance house was still cold, in spite of the constant heating from the four adjoining house lamps, but it was new and bright and utterly clean. The young girls had sprinkled the whole floor with soft new snow, had tramped on it and had swept it smooth with goose-wing brushes.

Everywhere there was much coming and going with tremendous excitement. I was with Kangiak in the house of Sowniapik, helping him tighten the single skin of the big flat drum. Many men offered us help and advice. We had dampened the skin carefully, and now we held it near the lamp so that it would become dry and tighten. Turning the drum in our hands, we tested the skin. Sowniapik took up the short drumstick and struck the wooden frame of the drum, gently at first and then twice strongly. The skin vibrated with a rich booming sound. People in the big dance house shouted with pleasure to hear the drum after its long silence, for with us the drum signified good times, exciting times, times of thankfulness, times of plenty. The drum meant eating and laughing and wild unseen women hiding and waiting to be caught in the darkness. In bad times the drum lay useless and forgotten, its skin slack or broken.

I will always remember that dance, for it was the very best of times, when Sarkak was full of power, when the foreigners were still new and exciting to us, when my three brothers hunted both seals and women until they dropped with the pleasures of fulfillment. It was a time when I could wait alone beyond the snowhouses and listen to the stars murmuring their songs down to me, and I could sometimes feel the snow tremble beneath my feet as the hidden creatures shifted in their tunnels within the earth. At that moment I seemed to be a part of the earth and a part of the sky, and it did not matter that my legs were twisted. I dreamed sometimes that I could see my soul flying over the soft summer tundra, mirrored in a hundred lakes, and my soul was not at all like me, not a poor cripple emptying urine pots. It was like some swift gorgeous bird with countless wings and many flashing colors.

Sowniapik again struck the drum, and the deep tone seemed to fill the dome with a rich booming sound. As if at a signal, everyone in the village filed into the dance house.

Every woman had on her best dance costume made of thin summer caribou skins, with carefully married fur sewn for contrast into many stripes, light to dark, Each costume was subtly different from the others. Men wore *kakuktak* boots of sealskins bleached in urine and frost-dried to a snowy whiteness, and many boot tops boasted elegant puppy fur, with little paws dangling so that they, too, would prance in rhythm with the action of each dancer's foot.

Sowniapik rushed inside the big snow dome, holding the drum high above his head, chanting the rhythm of our favorite song, and many women's voices answered him in chorus. People gasped with delight. As he turned, Sowniapik made the sign that the men and women should separate, and some women took the male children out of their hoods and handed them to fathers or older brothers, because it was wrong to have a male, no matter how young, be with the women on their side of the dance house. Poota, Kangiak and I went over to the *kalunait*, who did not understand what was about to happen, and pulled them gently to the men's side of the dance house.

At first everyone pressed back against the snow walls to give Sowniapik room to move freely. Slowly and ceremoniously, Sowniapik danced each position of the hunting moons. He moved bit by bit from east to west, chanting a different song as he stepped into each new position. In his left hand he held the big tambourine-shaped drum by its short strong handle. In his right hand he held a thick wood drumstick. Moving the big drum as much as he moved his drumstick, he struck the wooden rim, causing the stretched caribou skin to give off a dull booming sound. This first dance was very formal, and Sowniapik scarcely raised the drum above the level of his shoulders. It took some time for this to end, and I could see that some of the young people were growing impatient and feared the real dancing would never start. But they were wrong.

168

When Sowniapik's dance was ended, the three strangers clapped their hands together many times, in a way we had never heard before. We were amazed by this, but we could see by their faces that it was their way of showing approval.

Sowniapik flung the drum at Shartok, the mimic, who leaped into the air, whirled the drum and began to dance, imitating a mating raven. Shartok's shadow seemed to wing its way around the dance-house dome. He began to sing. The words of his song were scandalous, and everyone laughed and joined in the chorus of his outrageous performance. The children shrieked with glee and ran around and around the dancer. The room warmed with the heat of bodies, and people drew in closer.

Sarkak walked over to where Sowniapik's daughters were standing and spoke to them. Seeing their shyness, others joined him, and they half dragged the girls into the center of the dome. Once there, the two sisters knelt down and could only stare at the floor in their nervousness. But finally Evaloo started humming softly, and everyone became quiet. She laid her hands on her sister's shoulders and placed her mouth against Mia's half-open lips. Gently she began to blow into her sister's mouth, and the rush of air caused the cords in Mia's throat to tremble like tightly drawn sinews. From her throat came a high-pitched inhuman noise like no other sound on this earth. Evaloo blew and played on her sister's throat cords and set up a haunting rhythm that once heard could never be forgotten. All through my lifetime that sound has come back to me again and again.

I watched the faces of the foreigners to see what effect these sounds would have on them. After a while they moved in near the girls, and Portagee and Kakuktak bent close to them to hear better that unearthly sound, for they could not believe their eyes or their ears. Pilee did not bend to hear them. He stood short and straight in his black jacket with its shiny buttons, staring first at these two young wives he had purchased and then around at the audience who watched them. I could tell that he did not know whether to be proud or ashamed of his two females kneeling there before the whole camp with their arms around each other, their lips clamped together and their throats trembling as the wonderful ethereal sounds rushed out of them.

When they were finished, the two girls jumped up and ran from the big dome and hid in the half darkness of one of the four igloos attached to the dance house. I could just make them out in there, lying together, exhausted, on the side of the bed, and I saw Pilee peer into the darkness, then step down through the entrance to join them. It was not until the food came that they returned.

Some of the young men brought in caribou meat that had been partly thawed in the entrance porches, and we all squatted together, men here and women there, eating our fill. Some people than went to the wide beds in the side houses and rested, but it was not long before the big drum began to boom again and they returned to the dance house, although many of the younger children remained asleep or were left in the care of older children.

One by one, men took the drum and whirled it in the air. They danced heavily, imitating the movements of animals and people. Everyone was caught up in the pounding rhythm, and the heated room gave all of us a sense of luxury and companionship. Some seemed entranced and rolled their eyes back into the sockets until the pupils were gone and you could see only the whites. The tempo increased, and some of the drummers stripped off their parkas and danced naked to the waist. A white fog spread inside the dome of the dance house, and you could feel all the magic and excitement pumping your blood and shaking your bones. In a way, it was as though all the people in the dance house had melted into a single quivering animal whose nerves twitched with each beat of the drum.

At the very height of the dancing, when Poota was thundering on the big drum, swaying, chanting, gasping, he fell down like someone in a trance. The drum was then snatched up by a dozen hands and forced into Okalikjuak's grasp. Okalikjuak was the greatest dancer who ever lived among us, greater than all others, and I do not believe that such a dancer will ever come to us again. That evening, with a serious face, he took the drum from the many outstretched arms, and because he had led the caribou hunt and had supplied the meat for this feast, he agreed, after much begging, to re-enact the hunt for us.

Okalikjuak started slowly beating a steady rhythm on the drum, the kind of beat that crawls inside of you and demands that you obey it and move with it. He started twitching as he struck the edge of the drum, and everyone twitched with him, for they were helpless to do otherwise, so strong was the magic hidden in his slow-moving rhythm. His eyes closed, and he shuffled his feet, carelessly at first, imitating the men and dogs and sleds as they slowly dragged through the deep snow of the mountain passes, struggling to reach the great inland plain. Then his eyes flew open, and the beat became light and quick as shattering ice as he beheld the mighty sweep of the plain.

Suddenly we knew by his nervous turning that he had become a year-old female caribou, and we watched as she caught the first dread smell of the dogs and of the men. Then his head flung back and his chest expanded, and we knew by the great weight of his unseen antlers that he had changed into the bull caribou driving his sharp hoofs into the snow, anxious to run the herd away from the hunter. Then, like a dog shaking off water, Okalikjuak seemed to break himself into a dozen caribou that raced across the plain like silver shadows, their long gaits perfectly matching the pulsing sound of the drum.

But then, in an instant, Okalikjuak was once more the hunter, crouching, crawling on his belly, with his bow and arrows in his mouth, testing the wind, using all his cunning. Holding the big drum flat like a drawn bow, he seemed to launch the drumstick like an arrow through the air. Immediately he transformed himself into the bull caribou, rearing up

171

madly, eyes rolling back in shock and pain. I, along with every other person in the dance house, could see the arrow standing buried almost to the feathers in his naked chest. With five trembling drumbeats, each one heavier than the last, the rich artery blood seemed to drain out of him. We heard his heart falter, flutter once and stop forever as he crumpled forward onto the snow, his back glistening with sweat.

When I could compose myself, I looked at the strangers. Portagee stood rooted to the floor in wonder, as did Kakuktak beside him, and I knew that they had been so caught in the rhythm of the drum and the power of Okalikjuak's dancing that they believed they had witnessed his death, or at least some magical animal's death. Pilee, of all the people in the house, alone remained unmoved. For some reason this magic of the dance had not touched him, and he had not in any way understood the human telling of the story. He was the first to walk out and help Okalikjuak to his feet. Of course, there was no arrow and no blood, but Okalikjuak was as pale as death. Then other men surrounded him and helped him to the bed in his adjoining snowhouse.

It was time to eat again, but people had been so moved by Okalikjuak's dance and the power of its telling that they crept silently out of the dance house and returned to their own igloos and slept until it was almost time to dance again.

Skin Drum

26

Everyone was shocked to hear a great dog fight erupt in the very center of the village. The sound of its unfamiliar violence could mean only that many strange dogs had arrived. Rushing out into the darkness, we found three big teams from the nearest camp, with as many men and young women as the long sleds would hold. The drivers were running among their fighting dogs, lashing out furiously with the heavy butts of their whips, and our villagers quickly joined them, kicking and roaring at our dogs until the fighting stopped. Laughing with delight at seeing these favorite neighbors, who had heard of our good fortune with the caribou, we helped untangle their dogs and unload their sleds. We were overjoyed that they had hurried to help us devour this gift of meat, and we would not allow these guests of ours to build any new snowhouses. We insisted that they crowd into our wide beds and sleep with us. The visitors welcomed with pleasure this generous gesture, and in a few moments they had all disappeared down into the warmth of our snowhouses.

I alone stayed outside, peering upward into the darkness of the night. Countless stars flashed their icy messages down to me. My eyes watched the cold face of the moon cast its ghostly glow over the frozen bay, across the wind-swept mountains and out over the white vastness of the inland plain. Yet I believed that in all its shining length the moon's beam touched not one other human eye, so wild and lonely is our homeland.

When the snow had been beaten from the clothing of the guests, their boots drawn off and their feet warmed with dry fur stockings, they were fed blood soup and made welcome with the most honored places in each bed, for the people in Sarkak's camp were rich and grand, and there was nothing they liked so well as familiar guests to join them in a party.

When the visitors saw the three *kalunait*, they stared at

them in wonder and in horror, and we shuddered with pleasure to think that we alone possessed such unbelievable oddities from another world. But with all the thoughts of feasting their amazement did not last long.

On this night Sarkak expanded himself beyond measure. Ikuma and Nuna were thrilled to have visitors; they smiled and laughed like young girls. Last night's dancing and the feasting had only been a hint of the wild things to come. Two pretty women from the visiting camp sat laughing in the warmth of the igloo, their cheeks on fire from the stinging cold of the long sled journey. Sarkak's dark eyes were shining, and as I looked at him with the best hunters from the near camp seated next to him, I could tell that he, too, was excited. Sarkak called to me, saying that I should haul in the half-frozen haunches from the entrance porch.

We started eating, and as other guests arrived, Sarkak waved grandly, indicating that I should bring in more and more meat, until each guest had devoured more food than he could ever hope to have his stomach hold.

I knew that at the end of this feast, if it lasted long enough, we would have nothing to eat. Yet if Sarkak had not shown his guests the grandness and generosity of our camp and our disdain for hunger, I would have been ashamed of him. I, like all the others in our camp, thought of us as being more privileged than our neighbors. I thought of us as possessing great hunters, huge meat caches, clever women and swift powerful dogs willing to obey our commands. For in our camp Sarkak wanted only the best.

We are not afraid of starvation, for we know that we cannot change the things that will happen to us, things that must have been decided a very long time ago.

As we lay there on the wide bed, each absorbed in his own thoughts, we heard the throbbing of the drum again. It sounded like a heartbeat buried somewhere out in the snow. It called to each of us with a promise of hidden, secret things we could never fully understand. Everyone slowly came to life and stretched his muscles luxuriously; then we leaped down from our wide bed, so powerful and promising was the trembling sound of the drum. It promised us all the goodness and badness in this world, deeply religious things and hot carnal things, insight into the life hidden beneath the earth and the sea and passionate grabbings in a darkened igloo. It was often said that children sometimes turned into adults during this second part of the dancing.

We hurried out into the stabbing cold of the night and followed Sarkak across the moon's path toward the glowing dome of the new dance house. This second night was the one most people looked forward to. On this night all formalities flew away from us, and yet we still possessed the desires, the strengths and the passions that make a midwinter dance so famous.

On this night a little child started the dancing. He had begged to be breast-fed, but when his mother squatted on the snow floor to nurse him, he stayed only a moment with her and then scrambled away, running by himself into the very center of the dance house. There he started jerking violently in imitation of Okalikjuak's caribou dance. Like so many children, this child possessed a splendid power to mimic, and everyone instantly recognized Okalikjuak's gestures of the night before. This boy, who had not yet seen four winters, was scarcely out of his mother's hood, and yet there he was, bold and alone, out in the very center of the dancing place, seriously following the dancing movements of a hunter.

Everyone roared with pleasure, and the boy's mother's eyes grew big with pride, for such was the feeling within our camp. We knew we had been born in this land, were now living out our lives and someday would die, only to reappear all fresh and unknowing within the body of some newborn child. Was this dancing boy not the very image of his grandfather? At birth he had been given his dead grandfather's name, and we could plainly see that he possessed his grandfather's face. He also seemed to possess his grandfather's sureness and his

175

dancing skill. So the spirit leaves the dead body for a little while and then returns to live a new life again among us. It seems to me that we are like the moon that is born, grows slowly full, then fades away and reappears again, following some ancient never-ending cycle.

Seeing before us this promise of continued life excited everyone, and Sarkak called for meat for the child. Resting on his haunches, he smiled and beckoned to the small child, who, in the center of the dance house, stood alone staring at the adults who surrounded him.

"Uncle of mine, come and eat with me," said Sarkak.

The mother led her son over to him, and the small boy accepted the rich piece of marrow that Sarkak offered. The boy then ate it with all the dignity of an old man.

Slowly the dancing began again with Atkak. Then the drum was passed to one of the visiting hunters, who sang a song about poor people come to visit neighbors rich in meat, persons to whom the sea beasts gave themselves with pleasure. The song was answered by Sarkak, who complimented the guests:

> *"These relatives of ours,*
> *Uncles, cousins, companions,*
> *Friends from the near camps,*
> *Guests of ours*
> *Make our house grand."*

Then a sly man from among the visitors sang a very ribald song about the wildness of their women, whom he compared to hot-blooded ravens that mate in the air. It was a scandalous song, the kind those visiting people loved to sing. There was much laughter, and I must say that it was a funny song. Our women eagerly took up the chorus and started dancing, jigging up and down, shaking themselves without moving from the spot on which they stood. The men paired off and tried in their strength to dance each other down, their feet moving fast with intricate cleverness. The dance house grew hot again, and the inside walls dripped and glistened like ice. The rhythm of the big drum went faster and faster, making the blood rush to my head, and the dancers turned and turned until the house seemed to whirl and tip before their eyes.

Then there was a pause, and the drum was still. People looked this way and that way, expecting some trick. Slowly at first, and faintly, a new drum sounded from inside one of the adjoining snowhouses, and suddenly a wild figure leaped through the entrance and rushed among us. This man, if it was a man, wore a tight sealskin mask, with a dog-hair ruff around the face and black chin tattooing. I had certainly never seen this mask before, nor did I ever see it again after that dancing. I also saw for the first time the little hand drum he carried. If it was someone from our camp who wore the mask, I could not guess his name, for he crouched and moved in a strange way, and all his clothes were turned inside out to disguise himself. Around his neck he had a braided sinew, and from this, on each side of his chest, hung a large dog fang.

This dancer in the mask, this spirit, this dog man, took command of us. He became the ruler of Sarkak, and when he ordered Sarkak to move to the east side of the dance house with the other men, I saw Sarkak hurry to obey his command, with a great show of false fear. Sarkak went to stand next to Kangiak and the three foreigners, who were staring intently at the masked figure.

The masked man waited, holding his hands up until the dance house was silent. Then he made a clever pantomime of listening at three of the entrances. Each was silent, but from the darkness of the last, the fourth adjoining snowhouse, we all heard a sharp clicking. The sound came to us softly at first and then louder and louder as it repeated a short triple beat, and I heard a soft boot strike the hard snow floor twice. Then the triple beat came again. The sound was made by someone cleverly flexing a goose quill against their front teeth, using their mouth as a sounding box to amplify the noise, and stamping their foot to keep the rhythm.

177

Then a masked woman appeared. She was so short that she must have been a young girl, and I believed that she was not from our camp, but perhaps one of the guests. Her clothes were also turned inside out, and her mask was of scraped sealskin, with narrow slits for eyes and a grinning mouth with two small round bone ornaments, the sun and moon, inserted on each side of the mouth. She danced in a weird unwomanly way, for, of course, she represented the spirit of Tivajuk, the one who always appears during the wife-changing game.

When you watch a clever masked dancer, you always forget the person who hides beneath the mask, and you think only of the spirit that the mask portrays. The dancer's jerky movements seem to belong to some ghostly person from another world. I still have the feeling that if I had captured that dancer and stripped away the mask and clothing, nothing would have been there before me, nothing but air.

Portagee, Pilee and Kakuktak had been herded with all the other men and stood near Sarkak, crowded against the east wall of the dance house. I could tell that the three *kalunait* had no idea of what was about to happen, but anyone could see that they were fully caught up in the excitement of the game and were impressed by these strange masked figures.

The female dancer waved her arms and herded the women like nervous flightless geese into their places against the west wall. When this was done, the male dancer returned to the center of the big dome. Whirling as he beat his drum, he shouted, "*Sila-me, sila-me.* Outside, outside under the sky," and with a rush he herded all the men out through an entrance passage into the blackness of the night.

I was the only one who did not go. I could not run or dance, but I could see and listen, and perhaps in the end this was almost as exciting for me as for the others. I went and lay quietly in the shadows on the wide bed in Sowniapik's igloo, where I could look through the newly cut entrance and see all that happened in the dance house. I have found that if you lie quietly, people soon forget that you exist, and so it was on that evening, for I was the only man looking into the dance house crowded with women and ruled by this masked dancing girl.

I saw many women quickly unbraiding their hair. I do not know why they did this. Perhaps they had some taboo against lying with a man unless their hair was free. Perhaps it was because women know that hair braids are the first thing a man grabs in the heat of passion, and once he has hold of a woman's braids, he can control her and force her to do what he wishes. All the women pulled up their boots, which had sagged during the dancing, and held their cheeks and blew out their breaths. Mothers pointed at their daughters, and nieces at their aunts, and they giggled into their hoods so the men would not hear, and they trembled with excitement.

From the entrance I heard the dog dancer call to the girl. She placed her arm over her mask to hide her eyes and whirled around. With the thin penis bone of a seal she pointed at a woman, then rushed and grabbed her and forced her out of the passageway into the night. I heard the men shout with pleasure, and I heard the snow creaking as two persons ran past the outside of the igloo in which I waited.

The masked girl whirled again and chose another woman. Again there was a running sound and two people came bursting into the house and leaped up onto the other end of the bed. I saw the girl reach out and with her hand brush out most of the flame that flickered along the wick of the stone lamp, leaving the house almost in darkness. She was strong and agile, and she made a great show of getting away from him. They were both wildly excited, and I could see that she was losing the struggle. He held her so tightly that she gasped for breath and pounded the soft bed with her heels.

From the struggling girl on the bed I looked and saw the women and girls lining up to go out of the passage, and I was shocked to see that instead of hanging back, they pushed and joked with each other, eager to be the first in line, lifting the long tails of each other's parkas and grabbing at the short pants strings that held their fur trousers. As the young girl

179

dancer touched them, they pulled their hoods low over their faces and rushed outside. Again and again I could hear the shout of excited men, the squeal of the women and the sound of running feet.

The next person into the house and onto the bed where I lay was Sarkak, his big shoulders shaking as he brushed the snow from his back. His long hair was flying as he seemed to dance. I hardly recognized him, for he acted like a youth, laughing gayly as he flung the girl up onto the center of the bed and leaped after her. This was not surprising, perhaps, for he had drawn a visiting girl so young and slight and nervous that she made not one sound or movement on the bed. She answered none of his questions and lay like a dead person, so overwhelmed was she at being in the intimate naked presence of this great man, this giant who stood above all other people.

I could see the other three snowhouses filling up with couples, and I could hear laughing and squealing and the slap of naked flesh and even snatches of the songs we had been singing. I heard running feet again and a struggling in the passageway, and Kakuktak burst in upon us, frighteningly tall, his head above the door. He had a girl by the wrist, and I immediately recognized her as Nuna. But once inside the house Kakuktak just stood holding her wrist, not knowing what to do. Nuna stood quietly beside him, and I could imagine her embarrassment. Sarkak called to Kakuktak to come to bed with her, but he did it in a subtle way that, of course, Kakuktak did not understand.

Then I found myself feeling sorry for Kakuktak, and I wanted him to bring Nuna to bed and lie with her, to play out the game and save her pride and his own so that later there would be no gossip about either of them, for some of the older women in our camp had sharp tongues.

Nuna knew this, and I saw her take Kakuktak by the sleeve and gently pull him toward the bed. She was careful to take her place away from Sarkak, and I could see that she was nervous and probably did not even see me, although I now lay so close to her that I could easily have reached out and touched her.

As soon as Kakuktak took his place on the wide bed beside Nuna, I could see that the whole meaning of the game came to him. His back was almost touching Sarkak, and with grunts and chuckles the old man called out encouragement to Kakuktak. Kakuktak understood and pulled Nuna closer to him, and Sarkak laughed with a deep chuckling sound that shook his shoulders. The other two people who were near the lamp laughed and panted and spit out caribou hairs from the coverings and thrashed until the small single flame in the lamp wavered and threatened to go out. Kakuktak knew that I was lying in the shadows, but so filled with passion was he, so entwined in the hot richness of Nuna, that he did not even see me with his eyes.

I turned my gaze away from the bed. So filled was I with all the wild excitement of life that I lay there trembling. I looked once more into the dance house made of bright new snow and saw that it was entirely empty except for two figures. One was the masked male dancer, real or unreal, with his dog teeth dangling on his chest, his broken drum cast down on the snow floor. The other was the little dancer, the spirit woman hidden behind her grinning yellow mask. These two, with arms outstretched, circled each other slowly in a ritualistic dance. Then she turned stiffly as they moved close together with tiny mincing steps. Still in their furs, and trying to balance on their toes like animals, I saw them, under the very center of the big dome, bend and couple like the ghosts of foxes.

Skin Mask

27

It may be difficult to believe, but these neighbors stayed with us for more than half a moon, which was not an unusual thing for them to do.

In our camp we had a mad passion for dancing, for it is then that we send our feelings flying out before us. We loved the pleasures that these visitors brought to us. During this long party so full of borrowing and lending of wives, husbands, daughters and sons, not one person lost his temper. There was not one hint of trouble; there was not so much as a single song of ridicule sung against another man, for in our camp we were placid, gentle people, kindly to our guests.

A wonderful mood came over Sarkak, and he freely shared our abundance of meat and women and laughter with the visitors. They responded fully with all their mystical legends and all their scandals told in their special way, loaded with slyness and humor.

We were famous as big eaters in our camp, and we were unstinting in our desire to stuff ourselves with food. But it seemed to us later that we were like children in this matter of eating compared to our guests. These men and women, these visitors of ours, were well known for their eagerness in the bed, but they were far more remarkable when they squatted down to eat great quarters of our kill. They talked and listened and laughed gayly at the gatherings, and then suddenly when food appeared, they stopped talking and tore into our huge sides of caribou and walrus meat, leaving the carcasses so white and clean that even their ravenous half-starved wolf dogs would not find it worth their time to lick the bones. But slowly the visitors and even their dogs grew fat and lazy, and one by one our great walrus caches were opened and lay empty beneath the stars.

After a grand feast on the day when we had opened our last

meat cache, two of the visiting hunters hitched their fat dogs and journeyed out of our bay and far beyond the land until they reached the thin salt ice. Here they hunted with success and returned on the following day, bringing only two small seals, for they had carefully cached the others. They said that they had found the ice covered with countless seal holes and that we need only go near that place to have the seals give themselves to our good hunters.

Sarkak and the strangers and all the other people in the camp crowded around these two small seals. The rich meat was cut up and carefully divided so that it would feed as many people as were present. This small portion of fresh meat tasted better to us than any food that we had ever known, for it was soft and sweet and tender, not at all like the frozen oily walrus meat that we had been eating.

Now the visitors' camp was poorly situated in almost every way. They had few birds, bad fishing, no caribou or walrus, but we had to admit that their winter sealing grounds were excellent, much better than our own. So, hearing of this great new run of seals that had come to them beneath the ice, they could scarcely wait to harness their dogs, gather their stray wives and be off for home. Laughing and belching and politely farting with pleasure and gratitude, they left our camp as suddenly as they had come.

We were stripped clean of food, and yet we were sad to see them drag their willing women from our beds and go. The three *kalunait* had come to know and like our visitors, and perhaps they, too, were sad to see them go. But because we were out of meat, they grew nervous once more, and you could see that they did not really trust the future. They did not know that if you live a good life of sharing, somehow you will be provided with food.

Early the following morning Sarkak started the move, and there was a joyful feeling of expectation in the camp as we prepared to journey out onto the ice. As usual, he sent his favorite son, Kangiak, forward on the first sled with Tungilik, a quick and splendid snowhouse builder. Sarkak said that I should go, too, to help them, and at the last moment, because Kakuktak stood by the sled as it started to move off, Sarkak shouted to him, "*Ataii*," meaning to go ahead. Kakuktak ran with us down through the rough ice, jumped across the narrow tidal crack and leaped onto the soft load of sleeping skins piled high on the sled. We were going to choose a camp site and build a house for Sarkak.

The dogs raced across the snow-covered sea ice, yapping with pleasure at being free to run together once more, pulling as a team, willing to work the fat off themselves after their long idleness. Behind us the hills faded in the winter gloom. I felt the sharp sting of the wind against my face and saw each man draw his head deep into the warmth of his fur hood and hunch against the cold. Dawn came to us at midday as we traveled outward on the frozen sea. Above the horizon the hanging bellies of night clouds glowed faintly red, then faded once more, leaving the world to freeze beneath the winter moon. Our sled thumped steadily across the hard-packed drifts, and I felt that this frozen sea had no beginning and no end. Overhead the stars appeared, flung like bright birds across the sky, and probing like long pale fingers downward through the stars came the weird lights of winter, trembling, shifting and slowly strengthening until the snow around us glowed with a green and eerie light.

I had no way to mark the passage of time, but I could tell that we were approaching open water, for in the distance a black fog rose and blotted out the stars. Beneath the fog I could hear the ice scream and moan with the tremendous pressure of the rising tide. In the blackness to the west I could see newly formed ice ridges heaved up like jagged ghosts by the power of the sea. Before us spread a maze of cracks through which dark water seeped upward and flooded into slick freezing rivers.

Kangiak shouted at the dogs and drove them eastward. We were afraid to go forward in the darkness on this dangerous ice, yet we did not wish to leave, for we knew that there would be many seals coming to breathe in these newly opened places. Twice Kangiak stopped the sled, and twice he and Tungilik probed the depth of the snow and gauged our nearness to the edge of the broken ice. The second time we stayed, for it was a good place to build our igloos.

Tungilik and Kangiak each paced a circle. With their tongues I saw them lick their long ivory snow knives to coat them with ice. Quickly they began to cut the big blocks, and I heard them grumbling, for the snow was grainy and shot with ice crystals from the dampness of the sea.

Kakuktak and I knelt and chinked the outer walls with snow. Without words I had to teach him how to do this. It looks easy to chink a snowhouse, but it is difficult. If you do not force the fine snow into the cracks and hold it there for an instant in order that the cold may freeze it, the chinking falls away like sand.

When both houses were finished, we all joined together and built a side room onto the big igloo and a long tunnel that turned at the end against the wind. We left all the refinements to someone else, for it was dark, and we were tired. I could feel the dampness and the cold run like freezing wet hands down my back. Ice windows, meat porches, smoke holes and supporters for stone pots and drying racks would have to come later.

I unharnessed the dogs, and they howled insults at us when they found we could not feed them. I took their sealskin harnesses and lines inside one of the new houses, dug a hole in the snow beneath my bedding and slept on top of them. After their long day's work the dogs would gladly devour their harnesses or our boots or mitts or anything else we did not keep from them.

I threw chunks of fat into the big stone lamp, whirled the bow drill in the wood socket until the dry tinder smoked and carefully blew it into flame. When the long oily wick caught fire, it filled the new house with warm light that reflected back from endless shining crystals of ice in the new snow dome. Slowly the lamp spread its warmth, and our cheeks burned like fire in the faint heat.

We lay down together in the soft pile of caribou skins spread over one part of the wide sleeping platform, and little by little we removed our inner clothing and felt the human warmth spread beneath the fur. We relaxed and sighed and slept like dead men.

Sometime in the blackness of early morning I remember hearing the sounds of the other dog teams arriving and the soft squeaking of boots as men and women unloaded the sleds and started building their new igloos. It must have been cold work, for the wind had risen sharply and I could hear it moaning around the house. Sarkak, his wives, Nuna's mother and Neevee came into the new igloo, and I heard them coughing and beating the snow out of their clothing. They hurriedly pulled off their outer pants, boots and parkas and quickly crawled under the fur robes beside us. The bed must have felt wonderfully warm to them after their long journey, but because they still shivered and longed for real warmth, they stripped away their inner clothing to lie naked beside us, to feel our body heat surround them.

I awoke once and heard the ice crack beneath us. The chinks between the snow blocks showed the pale light of midday. I was hungry, but there was nothing to eat. I didn't mind, for as I lay in the warmth of the bed and fell backward into sleep, I seemed to see and feel sleek forms of fat, round-eyed seals that swam under our bed, beneath the ice, warm, too, in their thick layer of white fat. I could see in my mind's eye the many deep cone-shaped holes that the seals had kept open in the ice so that they could rise from their hunting grounds deep in the dark sea and breathe the same air I breathed.

Men were not the only hunters in this place. I thought of the killer whales, swift and high-finned, with blue and white markings. Perhaps they, too, had slipped beneath my bed, hunting with their terrible teeth, hunting for me.

186

We lay in the igloo and saved our strength, waiting for the wind to turn around and die. The only work that took place that day was when Ikuma cut clean snow from the wall and melted it in a pot above the lamp so that we might quench our thirst. I heard Kakuktak learning many words from Neevee.

Igloo with Snow Porch

28

In the morning the wind was down. Sarkak was the first to rise. With a great hacking, coughing, spitting and grunting he hauled on his clothing and struggled into the soft fur stockings and new boots his wives had given him. He stepped outside and admired his new camp, with igloos all around him and many dogs sleeping half covered with newly drifted snow.

Slowly moving his hips, Sarkak started to draw his burning yellow cross in the snow, retracing the directions of north, south, east, west. Wherever his urine ended, in that direction would he hunt.

"There to the west," I heard him say aloud as he examined the sky. He knew that he was right, that his body juices had shown him the best place to find the seals.

Kakuktak sat up naked in the bed, felt the cold strike him and then lay down quickly in the warmth beside Neevee. I heard her whispering as she helped him pull on his inner parka. Perhaps she pinched him somewhere, for he sat up again laughing. Puffing fog and shuddering, he beat the white hoarfrost from his outer parka and hurriedly pulled it over his head.

When I went outside, the gray bitch was waiting for me,

and almost every man and even some women and children stood in the half darkness. The men were gathering their hunting gear of slender harpoons and neat coils of seal line, which they slung over their shoulders with their hunting bags. I saw three old women walking out over the ice, each of them guided by a bitch on a long sealskin line. They were searching, letting the dogs sniff out new breathing holes beneath the snow, which they would mark for the seal hunters.

I, myself, took the gray bitch Lao, and borrowing a child's sled, attached it to her harness by a short skin line and sat on it. She slid me along easily over the hard snow while I pushed with one foot and helped over every drift and hummock. Not far from the camp she suddenly veered off to the west, and sniffing wildly, stopped and whined and started to dig. I yanked her line and drew her away from the hole. Then, using the harpoon to hobble after her, we searched together and found three more breathing holes that some seal was keeping open. I remained at the last hole, and as the old woman Ningiuk passed me, I gave her the gray bitch's line and little sled so that she could take them back to the camp. It is best to be alone out on the sealing grounds. One must be quiet and guard against any noise, for seals beneath the ice are very sensitive to sound.

Taking a stand directly above the hole, I opened my hunting bag and took out a square of thick white bearskin, and placing it on the snow, stood upon it. I then lapped it up over my feet and tied a piece of line around both my ankles so that it held the bearskin bound like a warm single boot around my feet. In this way I also prevented myself from taking one step or making any sound on the snow. I drew out a bushy white foxtail and stuffed it in the neck of my parka so that the warm air of my body would not creep out and leave me trembling with cold. Beside the hole I placed two small notched pieces of driftwood upright in the snow so that I would have a place to rest my harpoon. I then fitted the sharp head onto the end of my harpoon shaft and lashed it tight with a skin line to the shaft. Quietly I placed the harpoon on the stick rests. Then, drawing a thin wooden wand from my hunting bag, I probed very gently through the snow at the very spot where the hot muzzle of the bitch had made a mark in the snow. The probe passed down into the breathing hollow in the snow, then struck ice. I moved it around gently until I felt the seal's true breathing hole in the ice. It was not much larger than the size of a man's eye. I left the flat part of the probe floating just inside the eye-shaped opening, and taking out a soft goose-down underfeather, dampened its quill and instantly froze the feather to the upper end of the probe. This was to be my alarm.

I bent double, comfortably resting my elbows on my knees, making myself as small and compact as I could against the deadly cold that surrounded me. At first I was aware of the coming of darkness and of the cold, so sharp that it made the hair stiffen in my nostrils. I drew strength from the knowledge that other unseen hunters bent as I did, waiting motionless above other seal holes in our common search for food. As time passed, I forgot the cold, the stars grew bright and there was only me staring at the thin wand upright in the snow, nothing else in the whole world.

All day and night I waited, knowing that the seal was feeding in the dark waters beneath me, cautiously breathing at each of the other places, never once coming to the one I had chosen. Perhaps he knew that I was there. A dozen times my mind commanded me to leave this useless breathing hole and to move to the other three that the seal still used. But patience is the true art of the hunter, and I watched and waited until the first white streaks of dawn. Then I had a feeling as though I sensed someone listening, and the pains of cold and hunger rushed back to me, awakened me.

I saw the feather tremble and start to rise on the end of the wooden wand. I reached down silently, took up my harpoon and held its sharp point above the hole. Of course, I could see nothing, but I knew something alive was there beneath my

189

feet. I politely allowed the seal one breath. Then I drove the harpoon straight downward through the snow into the water and felt its point strike deep into flesh and bone. I flung the harpoon shaft aside, knowing that its sharp point was firmly set, and the harpoon line whipped downward through my hands. I drew the end of it around my body, using myself as an anchor against the animal's strength. The seal was almost as heavy as I was and fought desperately, but the harpoon's point had done its work, and slowly I felt the line grow slack. Then, using the bone chisel on the butt end of the harpoon shaft, I cleared away the snow that covered the small hole and chopped away a thin layer of ice. When the hole was large enough, I drew the dear dead beast up out of the water onto the snow.

It was my first seal of the winter, and to show my grateful-ness, I cut away a small piece of lip flesh and placed it back into the water of the seal hole. Our people know that this al-lows the seal's body to grow again in the sea. When I removed the harpoon head from the seal, I took a wound pin from my bag and plugged it carefully in the hole to save the blood, for all food is precious in a time of hunger. I longed to cut the seal open and eat, for I knew that the rich meat would be steaming hot and delicious, but I held back my hunger, for it is not the custom of our hunters to drag home half-devoured carcasses when others in the camp are hungry.

I packed my hunting bag, and because I could not pull the lifeless weight, I left the seal lying alone, its mouth open to the sky, its dark skin glazing white with frost. Using my har-poon as a crutch, I hobbled along in Ningiuk's tracks to see if she had found a new set of breathing holes for me. As I walked, my eyes searched the vast expanse of ice. To the east I could see Okalikjuak and Tugak and farther on two figures who must have been Sowniapik and Pilee. I could not see Ka-kuktak but knew he must have been with Kangiak beyond the pressure ridge.

Walking toward me, by himself, came Portagee. He rolled

and swayed like a bear as he moved carelessly across the ice. He carried a harpoon, but he did not use its end to test the snow-covered ice, a foolish thing to do, but I could see that he would pass well to the left of a round white patch of snow that I considered dangerous.

I had just set my wand and feather in a new breathing place when he reached me, smiling broadly. He was warm from his long walk, and he was delighted to see the new-killed seal lying out on the snow. He had made so much noise walking across this sealing place that the hunting was spoiled for the moment. So I took my harpoon chisel and walked a few steps, driving it hard into the snow before me. Portagee watched and then imitated me, laughing aloud and saying, "Goood!" He stamped his foot on the ice, then leaped in the air and came down hard. I could see that he completely trusted the great thickness of the ice.

I walked farther and waved to Portagee, and he caught up behind me. I pointed at my track in the snow and walked and pointed again until I was sure he placed each footstep in mine. He smiled, and I smiled. He thought I was teaching him a game, which in a way I was. It was the game of staying alive.

I came to the strange white place where the snow lay concealing every danger from our eyes. Indeed, I did not know whether it was good or bad, but I had a frightening memory of such a place. I stopped and pointed before me. Portagee stared, seeing nothing different. I took one more pace forward, stabbed down lightly with the harpoon, and it disappeared up to the place where I held it. Black water flowed over the ice. I withdrew the harpoon and tapped the snow lightly just beyond my feet. With a soft flop a chunk as big as a man collapsed into the freezing water exposing the hole where the tide had ripped away the ice beneath this thin layer of snow. I looked back at Portagee, who stared at the black water in horror and disbelief.

Together we turned and walked carefully out of that place, stepping in our own footsteps until we reached the seal holes. I

191

showed Portagee how to strike down with the *touk* end of the harpoon to test the ice ahead of each step. This he did with great care, for without words I had been able to teach him something about the treachery of ice.

I showed Portagee the place where a seal's breathing had made a small hole in the snow, and for him I placed a thin wand into the hole, attached a feather and showed him how to strike down with the harpoon if the wand rose. I taught him quickly and carelessly, for I did not expect him to have the patience to wait for a seal to come.

Scarcely had I set myself at the second hole when I saw Portagee strike down with great force. In a moment he was struggling violently with something on the end of the harpoon line. He did not know how to use his body as an anchor, and I thought as I hurried toward him that the jerking would haul his arms out of their sockets. But Portagee was strong and determined to hold this prize. I knew by the power of the seal that the harpoon head must only have pinned the seal through the skin at the side of the neck. Taking hold of the line, we played it together, back and forth, until the seal tired. Then I enlarged the opening of the ice of the breathing hole, and with my ice chisel I killed the seal.

We hauled this prize out of the water, wondering at its immense size. It was a huge dog seal. Falling onto his knees, Portagee quickly exclaimed in his language and ran his big brown hands over the silver sheen of ice that was forming on the short smooth hair of the seal. So pleased was he with his first seal that he gave a whoop of joy, and as I looked across the ice, I saw other hunters straighten up from their seal holes and look at us and wave their arms, for they guessed that Portagee had taken his first seal.

We both took up new holes and waited patiently in the gloom. But no other sea beasts came to the holes. Portagee grew restless and twice left his place and went over to examine the big seal that had come to him. He called softly to me, pointed at the seal and at his mouth and took out his knife.

But I did not want him to spoil his reputation in camp by bringing in meat that had been eaten, and so our hunting ended. We started back toward the igloos.

We tied a line to his seal and dragged it over the hard snow to mine, which I also tied and started to drag behind me. But the big brown man took the line from me and easily pulled the two seals along behind him. He stopped walking for a moment, and when I hobbled up to him, Portagee reached out and took me under the arm and urged me to place my more crippled foot upon his foot. We laughed and walked together in this way like a three-legged giant with a growth on his side. Portagee sang a song to me, and then I sang a song to him, and neither of us understood the words of the other. But it did not matter, for we both knew that we were hunters together, returning home with meat.

We reached the camp in the semidarkness of midmorning, and many people came out to greet us. Some hunters were already in, and others would soon follow. Okalikjuak and Tugak arrived after us with three seals, and Kangiak and Kakuktak brought two more. A sled had gone out and returned with five seals from beyond the pressure ridge where Sarkak, Tungilik and Poota had been hunting. This was the beginning of the hunting on the ice, and this first day of good fortune was said to be a wonderful sign for the future.

Of course, no hunter told the women who among us had actually harpooned a seal and who had not, for women have a foolish way of attaching importance to this and praising a husband when he has good fortune and looking upon him with disdain if on some days he fails in the hunt. Generations ago it was decided that it is best not to tell the women too much about success or failure. Now they scarcely try to guess, for they know that a hunter coming in with many seals may be simply hauling them for another person. Another man returning with nothing may have cached a walrus or even a small whale of such great weight that it could not be brought into the camp. So the women, like the men, share the meat without question, both in hungry times and in times of plenty. In this way we accept what is given to us.

When all the hunters were in and Sarkak looked at the seals, which numbered the fingers on both my hands and the toes on one foot save one, I walked up and pointed to the big dog seal and said, "Portagee got that one. That is the first one to give itself to him."

Everyone called out, "Is that truly so?"

And I answered, "Yes, yes. It is so."

Portagee, who was smiling and excited, pointed at the seal and at himself and called out, "Yes, yes, me."

Sarkak said, "Who is to be his mother?" and without waiting for an answer, he waved toward the old widow and said, "You shall be his mother."

The children kept the dogs away, and the old widow cleverly slit open the thick blanket of fat and lay bare the red carcass of meat. When she had finished cutting the meat into small pieces, she flung them up into the air. They scattered down among the people, and we shouted with joy and ran and snatched up the meat. All of the children and even the dogs ate some of the meat, for everyone should share in a hunter's first catch. In the sharing Portagee had tried to grab a piece for himself, but Kangiak held his arm and warned him off, for the provider must never eat of his own first kill, to show others that he will always be generous with the meat.

After all the laughing and excitement that accompanies the dividing of meat, we fed the dogs and dragged the seals into the safety of the meat porches. We then squatted around as some of the other seals were cut open. The life-giving meat filled our empty stomachs and sent a warm feeling of pleasure spreading through our bodies. Drawing off their heavy parkas, men grunted with contentment, and our women took the naked babies out of their hoods, shoved them up under their aprons and breast-fed them in the warm furry darkness.

When we had stuffed ourselves with meat, we lay down and slept like dead people until the following day, and when I awoke, I did not know whether it was night or morning. But I did know that a great blizzard was gathering its strength. I could hear its savage winds come moaning down to us from the sky. Sarkak started coughing, and a little later I heard him heave himself down off the bed and make his way outside. I knew that he would be gauging the wind, assuring himself that it blew in off the water and that there was no danger of the wind and tide breaking us away from the main ice and floating our camp away like a drifting island in the storm.

The blizzard lasted for four long days. It was a time when we could only eat and sleep and cough and mumble to each other and fill the urine pots. On the fifth morning the wind was gone and so was almost all the meat. The old women went with the dogs again to search for the deeply covered seal holes, and the hunters followed them. So sure were we of success that I did not even go with them. I stayed in the igloo, since Ikuma had asked me to help her scrape and stretch the new sealskins.

The hunters were gone for an endless time. First Pilee, Kakuktak and Portagee came in with Kangiak. They had nothing. Then the others also returned without seals. Nothing, absolutely nothing, had come to the breathing holes.

On the following day and for the next three days we went out and returned without seals. During this time Portagee and Pilee did not go hunting with the men. They wasted their time in the igloo.

One afternoon when Portagee was bored, he sent to Ikuma a sealskin boot for patching, and when she had finished doing this, Ikuma asked Nuna to return it to him. Nuna stayed in Portagee's igloo just long enough to have lain with him, if they had wished, then hurried back to her place in Sarkak's bed.

Many eyes in the village had watched her visit and had marked the time it took. It was a foolish thing for her to do, for all men become enraged when their wives visit or receive other men without permission while their husbands are away hunting. Indeed, neither Nuna nor Ikuma had the courage to mention this incautious, perhaps harmless, act to Sarkak. They made the mistake of trying to keep it secret.

One day when my legs pained me too much to hunt, the foreigners came into the igloo and borrowed snow knives. When I hobbled outside later, I was surprised to see the immense figure that they had built out of snow blocks east of the snowhouses. By the time the hunters returned, the *kalunait* had built three more snowmen with the help of the children, and these stood facing in four directions, like winter spirits around our camp, perhaps driving the sea beasts away from us.

All of our meat was gone, and the dogs roamed through the camp like starved wolves, afraid of humans, yet cunning in their thievery, for they would gobble up a dropped mitt or gnaw the sealskin lashings off a sled. Sarkak paced among the snowhouses like a bear, staring at the bleary moon, trying to gauge the weather. That night he tossed on the bed without sleeping, and perhaps seeing some vision in the shadows, he called out, commanding Kangiak and Yaw to hitch a team and travel back to the land, to go to the shaman's camp. He told them to bring the shaman to our camp as quickly as they could, for something was wrong. It was strange that the seals had gone. Someone must have broken a taboo, and for this we might die. If we returned to the land starving and without meat, we would never again feel the warmth of summer.

Ice Scoop

29

We gave up hunting and waited for the shaman, fearing now that anything we did might make the situation worse. Our women stood in the entrance porches, jogging to keep warm and to soothe their hungry babies. They stared to the northeast, eager to have a glimpse of the returning sled, and when it finally reappeared, we were all relieved to see that the shaman and his dirty boy were on it with Kangiak and Yaw.

The shaman was tired, he said, and marched straight into Sarkak's house before he was asked, lay down in the center of the bed and went to sleep. Just before arriving at our nearly starving camp, he had slyly eaten some meat, and it was not until the twilight of noon that he arose on the following day.

Many gathered in Sarkak's big igloo, as many as could find room to stand. Even the side house, the empty meat porch and the entrance tunnel were jammed with women and children who could not see but hoped to hear some of what was said. I stood in a place where I could watch both the shaman and Sarkak. The three foreigners placed themselves boldly before this magical man, who sat on the snow platform. They eyed him intently, and Pilee had a half smile on his face, not at all friendly, but mean and sneering.

I could see that the shaman pretended to look at others, but he was always aware of the *kalunait*. He had never spoken to us about these three, and it had been as though he did not recognize their existence. But now he spoke out. He pursed his lips and spoke quickly, using words strung together in a way that was hard to understand. I could tell that Kakuktak was listening carefully, but I think he understood none of it.

"Have you been visited by foreigners?" asked the shaman, as if he did not know.

There was a pause. Then everyone answered, "Yes."

"Perhaps they have brought with them some kind of evil that drives away the sea beasts," said the shaman.

"Yes . . . perhaps," answered all the people.

"Have these foreigners been fortunate in hunting?"

"No," answered the people.

One of the hunters spoke up. "Only the big one, who has had three walrus and one seal, and the yellow-headed one, who has brought us many birds."

"Birds! Only birds," sneered the shaman. "That is no wonder with those great snowmen standing in this camp."

He tied a band of skin around his forehead, grabbed up a snow knife, and tossing another to the dirty boy, ran out of the house. We hurried out after them, not wishing to miss anything, but, as always, because of my legs, I was the last to struggle outside, just in time to see the first snow figure come crashing down. Then over the top of Poota's snowhouse I saw the second figure, facing north, lean and break into pieces as it fell. The figure facing west toppled next, and I saw the shaman run up, gasping for breath, and with his snow knife slash down the last figure. He tramped and kicked apart its crumbled remains, and when that was done, he turned away in disgust and led us back down into the big snowhouse, all except the children and some of the women who were afraid.

No one spoke, and every eye turned toward the three *kalunait*. Some perhaps started thinking of them in a new way.

"These three strangers, these dog children," said the shaman, "they have returned to this land. Who can say if that is good? We can try only to listen and to understand the signs.

"I will tell you of the dog children again, for some of you may have forgotten and some young people may not have heard the story. A long time ago there was a seal hunter who had a daughter, and she thought that the young man whom her father had chosen for her was not good enough. So her father grew angry and said to her, 'For a husband you should have my dog.'

"That night a handsome stranger entered their igloo. No

one had ever seen him before. They noticed that he wore a beautiful close-fitting parka, and he had a sinew necklace around his neck. On each side of his chest hung large canine teeth. The stranger was welcomed into their bed, and he coupled with the hunter's daughter in a strange fashion. When they awoke in the morning, he was gone.

"The father worried about the visitor for five whole moons, and then he was certain that the stranger must have been his dog disguised as a man. He was sure that his daughter was with child, and being ashamed of this inhuman affair, he made the girl lie on the deck of his kayak. He paddled her out to a small island and left her there. But the girl did not die, for the dog man reappeared, and holding meat in his teeth, each day he swam over to the island and fed her. One day the hunter saw the dog man doing this and struck him over the head with the sharp edge of his paddle and drowned him.

"When the girl was weak with hunger, she brought forth six children. Three were *innuit*, true people like ourselves, and the other three were half dog and half human. She was ashamed of these dog children and knew that they would all starve. So she took a sealskin and fashioned a boot sole, curled like a boat. In it she placed the three dog children and shoved them off, southward toward the open sea. As they floated away, she called after them, '*Sarutiktapsinik sanavagumark-pusi*. You shall be skillful at making weapons.'

"Now look before you at these three, the offspring of those dog children, bastards, returned to us now with their sharp weapons, their iron knives."

I saw many people in our camp draw back in shock and horror. Our people had only vaguely thought of these three as dog children, but they had forgotten its real meaning, and now the ghostly impact of the inhuman father came to them. It would cause the women to fear the foreigners and the children to run from them.

"*Ayii*," said the people, full of uneasiness and suspicion. "We understand you."

199

The shaman held up his hands and said, "Someone is trying to speak to me. Listen. Listen."

We all listened, and the shaman began to cough. His coughing continued until he went into a great fit of hacking and strangling. When he straightened up, his face was flushed and red, and he growled like a dog. He whined and said words we could not understand.

The shadows of so many people standing in the snowhouse made the light faint, but I, myself, clearly saw what happened next, and Sarkak saw it and the three strangers saw it. The shaman swayed back as though he had been struck a powerful blow on the head, and he let out a horrible inhuman howl. As he opened his mouth, I could see great curved white dog teeth on either side of his jaws. He began snapping his teeth, and foam appeared at the sides of his mouth. It was flecked with blood. He was like a man gone mad.

Tugak reached out and held him by the arms, and the dirty boy leaped forward and also grabbed the shaman. They all three struggled violently. Everyone drew back in fear and horror. Had we not seen the mysterious dog man appearing before us, half hidden in the fat body of the shaman? At last the violent struggling ceased, and the shaman lay in their arms, pale and trembling, his face and hair streaming with sweat.

"Open your mouth. Show us your teeth," many called to him.

The dirty boy took him roughly by the chin and pulled back his lips, but the great dog teeth had disappeared. A babble of frightened whispers raced around the snowhouse, and those inside called out to the people in the passage, telling them of the magic teeth and of how they had suddenly appeared and just as quickly disappeared.

The shaman was given water, and slowly he revived. He talked of seals, carefully referring to them only as *puyee*, sea beasts, so that those hidden listeners beneath the house would not fully understand his plans. Shamans have a whole language of their own, with different words for every animal and fish and bird. I could tell that our shaman had been teaching the dirty boy this language, and sometimes his helper understood, and sometimes he did not. The shaman now raised himself up on the bed, and he said a word many times, but we could all see that the dirty boy did not understand. The shaman grew angry, struck him across the side of the head and made him get out of the snowhouse and be by himself in the cold and darkness.

When the boy came back, Sarkak and the shaman were talking, and everyone else was listening. So excited was I that this time seemed endless.

The shaman suddenly coughed again and then howled like a dog and curled his lips into a snarl. His eyes narrowed, and his shoulders hunched like a dog ready to fight, but in an instant the expression was gone. Then it came to him again and left him once more. The shaman gasped like a running man and begged for a harpoon. We believed that he would use it to fight off the dreadful dog spirit that tore at his anus, trying to enter his body.

Sarkak called for this weapon, and in a moment one was handed to him, a short broad walrus harpoon with a strong driftwood shaft and a long ivory shank holding a sharpened blade in place.

When the shaman had the spear, he placed its butt on the floor of the snowhouse, and kneeling on the sleeping platform, he held the harpoon shaft with the point directed at his chest. Fascinated, horrified, our people drew back, crushing each other against the snow walls, yet frantically anxious to see everything that might occur.

The heavy shaman started swaying his soft womanlike body from side to side, rolling on his knees, singing in a high unreal voice. We could understand only some of the words:

> "*Ayii, ayii,*
> *Come. Come to me again,*

Father of these dog children.
You with the big teeth,
Enter into me. Enter into me."

Then he stopped singing and started to tremble. A howl escaped from his lips, and snarling, he howled again and lunged forward, straight onto the upturned point of the harpoon. He screamed as it pierced his soft belly and forced its way through him. He flung back his head and stared at all of us with terrible bulging, dying eyes. Blood gushed out of his mouth and ran down his parka and splashed over the snow floor. He fell from the bench and lashed and twisted in his death throes, clutching madly at the shaft of the harpoon.

Women and children screamed, and even the men in the passageway rushed out in fear. Roaring, he followed them into the blackness. He ran once around the snowhouse and then darted back into the passageway. We gasped in disbelief to see that he was once again a whole man.

He leered and smiled at us, holding his arms outstretched. He flung down the red harpoon and wiped the blood away from his face carelessly with his sleeve. We could see the gaping holes in the front and back of his parka where the sharp head of the harpoon had entered and emerged from his body, for he turned for us to see them. Then slowly he raised his parka and exposed his great round belly. It was smooth and unmarked, showing neither wound nor blood.

There was absolute silence in the room.

The shaman said in a wild strong voice, "The dog man is dead." He stood in triumph, staring scornfully at the three foreigners, these true descendants of the dog man.

I thought of them again and looked into their faces as they examined the shaman with looks of horror, for they, like ourselves, had been standing almost beside him and had watched him fall heavily onto the killing point of the harpoon. How could he now stand here before us unharmed?

Pilee and the big Portagee turned and left the snowhouse, but Kakuktak remained, sitting motionless beside Neevee. This should have been a time to eat, to feed our guest and to think of all that had happened. The fact that we had no food and the lamp burned with short flames for want of seal oil reminded us of all our troubles. No one moved or said a word.

The shaman called for a sleeping skin and went into the small side room that had been built for guests and the foreigners. He tied one end of this cover to a drying rack that had been driven into the snow wall, and he handed the other end to the dirty boy to hold. Then he asked for the small drum that he had brought with him. The light of both lamps was extinguished, and those who most feared darkness left the house. The old widow started singing madly, and they asked Nuna to take her mother to another igloo.

The shaman sat for a very long time behind the sealskin cover. All I could hear was his heavy breathing and an occasional tap he gave his drum. Suddenly he gasped and began talking in a deep heavy voice, and then he answered in a high voice, calling out the words, "Moon. Moon. Moon." The drumbeats became sharp and rapid, and the stiff sealskin trembled as though it were held in a high wind. The voice behind the hanging skin grew weaker and seemed to go away from us, calling, calling as it flew farther away, until there was a long silence, and I believed that the fat shaman had flown from the house. Then a sound seemed to come to us again, high in the air, and it rushed down to us, the voice growing louder and louder. It was not the sound of the shaman any more, but a deep booming voice. It came into the igloo and sat behind the trembling blanket.

On that night I heard for the first time the throbbing voice of the moon spirit. Like the others, I held my hand before my eyes, so afraid was I that I would go blind if I saw this monstrous glowing *tornraksoak* with his great dog team. It was said that he sometimes came among our people like a night shadow and secretly lay with our women. Indeed, sometimes I feared that he might have been my father. I trembled to think that he was so close to me.

The frightened women started singing, "*Amayii, amayii,*" trying to find courage in their endless choruses. But the bitter body smell of fear filled the house, and the older women placed their hands between their legs to protect themselves from the penetrations of the moon spirit.

Then I heard the moon spirit strike the drum edge twice and fly away from us, his voice growing weaker and weaker as he rose again into the night sky. For some time there was silence in the snowhouse, and you could hear the sound of people breathing. Then with a slow tapping the drumming began again, and in this way we knew that the shaman had returned to us. The dirty boy called for the lamp and took down the sealskin cover, and again we saw the shaman. He lay face down, pale and trembling, and it seemed to me that his body had been used by Takkuk, the moon spirit.

As the shaman was reviving, he called for bone chisels and directed that a hole be cut down through the ice floor. Sowniapik and Tungilik began this with great vigor, then changed with others, their faces glistening with sweat. Portagee and Kakuktak each took a turn, laughing and chopping down with all their strength. The young women, hot with excitement because they had felt the moon spirit so near them, chanted chorus after chorus, faster and faster, in time with the pounding chisels and the flying chips of ice. Okalikjuak gave a shout as his point broke through and the dark waters of the sea flooded the hole.

The shaman raised his hand and approached the hole cautiously, peering down into the water. Then he called out strange words and shouted, "Nuliayuk. Nuliayuk." Without having to ask, Sarkak waved, and the people crouched in the entrance passage passed in a new sealskin line, tightly coiled and strong, about the thickness of my smallest finger.

The shaman listened and told the dirty boy to tie a running

204

knot in the line, but when he failed at this, the shaman flew into a rage and struck him again across the side of the head. To hit someone in anger in the presence of others is never done by our people, and everyone drew back in shock. The boy held his hands over his head, and the shaman pushed him violently into the entrance passage. He stumbled alone out into the blackness.

The shaman bent over the hole and became so stiff that he appeared frozen and alone under that dome crowded with people. In the end of the line he had himself made a running knot, and now with great care he lowered the loop down through the hole in the ice.

Of course, everyone knows of the great female spirit Nuliayuk, who lives in a house beneath the sea. Savage sea wolves guard the entrance to her house, and it is surrounded by long-clawed bears and bellowing walrus. Inside the house she sits and hoards the seals that swim in the immenseness of her lamp. Near the entrance passage sits her husband, Unga, a dwarf who still has feelings for the listeners at the breathing places, as he calls us, the true people who dwell above the ice of the sea.

Slowly the shaman lowered the long line until it was extended to its full length beneath the ice, and gently he called down into the hole, using kindly words, magical words. Suddenly I saw the line jerk violently downward, smashing the shaman's bare hands against the side of the hole in the ice floor. He lunged back, but the line was snapped downward again, and he braced himself against it. We could see it quivering like a bowstring.

"Help me! Help me!" he called.

But many were afraid to touch that line that stretched between ourselves and the awesome world beneath the sea.

Then Pilee stepped forward, with his hat on the side of his head and a smile on his face. He took the line. The shaman released his grip and Pilee was dragged to the floor and slipped and fell. Portagee and Kakuktak leaped forward and grabbed the line, and together, with tremendous effort, they drew the great weight upward, slowly, hand over hand. When the end was almost at the level of the ice, it jerked downward again, surprising them. The big Portagee let go, drawing back in horror. Kakuktak's face was pale and drawn. They had both felt the force of this unseen thing beneath the ice.

Sarkak called out, and his sons took the line and other hunters joined, including me. All together we hauled the trembling, jerking line upward. Women and children screamed with fear.

Then the shaman shouted, "Release the seals. Release the seals," and suddenly the weight on the line was released, and the men fell backward onto the people who crouched against the wall.

I looked at Kakuktak, Pilee and Portagee. I could see that the three foreigners were nervous and excited, for they had not known what to make of the shaman's performance. They were still with Sarkak, they were a part of his household, and yet they were becoming a part of all of us, and we seemed to be a part of them. I wished that they had not seen the shaman perform his magic. I knew that they did not understand him. Because he was dirty and sly, they thought he should be deceitful also. But this was not so. His magic was very ancient, and it had come down to him from powerful shamans who, people knew, could fly in the air and leap into the dark caves beneath the earth. I have heard that some useless shamans dwelling west of us perform tricks such as carving bearlike teeth out of bone and slipping these into their mouths to frighten people. We also know the old trick of filling a short piece of seal intestine with blood. When tied at both ends and hidden in the mouth, it will break when bitten and cause a most convincing bleeding. But these three strangers could not know all this, and we had no words to tell them. They did not wish to believe what they had seen, and yet they had all three seen it, as we had, and it would haunt them forever.

It was hot in the snowhouse and full of nervousness. A fog

had formed from our excited breathing and hung near the white domed ceiling that glistened with sweat. To cool my spinning head, I hobbled out into the darkness, where I happened to see the dirty boy running behind a snowhouse. He flung a coil of cut sealskin line and a knife up onto the igloo's dome so that they were hidden from my view, and this act of his made me suspicious. I followed his footsteps through the new salt rime on the snow and found the place where he had tramped around. Suddenly my foot slipped down through a newly made hole he had just covered, which had not yet frozen over. It was a small hole that he had chopped down into the sea. I was puzzled, for I could not at first imagine why he had made this hole and why he had then so carefully hidden it with snow. Then I thought that it might be part of a trick. I wondered whether the shaman had sent the line beneath the ice between two holes, as our fishermen do when they set our winter nets. If that were so, the dirty boy could have jerked the line to make us feel the hidden strength of the underwater spirit.

I put this stupid thought out of my mind and never mentioned it to a living person, until now.

Shaman's Teeth

30

After the shaman's séance, the big tide came to us and with it an abundance of seals. In this way the evil spell that had fallen upon our winter sealing camp was broken. As our meat caches filled and our bellies grew fat and the women and children laughed again, we relaxed once more, and the hunters slept late. It was known that some people ate as often as three times each day instead of once, which was our custom. You could tell who they were, for their eyes were glazed, and they were short of breath from eating and sleeping too much. We scarcely noticed when the shaman left, for now that food in plenty had returned to us we did not need him any more. Birds came in countless numbers along the edge of the white ice, and their wings darkened the sun. They filled the air with their soft calling: "*Akeeakunuk, akeeakunuk.*"

A whole moon passed, and the three foreigners seemed to enjoy this time at the sealing camp more than any other, for they felt sure of themselves once more. They could again see around them our richness of meat, and they could feel in their bones the warm coming of spring as slowly the light returned to us.

It seemed to me that there was no longer any place in the whole camp where one could sit and not be aware of the foreigners. Their sealskin cutouts were frozen into every wall, and their four gigantic snowmen lay tumbled like broken ghosts on the outskirts of our village. The *kalunait* seemed to amble endlessly among the snowhouses, calling out to each other or to the children who ran after them like a pack of unruly young dogs. One day I heard Panee shouting coarsely to Portagee. She sounded like a foreign woman, so well had she learned these new bad manners from them. I thought, Yes, this had truly become their camp. They could not even feed themselves, and yet they almost ruled us. I was surprised that our people did not talk about this, did not pay enough attention to the shaman's warning against the *kalunait*. Only Sarkak began to grow remote and cold toward the foreigners.

In the evenings, when we were all together in Sarkak's igloo and Kakuktak had nothing to do, he would take out his sharp sea knife, strop it on his leather belt and slowly shave his face. This always took some time, and the children would often come to watch him and joke with him. Neevee would fill a dark stone pot with water so that he could see his reflected image. She would warn him many times not to cut himself, but he would often make a nick or two under his chin. When the shaving was finished, he would wipe away the seal oil he had rubbed on his face to make the blade slip easily, and Neevee would sometimes kneel on the bed behind him, take his long yellow hair and with a piece of sinew tie it into a soft knot at the back of his head.

One night after Kakuktak had finished shaving, he took out his short marking stick and sharpened it with great care. He lay down on his stomach in his place on the wide bed, propped himself up on one elbow, untied the two hard covers and turned to the last white skins. We all knew that Kakuktak had covered both sides of almost all the flat white skins with drawings and with the marks that helped him remember our words. Of all the material between the two hard covers, he had only three unmarked skins left.

Neevee got a very small stone lamp, twisted and flattened a new wick of wild cotton and soaked it with seal oil before lighting it. Guarding its clear white flame, she placed it on the bed beside Kakuktak's book and climbed quickly into her place beside him in the bed. In one smooth motion she pulled off her parka and rolled it into a neat pillow. She lay down quickly and adjusted the light, for she wished to see the marks he would make on these last three precious skins.

Kakuktak looked at the white skin for some time and looked at Neevee and smiled. Then, using the back of his sea knife as an edge, he drew thin straight lines that slowly turned into a kind of house. As he drew these, he slowly explained each detail to Neevee as well as he could. I listened with care and could understand much of what he said in our language, and I leaned over sometimes to see the marks he made.

The house he drew was sharp and angular, and it filled the whole white skin. Kakuktak said it was all made of wood. The house was square, with a pointed roof, a wooden door and four windows each divided into four, with a thin sheet of ice in each section. The roof had neat little pieces of wood all over

209

the top and a huge stone chimney many times larger than the little snow snouts we place over our entrances. Two sea gulls sat on the top of the roof. On the outside of the house he drew a straight path with flowers growing along each side. Neevee said she liked the flowers and had Kakuktak draw more, but it seemed crazy to me, for what did flowers have to do with a house, and everyone knows that flowers grow only where they want to grow.

On the next-to-last white skin Kakuktak started to draw the inside of this same house. In the very center of the back wall there was a large stone place with fire in it, burning driftwood. I thought that they must have a lot of wood if they were going to keep a house warm in that way. On the flat stone above the fireplace Kakuktak drew a little ship, like the one he sailed in, with two big whale's teeth beside it, and on each side of the fireplace he drew pictures of animals with thin pieces of wood around them. One was, of all things, a dog, and I don't know what the other was. It may have been a whale. In his country it was the custom, he told Neevee, to hang nice pictures on the walls inside a house.

On the floor he drew a mat that was round, made in circles which, he said, were of different colors. He told us that his mother was very good at making mats and would gladly make one for this house. The colors, he said, would be red and blue. He drew a little animal sitting on the mat that looked like a white fox, for it had whiskers and a bushy tail. I wondered why people would have such a sly animal inside their houses, for a fox will give you a nasty bite if it gets the chance.

Kakuktak then drew two chairs, one on each side of the fireplace, and in one he drew himself, straight and tall, dressed all in black, with something stiff and strange tied around his neck. In the other chair he drew a picture of Neevee. But instead of her wearing the pants and leggings our women wear, he drew her in a long woman's parka without a hood. It completely covered her legs and touched the floor. Neevee laughed when she saw the clothes and said that she could never run beside a sled in that long parka, but when Kakuktak put dots all over it and made a pretty button at the neck, I could see that she liked it.

On one side of Neevee he drew a very fancy object standing on four legs. This, Kakuktak said, would be her sewing box to hold her needles, threads and thimbles. Kakuktak said that he would make the box himself as soon as he returned south and had the right tools and iron nails and wood.

In Neevee's right arm Kakuktak placed a small baby, not naked, but in a long dress like the one he had drawn on Neevee. Beside Neevee's left hand was a box with a hood built over it, and sitting in this box you could see another baby, a small boy with a cap like Kakuktak's drawn on his head. I thought there must be something wrong with a baby you keep in a box, for a baby belongs on its mother's back, but I did not say anything to him.

Neevee had been very silent through all of the drawing, but she seemed to understand every line, and even after Kakuktak was finished, she stared at the lines for a long time and would not let Kakuktak close the book. As he rolled over onto his back, she turned to him and said, "*Oona uvunga?* Is this me?" Then pointing at the two babies, she asked, "Are these our children? Is this our house?"

Kakuktak answered yes to her questions and then held his hand gently over her eyes so that she would stop looking at the drawing. But she would not, and so he closed his eyes and went to sleep beside her, wrapped in the warmth of her body. Neevee lay for a long time and looked at the picture and at his sleeping face.

After a while I saw that she was crying, but I could not understand why the drawing should have made her sad. Finally she stopped crying and wiped her eyes with her hair, and seeing that I was still awake, she said to me, "When the ice goes, he says the sailing ship will come again, and if it does, I will go away with him and live in that strange house. Did you see the two small children we will have, and the warm fire

211

burning? Oh, yes, I will go away and live with Kakuktak. When that time comes, I will not be afraid to go with him."

Small Oil Lamp

31

After winter comes the time when young seals appear in open water. Then the nights do not grow truly dark, and all through the long day the glaring light that leaps from the snow is so strong that without eye protectors it will blind you and burn your eyes until you see the world through a fierce red haze. In this season I liked to climb up on the high pressure ridge and look out over the stillness of the sea, to watch the huge broken pieces of floating ice that reach up to the sky and down into the water, stretched and distorted into strange mirages.

One morning when we awoke, we saw that the tide had opened an immense crack in the frozen sea and a field of ice much larger than our whole campground had drifted quietly away during the night. This served as a warning that we must move our camp back to the land. Only men would come hunting here after this, for when the ice started breaking, it was no longer a safe place for women and children to live.

Sarkak ordered all the families to move back to the land, but Pilee and Portagee could not understand his reason for a move and refused to let their women go. This was the first time that I had ever seen Sarkak's orders disobeyed.

Of course, in spite of their protests, we harnessed the dogs and broke in all of the snowhouses that evening. With their girls crying and threatening to leave them, Portagee and Pilee flung themselves angrily on the sleds and abandoned the sealing camp with us.

We journeyed through the soft blue night until early morning, when we turned into the bay and arrived once more in our land. The spring blizzards had covered our old houses of early winter, so we went near the hill, where we knew the wind would have packed the snowdrifts hard and deep. Some families occupied the igloos beside the big dance house to give it life again, while others, like ourselves, built new houses near the hill.

It was here at the end of winter that our worst troubles began. It is hard for me to describe the awful strain that came between our people and the three foreigners during the next moon. Our differences that had seemed only a small thing at the fishing camp, but that had grown much stronger when we broke up the sealing camp, now became so terrible in this second spring that the whole village was torn into many parts. Men would no longer hunt when the fog blew in, and I believe that Sarkak never forgave Kakuktak for leaving him so often, for fulfilling his desire to live with Neevee in the warmth of Poota's house.

Sarkak was not so powerful now as he had once been. Most people still respected him and continued to listen when he spoke, but they were beginning to lose their fear of him, and I could tell that he did not like this new feeling in the camp. I knew Sarkak sensed that his power was running out of him like blood. The *kalunait* were taking it from him, crudely disobeying him in every way.

Mixed with Sarkak's greatness was an unreasonable childishness, a fierce crazy jealousy. This he had kept so well hidden that most people had never seen it. But when it escaped from him, it was like an avalanche crashing down through the mountains, bent on destroying everything in its path.

On the day that changed everything I could see this raging jealousy swelling up in Sarkak. In the morning, as we lay in the snowhouse, ugly foreign sounds seeped through the walls.

We heard Portagee's rough laughter and Pilee's cackling, like a pair of sea gulls robbing an eider duck's nest. Their three girls screamed with laughter, harsh and bold as old women who rule households. I heard the foreigners shouting, "Dag-it! Dag-it," their name for Kakuktak, and I heard him answer them as he strode across the village, the snow squealing beneath his boots.

Hearing all this, Sarkak lay silent, staring at the gray dome of the igloo, his eyes squinting as though he were in pain. Then he sat up stiffly in the bed, pale and trembling, his head turning slowly, his eyes as cruel as an eagle's. It was as though his other self had entered his body and crouched there ready to lash out at the first person who came near him.

"Kangiak," he roared, "where is he? Send him for the meat!"

Kangiak was not there to hear his father, for he was away sleeping with Nowya's widow, testing her to see if she would make good material for a wife. Yaw jumped up and hurried out to get him.

Kangiak did not appear quickly enough for Sarkak, and when he did, he stared in alarm at the frightening change that had come over his father. Sarkak's face was deadly pale, his lips were sucked tight against his teeth and his jaw muscles were twitching. Sarkak jammed his feet into his boots and yanked his parka over his bulky frame, for he wanted to be dressed and ready when his rage burst forth.

Everything might have been different for all of us, but at that very moment the three foreigners crowded into the snowhouse, laughing and talking loudly to one another and ignoring us. Sarkak let a sound escape from his throat that sounded like a dog gone mad. His eyes glared, and his lips curled back from his teeth and he snarled at Kangiak and the foreigners.

"Ravens, all of you. Little hunters. Big eaters. Worthless children. All only good at sleeping late with women. These three whom I have saved from dying out on the ice, what good

214

are they to me, lying idly in every girl's bed, begging meat from worthless hunters?"

Sarkak spoke through teeth locked together in anger. "Look at him," he rasped at Portagee. "Look at that wife stealer—sends begging for his boots to be sewn, trying to lure a good woman into the bed we made for him. He is not content to accept the loan of a wife when she is offered to him by a husband trying to show him kindness. Oh, no. When that happens, he lies beside her fully clothed like a dead man in the bed.

"Slyly he waits until the husband goes away, foolishly hunting to feed these foreigners. Then he lures the wife into his house so that even the children will know what she is doing and laugh behind her husband's back.

"I suppose some big mouth has made a song of this, and it is sung beyond my hearing. Have I no sons to defend me?"

Sarkak's unforgiving rage was aimed at Portagee and Pilee, whom he trusted not at all. His words were also aimed at Kangiak and Kakuktak, and he spoke them slowly, so that each phrase would be remembered by them.

I believe Kakuktak understood many of the things he said. He listened carefully and stiffened his back when he heard "Little hunters. Big eaters," and Kangiak looked at the floor. Sarkak next turned his rage onto me. I felt like a lemming that has just seen the swift shadow of an owl swooping down upon him.

"You, Kangiak, and this little husband of the gray bitch, go now to the cache and get the meat. Take those three useless orphans with you."

Kangiak left the igloo, and I could tell that he was angry and ashamed to have been spoken to in this way before others. I rose to follow him, but before I could reach the entrance, the three *kalunait* turned and started to leave.

Seeing that they were going, Sarkak called to them, "*Tuavee!* Hurry!" Then again he shouted, "*Tuavee*," as though he were calling to dogs.

215

Kakuktak stopped instantly, for he and the other two had perfectly understood the rude command. He whirled around and leaped across the snowhouse so fast that Sarkak, with the instincts of a hunter, sprang back against the bed. Kakuktak stood directly in front of him.

"*Aagii*," Kakuktak said slowly, using our single word meaning no, rolling the word up from the bottom of his belly, using all our kind of guttural force.

I heard Neevee let out her breath hard, the way a woman warns of trouble to come.

Sarkak looked up into Kakuktak's eyes, and what he saw there must have unnerved him. Kakuktak's nostrils were pinched with anger, and he was breathing fast through his mouth. The color had drained from his face, and a hard crease ran down his forehead like a scar. I saw Sarkak's eyes flicker to the right and left of Kakuktak's face, and what he saw could only make things seem worse to him. On Kakuktak's left stood the big brown harpooner, his face a mask of anger, his nostrils blown wide, his whole body tense. On Kakuktak's right stood Pilee, red-faced and sly as a fox, his eyes not bothering with Sarkak as they searched the other people in the house, gauging where their weapons lay. His elbows jutted out, and his hands rested on his waist in that strange way so unfamiliar to our people. The only sound in the igloo came from Pilee as he clicked the nail of his right forefinger against the hilt of his sea knife.

Yaw sat on the bed behind his father. His face was calm, but his dark eyes were watchful. I think he was listening to that clicking sound against the knife. For myself, I heard nothing else. The nervous clicking and the cold blue of Kakuktak's eyes suddenly made me understand all that I had not known before. These strangers, these people who had danced and played with us, lain gently with our women and bounced our children on their knees, they were not at all as they had first seemed to us. They were not clumsy overgrown children.

They were strong men, with anger hidden deep inside themselves. They were dangerous fighting people.

Through it all, Ikuma continued to sew, but I knew that she was watching everything. Again and again she cut the sinew thread with the sharp half-moon blade of her knife. If anyone were to touch Sarkak, would they run the risk of being slashed with that ulu of hers? I wondered.

I do not now remember how much time passed, but finally the terrible clicking stopped. Kakuktak turned away, and the foreigners left the snowhouse. Sarkak stood motionless for some time, then heaved himself up onto the sleeping bench and sat there, staring straight at the entrance. No one spoke or made a sound. Sarkak seemed to slump slowly into himself, like an old, old man. Yaw and I left the snowhouse, and Neevee followed us. Even Nuna and Ikuma came out. Only Sarkak and the old widow remained inside.

Just at dark, when the igloos cast their glow against the night sky, Kangiak and I returned from the cache and heard the laughter of the *kalunait* coming from Atkak's house. Inside our snowhouse Sarkak lay motionless, staring at nothing, and when we entered, he did not move. When Ikuma offered him soup, he did not blink his eyes or speak. He was like a dead man.

Woman's Knife

32

The old widow, Nuna's mother, had knelt on the edge of the bed through all the excitement without moving or making a sound. But in the late morning, when things were quiet again, she started her crazy singing. I did not wish to hear her any more or to look at Sarkak, so I left the bed and hobbled out of the snowhouse.

Nuna told me later that her mother had risen from the sleeping platform, put on her best long-tailed outer parka, supported herself along the edge of the bed and halted at the place where Sarkak lay. She bent forward, stared into his eyes and whispered hoarsely, "Go while there is still time. Go while you have strength."

Then she hobbled out of the snowhouse. She stood beside me and flung back her hood with such a quick gesture that for a moment she looked to me like a young girl. Her eyes were shiny black as they searched the sky. The air had grown warmer, and a breeze was rising. We could hear a moaning sound, a monstrous sighing that came to us from the empty frozen wastes beyond our winter bay. The whole of the southern sky was filled with a towering whirling grayness that moved toward us as we watched it. Faint veils of whiteness swept slowly across the shapeless face of the storm as warm winds whipped the snow through the midday gloom.

"It is good to see the dear sun shine again and feel its brightness," she said as she faced the storm and the first big soft flakes struck her face and melted, running down her cheeks like tears.

The old widow stood for a long time, staring out over the long flatness of the ice, and then she turned slowly and made her way back down the long snow tunnel into the igloo. I followed close behind her, watching carefully to see that she did not fall. She moved gently in a way that made me feel that she was floating, drifting on air.

When we returned to our places on the wide bed, the thickly falling flakes had already blocked out the light from the ice window above the entrance. The lamps sputtered low, and inside the igloo it was dark and cold. We could hear the savage winds whirling around the house, chocking the entrance passage with drifting snow. Kangiak, Kakuktak and

Neevee were all gone, leaving empty places in the bed. Yaw tossed restlessly, as did I, and for most of that night we could not sleep. Ikuma and Nuna knelt in their places and sewed in silence. The old widow had stopped her singing, but now she swayed back and forth, back and forth, without a sound, stopping every now and then to stare at one or another of us. Her quick animal eyes frightened me.

I looked again at Sarkak. It was easy to imagine that he might be dead, for his face was still, his eyes half open, staring at nothing. Could you imagine that one small word would destroy such a powerful man?

If Kakuktak had known our customs, Sarkak would have given a party and sung a song of ridicule against him and the other foreigners, and that would have driven them out of the camp into exile and shame forever. But they were not our people. They did not use our language, which could be subtly twisted and turned into expressive songs. They were still too ignorant of our ways. Because he could not sing them down, Sarkak had lost. Now he would have to kill them or leave the camp. But killing men was not our custom, and it had not been done in living memory. Besides this, I knew Sarkak in some ways thought of Kakuktak as an unruly son.

Toward morning, when the storm spun around us at its worst, pressing down like a great hand upon the igloo, I saw Ikuma and Nuna nodding with exhaustion. The whole house seemed to throb helplessly in the center of a whirlpool of wind that sucked the air out of the house, and I found it hard to breathe. Finally I rolled over onto my belly and slept.

I do not know whether I dreamed or not, but I was awakened suddenly by the screaming of Nuna. Her mother was gone. The old widow's tattered sleeping robes were neatly drawn up to her pillow, and seeing her place empty in the bed gave me a profound shock. On top of her bedroll lay her warm outer caribou-skin parka and her short pants and leggings. Beneath them I could see the tips of her warm outer boots. Her clothes were folded neatly and precisely, the way a woman folds garments when sewing them into a tight skin bag for summer storage.

Nuna leaped from her place on the bed beside Sarkak and darted into the entrance passage. None of us had removed our inner clothing because of the violent storm that can sometimes break a snowhouse. I had only kicked my crippled legs to the icy floor when I heard Nuna give a long wailing cry, a sound full of despair and death.

When I reached her, she was leaning against the wall and did not speak. She only turned and pressed her face against the big snow blocks and pointed to the small footprints that her mother had made only a little while before. Already they were filling up with fine drifting flakes that sifted into the entrance passage.

I lay on my stomach and with my hands pulled myself through the narrow part of our entrance that had not filled with snow. Outside it was a terrifying world of wind-lashed snow. I had taken only one step, and yet looking back, I could not see our snowhouse. I could see no dogs, no sleds, nothing but whirling snow.

I felt Nuna brush past me, and as she moved forward I caught her and held her. It took all my strength, for she was like a person gone mad. But I knew that no one could live out there in that howling whiteness.

Nuna cried out, "*Ananaa. Ananaa.*" But the storm ripped the words out of her mouth.

I dragged her back to the entrance until we both fell to our knees, and I brushed the snow with my bare hand, searching, trying to feel just one footprint to show me the direction the old widow had taken. But there was none, not one mark, just a sandlike shifting smoothness and the sharp sting of the giants' whips against our faces.

I forced Nuna back into the snowhouse and brushed the driven snow from her clothing. She was like a dying woman as she stumbled toward Ikuma and slumped against the bed.

The older woman held her and stroked her head and tried to comfort her.

You will not believe me, but Sarkak did not move or show in any way that he had heard all of this, although it seemed to me that the house was full of women's screaming. I wanted my brother Kangiak's good advice; perhaps he could also arouse Sarkak. But Kangiak was away sleeping with the young widow. Yaw, the greatest sleeper in our camp, had remained asleep through all of this, and I was afraid to wake him, for sleep, we say, is next to death, and waking someone suddenly in the middle of a dream might cause him to lose his way back to life.

I went to my sleeping place and as I drew back the skin covering, I saw a strange amulet lying in my bed, one that I had never seen before. This charm must have belonged to the old widow's husband and worked powerfully for him, for he had always had good fortune in the hunt. After that, I always carried it with me in the kayak, but I must say that the weather seemed to become worse when I tried to use it. But then I am not one who has had much good fortune in this life. Charms have not helped me.

The storm raged all the next day and throughout the night, but in the early morning it passed inland over the mountains and was gone. Kangiak, Yaw, Tugak and all the men in the village went looking for the old widow. I took the gray bitch by the ruff and walked around behind the snowhouse, letting her lead me where she would. We went a little way along the path that led into the hills, and near a deep new snowdrift the bitch started whining and digging with her front paws. I helped her dig, and in a moment we uncovered the face of the old widow. It was frozen white and peaceful. Her eyes were closed, and she had lost that nervous crazy look. She lay comfortably on her back, clad only in her lightest, poorest clothes, her arms folded, her knees drawn up as though she were sleeping.

All of the women came to the path and mourned for the old widow. They drew their hoods down over their faces and wailed once together, making a long and terrible sound that ended as abruptly as it had begun. Then the men picked up her stiffened body and bore it to the high ground. Because Sarkak still lay like a dead man on the sleeping platform, we never brought the old woman's body back inside the house, for that would have meant we would have had to destroy it. The men laid her carefully on her side and covered her with heavy stones piled shoulder high so that no animal could tear apart the grave and so her ghost could not lift the heavy load.

Some say that we kill our old people. That is not true. Our old people have the strength and pride to kill themselves if they believe that their lives should come to an end. Sometimes they may command us to help them with their death, and so powerful is the word of a parent that his children may be forced to obey his wishes. That is our way, an ancient custom that we do not think is wrong.

When we went back to our snowhouse, the three foreigners were standing outside Sowniapik's igloo, watching us. Perhaps they knew that the old widow was dead, but they did not come near us. We entered our igloo and found Sarkak sitting up on the side of the bed. He must have known all that had happened.

Sarkak kept saying, "This ground is poisonous. This ground is poisonous."

I slept fitfully that night, so tired was I from the fear of the storm and the thoughts that had raced through my mind about the old widow. I dreamed the most terrible dreams.

In the morning Sarkak was up and fully dressed before any of us. When I looked at him, he thrust his chin forward and said, "Go. I shall go. I am leaving this place today. I am going inland for caribou."

I could scarcely believe what I heard, for he had not been caribou hunting for many winters. It would be a long hard journey inland at this time, for the spring sun would soon soften the snow in the valleys, and each step could drop a man thigh-deep through the crust. If the hunting was good, they would simply remain there, but if the hunt failed them during the summer, Sarkak and his women would not be strong enough to walk out through the mosquito-infested lakes and endless bogs of clinging mud.

But any action seemed better than this long silence we had suffered. We all got up, so pleased were we to see him come to life once more. Ikuma and Nuna shook out his warmest caribou parka and pants and stitched new soles onto his spare sealskin boots. Yaw gathered together the traveling lamp and the weapons and borrowed more arrows. Everything was hurried, for Sarkak planned to leave instantly, although he knew that it would be at least a year before he returned, or even longer than that, perhaps never. His wives were nervous, for he had not yet announced who would go inland with him.

"Two sleds I want," he said to Kangiak. "Twelve dogs, both wives, and Tugak and Yaw. You," he said to Kangiak, "and you," he said to me, "stay here and guard our kayaks and our meat caches, for there are bad people here—foreigners, wife stealers, dog people—whom I do not trust. Beware of them."

Bone Arrow

33

Tugak and Yaw were icing the runners of the two long sleds while Kangiak and I caught the dogs and harnessed them into a team. Sarkak selected the ones he wanted, and when we had filled almost every harness, he suddenly commanded me to tie the gray bitch, Lao, into the team. For a moment I was dumb with shock, then I called to her in a loud angry voice, hoping that it would frighten her and cause the dear bitch to run away and hide in the hills. Instead of this she ran up to me with more obedience than usual and lay down on her back, wriggling with pleasure, so delighted was she with the thought of our traveling together.

I looked coldly into Sarkak's eyes, and he glared straight back at me, silently daring me to say one word. I thought, I shall say no to him, NO, NO, NO, like Kakuktak, and he will be ashamed, and he will not take her from me. I lowered my eyes, for, of course, I could not do that to him. I made the bitch stand, and I started to pull the sealskin harness over her head.

"*Queeannak*," Sarkak called to me. "It doesn't matter. Chose a stronger dog for this team."

In this way my father, Sarkak, showed me more kindness than he had since my mother's death. Quickly I released the gray bitch, and she trotted away, unconcerned, and sat down in her place by the entrance porch, licking her nose and smiling.

Some of the people from the neighboring snowhouses came and watched us lash the loads onto the two sleds. Three more dogs were given to Sarkak as a gift from Sowniapik. Although I knew that these dogs were young and not much good as workers, politeness demanded that they be harnessed to the team. They could always be eaten, of course, if the going was difficult on the long journey inland.

When the loading was completed, Sarkak, Ikuma, Nuna and Yaw stood in their places beside the two sleds. Kangiak and I stood a little to one side to show everyone that we intended to remain behind. As I looked around the camp, I saw the foreigners standing silently in front of Poota's igloo. Sarkak hurried, leaving almost no time for farewells. His face was as set as a dead man's, and you could see that he wanted to let everyone know that he was being driven out of his own camp by these three hard-eyed intruders.

Tugak was missing. Tugak had been in a trial marriage with Meetik for ten whole moons, and now when he needed her most, she had run off like a crazy woman into the hills. She had fled, of course, when she heard that Tugak was going inland with his father. Tugak was away tracking her down, and everyone was waiting and watching with silent interest. Many guessed that Sarkak would not wait. But he did.

When Tugak caught her, he half carried her, kicking and fighting, down to the sled. You might think that some relative of Meetik's might have stepped forward to rescue her, but, of course, they did not, for we know that a girl who fights against marriage at first always makes the best wife in the end.

As they left, Tugak yanked her onto the sled and held her. Although she struggled and cried out to her relatives, you could see that she was almost willing, for he did not even need to tie her down. I was relieved for both Tugak and Yaw. I hoped that they would work out a way to share her between themselves. How else could they tolerate the vast loneliness of that inland plain without a woman?

Not long after Sarkak left us, the true spring came, carried softly on the south wind. But it did not help, for there was little joy left in the camp. Slowly the lamps sputtered out, and our big snowhouse died in the cold. For a few days the foreigners tried to live in their little side igloo, but it was a cold and lonely place, and they soon chose to sleep in other houses. Kangiak stayed with the young widow, and I was left utterly alone, like something useless that had been thrown away.

I killed a white fox that had gone crazy and run around the igloo and sent it to the old woman, Ningiuk, as a gift, and she came over with her young daughter and lit the lamp again and kicked out all the frozen dog turds. With her little goose-wing brush she swept the hoarfrost off the sleeping skins and remade the bed so that the igloo became a livable place once more. She sewed the torn places in my parka, and she even sang a song for me in her shaky old voice, to try to make the house gay again.

When this was done, Kakuktak moved back into the big igloo with Neevee, Kangiak came often to visit and Portagee kept his spare clothing there. It was a house without a true wife, but it had heat; it was a house once more. It may be hard to believe, but people started calling it my house, Avinga's house. Imagine suddenly possessing such a place, me, a slave to this family. Only a few bad words, a few bad days, and I had in one way become like Sarkak, the master. For the first time since I was young I started to think of Sarkak as my father.

I believed then, as I do now, that all our troubles had been caused by the three foreigners. They had come to us like help- less children, and we had fed them and clothed them and had even taught them to speak a few words with us. We had gladly shared our food, our houses and our women with them. In return for this they still believed themselves to be their own masters, three people somehow apart from us.

By the end of the first summer we had seen them as three very different beings. Portagee was full of bigness and strength and songs and crude boisterous laughter. Pilee lived by his cunning and his charm with women. We might have liked him if it had not been for his nervousness and his quick temper. Then there was the long, lean Kakuktak, who looked least like us on the outside but was almost one of us on the inside. However, he quickly joined the other two when trouble came.

The three foreigners had insulted Sarkak and had driven my old father away from his own camp in disgrace. Now he wandered like an outcast, like a murderer, somewhere beyond the mountains on the inland plain. Sarkak had saved these for- eigners' lives and had treated them like sons instead of slaves.

Because of his kindness, our camp was now without a leader. We argued among ourselves, we hunted little, went hungry, and for the first time in our lives we feared the changing of the seasons.

Sowniapik slowly took a kind of weak control over the camp. He was often silent and rarely spoke, for he did not wish to lead. But people turned to him for the final decision on when and how we should move and where we should hunt. The strangers walked among us like alien gods, proud of their victory over the old man, not knowing that he had been their protector, not able to imagine what the future held for them.

Hand Toggle

34

Everywhere it was spring. Most of the snow was gone from the south sides of the hills, and we saw the gravel bank appear once more beyond the igloos. Everywhere we heard ptarmigan calling for their mates. Soon the sun would grow strong, and the rains would come and soak the tundra until it held the water like a sea sponge. The rains would wash the gravel clean, and we would pitch our tents up there to have good drainage. I do not know whether this was because we were lazy or because we were afraid to move away without Sarkak to make our decisions for us.

One windless day when the sun had turned our whole world into a bowl of glaring whiteness, I hobbled after Portagee and Okalikjuak to the high bank. We were wearing our bone eye protectors with their narrow slits to ward off snow blindness. As we walked toward the gravel bank, we noticed two red-brown objects that stood out against the searing whiteness, and when we came to them, we saw that they were two of the sealskin buckets full of berries that the children had gathered in the autumn as a gift for the foreigners. Under some snow Portagee found the third bucket of frozen berries and easily uncovered it with the toe of his boot. They had not been stolen, as the *kalunait* had imagined, but had been buried during the first autumn storm.

The spring sun had softened the ice in the buckets, and the berries, still partly frozen, were loose on top. Portagee took one of the berries and bit into it. He spit it out and then stood thinking for a moment. Taking two more, he chewed them carefully. I tried one, too, but spat it out quickly, for I did not like its sharp bitter taste. I knew that if a person ate these berries, they would burn their way straight through him like red-hot pebbles and shoot out the other end with a terrifying force not soon to be forgotten.

When we started back down to the igloos, Portagee jerked one of the sealskin buckets out of the snow and carried it down with him. We came to Sowniapik's snowhouse, and I followed Portagee inside. We sat down on the bed beside Pilee, who was shaving himself with his sea knife. He had his jaws slick with seal fat, and before each stroke of the knife, he watched carefully his reflection in the water that filled a dark stone pot.

While Pilee finished shaving, Portagee talked to him and showed him a handful of the useless berries. Pilee put down his knife and with a white bird skin wiped the seal grease from his face. Together they ate a few of the berries, nibbling them slowly. They spoke briefly in their own language, nibbled again and laughed wildly. They gaily pushed each other and slapped their knees with delight.

Pilee rose from the bed, slipped the knife he had traded to Sowniapik into its sheath on his own belt and pulled on his parka. I watched from the entrance passage as the two of them climbed up the hill. After a little while they returned, each carrying a bucket of the rotten berries that had frozen and thawed in the autumn sun. They were very careful not to spill any of them.

I wondered why they cared about those berries, for we had plenty of good food at that time, and they could have all they wanted. But these two foreigners were very determined when they had an idea, and they became like stubborn children who had to try everything for themselves.

When Kakuktak returned from seal hunting with Kangiak that evening, Portagee and Pilee repeated their talking and laughing with him and kept looking at the berries, which they had placed beside the lamp and were now thawed out and floating in the buckets. Urged by the others, Kakuktak went to our big igloo, and without asking Kangiak or me, he borrowed a huge stone pot and one of our big stone lamps that Ikuma had not taken on their journey inland. Kangiak and I would have minded his taking these without asking, but we two could not help but think of him as a brother, one of our family, in spite of the terrible troubles he had had with Sarkak. Pilee borrowed two smaller stone pots from Sowniapik's wife, and the three *kalunait* started preparing something strange and foreign in Sowniapik's igloo.

I watched them intently, for I wanted later to be able to give people a detailed account of their strange actions. I wanted to know everything about these *kalunait*.

First they poured all of the rotten berries into the three stone pots. Then they covered the berries with ice water. They cut sealskin covers shaped to fit the tops of the pots, bound the edges tightly and carefully pierced a small hole in each cover. Over two of the big stone lamps they constructed a special rack using pieces of driftwood, lashing the pieces together with thongs, and using several of their clever knots. When the rack was finished, they suspended the pots from it by sealskin lines until the stone bottoms touched the yellow flames of the long lamps.

Sowniapik's wife was not always in a good humor, but new

ideas and new projects like this had always interested her. When the foreigners asked, she willingly piled chunks of seal fat in the lamps, made new wicks and added them to the old ones already lit. She carefully tended the long flame of each lamp until it burned with a high even heat and brightness.

We all lay back and watched the pots hanging above the flames. Slowly a terrible odor of hot rotten berries filled the house. Steam rose from the three ventholes in the skin covers, and a thick bubbling sound came slowly belching from the blackened pots. Pilee waved to Sowniapik's wife to lower the flames, which she did by tipping the lamp and reducing the flow of oil into the wick.

So concerned were the foreigners over the cooking of these rotten berries that Pilee and Portagee stayed awake all night, and only Kakuktak went away to find a warm place to sleep with Neevee. In all the time they had been with us I had never seen the foreigners so interested in anything. I had no desire to go to our big cold igloo, and so I squeezed into the bed and slept there for the night. I awoke early, with the vile stench of the cooking in my nose, and since I was tired of this foolishness with the pots, I left Sowniapik's igloo and returned to our own house.

That evening it was cold and still, with a bright spring sky that makes the stars seem pale. I went back to Sowniapik's house and found Pilee sleeping there. The three pots were no longer over the fire but were crowded close beside the heat of the lamps. They sat on pieces of driftwood to keep them above the snow. Their tops were even more tightly lashed with thongs and sealed with a mixture of thick blood and caribou hair that dries as hard as stone. Sowniapik's wife, red-eyed for want of sleep but faithful to her orders, continued to care for the lamps and guard the rotten berries. Pilee had made her realize how important it was to keep the pots warm.

In the midst of all this confusion Kangiak got a craving for fresh seal meat, so Kakuktak and I went away hunting with him for five sleeps. We cached many seals, and like the dogs, had as much meat as we could eat. We brought only a few seals back to share with the camp, for friendships were strained after Sarkak's leaving, and sharing food and wives with one's relatives was not the same joyful experience it had once been.

When I entered Sowniapik's igloo, the smell of the rotten berries was awful, and the roof of the snowhouse was dripping thin and icy from the constant high heat of the lamps. I could see starlight coming through newly opened cracks. The seal-skin covers lashed onto the tops of the stone pots were puffed upward with some strange kind of pressure. I noticed that the ventholes had been jammed tight with wooden plugs.

I could tell that the three foreigners were very excited. Some of the old people said that their madness was simply a sign of the coming of spring, and that as spring makes the dogs wild, so it must be with these dog children. But I believed that their excitement had only to do with the contents of the stone pots, and Sowniapik's wife agreed with me. She knelt endlessly on the bed beside the pot and said she could not even smell the evil odors any more.

Late one night Kakuktak came looking for Kangiak and me and urged us to come quickly to Sowniapik's house. We both got up and went with him and found Portagee and Pilee already there. The pots had been moved from their warm place beside the lamps and stood in a row cooling on the edge of the sleeping platform. We all stood around and watched Portagee as he carefully grasped a plug that was jammed in one of the ventholes. He wiggled it back and forth with his powerful thumb and forefinger. An ugly hissing sound came from within the pot.

"Shoooo," he said in a voice that imitated the sound from the pot, and he glanced at Pilee and Kakuktak with an evil smile.

"Shoooo," he said again as he eased the plug out of the pot. It popped, and the force of the pressure drove his hand upward. Foam bubbled up out of the hole.

"Shoooo," he said once more as he clapped his hands on either side of his head. "Whaa," he laughed, his white teeth flashing.

Pilee handed him a horn cup, and Portagee held it while Pilee and Kakuktak carefully tipped the pot. A trickle of dark-red liquid partly filled the cup. Portagee sniffed at it and wrinkled up his nose at the smell. Then, holding the cup in both hands, he closed his eyes and took a small sip. I saw his throat bob as he swallowed. He made another face, and his eyes watered. Then he said, "*Peerjuk, peerjuk.* It's good, it's good."

How it could be good when it had made him choke and weep tears I did not know. I would have thrown it all away. But Kakuktak next took the cup and drank and gasped. Tears ran down his cheeks.

Pilee snatched the cup from him, drained it and coughed until I thought he would fall down. The first word he said when he had regained his wind was "Goood!"

The *kalunait* talked excitedly among themselves, and Pilee replaced the plug in the cover. Then the pots were again placed near the lamps, and Sowniapik's wife was carefully shown how high she must keep the flame. I was glad that they did not offer the hot red poison to Kangiak or me.

Outside, Pilee shouted for Evaloo and Mia, who were visiting in a neighboring house, for he intended to have them keep him warm that night while he protected the evil-smelling pots. Lying in our snowhouse, Kangiak and I talked for a long time after Kakuktak and Neevee were asleep. We talked about the three foreigners and their fascination with the pots. We both believed that they had caused the berries to turn into a powerful medicine, and we wondered what ills it could cure.

Stone Pot with Cover

35

The first soft light of dawn caught the side of the big dance house that still stood between the four igloos in our winter camp. The dance house looked much smaller now, for, like the igloos, it had been half buried in the heavy snows of winter. The four inner entrances that had connected the dance house with the four houses had long since been sealed up to keep the heat in the igloos.

On this morning I had watched Sowniapik leave his snow-house early and pool his dogs with six other hunters so that they set out together using only three sleds. Moving quickly, they passed down through the barrier ice and out onto the snow-covered bay. The sealing grounds were not far away at this season, and I knew that they hoped to return to camp that night.

Pilee, who should have been out hunting with Sowniapik and the others, lay comfortably between the two girls he thought he owned. That is how I found him when I entered Sowniapik's snowhouse at noon. Pilee just lay there under a pile of furs, and as if planning his evening entertainment, eyed his pots that lay bound before him like treasured possessions.

Suddenly Pilee started saying a lot of words to Mia and Evaloo and myself, all words of his own that we did not understand. He sat up naked in the bed and made the girls help him draw on his long fur stockings, his skin boots and his sealskin pants. They held his parka for him, and he pulled it down over his head.

He pinched both girls to make them hurry and then jumped down out of the bed and searched for the long ivory-bladed snow knife. When he found it near the entrance passage, he turned and leaped back up onto the high bed. As we watched, he examined the big blocks for any sign of the old entrance to the dance house, and when he found it, he quickly hacked out a crude opening through the wall.

We all peered nervously inside the half-forgotten dance house. It looked like some weird blue cave. A film of ice had formed inside the dome, and great festoons of frost crystals hung thickly down from the ceiling. I had forgotten how big the dance house was inside. The little broken drum of the masked dog man still lay on the wide snow floor, reminding me of the wife-changing game and of all the other pleasures of the midwinter dancing. It seemed only a moment ago that we had crowded into this dance house, melting it with our hot bodies, shaking it with the wild sounds of our singing. But in that brief moment between then and now Sarkak had gone, and all the people I could call family except Kangiak had disappeared. The camp was full of trouble now, for we no longer had a leader. Some men stayed in bed and slept, and some men hunted. We had no plans at all for the future. We were not together in anything that we tried to do. We were confused like black brant geese caught in a blinding snowstorm.

These sad thoughts left me when I saw Pilee step through the new opening into the dance house. He picked up the broken drum and beat on it with his hand and sang and capered under the big glazed dome. We three watched him closely, and I could see that the girls were embarrassed by his foolishness and his bad imitation of our dancing. We remembered that he had not had the courage to dance among our kayakmen in the midwinter feasting.

Ignoring him, Mia said to me, "We could have a dance."

Evaloo joined her, saying, "Yes, we could have a dance tonight."

I found myself thinking that a good dance might help the people in the camp to unite and become friends again. Perhaps in the excitement of the dancing some strong man might come forward and take Sarkak's place as a leader. We did have enough meat for a party if it did not last too many days, although we did not have any guests or visitors, except for the three *kalunait*. But at that time people saw so little of each other in our camp that if they met together in the dance house, they could truly greet each other like hosts greeting guests.

Pilee brought the drum back into the house and gave it to the girls to replace the broken skin. Then he hurried out, and finding Portagee and Kakuktak, he told them that the hunters —it is hard to believe, *our hunters*, at a time like this—had decided to have a dance.

When the drum was mended, Mia and Evaloo ran to every igloo in the village and told the people that the three foreigners had decided to have a dance. Because these girls were the daughters of Sowniapik and he was now the most respected man among us, they believed Sowniapik had agreed to the dance and now sent news to them through his daughters, for who would believe that two young girls would dare to think up such a thing by themselves? As for the three foreigners, they were nothing; they had no houses, no meat, not even songs to give at a dance feast.

All four inner entrances to the dance house were quickly reopened, and the lamps burned high. Slowly throughout the day the great igloo warmed and glistened, the frost crystals fell and the big dome started to loose its gravelike chill. Carefully the women unwrapped and shook out their best fur dance costumes. They pinched their cheeks and helped each other braid their long black hair as tight as dog whips. They ran back and forth through the camp, visiting each other and whispering and shuddering with delight at their possible fate if the men dared to play the wife-changing game again.

The dancing did not start until very late, for we had to wait until the seven men returned from the sealing grounds. Fortunately their sleds were loaded with seals, and they were in good humor. The villagers started shouting at them even before they could unlash the meat, announcing that they were about to have a feast, a dance. Girls ran forward and urged the hunters to hurry, and the hunters laughed their tiredness away, so eager were they to believe that the tensions in the camp were at last broken. From the sleds the hunters hauled the fat young seals, not yet fully frozen, and they dragged these silver-skinned delicacies into the houses and split them open, spreading their thick white blanket of fat out around them like a cloth. The dark-red meat steamed as the spring feast began.

In a way it was all wrong, for there were no guests, no host and no plan for this feast, but in a little while most of the villagers were crowded into three of the igloos that joined the dance house, eating fresh seal meat. They ate sparingly at first, for they were excited by the idea of dancing and did not wish to make themselves heavy with food.

I feasted with Okalikjuak and a dozen other villagers, including some children, in his house, and from time to time I, like the others, stood up and peered into the dance house to see if anything was happening. I could see people eating in two other igloos that joined the dance house, but over the entrance to Sowniapik's igloo someone had hung a sealskin, even though there were people in that house, too. I could hear them laughing. The big Portagee sang a few words, and a girl squealed, and then Pilee started shouting, calling out our names.

"Kangiak," he called. "Kangiak, *kigeet*." He called to me also; "Avinga, *kigeet*. You come." Then he flung back the sealskin covering the entrance and added in a rough voice, "Neevee! Panee!"

The people eating in the three other snowhouses became silent and watchful. Slowly we four who had been called by name stood up and made our way into the dance house. With every eye upon us we trailed across the floor, and pulling back the sealskin cover, we stepped into Sowniapik's house and let the cover fall again, hiding us from sight.

I was the last person to enter, and I found the igloo hot and crowded with people. The three foreigners were standing tall above all the others. Then there was Sowniapik and his wife, sitting on the bed near the lamp, and Mia and Evaloo, Pilee's so-called wives. Sowniapik's brother, Tungilik, was there with his wife and their son, Shartok, and older daughter.

Portagee and Pilee were trying hard to talk our language, and I had never heard them do so well in using our words. I looked at Kakuktak and was surprised to find that he was bright red in the face, as though he had been working a heavy sled through rough ice. Sweat appeared across his forehead, and I wondered if he could be sick with fever. But this could hardly be, for as soon as he saw me, he placed both his hands on my shoulders and started singing into my face. His breath smelled of the rotten berries. Half of his song was in our language and half of it in his own. When he was finished singing, many people laughed, and I looked and saw that of the three pots near the lamp, one was already empty, save for some mashed berries drying in the bottom.

Pilee was busy cutting away the sealskin lashings on a second pot, the largest one, and when he pulled away the cover, he, too, began to sing. Then he dipped a horn cup into the pot, using it to scrape away the thick scum and then filling it with the dull red liquid from beneath. He danced his way across the crowded space, laughing, weaving this way and that, careful not to spill a drop. He held the cup for Mia, who drank half of it and coughed and turned pale. The other half he gave to Evaloo. Then he went and drank again and brought them both another cup.

Portagee leaned forward and filled a long bone ladle and gave most of it to his girl, Panee. The rest he offered to Sowniapik. It was offensive of the foreigners to have first offered food or drink to these mere girls, for, of course, Sowniapik should have been the first to receive everything here in his own household. But he took the ladle after the girl was finished, for he wished to be polite and did not want to spoil the party. He was also anxious to taste this foul-smelling liquid that seemed to have such a strong effect upon people. Sowniapik took a mouthful but could not stand the taste. Turning his head instantly, he spit it out violently against the wall of the igloo.

Portagee and Pilee and Kakuktak threw back their heads and drank boldly. This time I saw no tears and heard no coughing. Their eyes gleamed, and they slapped their chests with powerful blows and called out, "Goood. Goood. Goood driiink!"

Sowniapik's wife drank a full horn cup of the magic brew she had so faithfully tended, and in a little while she started singing, slowly at first and softly, but then her voice started rising and gaining power. She had always been such a shy and quiet woman that I could scarcely believe what I was seeing and hearing.

Kangiak was given a cup. He drank and coughed so hard that he passed it to me, fearing that he would spill it. Portagee shouted to me, "Driiink, Avinga. Driiink," and I put the cup to my lips and drank. I coughed and cried, and the red liquid burned its way down my throat and into my stomach, and then it seemed to come back up into my throat like waves of heat from a flame spreading swiftly through my whole body. I took another long swallow, then slowly drained the whole cup and passed it, empty, back to Pilee.

Evaloo called out dreamily, "*Okojualook!* It's hot in here. Hot! Hot!" She then dragged her parka off over her head, and her hair, which she had unbraided, hung like black feathers over her naked shoulders, showing that she was ready to sleep with someone. It was not the custom for a young girl to take off her parka and sit naked with her breasts exposed before guests. I thought that her mother would be angry with her and speak sharply to her, but she only stared blankly at her daughter and went on clapping time with her hands, laughing and singing in a gay crazy way.

Pilee sat down with his arm around Mia's shoulder and he, too, began singing, but it was another song in a different language, with a different rhythm. The two songs did not blend

238

together at all. It sounded terrible. Portagee started laughing. His great booming voice shook the igloo as the others kept on drinking and talking crazily. It was as though some strange magical force had come and gripped us all.

I tried to understand what was happening to everyone in that house, but I found that I could not think clearly after drinking a second cup of red juice. My crippled legs that often pained me felt much stronger than I could ever remember, and I tried desperately to dance on them. I tried to follow the rhythm of the house as it swayed and moved around me. Neevee was laughing with me and trying to dance with me, holding me, encouraging me to whirl around. Portagee kept lifting Panee, his arms locked around her waist, hauling up her parka, exposing her naked belly. Sowniapik's wife continued singing and eating handfuls of the rotten berries, trying to squeeze the last drops out of the pots.

Sowniapik, who had drunk nothing, stood up and left the house.

"Danasee. Danasee," shouted Pilee, and everyone in the house took up the cry. "Danasee. Danasee!"

The three foreigners each filled up their cups, and flinging back the sealskin cover, we trailed one after the other, singing and shouting and swaggering, into the big dance house. All the rest of the people who had not been in Sowniapik's igloo stood against the far wall of the dance house, staring at us in amazement.

Kakuktak shouted and waved gaily to his friends. Stumbling across the room, he offered Okalikjuak a drink from his cup and then let the woman beside him finish it. All this time Sowniapik's wife, without stopping her singing, leaned heavily against the wall of the dance house. Evaloo spun around, with her arms out like a bird. She did not bother to put on the top of her dance costume.

Tungilik, who had drained two cups of the fiery red liquid, started the dancing. He had never been thought good at dancing and had always been the last to perform at the feasts. But now he started off, whirling, flapping his arms and stamping his feet in a wild imitation of a red-throated loon about to mate.

I do not remember how his dance ended. In fact, I do not clearly remember anything about the rest of that night. But I do remember that for a while I felt like a tall giant with long straight legs and mighty arms. I remember hearing the drum beating wildly, men laughing and women screaming, and the sound of running in the darkness.

Dance House

36

The next day Kangiak found me lying in a strange bed with Tungilik's daughter sprawled out naked beside me. I hardly recognized her when I awoke. We two had never even thought of each other before, for she had been promised in marriage by her father since the day of her birth. Lifting her limp arm from off my chest, I felt around under the fur covers to find my pants and boots and parka, and when I had them on, I crept quietly out of the bed. She did not even wake as Kangiak and I covered her and left the snowhouse.

It was dark outside, and a whole day had passed since the feast. It had passed as if by magic. I had not seen it, had not even known it. The new moon was thin and bright, like a dog sled pulled by stars, its driver caring not what had happened in our little village.

Kangiak helped me walk back to Sarkak's old snowhouse. My head pounded, my throat was dry, my stomach trembled and I wanted never to see food again. This was the first time I had ever swallowed this kind of powerful liquid, and it seemed to drive straight into my soul like a harpoon's point.

Inside the igloo I drank cup after cup of cold clear ice water, for it helped put out the fire that still raged within me. I hoped the whirling in my head might stop when I lay down.

Kangiak and I found our places on the bed and saw Pilee lying there on his side, as pale as death. Kakuktak was fast asleep, with his arms flung out across Neevee's empty place in the bed. As we lay there, Kangiak told me about the feast. He laughed, and his words were thick.

"I tried to get more of the rotten berry juice," he said, "but it was all gone. Even the squashed berries that had been left in the bottom of the pots were gone, for those, too, could make your soul fly out of your body.

"The dancing," Kangiak said, "was wonderful at first, but then it became very wild and changed into madness. The noise was awful. I fell down once crossing the dance floor, and two laughing women tripped and fell on top of me. I rose again, brushed the snow off myself and crawled through the sealskin cover into Sowniapik's house."

"Was Sowniapik still there?" I asked.

"Yes, he was there, but he had not drunk the berry juice, and he was angry with everyone. His wife and one of his daughters were gone, and the other one lay naked on the bed, crying that Pilee was gone, saying that he was lost in the snow."

"How did you find him?" I asked.

Kangiak said, "First I went back into the dance house, and seeing that Pilee was not there, I looked into the other snow-houses that were attached. He was nowhere to be seen. So I found Kakuktak and caught him by the arm and shook him back to his senses and dragged him away from a woman he held pressed against the wall.

"Together we staggered out and climbed the hill behind the snowhouses. We were surprised to find that it was morning. From that high place above the village we looked all around us, and finally we saw Pilee. There he was, lying sprawled out on the snow beyond the kayak racks. He was sound asleep, as though he lay in the warmth of the bed. We hurried down to get him, for we knew that he would freeze to death if he stayed there any longer."

"Was he frozen?" I quickly asked.

"Not too much," Kangiak added. "Only his fingers and one cheek were white. When we picked him up, he was like a man with two broken legs. At first he could not walk at all. I took his white fingers in my mouth and blew until the life came back into them. Kakuktak rubbed and blew hot breath on his cheek where it had rested on the snow, and together we ran with him, bouncing him and dragging him, trying to wake him up and force the blood to move again in his body.

"Sometimes all three of us fell down in the snow together," Kangiak told me. "But being still half out of our minds, Kakuktak and I laughed and struggled up and ran again until at last Pilee, too, started laughing with us, and the color began to come back into his face. Soon he could walk a little, and we made our way back to Sowniapik's igloo, but I could tell that his whole mind had not returned to him, for when we tried to take him into the snowhouse, he put his feet against the entrance porch and cursed and fought against us. The big dance house was silent, and as we struggled with him, I saw a huge snow owl sweep silently over the village. I knew that was a bad sign, coming as it did just after the dawning of the new day.

"We entered the house and saw Sowniapik sitting by the lamp, grimly staring at the floor. His wife was gone from the igloo. On the bed was Portagee, his big brown body free of clothes, sleeping comfortably between Pilee's two girls.

"I felt the strength pour back into Pilee's arm as he gave a wild shout, broke away from my grasp and whipped out his sea knife. Kakuktak still held Pilee's left arm, and he jerked Pilee violently away from the bed. But Pilee had become a mad man, and he whirled around, his teeth bared like a wolf, and slashed open the whole front of Kakuktak's parka with his deadly-sharp knife. Kakuktak let go of him in horror. We both thought that he had been cut.

"Portagee awoke, sensed danger and was on his knees in an instant. With a murderous lunge Pilee slashed out, driving the knife toward Portagee's face. The girls rolled away from him in terror. His thrust was too short, and in an instant Portagee sprang his whole body forward, and his huge right hand closed over Pilee's throat, squeezing out his life. He lifted him up off the hard snow floor and shook him like a white bear killing a seal between his jaws. The knife fell out of Pilee's hand, and Kakuktak grabbed it and the girls screamed. Portagee relaxed his grasp and let Pilee fall gasping onto the snow floor. Portagee laughed aloud and lay down leisurely between the frightened girls.

"Sowniapik had watched all of this without moving. He got up slowly," said Kangiak, "and looked at me and said, 'These people are dogs. Dogs of the dog children. And there are others—those who run with them.' Then having said this insult, he walked out of his own house in disgust.

"Kakuktak and I helped Pilee back to this igloo," Kangiak continued. "He was choking and as weak as he had been when we found him asleep in the snow."

Kangiak finished talking, and we slept for a long time. When I next awoke, Kakuktak was propped up on his elbows, staring at nothing. He passed me a cup of water, and I noticed that his hand was shaking, and so was mine. Before I had finished drinking, we heard footsteps creak across the snow outside. We heard someone enter our outer snow porch and come into the passageway. We did not see who it was, but suddenly all of Pilee's possessions from Sowniapik's house were flung onto the center of the floor: his extra parka, boots, black hat and pea jacket. Then the footsteps walked away.

Kakuktak and I stared at the clothes for a while, and then we started to laugh. What else could we do, when everything was going from bad to worse?

37

One day had passed when Neevee came quickly into the snow-house. She came straight to me and said, "Sowniapik and the kayakmen who did not drink the berry juice went and sat to-gether in Tungilik's house. On my way here I saw them com-ing out, and the children said they had been in there a very long time."

I did not like the sound of what Neevee said to me. It was not like those people to hold a secret meeting in that way. Such a thing had never happened in my lifetime. The dance and the feast, which I had hoped would improve the feelings in the camp, had made everything much worse because of the craziness that the rotten berry juice had brought us.

We all stayed in the big snowhouse, separated from every-one, until we started to run short of meat. Then Kangiak and Kakuktak and I took the sled and the dogs and went out to bring in the seals we had cached. When we returned, Pilee and Portagee were standing outside the entrance passage, waiting for us.

"Neevee has taken her things," they told us, "and returned to her father's snowhouse."

A little later Kakuktak went over to Poota's igloo, but find-ing no one inside, came back to us with a puzzled look upon his face. We ate our meat in silence, for we were now woman-less and alone, without a friend in the village. In the days to come even the children were afraid to come near our house.

Early one morning a strong dog team came out of the north, with three men riding upon the sled. We stood out in front of our igloo, separate from all the rest, and watched the sled sweep up through the barrier ice and stop before us. The shaman and the dirty boy stood up and looked at the five of us and then at the much larger group of people who stood near the dance house. Without hesitating, the shaman turned his back on us and walked toward them. For a short time they stood together speaking quietly and then went down into Sowniapik's igloo. They stayed there until noon, when the driver from the north harnessed his dogs once more and continued on his journey south, leaving the shaman and the dirty boy with the other villagers in our camp.

For five nights the shaman slept in the camp without ever once coming near our igloo, and life became like a bad dream for all of us because of this unbelievable rudeness. Kangiak, who was strong in so many ways, could not stand this isolation. After the second night he used to go and sleep with Nowya's young widow, and the time he spent with her seemed to increase each day. I would hear him come in early each morning, and then he would lie down among us, exhausted, and sleep until midday.

One morning, when the three foreigners were still sleeping, Kangiak told me that the young widow had told him that Neevee walked alone in the hills and cried much of the time. She slept little and ate almost nothing, but Poota had forbidden her to return to our house, and he said that now he was afraid to allow Kakuktak to come into his house.

Three nights and days passed without a single interesting event; nothing at all happened to us. Kangiak was our only visitor, and he, after all, belonged in our house. We only went out briefly to look at the stars, to chill our backsides and to make our little steaming yellow crosses in the snow.

Kakuktak became as nervous as a sandpiper running before a wave on the beach. Most often his mind was far away from us as he searched for every memory of Neevee. Every day Pilee and Portagee sat on the big bed and played the knife game, slowly flipping the sharp blade back and forth until I grew to hate the thudding sound. They had long ago cut away and bet all their buttons, and now they no longer seemed to care who was winning or losing.

On the third night it was cold in the igloo. When Portagee and Pilee finally grew bored with their game, they stopped playing and went to sleep. Kakuktak went over to the stone lamp beside a woman's place on the bed and sat down. It was where Neevee should have been. He shivered and drew a light caribou sleeping skin across his shoulders, since he had pulled off his fur parka for some reason and had buttoned on his tight-fitting black pea jacket, which was now covered with a light shedding of caribou hairs from the bed.

The yellow light of the lamp lit his face, and as I looked at him, I realized that he had grown lean again, as thin as he had been in those early days when he had first come to us. The shadows cast by the lamp revealed the hollows in his cheeks and the lines that had deepened on either side of his mouth. His hair was carelessly tied behind his head, and across the lower part of his face he had allowed a yellow stubble of beard to grow again.

Without women we no longer cared about appearances. The inside of the snow dome had grown black with lamp smoke, and the bed was a mess. The floor of the igloo was scattered with gnawed bones, like a den inhabited by wolves.

Kakuktak took his knife and carefully sharpened the pointed end of his marking stick. It was now much shorter than his little finger. He drew the thin bound bundle of white skins from his side pocket, and he opened it, exposing the last one. He turned it with care, and I could see that it was clear on both sides, without any marks or drawings. When he was ready, he smoothed the last white skin flat with his big hands and began slowly making his small careful lines.

With utmost care he moved his right hand, gently forming his secret images. As he worked, he bent farther forward to catch the light. His hand swept slowly across the skin, making long curving lines. His eyes narrowed as he lost himself in this dream he was drawing. When I tapped the side of the stone water pot with the bone ladle, he did not seem to hear me.

I must have dozed for a while, for when I awoke, I saw that the lamp beside Kakuktak had burned out at one end of its long wick, and the other end sputtered blue for lack of oil.

246

Kakuktak no longer seemed to notice the failing light as he carefully added the last lines to his drawing. He finished and held up the thin white skin and examined his work. He turned it over and looked at its blank white side. It was the end.

Then he did the only wild and crazy thing I had ever seen him do. He dropped his marking stub carelessly in the bed and violently tore this last piece of drawing skin from between the hard covers, its one side as yet unmarked. He crumpled it up into a white ball and held it out into the dying flame of the lamp. I was surprised to see it blaze up so quickly, not at all like caribou skin burning. The bright new flames flared back and touched his fingers, and only then did he slowly release his grip and allow the crushed ball to drop flaming into the lamp. When it touched the oil, it sputtered brightly and then turned slowly black and collapsed into ashes.

Kakuktak turned his head and stared at me for a moment, and then he closed the book and tied it with the thin flat cord. He tossed it gently across the sleeping forms of Pilee and Portagee, and it landed beside my hand.

"*Tuyuktagit.* A small gift to you," Kakuktak whispered in a hoarse voice.

He got up and moved stiffly away from the lamp. He climbed onto his place near the center of the bed and lay down, roughly covering himself with sleeping skins, not caring, not even bothering to remove his clothes.

Knife

38

On the following evening we were surprised to hear the drum beating. We went outside but could not tell whether they were just fooling or really tuning up the drum for a dance. Well, I thought, there will be nothing wrong with a dance. The rotten berries are gone, and people like to dance. Perhaps it will improve the mood of the camp.

The drum beat out a flat monotonous rhythm that continued almost without breaking long into the night. Kangiak might even be dancing with them, I thought with envy as I rolled over, with my face away from the three foreigners, and tried to sleep. I heard Portagee pounding softly on his thigh in time with the drum, and I knew he wished that times were as they used to be. I held the bound skins that Kakuktak had given me, but I was too tense and excited to stay in the house. I pulled on my clothing, crawled out of bed and went and stood in the pale starlight at the end of the snow passage. Night clouds turned white as they flew past the moon.

With the beating of the drum a song came to me. It was the song of a dead man, a song I could not sing aloud to others. But I knew each word, and I sang it to myself there in the darkness:

> *"I am afraid*
> *When my eyes follow the moon*
> *On its old trail.*
> *I am afraid*
> *When I hear the wind wailing*
> *And the murmuring of snow.*
> *I am afraid*
> *When I watch the stars*
> *Moving on their nightly trail.*
> *I am afraid."*

When I had finished my secret singing, I turned and went back into the bed and slept. I awoke early the next morning with a feeling of desolation. Kakuktak, Portagee and Pilee remained sleeping beside me, their white breaths rising evenly toward the ceiling. Outside I heard the soft creaking of footsteps on the snow. The walking stopped.

Because of what Neevee had told me, I had feared danger and had been sleeping with my boots and pants on. It took me only an instant to sit up and pull my parka over my head, slip quickly out of bed and hobble up through the entrance passage. The whole camp was silent. The dogs slept, and all the snowhouses lay wrapped in morning mist. Shivering as I stood there in the damp cold, I added to the big yellow urine stain on the side of the igloo. As I watched, the snow came down in soft wet flakes. It was spring snow, filling the sky like slow black rain, then turning white on white against the mountains to the north that lay in soft curves like sleeping giants.

When I turned to go back into the snowhouse, I saw the shaman. He stood dead-still, very close to our house, closer than he had been since his arrival. He stared at me coldly, like a fat bold raven, his greasy parka looking gray against the snow. He seemed to be in a kind of trance and did not move or even blink his eyes. I shuddered, more from the revulsion I felt for him than from the cold. I turned away from him and slowly made my way down into our entrance passage.

Once inside the igloo I sat down on the side of the bed near the sleeping foreigners. I listened carefully for a long time but did not hear a sound. Then, as I leaned over to tend the flame burning in the stone lamp, I heard once more the sound of soft footsteps on the snow. I knew that he was leaving. It was as though a great weight had been lifted from me. The shaman's presence had filled me with an unreasonable sense of terror. As soon as he was gone, that feeling left me, and I fell into a deep sleep that lasted until midmorning.

I awoke to the sound of girls laughing and Pilee calling out to them excitedly. Portagee began urging them softly with his deep musical voice to come inside, and Kakuktak sat up on the side of the bed, pulling on his sealskin pants and boots and his own black pea jacket, driving away the sleep by rubbing his hands over his face as though he were washing in water. I sat up, too, and listened to the soft laughter of girls in the entrance passage. I could not see them, but I recognized Mia's warm voice.

"*Kigeelaritsi*," called Pilee. "Come in," and he sat up, dressed quickly and smoothed back his long brown hair.

"*Keenukiak?*" called Portagee. "Who is it?"

"*Etiri*," called Pilee. "Enter."

The girls laughed nervously and pushed each other until finally Mia was shoved through the entrance into the igloo; then Evaloo and Tungilik's daughter followed. The three girls stood together before the bed, red-faced and shy, looking down at their feet.

Pilee made room beside himself on the bed, and patting the soft caribou skins, he said to Mia, "Come, sit here. Come lie down here beside me."

He was excited. All three foreigners were full of desire, for it had been a long time since any girls had lain in their beds or had been in any way friendly with them. Portagee did not put on his parka but left the caribou robe across his shoulders. Still kneeling on the bed, he started to hum our favorite song, clapping his hands softly and weaving his big brown body in a way that always excited people. The girls laughed and shuffled their feet, but they did not immediately come into our bed as Pilee had asked them to do.

The three girls waited for some time; then Mia shyly reached into her hood and drew out a large new pair of long mitts. I was surprised to see the other two girls also draw new mitts from their hoods. I knew that older women must have done the sewing, for these young girls could not make such splendid blendings of fur, and men must have suggested these rich designs, all of which could mean only that the people had decided to be friendly again with the *kalunait*.

At that moment I wished Kangiak could have been there to see this important change of events. I remember thinking that when the foreigners finally got these girls into the wide bed with them, I would watch only for a moment, then give up my place and go to find Kangiak and tell him about these gifts, for I believed that the whole camp could be drawn together again.

Mia held one mitten under her arm and with both hands shyly offered the new right mitt to Pilee.

"*Mikilawaktok udliavok?*" she said. "Perhaps they're too small?"

Pilee shoved his hand inside eagerly and said, "*Namuktok. Namuktok.* It is enough. It is enough," and as soon as she held the left mitt up for him, he slid in his other hand.

At the same time, the two other girls fitted the long sealskin mitts onto Portagee and Kakuktak.

Pilee was the first to notice that there were no thumbs in the mitts. "No good!" he shouted loudly. "*Peeungituk.*"

"You didn't chew them," Kakuktak said. "The palms are stiff."

At that instant I noticed that all the long mitts had strong leather drawstrings, like a boot, and before I knew what was happening, the girls had whipped the laces together, tangling them into loose knots. The three men stared at each other trussed up in this way in their new stiff thumbless mitts. They started to laugh at each other, trying to jerk their hands apart, which only served to tighten the knots.

I saw Kakuktak look at Mia. Her eyes were wide. Her mouth was already open as she screamed into the entrance passage, "*Tuavi! Tuavi! Tuavi!* Hurry! Hurry! Hurry!"

In horror I saw Tungilik come lunging through the entrance. He clutched the dead man's sea knife in his right hand. Sarkak had owned that knife, I thought. How could this man have it now?

Pilee knelt on the bed in front of him, shouting, writhing and fighting to free his hands from the binding mitts, trying to reach around for his own knife. Tungilik lunged straight at him and drove the sea knife downward into the side of his neck. Then with his left hand he swiftly raised Pilee's parka and drove the knife blade up under his rib cage until it must have touched his heart. The three girls stood huddled against the wall, watching intently.

As Pilee fell sideways toward me, I saw Atkak, the strong man, leap into the snowhouse, knife in hand, and fling himself at Portagee. The big brown man, struggling against his bonds, rolled back on the bed, drew up his legs and in one smooth motion lashed out at Atkak with both feet. Portagee struck him in the chest and drove him back with such force that he loosened the wall. Atkak sprawled on the icy hardness of the snow floor, and Portagee, naked to the waist and still tearing at his bindings, roared and stamped over Atkak's body and threw his full weight against the side of the igloo. The curved snow wall gave away, and almost half of the roof blocks fell around him. His arms were still bound, and so great was his momentum that Portagee could not regain his balance. He stumbled and rolled across the snow outside the wall, jerking wildly at his lacings. Almost half of the house was gone, and as the whirling particles of snow cleared, I had a full view of all that had happened.

Shartok, the comic, the fool, separated himself from the crowd of onlookers and ran, crouching, to the entrance. So excited was he by all that was happening that he snatched up a long, sharp killing spear and reared back in a slow comical way that had often made people laugh. He aimed and launched the harpoon. But this time he was not fooling. The point struck with great force, driving deep into the center of Portagee's naked back.

The big brown man stiffened in horror as he felt his death-blow. He struggled for an instant, but I could see his movements weaken as thick artery blood ran out and stained the snow. Shuddering, he drew his knees up to his chin, then straightened out and died without uttering a sound.

I whirled around to see what had happened to Kakuktak. He stood upright among us, not moving, his eyes alert. His arms were now magically free of the mitts and lashings, for he had torn them off while we had all tried to catch a glimpse of Portagee's departing spirit.

Kakuktak whirled away, his sea knife held in his right hand. As I watched him, he slashed out dangerously at anyone who came near him. He rushed straight at the three girls. He could easily have cut them, and I believe that he should have cut them for their terrible treachery, but they fell down before him, screaming in terror, and he veered away from them. He leaped out of the broken snowhouse and ran, changing his course again and again, whirling around twice, slicing the air crazily with his iron knife. I can still see and feel the terror that he must have known at that moment after seeing his two companions cut down and feeling that the whole village was against him, not knowing that one and only one executioner had been sent to kill him.

Kangiak must have been awakened by all the unfamiliar sounds, for I saw him pulling on his parka and running as fast as he could from the widow's side igloo toward Kakuktak. When he saw what was happening, he drew his thin flint-stone blade and cursed them, shouting, *"Unalook. Unalook,"* at the people who ran behind Kakuktak, for they were anxious to see how their appointed executioner would make the kill.

Kakuktak must have believed that Kangiak had called out the insult against him, for he glanced back only once at Kangiak as he started running westward along the beach. He ran gracefully like a strong young caribou, his long even strides carrying him swiftly over the hard-packed snow.

The others were after him like a pack of wolves. Many of the women cried out, "Run, Kakuktak. Run," for they could not bear to think of his being killed. I caught the gray bitch by the ruff of her neck and hobbled after all of them. But even the little children were running far ahead of me. They cried out with fear and excitement, for some were too young to understand what had happened or what was about to follow. I turned and struggled painfully up the high knoll that had often been a lookout place for me, for I knew that my crippled legs would not carry me much farther. From the knoll I had a long view of the beach. I knelt and leaned, gasping, against the bitch, clasping my arms around her neck in terror, fearful that she, too, like all the others, would run away from me.

I could see Kakuktak loping gracefully across the big patch of spring snow. Following some distance behind him, Kangiak ran with his head down, his short legs moving fast, as he tried to keep pace with Kakuktak. Even as I watched, I could see the two of them slowly increasing the distance between themselves and the wolflike pack of people strung out in a long line.

Behind them all, following the dogs and the last small child, walked Neevee, slowly, stiffly, her parka hood flung carelessly back, her long hair tangled and drifting loosely out on the breeze. I could tell by watching her trancelike way of walking that she had given up hope for him, and when Neevee saw the cliff that barred Kakuktak's path and knew his mistake, she stopped walking and let out a long piercing cry of hopelessness. It was a woman's wail, and it set the gray bitch into a crazy trembling of fear. It was all I could do to hold her steady in my arms.

At the end of the long shore I saw the steep red stone cliffs of Aupaluktok glowing in the morning sun. My heart sank, for I realized then that Kakuktak had blindly chosen the wrong direction, and it was too late for him to save himself. He was running straight into a trap, for no man could climb those crumbling red shale cliffs. He should have turned inland. Now he was caught.

Faintly, far away, I heard Kangiak calling to him, "*Akilini, akilini.* Across the land," but Kakuktak still did not trust him or did not understand him, for he ran straight into the little red stone canyon. He stumbled up over the rough tumble of stone that lay beneath the rock wall that barred his path. Desperately he searched for a foothold, and then seeing that all was lost, he turned slowly to meet the panting mob of villagers who followed him.

I saw Kangiak run close to Kakuktak and stop dead. Then I saw Kakuktak extend his right arm to its full length, pointing his knife into Kangiak's face. But I was not surprised when I saw Kangiak carelessly turn his back on Kakuktak and point his own knife toward the villagers. As I started down the knoll toward them, I heard Kangiak's voice boom over the snow. It rumbled up from inside him exactly like the deep voice of Sarkak as it called, "*Aauuu*," to halt a team of dogs.

The people stopped and stood dead still, each one of them remembering the power of Sarkak, remembering the bear killing. Some became uncertain of what they should do. But again I heard Sarkak's rough voice thunder out of Kangiak's mouth as he snarled, "*Aauuu, aauuu!*" The sound rose up from his belly with such power that many people took a step backward.

As I leaned against the gray bitch and hobbled along the shore toward the canyon, I met the shaman's dirty boy running back toward the village, his shabby clothes fluttering around him in tatters, his grimy face open-mouthed, gasping for breath. I do not think he even saw me as he passed. I wish now that I had grabbed him by the throat and choked the life out of him.

When I reached the edge of the crowd of people who faced the two men, I was so exhausted that I fell trembling to my knees and had to wait for some time until my strength returned to me. No one saw me, for they were all so intent on watching Kakuktak as he stood, knife in hand, and they listened carefully to the words of Kangiak.

"This man, what has he done to us that would cause us to kill him? Why did some among us break in upon the sleep of morning with stabbing knives? What had Portagee done to us to deserve killing? Who appointed that mumbling fool who always fails in the hunt to do that vile work with a harpoon?

"I warn you that killing begets killing, and this man standing here is like a brother to me. Before you do him harm, remember that he is my brother. Which one of you has been appointed to murder my brother? And who were those who appointed that man?"

Kangiak directed his knife in turn at some of the kayakmen he suspected. He stared longest into the eyes of those he trusted least. Shartok, the mimicker, who had given Portagee the death thrust, and Tungilik, the one who had stabbed Pilee, turned to walk away, for their work was done. The dirty boy rushed up to them with his hand clasped behind his back.

The crowd grew restless and started to shuffle around and to talk to each other.

"He's better than the other two," called Poota. "See, he still has good fortune. He still lives life."

Not daring to use the two dead men's names, one said, "The little one and the big one were bad. This one, Kakuktak, is not so bad as the others."

"He came from nowhere. Let him go back to nowhere," called another.

"Let him stay among us," called Nowya's widow. "He has the will to live, so he lives."

I knew that Kakuktak could understand only a little of what they said, but he could sense the change that was coming over the men as he watched them relax. Some young children on the edge of the crowd started to run and play. One woman laughed nervously, and another called to her husband and her son to come home with her. I felt somewhat better and stood up, so relieved was I at the change in the temper of the people. Kakuktak had put his knife away and stood tall and straight, his back almost touching the red cliff, his yellow hair shifting

256

lightly in the breeze. His face and his whole body were relaxed after the long ordeal.

I saw the dirty boy hand something into the crowd of kay-akmen, and his action was so sly and secret that I felt my breath catch in my throat. I hobbled around to see what he had done. Too late, I saw Okalikjuak, the archer, his brown face expressionless, his white lip ornaments protruding like ugly little tusks, as he knelt and drew the bow. He held it flat, parallel to the ground, in that deadly way of the caribou people. In that instant I realized that he was Kakuktak's executioner. I tried to shout, to warn Kakuktak. I thrust out both my hands and lunged out in front of his murderous arrow. I do not think Okalikjuak even saw me, so intent was he upon his target. He released the slim bone shaft, and my fingertips just touched it, as the broad hunting point sheared away my two fingers at the second joints. This may have deflected the arrow by a hand's breadth, for as I fell, I saw it strike Kakuktak in the belly just above the right hip. It disappeared almost to the feathers. Kakuktak reared back with the shock. Blood spurted from my fingers, and as I tried to rise, the second arrow whistled over my face and struck Kakuktak deep in the chest. I shouted. Kangiak turned to see Kakuktak stiffen.

The second arrow must have touched a vital spot, for Kakuktak's blue eyes opened wide, and with his last breath he tried to call out. But no sound would come. He looked wildly among us. I know now that he was not searching for his assassin, but for Neevee. Not seeing her, he fell forward, and the frozen ground forced the arrows deeper into his body.

Kangiak turned him over and held him gently as the life ran out of him. Kangiak sat in this way for some time, with Kakuktak's head in his lap, just looking into his face.

Finally he stood up and said to everyone, "I shall not live among people who would do that. You, friends of his, who used to sing with him and dance with him. Perhaps I shall not even seek revenge on the one who sent that arrow to his heart, for he was appointed by many of you. But I tell you this," he said, waving his knife slowly back and forth at them, "if anyone touches this dead man's clothes now, if they take his coat or his pants, or his buttons or his belt or his knife, I will kill him. Or if they are touched later, I will come back and I will kill him. Do not try to cover him with stones. Do not weight his body or his soul. I hope that it will rise each night and stalk among you and tremble in your entrance passages, moaning like the wind and weeping for the wrong that you have done to him. I believe that this man, Kakuktak, has the power to avenge himself upon every one of you."

With that, Kangiak slipped his knife up the sleeve of his parka and walked straight through the crowd of kayakmen where the arrows had come from. Okalikjuak was not ashamed; he stood his ground, the bow still resting in his hand, his face relaxed, his lip ornaments shining.

Kangiak stopped beside me and placed his arm under mine, a kindly gesture that he had rarely made since we were children. He examined the tight cord I had bound around my wrist and the mitt I held against my hand to stop my fingers from bleeding. Then he helped me to walk, and we two slowly and silently started back to the deserted village. The others followed us, strung out in a long line.

We were scarcely out of the canyon when I saw Neevee running across the valley toward us, stumbling through the soft deep snow. She pushed past us, wide-eyed with fright, as she caught sight of Kakuktak's body lying alone, sprawled at the base of the red cliff.

She ran and fell on her knees beside him, touching with horror the feathered ends of each arrow. I saw her feel his pale cheeks, then grasp his shoulders and try to shake him back to life, but as she did this, she saw the blank-eyed emptiness of death. Slowly she ran her hands along his arms until she lay outstretched on top of him, trying to warm him with her body, not caring about the arrows or the blood. Her loose black hair fell across his face, but I could see her blowing her breath into

258

his mouth, trying to bring his life back to him. When this failed, she remained kneeling beside him, sobbing, shivering like a sick animal. Not heeding the voices of the older women, she hid her face from all of us.

Kangiak and I returned alone to our broken snowhouse and worked grimly together, removing the killing spear from Portagee's back. We pulled Pilee's stiffened body off the sleeping platform, and without a word to each other we dragged first one and then the other up to the rocky wind-swept hill and covered them as gently as we could with heavy stones. So grieved was I that I felt no pain from my bloody hand.

I was anxious to leave this place, fearful that we might meet the ghost of one of these poor killed men, for it seemed to me then that all of the ground beneath our feet had become poisoned by this violence. The others in the village stayed inside their igloos, and that was just as well. Kangiak and I flung our few belongings onto the sled, and not bothering with dogs, we hauled it ourselves out of the village and half-way to the place where Kakuktak lay. There we stopped and built our new snowhouse. Its entrance faced the village instead of the sea, and we drove many spy holes through the walls to show those people that we watched them always with mistrust.

All that day I watched and waited, but Neevee did not come out of the canyon, and that night the stars gleamed faintly and the cold drifted in on a breeze from the sea, and still I did not see her leave that place. I watched and waited and spoke to Kangiak, but so stricken was he with the death of our friends that he could not even answer me.

My fingers throbbed so that I could not sleep, and just before the false dawn came, I left the snowhouse, and gathering all my courage, I made my way up the dark path to the canyon. The whole place lay in shadows, and at first I could see nothing. I moved farther in toward the cliff and found myself almost upon him before I could make out Kakuktak's form lying alone, staring stiffly at the sky. A light powder of snow had blown down and partly covered him. Kakuktak's body looked so empty with its spirit flown that I could not feel afraid. Neevee was gone, but where? Hobbling forward, I stood beside his frozen shell. There at my feet I saw a sharp crude drawing in the snow. It was of a square house with a pointed roof and many foreign windows and a high door. Four people—a tall man, a short woman with a long dress and two small children were walking toward it.

I saw where Neevee's small footprints led away from her drawing in the snow, and I turned and followed them. She had moved through the big stones west of the canyon's mouth, and I could see where her steps in the snow trailed down the embankment and stretched in a long curving line far out over the newly broken ice that drifted toward the open sea. Every crack in the ice spewed white steam into the freezing air. Neevee was gone, gone forever, carrying her children within her. No one from our village ever saw her again.

Bound Bow

39

For many days and nights we took turns watching the little red canyon where Kakuktak's body lay. Dogs went into that place, and we heard them fighting over his remains. We could not help that and did not really care, for we knew that his soul had long since gone. Kangiak's warning had been to the people, and they did not try to enter that place or to take Kakuktak's knife or clothing.

Almost everyone whom I loved or respected was gone. For the first time in my life I felt utterly alone. Only my half brother Kangiak was left to me, and he moved stiffly like Sar-kak, his face cold as stone. His dark eyes glittered cruelly, and I knew that he still carried a knife in his sleeve.

But in spite of this, he and I knew that the killing was ended, that there was nothing more to fear. Sometime after the drinking the villagers had met and decided that the foreigners were dangerous in the camp. For one thing, these visitors of ours had taken our food and our women and clothing and had given us nothing in exchange, not even clever songs or stories. They had demonstrated their power by forcing Sar-kak, the strongest man we had ever known, to flee from his own camp.

Acting together, the villagers had selected Tungilik, Atkak and Okalikjuak as their three appointed executioners. Then they had carefully planned their attack. I suppose the women must have devised the idea of thumbless mittens with strong arm lashings to protect the executioners against the seamen's knives. They must have selected the girls, too, knowing that those three had most often bent beneath the strangers and would best know how to excite and deceive them.

Two of the executioners had been able to carry out their killings as planned. Only Shartok, the fool, had not been appointed. He had murdered the brown man without permission, and for this the people of the village would cast him out, banish him forever from the camp. To them, unplanned passionate murder was the most terrible of all crimes.

As for the three executioners, all relatives of mine, they had simply tried to do what the community had ordered them to do. I knew that they would be as safe as anyone else against the roving vengeance of the foreigners' ghosts. Imagine how simple we were, believing that these three *kalunait* from the south would have no relatives to come feuding against us, with the power to destroy us all in countless subtle ways.

The hot spring sun caused our snowhouse to collapse, and finally, like the other villagers, we moved to higher ground and pitched a small sealskin tent, but we remained far away

261

from them. I noticed that Kangiak was growing more relaxed. He slept quietly now and watched the red canyon less. He told me that we should repair the kayak covers, for he planned to travel east along the coast with me and then northward up the whole length of the Shukvak fiord, as soon as it was free of ice. There we would hunt, he said, until the first winter moon, when we would leave our kayaks and borrow a sled and dogs from the people of Okoshiksalik and journey inland to search for our father.

I was anxious to go, for I had grown to hate living like an outcast on the edge of the big camp. Now it looked like a haunted place with all the good forces of life drained out of it. Men, unless they were away hunting, stayed in their tents, as though they feared the light of day. Women and even children were rarely seen, and hungry dogs roved there in wolflike packs, as though they owned the whole place.

The only people who came to visit our tent were the old woman, Ningiuk, and her young daughter. Some people said that Ningiuk was becoming weak-minded and forgetful, and I admit that she sometimes talked to us in a foolish way, but she was always helpful and kindly to us, because she knew we had no woman in our house. She was accompanied by her young daughter, a girl of at least fourteen winters, who had short strong legs and long tangled hair, who was so shy that she could hardly speak. Ningiuk leaned on her and used her like a crutch when walking over the rough ground.

Because I often allowed Ningiuk and her daughter to look at the bound skins with Kakuktak's marks and drawings, the old woman helped us sew the kayaks, and she mended our clothes and gave us all the gossip that the village had to offer. She told us that the shaman had tried to trade that useless dirty boy he was training for Sowniapik's two daughters, who were both starting to swell, each with a child growing inside her. But Sowniapik had refused, for everyone in the camp was anxious to see what kind of young they would bear.

The shaman and his dirty boy had left early one morning,

262

and no one had stood near them to say good-bye. People, Ningiuk said, were forgetting the taboos the shaman had placed upon them, and she herself was again using for her sewing the fine sinew from a fox tail, in spite of the harm he said it might do to the summer fishing. It was clear she did not like the shaman, and she said she had all along been against the killing of the three foreigners, although she had, of course, known every detail of the planned assassination and had said nothing that might have prevented it, for that is our way.

One evening when I sat talking to Ningiuk as she sewed our clothing, I saw Kangiak lure her daughter gently back onto the darkened bed. Taking advantage of the fact that she was so shy and made no sound, he pulled off her lower clothing and eased himself on top of her before she knew what he was doing. I talked slowly to the girl's mother and watched until I could see that it was over. Then Kangiak looked at me with compassion, and holding the girl in place for me, rearranged his own clothing, and we smoothly changed places. He carried on the conversation with the old woman, and I replaced him over the daughter. I remember shivering with excitement as I felt the willingness of a young girl's hot gentle body, lying there like a timid animal among the soft caribou skins.

This is how we waited for the summer moon to come. We hunted only a little, barely enough to feed ourselves and the dogs, and as often as they came, one of us talked to the old woman while the other lay with her daughter.

Arrowhead

263

40

On one of the first days of summer, when the old snow crust had collapsed and melted away in noisy torrents, the new moon still rode in the bright morning sky like a thin white hair, and I was rudely awakened by Kangiak, who shook me violently. I had never seen him in such a state of excitement.

"A ship," Kangiak gasped, "a huge ship out there beyond the hills!"

I flung my parka on as he helped me, half dragging me on my crippled legs, out of the tent, and we climbed the big hill that protected the village from the winds of the open sea. No one saw us go. When we reached the top, he did not have to point it out, for there in the distance beyond the nearest ice floe lay the immense ship. It was huge, as he had said, larger than my wildest dreams of the sea vessels Kakuktak had drawn or Sarkak had described. Its three great masts jutted boldly into the clear morning air, and its vast sails hung slack and yellow in the dazzling light. The hull was black as a whale, and I could see countless dark lines running up to support the masts and sails. Below these, several tiny specks that must have been men moved restlessly on the deck. That first vision of the power and mightiness of the *kalunait* stands forever in my memory.

Two figures in a small white boat detached themselves from the huge ship, and I watched in wonder as one rowed in the middle with two long oars and one paddled in the stern. They seemed to stroke the boat in a slow lazy way, and yet it moved with surprising speed across the open water until they reached the long floating field of ice. There I saw the two men get out, as we would do, and easily slide the short wide boat across the heavy ice until they reached the other side. Then they neatly slid the boat into the water again and stepped aboard and continued their rowing and paddling. Quickly they came straight toward our beach.

Kangiak and I waited there, motionless, on the hilltop in the shadow of a big rock, watching them and knowing that they could not see us. The big summer tide was in full flood, coming against the whole of our long beach, slowly covering each white pebble and straining to touch the highest tide mark left on the beach in ancient times. As the boat neared the land, I saw the oarsman turn and study the curving shore. They both had tanned faces and wore the same dark clothing we had come to know on Kakuktak, Pilee and Portagee. The man with the paddle pointed to a good landing place on the beach, and the oarsman turned again to drive his long pair of oars smoothly through the water.

I heard Kangiak draw in his breath. He started to move out into the sunlight, to leave the dark protection of the rock that hid us from their view, and I remember that I reached out and caught him by the arm. I tried to hold him back with all my strength, for I could not stand another encounter with these unfortunate foreigners. Kangiak stopped and turned his head, looking straight at me, and I knew that he understood my feelings, but I also knew that he had to go down to them, no matter what I said or did. I released his arm and instead held out my own to him. Gently he helped me down the long boulder-strewn hill that led to the beach.

The two boatmen saw us coming, and for a while they sat and watched us, allowing the tide to carry their small boat toward the shore. When they touched the gravel beach, the man in the middle quickly lifted his oars and placed them neatly in the boat. He turned and sprang forward out onto the shore and caught the bow in his hands. The paddler from the stern of the boat walked forward and jumped out onto the shore, still holding his short paddle nervously, as though he might use it as a weapon. Then the two men ran the boat up clear of the tide and stood watching us as we approached. I could hear them talking together in low voices. They sounded exactly like Kakuktak and Pilee, and I had a terrible feeling for one moment that this might be the magical way in which *kalunait* delivered their souls back to the lands of the living. I listened carefully to their conversation as we drew nearer, hoping to catch some word that I could recognize, for I felt that if I paid close attention, I would somehow understand all the words they were saying.

Kangiak and I crossed the beach slowly because of my crippled legs and stood a little distance from them, empty-handed, for they could not see the knives concealed in our sleeves. Each of us carefully studied the other.

"Halloo," said the taller of the two men. Then he said again, "Halloo."

He pointed back to the big ship, whose sails had now turned blazing yellow in the full sun of morning, and made a gesture as though we had not seen the ship, then stiffly pointed at himself and at the shorter man. The two strangers smiled at us, showing their upper and lower teeth, and we smiled back formally, showing all our teeth.

There was a long moment of silence. Then Kangiak said to them, "*Tikiposi*. You have arrived," for this was a term he had taught Kakuktak to know and to use.

But these new strangers did not understand him, and to fill the silence we all laughed with nervousness.

The two strangers seemed younger to me than either Kakuktak or Pilee. The short one was scarcely taller than Kangiak. He had only the first few yellow hairs curling on his lip and chin. He had wide shoulders and a thick neck, and you could tell right away that he would be good at the wrestling game.

The short man reached down into the bottom of the boat, and gripping a rope handle, he lifted out a wooden barrel. It was the first one I had ever seen. It was round, made of curved pieces of wood bound with two iron hoops. Each end was butted with smooth wood, and in the center of the barrel there was a hole the size of a man's head, with a lid to cover it. With his other hand the short man reached in the boat and lifted out a long-handled wooden ladle. He knocked this ladle several times near the opening in the barrel, then held it to his lips and tilted his head back, making sounds as though he were drinking water. Then he opened the lid and dipped the ladle into the empty barrel and pointed in both directions, first east and then west along the beach.

We knew instantly, of course, that they wanted fresh water, as any man would who traveled by sea, so we helped them drag the boat up beyond the rising tide and led them west along the beach for a short distance until we came to a stream that emptied the melting snow from the mountains down into the sea.

When we arrived at the stream, one of the strangers knelt down and with the ladle scooped up the cold fresh water and drank. The other one remained standing, watching us; then they changed places. I looked at the knife cases on their belts, but they were both empty. Their sea knives must have been hidden in their clothes, as were ours, lying smooth and cold against our wrists.

The tall man held the barrel to steady it while the man with the thick neck carefully ladled water into it until it was full. After they replaced the lid, they seemed in no hurry to go. They stood up slowly and stretched themselves, enjoying the firm feeling of land beneath their feet, as kayakmen do when they come in from the sea. They seemed to gain trust in us, and they looked around again at the far mountains that hung blue in the distance and at the near hills covered with gray-green tundra moss. They studied the gullies full of old snow and the high ground covered with new white and yellow flowers and noticed everywhere the huge tumble of boulders that the giants had flung down so long ago.

Choosing a rock beside a smooth damp sandy place, the two strangers sat down and motioned us to come and sit beside them. We squatted on our heels near them, not wishing to chill our bowels against a freezing stone. To be polite we all stared quietly out to sea.

I could feel the eyes of the short man upon me, and I looked at him. He started speaking slowly, his lips moving in the terrible way of those people. He spoke loudly, as though I were an old man gone deaf. I did not understand any of his words. I looked at Kangiak to see if he had understood, but he blinked to show me he had not. Then, in the way of foreigners, we both shook our heads vigorously, like dogs coming out of water. They understood the gesture perfectly, and Kangiak and I were both pleased with our clever imitations.

The two strangers spoke quietly together for a moment, and then the thick-necked man took the wooden ladle in his right hand and with its handle started to make lines in the wet sand. First he made a crude drawing of the big ship and pointed out to it. Then he drew another very small boat, and he pointed at the one they had used to come to shore. We understood this easily. Then he drew another boat much smaller than the ship but larger than their small boat. In this boat he carefully drew the images of six men. At the stern one stood up steering with a long paddle, in the middle sat four men, each with a long oar, and standing in the front, there was a bigger man holding a harpoon.

He pointed at his drawing of the six-man boat and out at the ship, and he made a motion showing the boat coming to the land. Then he pointed at his drawing of the man holding the harpoon in the bow of the boat and held his black sweater up over his face. With his left thumb and forefinger he made a circle and held it to his ear.

I looked at Kangiak. He opened his eyes a little. Yes, there could be no question. This stranger was trying to ask us about Portagee with the ring in his left ear.

The stranger went on with his description, and we became confused, for he described in mime three men whom we had never known or seen alive, but then suddenly he was describ-

268

ing the blondness of Kakuktak, his thick wrists and big hands. Then last of all, he spoke of the steerer, Pilee, short, brown-haired, quick and full of rude orders.

So here they were, the very men who had lived in the ship with Kakuktak, Portagee and Pilee. With marks and gestures they had made us understand that they were searching for these missing men. I thought, Yes, I could lead you to the graves of Pilee and Portagee. They lie under the stones on the path leading to the children's playing place in the gully. Yes, I could also take you to the little red canyon and show you the scattered bones of the dear Kakuktak, his clothes, his boots and his iron knife rotting there with him. I suppose also, although I have never looked, that we could go to the valley near the cache and find what remains of the first dead man we found, the one with red hair. Yes, I could say the words, "Dag-it. Dag-it," for you would surely understand Kakuktak's other name. But I did nothing, for after all that had happened, I could not bear to have other *kalunait* here again.

While these thoughts moved through my mind, I looked at Kangiak. He blinked at me, meaning no.

We both shook our heads again like wet dogs and pretended not to understand. "*Kowimungilunga,*" we both said several times. "I don't understand. I don't understand."

They shook their heads, too, meaning they did not understand us, and this strange gesture was the only bond we had between us. They spoke together again in low voices, then both got up stiffly from the cold rock, and we helped them carry the heavy water barrel back along the beach. Together the four of us easily carried their small boat down to the water, where the tide was running out. We all looked at the ship riding easily in a smooth sea beyond the ice. Although we had no words that we could understand between us and we dwelled in two worlds distant beyond our dreams, still we stood together on the empty beach like four brothers reluctant to part, trying to hold together like a family.

The tall man reached into a secret pocket and drew out a

round shiny flat case attached to his pants by a thin length of bright chain. He opened this and showed it to Kangiak and me. It had marks around its white face. He held it to my ear, and I heard a soft clicking sound. I thought then and for a long time later that such a shining box was a crazy place for a man to keep lice. Lice are useless, I thought, not worth keeping. The tall man let Kangiak hear the lice clicking inside the precious round box, and then he closed the lid and carefully returned it to his hidden pocket.

We lifted the boat forward again into the water, for the tide was running out fast. The tall man climbed into the boat, stepped over the center thwart and sat down in the stern, with the paddle resting across his knees. The short man with the thick neck held the bow of the boat, ready to shove off. He looked at both of us again and did not seem to wish to go. I knew how he must feel, for we had countless things to say to each other, and yet we had no words with which to speak.

Suddenly the short man reached out and touched Kangiak's shoulder and then pointed at him and pointed at the ship. He made a motion as though he were throwing a harpoon, and he again pointed at Kangiak, motioning him to come with them, inviting him to enter their small boat and leave with them for the ship.

For a moment Kangiak did not move. Then he turned quickly and looked at me, and I could see in that instant that he would go with them, that he wanted to see the inside of that great ship and to be with them and hunt whales with them. He sucked in his breath, meaning yes, he would go, and I looked into his eyes and answered yes by drawing in my breath.

Kangiak stepped quickly into the little boat, balancing himself gracefully like a kayakman, and squatted down by the water barrel between the two strangers, with his back to me. I was glad that I could not see his face.

The short strong man reached into the pocket of his black jacket, and stretching out his arm, he handed me a shining iron box. It was so small that I could almost make it disappear

270

when I closed my hand over it. He then gave the boat a hard driving push with the full weight of his shoulders and as it ground free of the rocky shore, he leaped neatly onto the bow, balancing himself briefly before swinging his left leg inboard. He sat down facing me and placed each of the long oars into their sockets, and with a single stroke he drove the boat safely away from the rocks. Then he paused, and the tall man turned in the stern, and Kangiak turned, and they all three stared at me.

The short man started to wave in the way of foreigners, and the tall man joined him, and they both called out, "Goo-baay. Goo-baay."

A great feeling of sadness came to me, for I could remember Kakuktak and Portagee and Pilee calling this to us when we used to joke together in the little stone gully and on the long arm of rock after the walrus hunt.

I waved back at them in a stiff formal way and imitated them, calling out as best I could, "Goo-baay, goo-baay." And Kangiak called, "Goo-baay," to me, already using their language.

Motionless, I stood watching them as they rowed toward the huge ship. The tall young man only steered with his paddle, so swiftly were they carried on the outward flood of the tide. I watched them as they reached the long ice floe, leaped out and easily dragged the boat across, working together like three small black insects. By the time they reached the ship, I could no longer see them, for they were lost in the long pale skeins of morning fog that drifted in broken patches over the water. Then I saw the bottom of the little white boat flash in the sunlight as it was hauled aboard the great ship. Only then did I remember the gift.

I opened my hand, and I examined the small box. It had a wonderful way of opening when I pulled its end, and inside the box there were many thin wooden sticks. Each of these had a small blue-colored head, waxy, with a bitter taste. I closed the box and slowly and painfully made my way up the

271

long hill. In many places I had to crawl among the boulders, and I was glad there was no one there to see me. I felt like a wounded animal. I moved as slowly as I wished, for now I had no place to go and no person I wanted to see in this whole land.

When I reached the top of the hill, I looked out to sea again and saw that the ship was moving slowly down through the great opening that ran like a river through the ice toward the open water to the south. I rested for a long time, looking down now at the small bay and the camp, the very place where I had been born. In a while I saw the gray bitch tracking me up through the rocks. She moved cautiously, the way a woman moves, her nose to the ground, following my trail. She came right up and lay down to rest beside me. Seeing that I was not inclined to move from that place, she waited for a while, then stood up and rubbed against me, nudged me, offering her heavy neck ruff for me to support myself. With her help I rose, and together we made our way down toward our tent. A light wind came up, and clouds swept in, and the day grew damp and gray. A light rain was falling when I reached the tent.

The lamp was out of oil, and it was dark and deadly cold inside. I could smell the urine of strange dogs that had been there, and I could see that they had devoured my only spare boots and Kangiak's old sealskin mitts and had left the tent in a tumbled mess. It was so sad and deserted without Kangiak that I went outside again and squatted on the tundra, trying to set my thoughts free of the place, not caring about the cold summer rain.

I saw the old woman, Ningiuk, and her daughter coming toward me. The old woman asked me if I had seen the ship, and instead of answering her, I handed her the small box with the little blue-headed sticks. She would not touch them at first and only stared at them in alarm, asking me where they had come from. I told her briefly of the two men that morning and of Kangiak's sudden leaving. She thought it was all magic, that the two strange men must have been the ghosts from beneath the sea come to avenge the deaths of their kinsmen. But even she could see that the strange box and little sticks were real.

Because she liked the color of the blue heads, Ningiuk's daughter wore the little sticks in her hair until one by one they fell out and she lost them all. Sarkak would have known what they were for, and he would gladly have told me how to use them, but he never returned. I heard from some visiting hunters that a thaw had come, and terrible storms of winter rain had raged across the inland plain, turning it into one vast sheet of ice where no animal could dig for food. Every bird and beast had fled, and it was no longer a place of feasting. It was a place of death. Sarkak and his wives, my two brothers and Meetik, and all their dogs had disappeared forever.

Fire Makers

41

Countless winters came to us and slowly turned into spring and foreigners like yourself came to our land again before I learned what the little sticks with blue heads were for. I found out that those two strangers had given me a little box of fire makers in exchange for my brother, and then he, like all the others, was lost to me forever.

One evening at the end of summer, when the air was still and the huge tide was running fast, I thought that I would take the old widow's kayak and go searching for the lost ones, that I would wander out on the open sea and drift until some violent storm caught me and carried me to them, to Kakuktak and Neevee, to Sarkak and to my brothers, and Ikuma and Nuna, Portagee, Pilee and all the others.

But as I stood up to go to the kayak, the sun's rays came slanting across the hills in a way that made me catch my breath with joy, and I remembered the words of a song well known to our people:

> *"Ayii, ayii,*
> *There is one thing*
> *And only one thing,*
> *To rise*
> *And greet the new day,*
> *To turn your face*
> *From the dark of night,*
> *To gaze at the white dawn.*
> *Arise. Arise.*
> *Ayii, ayii."*

These words seem true to me, for I have an endless curiosity about life. Look at me, old and crippled, and yet still waiting for all the good things and bad things that life will bring to me.

Abstract from the log of the sailing bark *Escoheag*, 822 days outbound from New Bedford, Massachusetts

---

Sunday, July 18, 1897
Scattered ice seen to the south, wind NNE, light. Two whales sighted. Will go west to look for missing crew we had to leave a year ago, since we are near that place and hunting is poor.

Tuesday, July 20
Big tide here and heavy ice. Dropped anchor off shore of island where whaleboat was lost. Sent the mate and Atkins ashore for fresh water and to look for Esquimeaux or any sign of the lost boat crew. They came back soon, bringing a little fresh water and a likely Esquimeau lad to replace the ship's hand who died off the Labrador sealing grounds. No sign of the boat crew. God rest their souls. Wind shifted to SW. We are leaving on this tide. So ends this day.